McAlister
and the
Great War

by
Richard Marman

Artwork and Graphics by Richard Marman

Published in England
by
Abela Publishing
Sandhurst, Berkshire, England

Email: Author@RichardMarman.com
Website: www.RichardMarman.com

ISBN: 978-1-92583-3-034
Republished 2018 with Ocean Reeve Publishing

First Edition, 2016

As an Australian Vietnam War veteran, I'd like to dedicate this book to my family of warriors.

To my Grandfather Reggie, who served in the Boer War and to my Granddad Jack, who was wounded on the Western front during WWI, but returned to battle. He married the widow of his mate Bert Novis who was killed in action. Granddad went on to live to be ninety-seven.

To my Uncle Barnie, who served on the North West Frontier and was killed in action in Africa during WWII.

To my dad, who flew spitfires and hurricanes for the RAF during WWII and met my mum in Ireland where she worked as an aircraft mechanic.

To my Uncle John, who piloted RAF V-bombers during the Cold War.

To my brother Chris, an RAF patrol boat skipper who then flew as a C-130 navigator during the Falklands War.

And finally to my eldest brother, Major Michael Marman, a tank commander and helicopter pilot with the 9th/12th Lancers in Germany, Northern Ireland, Hong Kong, Cyprus, Zimbabwe and Oman, who was tragically killed in a car crash on 11 November 1986.

Richard Marman 2016

Glossary & Notes

Admin-O   administration officer
AIF   Australian Imperial Force
ANZAC   Australian & New Zealand Army Corps
Asquith, Herbert   British Prime Minister in 1916, succeeded by David Lloyd George in December
Batavia   present day Jakarta
Blighty   Great Britain — a term coined in the Boer War and in popular use during WWI
Bodhrán   hand held goatskin Irish drum
Bumboat   small marine craft used by native hawkers, selling wares to ships in port
CGM   Conspicuous Gallantry Medal
Chooks   Australian term for chickens
Cumann na mBan *League of Women*, Women's Auxiliary of the Irish Citizen Army
Currach   Irish wooden-framed rowing or sailboat with an animal-hide hull
DCM   Distinguished Conduct Medal, awarded to non-commissioned ranks for acts of gallantry in the field
Deena   Australian pre-decimal shilling coin (ten cents)
DFC   Distinguished Fly Cross — awarded to officers for gallantry in aerial combat
DMP   Dublin Metropolitan Police
DSO   Distinguished Service Order — the second highest British Imperial military award below the Victoria Cross
Equip-O   equipment officer

FANY	First Aid Nursing Yeomanry founded in 1907, known as the Princess Royal's Volunteer Corps today
Flimsies	metal petrol cans of various volumes, named because of their lack of robustness — the ubiquitous jerry-can didn't appear until WWII
Forlorn Hopes	advance parties sent to soften up well defended enemy positions, mostly consisting of ambitious young officers seeking to make their name, and troops condemned for some crime and given the opportunity to dodge the noose. The outcome was usually death
Gam'in'	Aboriginal term for fooling or joking, thought to have derived from the English expression 'gammon'
Gubbah	Aboriginal term for white people
Hairbrush Bomb	WWI hand grenade with a throwing handle shaped like a hairbrush
Havildar	Indian Army rank equivalent to sergeant
HE	high explosive
HQ	headquarters
Hungry Lizzie	ambulance used to carried injured trainee pilots to hospital after they crashed
ICA	Irish Citizen Army — military arm of the IRB
Intel-O	intelligence officer
IRA	Irish Republican Army — a term first coined after the 1916 Easter Rising
IRB	Irish Republican Brotherhood, an Irish independence movement that would become the IRA
ITGWU	Irish Tram & General Workers' Union

Jagdgeschwader	German air force wing consisting of several jastas (squadrons)
Jagdsteffel	another term for a WWI German air force squadron
Jamadar	Indian cavalry officer equivalent to lieutenant
Jezail	Arabian long rifle with a distinctive curved stock
KIA	killed in action
Kites	aircraft, a term thought to have been coined by American aviation pioneer Sam Cody who experimented with kites before developing powered aircraft
KSAM	King's South Africa Medal
Lafayette Escadrille	WWI French aviation squadron crewed by American pilots
Levant	present day Middle East, especially on the Mediterranean shore
Luftstreitkräfte	German air force in WWI
MC	Military Cross — medal awarded for bravery in action
Mention in Despatches	bravery commendation signified by a bronze oak leaf worn on a campaign medal ribbon
MIA	missing in action
Mufti	civilian clothing worn by someone who usually wears military uniform
Naik	Indian Army rank equivalent to corporal
NCO	non-commissioned officer — lance-corporal, corporal, sergeant and warrant-officer
NSW	New South Wales
OC	officer commanding
O's	officers' mess

Panguian	a sultan's first wife
PE	physical exercise or physical education
Persia	present day Iran
Pom (Pommy)	Australian term for the British
POW	prisoner of war
QSAM	Queen's South Africa Medal
RIC	Royal Irish Constabulary — Irish police force
RIR	Royal Irish Regiment
Risaldar	Indian Army cavalry officer equivalent to captain
RNAS	Royal Naval Air Service
Sarnie	Cockney slang for sandwich
Seltzer Water	carbonated water
Shemagh	Arab head-gear
Siam	present day Thailand
Simoom	sandstorms experienced in North Africa during summer
Sinn Féin	political party formed in 1905 to support Irish independence
Smoko	Australian expression for a rest break from work
Sowar	Indian cavalry trooper
Subaltern	most junior commissioned officers — 1st and 2nd lieutenants
Tipper	wooden drum stick used to strike a bodhrán, sometimes know as a cipin
Tommies	British troops, WWI term used universally by allies and enemies alike
2IC	second in command
UVF	Ulster Volunteer Force, an Irish organisation opposing home rule

VAD	Volunteer Ambulance Driver
WA	Western Australia
Wadi	Arabic term for a creek, riverbed or small canyon
Waler	Australian mixed-breed reliable cavalry or stock horse
WIA	wounded in action
Zack	Australian pre-decimal sixpenny coin (five cents)

Part Three — Emerald Isle 1916

Part Four — Western Front 1916-1918

Part One — Middle East 1914-1916

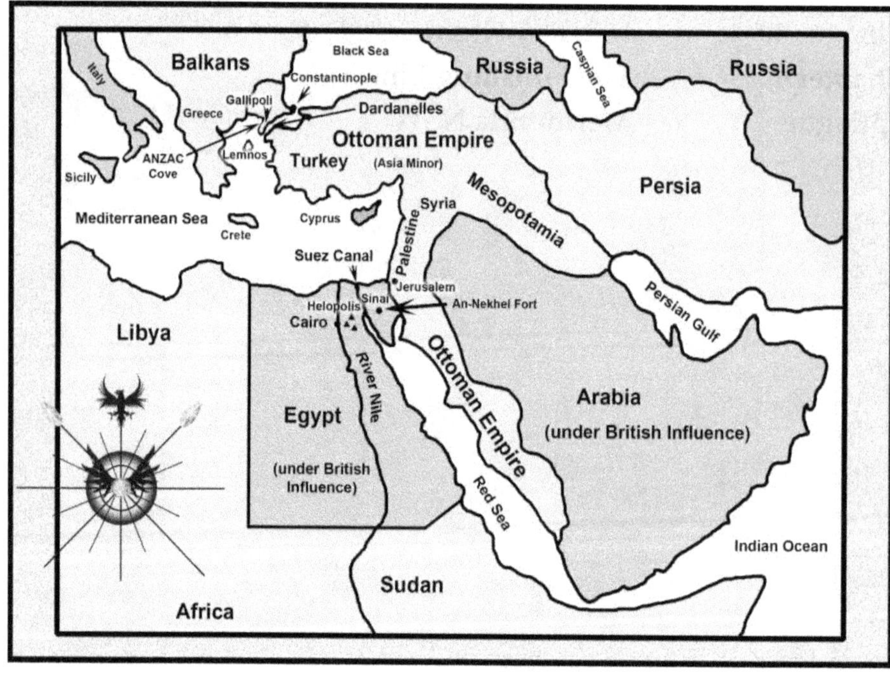

Prologue — Merimbula New South Wales

My name is Zach McAlister and I have been documenting my Grandpa Danny's and his girlfriend Angela's adventures back in the 1950s. If you've read my earlier books, you'll know what I'm talking about. Angela and Danny now live on a property half-an-hour out of Merimbula on the New South Wales Coast near the Victorian border. If you want to know all about those early stories, grab a copy of my books or download them onto your tablet.

I visit Grandpa Danny and Ange during the school holidays. My dad reckons I should be hanging out with kids my own age, but I tell him at least I'm not doing drugs or getting girls pregnant so he can't complain. I think Dad reckons Grandpa's yarns are mostly hot air, but there are any numbers of historical records to back Danny up and I certainly believe Angela. I reckon Dad's plain jealous because he works at an office job in the city and has never been on any adventures except a European Contiki bus tour where he met Mum.

What I especially like about Grandpa's place is the neat stuff he has and the fact that he can do pretty much anything. He paints, sketches, plays musical instruments, is a handy marksman, cook, archer, surfer and can fix gadgets given time. He classes himself as 'adequate' at these skills, but he seems damned good to me.

The property has a whopping three-bay shed where Grandpa stores souvenirs from his past. He calls them artefacts. I sometimes rummage around and discover items which have a story to tell — mostly by Grandpa, although Angela adds her piece often enough.

On one occasion I found some sepia photos, artwork, bundles of correspondence, news clippings and two more sets of medals, which I knew weren't Grandpa's and a single medal Angela identified as a French *Croix de Guerre*. When I asked him about the find, he explained they belonged to his grandfather, Robert and his great uncle Callan, who must have passed them on to Danny's father, George.

'I found those papers and photos after my mother died,' Grandpa said. 'She remarried a chap called Stanley Hallet when Dad didn't return from New Guinea after the war. I blamed Stan for persuading my mother to send me to boarding school, but actually he wasn't such a bad bloke. He treated my mother fair and square and I could see he was really cut up when she passed away. Stan packed up all the stuff he thought might interest me and I brought them back here.'

Grandpa's mother — he never referred to her as 'Mum' — had lived in Rockhampton, although they'd barely been in touch over the years.

Angela and I eagerly examined the box contents. There was a wealth of interesting items pertaining to my heritage which I had no idea about.

'There's a load of cool bits and pieces in here,' I said. 'I wonder why no one has mentioned them before.'

'I guess there was too much pain after the Great War. Diggers seldom talked about what'd happened to them so the family history was never handed down. Over the years I've just put these things aside, but I'll tell you what I know...'

Grandpa had never met his great uncle, but Grandpa's dad George, had told him some of the story. Angela and I were going to dig up the rest...

Chapter 1 — It's War!

McAlister Property Northern NSW Hinterland — 1914

Callan McAlister was a fine horse rider and natural bushman. Mind you he'd been brought up to it. He and his brother Robert were raised on their family property in Northern New South Wales just short of the Queensland border. The area was well-watered, fertile farmland which was a blessing — other than during flood season — in Australia. The McAlister property was situated on gently sloping high ground, thus gaining the benefits of summer wet seasons without fear of inundation. It may have been some acres short of a vast outback station, but was still a profitable cattle farm and self-sufficient with an abundant herb garden, vegetable patch, orchard, chooks and a pair of breeding pigs.

McAlisters had owned the land since Jonathan and Christina McAlister sailed to the colonies nearly a century before. He'd chosen wisely and the family had lived comfortably ever since as the property was inherited through following generations. Initially Jonathan had made a pile from logging and when he'd cleared the pasture, turned his hand to rearing Merino sheep. This wasn't a great success because the humid climate was inclined to cause footrot, so the McAlister's became beef and dairy farmers, which worked out admirably.

Callan's older brother Robert had gone north cattle droving for the Queensland stations where he'd met a feisty jillaroo called Henrietta Clark, fallen in love and married the girl. Robert and Henrietta hadn't actually settled down, as a nomadic life suited them. So Callan was surprised when the couple turned up in their sulky drawn by a redoubtable waler with their mustering stock tethered behind. Robert and Henrietta travelled lightly and all their worldly possessions fitted into the cart with room to spare.

Of course Ma and Pa McAlister were overjoyed to see their oldest boy home especially when they heard that Henrietta was expecting a baby in six months.

'So, you've decided to settle back home and work the farm,' Pa Mac suggested, lighting his pipe while Ma poured tea all round.

'Well, not exactly,' Robert replied uneasily.

Pa arched his bushy eyebrows.

'I sort of joined up, Pa,' Robert confessed.

One of those awkward pauses followed. The silence was only broken by the occasional kookaburra and crows rattling away in the bush accompanied by lowing cattle streaming in from the paddocks for milking.

'Sort of?' Pa challenged. 'Exactly how much "sort of"?'

'It'll be such a lark, Pa,' Robert continued. 'They say the war'll be over by Christmas, so I'd better get in quick and do my bit to sort out the Hun.'

'And why would you want to go and stick a bayonet into some German fellow you've got no argument with?' Pa asked, quite reasonably many people would add.

'For King and Empire,' Robert sprouted, rather too glibly in Pa's opinion.

'I can guarantee it won't be a lark. War isn't like that. It's mostly boredom, sickness, discomfort or downright frightening horror.'

And Pa Mac should have known. Like many Lismore men, he'd volunteered for the NSW Mounted Rifles at the very turn of the 20th Century, and before he knew it, he'd been shipped off to the Transvaal to chase Boer guerrillas for a couple of years. Nearly six hundred Aussies lost their lives in battles or from disease during the conflict and many who returned were thoroughly disenchanted with the British military and colonial system they'd served.

'The Poms used us because we could play the Boer at his own game,' Pa Mac explained. 'We could ride, shoot and ride again. We'd keep that up for days — weeks even.'

'But you beat the Boers in the end, Pa,' Robert declared.

'Dunno about that, son,' Pa reflected. 'Mostly the Poms rounded up all the Boer families and stuck 'em behind barbwire — concentration camps they called 'em — then burnt all the Boer farms and paddocks. Finally the men-folk gave up after so many of their loved ones died in captivity. I reckon disease and heartbreak did for 'em in the end. Our generals didn't know what they were about more than half the time. Hector MacDonald was the only one worth his salt, but he barely stayed in South Africa for eighteen months before they shifted him off to Ceylon.'

'We have good generals now, though,' Robert insisted.

'Haig, Kitchener, French, they're the same re-hashed bunch. Fighting Germany and the entire Austria-Hungary Empire is going to be a lot stiffer than a bunch of African natives or a handful of

Boer cavalry. Not to mention Johnny Turk, who's been drawn into the whole mess just because the Ottoman Empire lies between Europe and the Persian oilfields.'

Pa Mac's bitterness towards British military brass had been further inflamed back in 1902 when Captain Harry 'Breaker' Morant and Lieutenant Peter Handcock faced a firing squad after being convicted of murdering Boer prisoners. In truth Morant and Handcock hadn't committed any worse atrocities than others on both sides. They'd simply been foolish enough to shoot their prisoners after they'd captured them rather than before. But it was General Herbert Kitchener who'd signed Morant and Handcock's death warrants, which many Australian troops thought was an unjust punishment.

Pa Mac prided himself on being well informed. The dairy co-operative truck regularly delivered copies of *The Northern Star* and *The Queenslander* before transporting full milk churns back to Lismore. Ma and Pa avidly read every page. So they were well aware that Serbian malcontent, Gavrilo Princip had shot Archduke Franz Ferdinand and his wife Sophie in Sarajevo. Franz Ferdinand wasn't any penny-ante European nobleman either, he stood a good chance of becoming Austria-Hungary's next emperor if no other Hapsburgs popped up to gazump him, which looked extremely unlikely.

Ma and Pa had discussed the outcome at length and agreed that war was pretty well inevitable and the royal assassinations were merely a catalyst. Russia wanted to grab a piece of Balkan territory as well as accessing Middle-Eastern oilfields and Austria-Hungary planned to stop them. Germany and Italy had a triple alliance with Austria-Hungary, while France and Russia had another pact. Britain was in league with France with their *Entente Cordiale*.

'"Cordial agreement" for heaven's sake,' Pa declared. 'Cordiality between Britain and France — that'll be the day.'

With such a Gordian knot of international wheeler-dealing and intrigue, it was a wonder anyone knew which side they were on. Meanwhile the Ottoman Empire was sandwiched between east and west and trying to keep a low profile, but badly in need of powerful friends because its economy had collapsed reaching basket-case status. The Ottomans opted for Germany which was a mistake, but none of the other big kids wanted to have anything to do with the Turks.

But it all started in the Balkans:

- After the Archduke was killed Austria-Hungary demanded that Serbia suppress all anti-Austria-Hungary sentiment and ensure it didn't rear its ugly head again.
- The Serbs declined and sent their army across the Danube to protect the border. Austria-Hungary responded with troops to oppose the Serbs and declared war.
- Russia mobilised just to be on the safe side, which was a bad move because Germany immediately declared war on the mighty East European bear.
- Italy and the Low Countries thought it best to sit on the fence.
- Germany then invaded Belgium in an attempt to steal a march on France. The two armies now faced off along the Belgian and Luxembourg borders.
- Britain warned the Germans to withdraw, but to no avail so she declared war along with her colonies and dominions.

- The Ottoman Empire closed the Dardanelles cutting off the route to the Black Sea oil wells and the back door to the Austria-Hungary territories.

- Serbia and Montenegro declared war on Austria-Hungary and soon pretty well every European power was in conflict with someone or another and to make matter worse, Japan — with an eye on flexing its martial muscles in China and any South East Asian territory it could lay its hand on, declared war on Germany too.

In a matter of weeks the whole of Europe, while not yet ablaze, was a simmering powder-keg ready to explode. And explode it did when German and *Entente* armies slammed into each other at Mons and Marne in a bloodbath that degenerated into both sides slugging it out in trenches, which became the Western Front.

'What a mess. Anyone who claims to understand it all is telling fibs — talk about falling dominoes,' Pa Mac declared. 'This can only end badly.'

Yet, whatever his parents felt, it made no difference because Robert had signed up with the Ninth Australian Infantry Battalion which planned to ship out to Egypt within days. The following morning Ma and Henrietta wept while Pa solemnly shook Robert's hand.

'You'll have to grow a moustache,' Ma said sniffing into her handkerchief. 'You'll need one if you want to be a general. They're all sporting them, you know.'

That was an astute observation on Ma's part, because growing moustaches had actually been a regulation for British soldiers since 1860 although colonial forces didn't enforce the requirement.

Robert embraced Henrietta for a final kiss before mounting up to ride to Lismore. Young Callan accompanied his brother to lead his horse back to the farm. Callan and Robert rode two stalwart gelding walers, Flash-Jack and Clancy who like all the McAlister horses were named after favourite bush-ballad characters.

From Lismore it was a fractured rail-road trip to Brisbane where Robert was to embark for overseas. The direct seaboard railway track between Sydney and Brisbane was still some years away.

'I should be coming with you,' Callan sulked.

'Don't be mad, Callan,' Robert said although not harshly. 'You're too young.'

'I'm seventeen...'

'You'll be seventeen tomorrow...and that's still too young. Anyway someone has to stay and help Ma and Pa with the cattle.'

They didn't talk of war again, but enjoyed the ride. North New South Wales was one of the few permanently lush areas in Australia. Although there'd been a rare drought at the turn of the century, Lismore had enjoyed bountiful rainfall for years. The bushland surrounding the pastures abounded with wildlife and kangaroo meat often supplemented the settlers' diet. Cockatoos, vividly coloured parrots, lorikeets and galahs squawked in the tree-tops. Callan spied a wedge-tailed eagle soaring on high, pointing it out to Robert. Unlike sheep farmers, dairy producers were more tolerant of the giant raptors as they culled the rabbit population and left the cattle alone. Lambs were a different story. Sheep station owners offered a bounty for eagles and thousands were slaughtered over the years.

'You'll miss this, I bet,' Callan commented.

'Maybe so, but I've been droving up north where it's a lot hotter and dustier than this. It's great to come home, but I like to wander.'

'Is that why you volunteered?'

'To see the world, you mean? Yeah, I guess that's part of it.'

'But you're going to be a father. Don't you want to be around when the baby is born?'

'Yes, but this is a once-in--lifetime opportunity. I can't pass it up whatever Pa says.'

Neither brother seemed to entertain the fact that Robert might well get shot in the process, but that was the nature of young men at the time.

When they reached Lismore, Robert presented his papers at the City Hall on Ballina Street. The building bubbled with activity as a number of local men and youths clamoured to enlist there and then. That wasn't particularly surprising because Lismore was the 4th NSW Lancers' HQ, commanded by Lieutenant Colonel F J Board. Although Robert wasn't joining that unit, its staff knew how to process new recruits and the town hall was the best location to go about it. A military clerk appeared well informed and promptly issued Robert's travel vouchers. Virtually every town in the country had a recruiting agency of some sort where gung-ho lads clambered over one other to join up.

Callan waited outside with the horses. It was a pleasant spring day and the jacaranda blooms were appearing unusually early that year. He'd nothing better to do than stand in the shade and gawk at the townsfolk passing by. He didn't get to Lismore often and enjoyed seeing the office men dressed in their striped jackets, suits, bowler hats and boaters, but he especially liked the ladies in their fine dresses, broad-brimmed hats, floral bonnets and parasols. They all looked so glamorous compared to the homespun country-style outfits he was used to. It never occurred to him to feel jealous. He'd liked living on the farm, but he loved visiting town as well.

Callan owned a Matthias Hohner diatonic harmonica, which was his prize possession. Right now was the perfect time to sit in the shade and blow a few tunes. Townsfolk enjoyed his playing, nodding as they passed by.

About then one of the most daunting challenges facing any adolescent lad appeared. A quartet of coquettish teenage 'young ladies' sashayed out of Riverside Park, crossed Molesworth Street, heading straight for City Hall. Their young bodies had just developed from girl to womanhood and they were out to impress. They were the private-school darlings of well-heeled townsfolk, un-chaperoned and out to make mincemeat of anyone who crossed their path.

Three of the girls were striking beauties while the fourth was a plainer, bespectacled lass but with fetching dimples nevertheless. Bored and mischievous, the two ringleaders were poised ready to strike, and what better prey than a lad from the sticks smelling of horses and cut grass and playing such a crass, lowly musical instrument.

'Well, good day to you, Mr Music Man,' the leader of the pack chimed in a voice as sweet as molasses. 'We haven't seen you around here before, have we?'

'N...n...no,' Callan stammered, pocketing his harmonica.

He wasn't normally a babbling idiot, but being bailed up by a bevy of feisty females knocked him squarely out of his comfort zone.

'Goodness me, the poor wee soul seems to have trouble speaking, Lydia dear,' the second girl in the pecking-order remarked. 'Are you fully in command of your faculties, young man?'

'I'm...I...'

'Oh dear, he does appear somewhat addled I fear, Cecily darling,' Lydia said.

'I wonder if we should direct him to the nearest physician,' Cecily suggested. 'But might he lose his way?'

'Yes, I do believe he may well be in need of therapy...'

'I'm fine!' Callan finally managed to utter words without stuttering.

'Goodness me,' Lydia declared, 'how rude of you to raise your voice to ladies.'

Callan had pretty well recovered by then and he didn't care for being teased or taken for a fool.

'I don't believe I was the one being rude...and...I was unaware I was speaking to ladies, but I apologise for raising my voice in any event,' he said with just the hint of menace.

'This is intolerable for you to address me so!' Lydia hissed.

She raised he hand to slap Callan's cheek, but he easily blocked her arm. Lydia's palm slammed into his forearm. Callan felt the force jar to his shoulder. The girl packed quite a wallop, but he reckoned she'd hurt herself more than him.

'Ow, you beast,' she wailed. 'How dare you strike a lady?'

'Me strike you?' Callan replied in dismay. 'You've got to be joking. I'm standing here minding my own business when you and your hoity-toity mates come along and start insulting me. Why don't you just shove off?'

Tears welled in her eyes. Apparently it didn't take much to reduce those fragile misses to vapours.

'All I can say is you're no gentleman,' the girl snivelled. 'Just because you have come to enlist does not mean you can behave like a complete larrikin.'

'Enlist? Who said anything about enlisting?'

'Why, of course you are,' Lydia glared at him, 'that is the only possible reason you are in town, is it not?'

'No. My brother has joined the AIF...'

'Then why not you, pray tell me that?'

'I'm too young for a start and I'm needed to work on our property.'

'Poppycock! You look old enough to me. I believe you are a poltroon, Mr Country Bumpkin.'

'You can believe what you like,' Callan flared. 'I don't have to justify myself to you.'

'Not to me I daresay, but to your king and country!'

And then something most perplexing occurred. Without a further comment, and as if rehearsed, Lydia and Cecily opened their shoulder bags in unison. Callan was unable to see the usual female paraphernalia the bags contained because it was hidden by white goose down. Both girls took a single feather from her purse and before Callan realised, had clipped them to the metal adjustment clasps on his braces — one on each side.

Lydia and Cecily's two companions looked on with what Callan detected as some sense of discomfort and embarrassment.

'Come ladies,' Lydia commanded.

With a collective huff Lydia and Cecily flounced past Callan while the other girls meekly followed. Lydia furled her parasol and thwacked Callan on the shoulder as she went by.

'So there Mr Cowardy Custard, wear the shame for all to see,' she snorted and marched away.

Now what the blue blazes was that all about?

At that moment Robert emerged from the city hall. He noticed the feathers instantly, glanced about him in case anyone was paying attention, then ripped the feathers from Callan's brace-buckles and ground them under his boot heel.

'I didn't think they suited me either,' Callan said.

'Damn right, they don't,' Robert replied with true anger in his voice that puzzled Callan.

'I know I don't have much dress sense...'

'You don't know what they mean, do you?' Robert hissed.

'No...'

'Who gave them to you? Those four bitches heading down the street.'

Callan nodded. He'd never seen his brother so angry — not even when he hit his thumb with a hammer — and he'd rarely heard him use strong language. Those four girls may have been a handful, but Callan would never have considered calling them bitches.

'What does it mean?' Callan asked.

'It doesn't matter. Forget it,' Robert said as he calmed down. 'It's just the way some of these stuck-up silver-spoon sheilas have of making blokes feel bad. They're probably handing stupid feathers out willy-nilly all over town. Don't take any notice, understand?'

'OK.'

'No, promise me you won't take those silly cows seriously.'

'Yes...fine,' Callan was becoming a little upset, seeing his brother so disturbed about something so trivial. 'I promise.'

'Good, now I must go to the station. My train leaves in an hour and you have to get the horses back home before dark.'

Although Callan wanted to stay with his elder brother, Robert said he preferred to simply shake Callan's hand and say cheerio. Hanging around on the railway platform wondering what to say to each another wasn't their style. So with a brief nod, they parted and Callan led Flash-Jack and Clancy to one of the remaining town stables for feed and water. Horse transport was still vital for the surrounding countryside, although road, rail and river traffic had become usual.

Pa regularly used the stable before returning to the farm. Callan knew the proprietor Bernie Smart well, and they chatted idly while the horses drank.

'Tell me something,' Callan asked the old timer as he mounted up to leave. 'What do white feathers signify..?'

Chapter 2 — Raw Recruit

Lismore Northern NSW — Early October 1914

After Bernie explained, Callan dismounted and left his horses at the stable, knowing they'd be lovingly cared for. He returned to where Robert had ground the feathers into the dusty street. Callan picked them up and placed them in his pocket before climbing the steps to City Hall. There were several desks manned by moustachioed NCOs with several young men queuing at each table. Callan chose the shortest line and waited his turn.

City Hall was decked with red-white-and-blue bunting, Australian flags, Union Jacks and lurid posters of the spike-helmeted Germans with gorilla faces bayoneting babies and violating particularly virtuous and vulnerable-looking young women. But mostly there was the image of Lord Kitchener gazing sternly ahead while pointing directly outwards and declaring patriotically, 'Your Country Needs You'.

Such was the demand for cannon-fodder the men were quickly inducted and before long Callan faced a burly sergeant. Colourful QSAM and KSAM campaign ribbons were sewn above his left breast-pocket. Callan recognised the awards because Pa Mac had shown him the same medals he'd earned during his South African service. The sergeant also wore the blue-and-red striped DCM ribbon, indicating not only had he fought the Boers for a long time, he'd gone about it with considerable intent and courage.

'G'day to you, young fella-me-lad,' the sergeant said jovially, which Callan noted was not always the case. Some of the recruiting officers simple greeted prospective recruits with a terse, 'Name?'

'I presume you wish to join up and ride to fame and glory while butchering as many of the Hun you can.'

Callan nodded, although he hadn't actually thought of putting that way.

'Know anything about guns?' the sergeant continued.

'I can shoot a rabbit's eye out at a hundred yards.'

'Shooting rabbits and shooting men ain't quite the same thing...'

'I hardly ever miss.'

The sergeant was a shrewd judge of men and detected a look of steely determination and gritty resolve in Callan's eyes while sensing the same attitude in the tone of his voice.

'Can you ride, son?'

'Ride..?'

'Why yes. The Fourth is a mounted regiment. Who wants to go foot-slogging all the way to wherever it is we wind up?'

'Yessir, I can ride,' Callan replied with justifiable pride. 'I was in the saddle before I could walk. I've got a fine gelded waler over at Bernie Smart's place right now.'

That was the clincher as far as the recruitment sergeant was concerned.

'You'd better sit down and tell me your name then,' he said, producing a copy of the required enlistment papers. 'And don't address me "sir". I am Sergeant Blake and you will call me, "Sergeant".'

'Yes sir...Sergeant.'

'You'll get used to it. Now what's your name?'

'Callan McAlister, Sergeant.'

'I remember a McAlister from the Boer War, but we served in different units.'

'Probably my pa. He fought in South Africa.'

Sergeant Archie Blake was a wily devil and recognised an A-grade recruit when he saw one. He didn't want to let this one slip through his fingers. He also recognised a kid when he saw one. Callan had barely started shaving and it wasn't something he had to do every day. Sergeant Blake knew very well that the minimum eligible recruitment age was eighteen, but hundreds, probably thousands of lads lied about their age and there was certainly no time to check on all their birth certificates even if they could be produced.

In 1914 there was no shortage of willing recruits and many were turned away, especially if they were under-age, so Sergeant Blake had to tread warily.

'Now, McAlister m'lad, the youngest age required to join up is eighteen so I'm obliged to ask how old you are.'

'My birthday is tomorrow,' Callan beamed.

'And you will be..?'

Callan returned Sergeant Blake's fixed gaze.

'...Why eighteen, of course.'

The sergeant nodded and grinned. He knew they understood one another.

'Then sign on the dotted line with tomorrow's date right next to your moniker.'

*

Sergeant Blake instructed Callan to return the following day. Unlike Robert, he was to be transported to Sydney for induction, medical examination and uniform issue. There was no time to go home and Callan wasn't certain he wanted to do that anyway. He was unsure how his parents would take the news and he didn't want Pa charging into town blabbing that his youngest son was under-age.

Bernie Smart was ambivalent about Callan's enlistment, but when Callan asked to be put up for the night Bernie agreed. The stableman lived alone and it was a nice change of company from the usual crowd at the Richmond Hotel public bar — not that there was anything wrong with the usual crowd, mind.

Callan had one more task to complete, before the day was out. Discovering the whereabouts of the four girls wasn't as hard as he'd thought. They'd left a trail of bristling indignation behind them. Not that everyone had been presented with white feathers, but Lydia and her feline chums had visited every fashionable lady's wear establishment in town, leaving a dozen harassed and distressed shop assistants in their wake.

Lydia and Cecily Fallon were sisters from an old-money NSW family who'd been thick with John McArthur when making dubious fortunes from sheep and rum was fair game. The Fallons believed they ruled by divine right and tended not to bother with any due process of law or worry about whose feet they trod on.

Everyone knew the Fallons lived in a palatial home just above the flood-line set on two acres of sprawling lawns and manicured colonial gardens. Most retailers made deliveries and a Conway Street butcher gave Callan directions although he couldn't fathom why a country lad wanted to go there. The main entrance was a double wrought-iron gate supported by sandstone pillars. Undaunted, Callan opened the latch and marched towards the house along a jacaranda-shaded driveway.

With his heart in his mouth, Callan rapped on the ornate lead-glass front door. In moments it was opened by a young aboriginal woman dressed in black-and-white maid's livery.

'Good afternoon,' Callan began, 'I'd like to talk to Miss Lydia...'

'You crazy, gubbah-boy,' the maid hissed. 'You make delivery-business out back?'

'I'm not delivering anything...well I am actually...'

'You gam'in' me? *You* can't use *this* door.'

'Why not, it works fine?'

'Mr Fallon gonna kill me yabbering on here...'

Right then Callan had no idea of the whole class system that was supposed to no longer in Australia, but thrived through a wealthy pseudo-aristocracy.

'What is the matter, Margaret?' a soft lilting voice called from beyond the hallway. Before the maid could reply a girl about Callan's age approached the front door. Callan immediately recognised her as one of Lydia and Cecily's companions who'd appeared averse to playing cruel pranks on passing strangers.

'That is all right, Margaret,' the girl said pleasantly, 'I will talk to this young gentleman.'

Margaret stared suspiciously, but relented and retreated to her duties.

'Well hello again,' the girl said extending her hand. 'We weren't formally introduced before. My name is Ivy D'vere-Brown, but Ivy Brown suits me fine.'

'Callan McAlister, Miss Brown. I...'

'We cannot stand in the doorway all day, Callan. Come let us walk around these lovely gardens, it is such a pleasant afternoon. And please call me Ivy.'

She took Callan's arm as if it was the most natural thing to do. They strolled across the lawn, admiring the flower beds until they found a bench in the shade of a Moreton Bay Fig. A sketch pad, coloured pencils and watercolour paint box had been left on the seat. Two finished works of garden scenes lay beside the artist's tools.

'Are these yours?' Callan asked.

'Yes, but I do not think they are very good,' Ivy replied with genuine modesty.

'I wouldn't say that — I wouldn't say that at all. I really like them.'

'That is very kind of you to say so,' Ivy said, blushing coyly. 'Mama believes all true young ladies should have a hobby. My equipment is quite easy to carry around. Look, everything fits into this satchel. It is wax-coated with a rubber lining to make it water-proof so I can take it everywhere on my travels. Mama had it specially made after some of my early drawings were ruined in a rain storm. I was so upset, I cried for days. I keep a journal too, so I do not forget any of the wonderful places I have been to, what I have seen and...who I meet.'

She eyed him coquettishly.

'That sounds very sensible to me,' Callan observed politely.

'I must apologise for Lydia and Cecily's behaviour this afternoon,' Ivy said as they sat together. 'They can be such little rascals.'

'You and the other lass didn't look too happy about Lydia and Cecily's manners. Why are you their friend if they're so mean? You seem very nice to me.'

'Thank you,' Ivy blushed slightly. 'The Fallon gals can be charming when it suits them. Georgina, our other companion, is sweet. I think she only tags along hoping to snare a chap at dances.'

'Attraction by association then, using Lydia and Cecily as bait.'

Ivy smiled.

'I hope it works for her having to put up with those two little madams. What about you?'

'I really do not know the Fallon family at all,' Ivy replied. 'Papa met Mr Fallon in China during the Boxer Rebellion. I cannot remember any of it. I was just a wee girl. Papa was a major then and I think Mr Fallon had a contract to provide rations for the troops. He is a businessman, not a soldier. We are here with Mama on holidays. I love the weather and the beautiful bush, but we shall be returning to England soon.'

'So that's your accent.'

'It is a bit of a mish-mash actually — half-Irish and half-English I suspect.'

'Not at all, I think it's lovely.'

She blushed again. For a lad with no experience with girls, Callan was doing pretty well, but Ivy was so easy to talk to and he'd liked her instantly.

He told her about growing up on a farm, how he could ride, and muster cattle, shoot and how he'd learned bush-craft from the local Bundjalung people. Later he couldn't believe how he'd babbled on.

In turn Ivy said she lived on the family's country estate in Shropshire near the Welsh border. Her family also spent much of their time at their holiday 'cottage' in a small Southern Irish town called Crosshaven, by the coast close to Cork. Then Callan explained how Robert and he'd joined up and even that he was staying at Bernie Smart's stable overnight. Although Callan was unused to sociable conversation, the words just poured out.

'I came to bring these back since I've joined up,' he said producing the feathers that were now dusty and a bit the worse for wear. 'It doesn't really matter anymore, but I'm pleased I did because I met you.'

Ivy was charmed by Callan's innocent sincerity. He said exactly what he thought without the pretentious etiquette she was so accustomed to. People in her world spoke in riddles most of the time and were forever on edge in case they tripped over some pointless societal faux pas or another.

'Ivy, where the devil are you?' a male voice called from the front porch.

She'd lost all track of time and had no idea how long she and Callan had been together. Just then a contingent consisting of Mr Fallon, her father and Lydia trailed by several household staff, marched towards where Ivy and Callan sat.

'We've been looking everywhere for you,' Major D'vere-Brown said. 'Your mother was concerned...Who is this?'

'I would like to introduce Private Callan McAlister who has just enlisted and is leaving in the morn...'

'Why it's the cowardy-custard boy,' Lydia declared.

'I came to return these, Miss Lydia.'

Callan took the feathers and tossed them at her feet, but they floated with the light breeze and both landed on Lydia's breast, which had a better effect than he'd intended.

'Ewee,' she wailed, screwing up her nose and flicking the feathers away as if they were spiders.

'Yeah, I didn't like them on me either,' Callan said.

'How dare you trespass on my property?' Mr Fallon barked.

'I am sorry, Mr Fallon. I asked Callan to stay...'

'Keep out of this Ivy. You, young man, will leave immediately.'

'Steady on, old boy,' Major D'vere-Brown said. 'I don't think the lad meant any harm and he's off to war tomorrow.'

Major Humphrey D'vere-Brown didn't care for the way Fallon had spoken to his daughter, but the fellow was 'trade' after all, so what could you expect? The D'vere-Brown family had only visited Lismore when Fallon insisted. The Northern Rivers country was beautiful, interesting and the weather delightful, but Fallon was tiresome and it was time to head home. Although the major was well respected and looked to the welfare of his men, he normally wouldn't tolerate Ivy associating with a common private, but the lad would be gone, so no harm done and he could afford to be magnanimous. Soldiers had to stick together, what?

Soon Cecily, Mrs Fallon and Mrs Meredith D'vere-Brown arrived to see what all the fuss was about. Callan figured, much as he'd like to stay and chat with Ivy, he was now seriously out-gunned and it was time to leave.

'It's been a pleasure meeting you Ivy,' he said, 'and you too Major, Mr Fallon, and of course you lovely ladies. Good afternoon to you all,' he added with a cheeky grin. Callan touched the brim of his bushman's hat, spun on his heel and walked casually away. He took his harmonica from his trouser pocket and started blowing *Waltzing Matilda* before reaching the gate.

*

The following morning Callan woke early. Bernie was already up and boiling a billy for tea.

'Well, today's the day,' Callan announced. 'I'd better get a move on and take Flash-Jack to the muster area. We have to board the train today.'

'Not before a hearty breakfast, you don't. I've sausages and bread frying in the pan. You'll need something to stick to your ribs. You've got a big day ahead of you.'

'Thanks, Bernie. I really appreciate you putting me up.'

'No problem, Cobber, but you'll have to let your folks know what you're up to. They'll be worried.'

'I bought a writing pad and pencils yesterday. I've written Ma and Pa a letter explaining everything. Can you give it to the co-op truck driver before he makes his rounds please and look after Clancy until Dad can collect him?'

'Leave it with me, Callan. I'll ride out to the farm with Clancy myself,' Bernie said. 'And talking of letters, a very dainty little miss left this for you...'

'Ivy Brown?'

'I do believe that was the young lady's name and might I say she's a bonzer looking sheila. You really weren't idle yesterday arvo, were you?'

Callan couldn't hide his chagrin at missing Ivy, but she'd caught the first train south at 6 am.

'She came to say goodbye before catching the Sydney train, but she didn't want to wake you because she knew you'd be flat-out today.'

Callan unfolded the note which was written in meticulously neat handwriting on high quality, textured paper.

My Dearest Callan,

You have no idea what a joy it was meeting you yesterday. It was so refreshing to chat to someone so honest & unassuming. We must return to England post-haste because Papa has been ordered to reform his battalion with the rank of lieutenant-colonel.

I am full of dread for him & all of you boys marching to war. I hope it won't be too terrible & you return safely & covered with glory.

I would truly love you to write to me about your adventures wherever they may take you.

Our address in Shropshire is:

Stanford Park Estate, PO Box 7

Ludlow, Shropshire, England or:

Peachtree Cottage, Carrigaline Road,

Crosshaven, County Cork, Ireland.

God bless & please do write to me.

Your dear friend

Ivy Brown.

Hmm, 'dear friend' already, that's encouraging.
Callan smiled as he placed the letter into his shirt pocket. Of course he had to remember Edwardian girls were prone to sentiment and romance. Apparently Ivy was no exception.

Callan hadn't really thought about a change of underwear or toiletries. Bernie had given him a spare toothbrush and a small tin of his home-made concoction containing baking powder and salt mixed into a paste with peppermint oil.

'The main thing is that your teeth are clean and your mouth smells fresh. You can always jump in a creek to wash the rest of you,' Bernie advised.

So Callan shook Bernie's hand and led Flash-Jack towards the railway station.

Chapter 3 — A Born Soldier

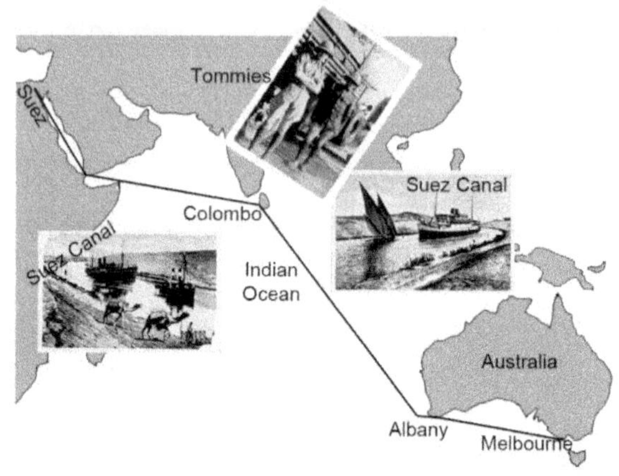

Sydney, Melbourne, Albany, Indian Ocean, Ceylon & the Suez Canal — October-December 1914

Callan's head spun for the next two months. He travelled south by rail with Flash-Jack. Upon arrival at the NSW capital, he was issued with a uniform, which fitted reasonably well. He also received pretty much everything he'd need to survive army life. Underwear, boots, peaked and slouch hat, toiletries, metal water-bottle, eating utensils, metal plate and pannikin, even a sewing kit aptly called a 'housewife' and most importantly a Lithgow manufactured Lee-Enfield short rifle and bayonet although he was yet to receive any ammunition.

Caring for Flash-Jack took up much of Callan's time, but he also got to know the men around him, most of whom were not much older than he was. There was great excitement as they reached Melbourne where more soldiers joined not only Callan's ship, but an entire convoy which had formed ready to sail for Europe — or at least that's where Callan assumed they were going.

Callan and his fellow recruits found themselves absorbed into Colonel Harry Chauvel's Mounted Brigade. One of Callan's fellow recruits was a bit of a toff who'd studied French at school and thought 'Chauvel' was a most appropriate name for a cavalry commander.

Fortunately Sergeant Blake had accompanied the recruits, which was reassuring. He suggested not many private soldiers were pleased to see NCOs, but he represented order and stability to Callan. Blake kept his men busy with weapon drills, animal and kit inspections and lengthy PE sessions. The sergeant was in excellent physical condition and didn't expect the recruits to do anything he wasn't prepared to, which included the spit-and-polish of his gear.

When their ship docked at Port Melbourne there was a great fanfare as Colonel John Monash's 4th Brigade marched through the city streets to the stirring music of several military bands. Flag-waving crowds cheered from the pavements and every shop-front and office window was jammed with onlookers.

Callan watched from the ship-rail as the troops struggled up the gangplanks with their rifles and kit-bags. They were cheerful to a man, joking and ribbing one another with wonderful camaraderie. John Monash wasn't quite what Callan expected — although in truth he didn't really know what to expect about anything in the army.

Monash was a chubby engineer and long-time army reservist, but the 4th Brigade was his first actual fighting command. He was a perplexing mixture of disciplinarian and comrade who genuinely cared for his troops' welfare. His men liked and respected him.

The voyage across the Australian Bight was uncharacteristically calm and few men or horses succumbed to seasickness. There was little time for actual training. Shipping a battalion half way around the world was a difficult logistical project, but at least Callan received news of their task.

Over the next few days, company and platoon commanders were summoned to the brigade major's cabin for briefings. Sergeant Blake was among them and returned to his men with the news. He battled his way past the hammocks stretched where men had found a minute space to call their own — as long as they were prepared to defend it. A dozen men now formed the mounted squad.

'We've been attached to the 4th Infantry Brigade,' Blake began, '...but that's not bad,' he added when he saw the crestfallen looks of the men. 'Colonel Monash wants an exploring unit. That means he needs us to act as the brigade's eyes and ears. We'll be riding far and wide and keeping an eye on things for the colonel. Our official title is 'A' troop, 1st Scouting Unit. Other troops will be formed, but we're the first. '

'Like an independent command,' Shorty Malone, one of the recruits suggested with some relish.

'Precisely,' Blake replied, 'but that don't mean we go prancing around like a bunch of punch-drunk larrikins. You may not have had much training, but you're natural horsemen and we've been given a golden opportunity to show the infantry what we're made of. I know I can count on you blokes not to let me down.'

'Too right, Sarge.'

'No worries.'

'Bloody oath.'

'Righto then,' Blake concluded. 'I shall be reporting directly to Major McGlinn, Colonel Monash's chief-of-staff. He's a decent officer. I served with him against the Boers.'

Colonel Monash had especially requested John McGlinn as his brigade major, because of his indefatigable efficient work ethic and administration skills.

So 'A' troop's strength was:

SERGEANT JOHN BLAKE (OC)

LANCE CORPORAL SLIM BLIEVERS (2 IC)

PRIVATES: JOSEPH DALRYMPLE

                BILL JONES

                COL GRIMLY

                CALLAN McALISTER

                SHORTY MALONE

                CLARRIE MONROE

                BILL PRESTON

                CES ROBINSON

                BLUEY STURGIS

                TREVOR WARREN

All were excellent horsemen, crack shots, keen as mustard and, other than Sergeant Blake, not one of them had yet reached his twentieth birthday.

Callan had plenty of opportunities to write to Ivy and his parents although his letters were not delivered for months.

Dear Ivy,

Life aboard ship is mostly hot and boring. Luckily I have Flash-Jack to care for. We berthed at Albany where a couple of New Zealand battalions joined us. We're now a mighty armada sailing for glory. The En-Zedders seem like sound blokes, much the same as us except they can't say 'sixpence'. It sounds like 'suxpunce'. We rib them about it all the time.

There were lots of high-jinks when we crossed the equator with every one getting doused with seawater, which was pretty refreshing so no one minded.

As I don't drink I was seconded to the provosts to round up some of our boys who'd jumped ship in Colombo and gone on a spree. We got them all back much the worse for wear and nursing sore heads the next day. Colonel Monash chose to treat the matter leniently...as no harm was done and we're at sea once more...We have a great bunch of blokes who are

Callan found the more often he wrote to Ivy, the worse he missed her. So he tried to avoid being sentimental although endearments slipped out regularly.

Pull yourself together, you drongo, he admonished himself, *you only met the girl once for an hour or so. Stop acting like a love-struck sissy!*

The convoy reached Suez unscathed and was cheered by Allied troops and Turk-fearing Arabs who lined the banks. Monash's brigade disembarked and set up Mena Camp close to the Giza Pyramids and a couple of hours walk to Cairo. Blake's mounted squad started training immediately, which helped Callan concentrate on something other than Ivy.

By 1915 Imperial forces including Australians, New Zealanders, Nepalese Ghurkhas, Indian Sikhs, and British units were stationed along the Suez Canal to protect that vital waterway. The Ottoman Empire, made up of Turkey, Mesopotamia, Palestine and Syria, on the other hand felt obliged to capture the canal for their German allies who wanted a short cut to the Red Sea.

Turkish foreign minister, Enver Paşa, who'd brokered the treaty with Germany after early British and French setbacks on the Western Front, might have been having second thoughts about then. Now the Turks found themselves wedged between British forces in Egypt and the Russians to the north.

The upshot was that Turkish troops planned to move south, urged on and often led by German officers and advisors. Their aim was to march through Gaza into the Sinai Peninsula and seize the Canal. It didn't take a genius to work out what they were up to and even the British high command, which had not showered itself with glory thus far, saw to it that the waterway fairly bristled with cavalry, infantry, guns, bayonets, mortars, mines, machineguns and artillery — not to mention warships anchored with their great guns aimed towards a potential enemy advance.

Unfortunately for the British, the canal ran for over a hundred miles from Port Said on the Mediterranean coast to the Gulf of Suez, which was a long front to defend in anybody's language. The Turks weren't without problems of their own. They'd have to cross the Sinai Peninsula to reach the canal and that was a stretch of seriously inhospitable terrain.

Excerpt [censored] letter to Ivy March — 1915

Dear Ivy,

It looks like we've arrived where we're supposed to be, but it sure doesn't look like France. I don't think I'm supposed to tell you where we are, but there are three dirty great triangles sticking up into the sky right next to our camp.

It's all marching, drilling, spit and polishing and caring for the walers. Our tents look pretty smart in absolute straight rows, but every now and then some Tommy officer struts

Callan wrote to Ivy regularly, but was disappointed that he received no replies. He'd given his address as the 4th Infantry Brigade AIF, which he thought would be sufficient — letters from his parents reached him. Maybe she'd just been teasing him and leading him on. In any event he put all thoughts of Ivy aside when Sergeant Blake announced 'A' troop's first mission.

'Right, you jokers,' Sergeant Blake said. 'We take rations and water for a week, one-hundred-and-fifty rounds per man. It's time to earn your keep. We're off on a joy-ride.'

'Where to, Sarge?' Bluey asked.

'Need to know basis,' Blake replied, 'which means I'll tell you when there's a need.'

The Allies did know that in January the Turks under their German commander, Colonel Kress Von Kressenstein, had already attacked the Suez Canal at Ismaila in the centre of the canal along with several other strategic points. The Turks were beaten off and had virtually disappeared. Colonel Monash and his superiors were interested to find out what had happened to them.

Callan and his comrades all wore slouch hats. It may have been winter and often cold, but they still needed to avoid sunstroke. Conversely they carried overcoats and blankets because nights were expected to be freezing. The riders carried ninety rounds of .303 ammunition in bandolier pouches with a further ten rounds in the rifles slung across their backs. The remaining fifty rounds were shoved into their saddle-bags.

They also led four extra horses as pack animals to carry additional feed, firewood and water to the weight of a fully equipped rider. The troops knew the horses would have to be abandoned if it came to a running fight. The walers' chances of survival in the Sinai Desert were slim unless they could keep up with the mounted riders on their own, or were captured by Bedouin tribesmen.

The patrol left early, but it was still forty miles to Ismaila where they were ferried across the canal by barge and clattered ashore on the Sinai bank. So they camped on the eastern bank where they were joined by a sinister, hook-nosed Arab with piercing black eyes who'd act as guide and interpreter. His name was Hassan al-Wazir. He'd sided with the British, hoping they'd crush the Turks and help form an independent Palestine. To this end Hassan was armed with a Webley .455 service revolver, Ottoman scimitar and a long jezail-style rifle which had been converted to a breech-loader.

Hassan differed from many other Arabs who were vehemently anti-British, some of whom had even enlisted in the Ottoman Army.

The British had withdrawn all their units from the Sinai Peninsula to guard the canal, so patrols were the only way of gathering intelligence.

Next morning the Anzacs rode east. During the morning two bi-planes droned overhead. Callan wondered what it would be like to soar into the sky without considering the engine noise, vibrations, reek of aviation petrol or being splattered with leaking motor-oil.

Hassan's camel was a belligerent beast which insisted on spitting at anyone close by and spooking the Australian walers. The Aussies were relieved when they left the canal bank and Hassan, along with his camel, cantered ahead of the column on the lookout for trouble.

'Ruddy hell,' Bill Jones observed as the sun rose, 'this place is worse than the flamin' Simpson Desert. Who the blazes lives 'ere?'

Nobody much as it turned out. Some isolated settlements lay along the Mediterranean Coast, but it was essentially 'just-passing-through' country. A few Bedouin and Berber nomads camped in protected wadis or oases where there was at least some water and protection from summer's searing heat and suffocating simooms. But generally the terrain was rocky, rugged, barren and cruelly hostile.

The patrol travelled over Sinai's western plateau fringed by snow-capped peaks in the eastern distance. Fortunately Hassan either knew where to find water or who to ask. Whenever the patrol came across wandering Bedouin tribesmen, Hassan questioned them for intelligence.

These conversations always seemed animated and agitated to Callan. Sergeant Blake ordered his men to stay alert with their rifles ready. The Arabs either simply looked suspicious or downright hostile. Rightly or wrongly, the Australians didn't trust the locals on sight. It was probably just in-built prejudice and the first two days passed uneventfully.

Early on the second day out from Suez the horsemen reached an oasis already inhabited by a family of nomads who'd erected several tents under the date palms. There was no sign of young men among the nomads. A dozen women fussed around preparing food and gathering drinking water surrounded by a flock of children.

All the women wore black abaya robes and covered their lower faces with hijab veils. Callan wonder if they were pretty like the young Egyptian women walking the streets of Cairo, many of whom had abandoned their traditional attire for western fashions — no doubt influenced by the British. The patriarch and boys uniformly wore dishdashas, which seemed rather drab as Callan remembered the dapper and stylish Australian city-folk. But then the Sinai was a drab place.

As the troops brewed tea, Hassam questioned the headman and reported to Sergeant Blake.

'He says Turks are close,' Hassam explained. He spoke flawless English, which wasn't surprising as it turned out he'd won a scholarship to be educated at prestigious Reading Public School in Berkshire. 'They patrol all around. One day this direction, one day that. There is no pattern.'

'Intelligence gathering, like us?' Blake suggested.

'Possibly,' Hassan replied with a shrug, 'or just trying to look busy.'

'Does the old boy know how many?'

Blake handed Hassan a pannikin of black tea, which he preferred to the Aussie choice of as much sugar and condensed milk as possible.

'He does not know if he spots different units or the same one over and again. He is unhappy. His young men have either been conscripted or have made themselves scarce living in the mountains like outlaws.'

'If there are large numbers of troops in the area, they must have a base. They have to resupply. You can't carry more than week's supply of food out here.'

'An-Nekhel Fortress lies half a day's ride from here. It is abandoned now, but I believe the well still holds water. There is nothing but barren desert for miles. If I had to be here, that is where I would base myself. Maybe we should go and see.'

'It's worth a try. We haven't turned up much so far.'

Callan thought Hassan didn't appear nearly as ominous once you got used to his stealthy ways. At first the Australians thought their guide might be a bit aloof, but he joined them for a meal, using his right hand to eat rather than a spoon. No one commented.

'A' Troop rode off soon afterwards. A road actually linked Suez to An-Nekhel, which had been used by pilgrims for half a millennium, but the surround country was wasteland. Several miles short of the fort the terrain flattened into a vast plain with no remarkable features whatsoever. 'A' Troop had reached the limit of its range before having to return to Suez.

Sergeant Blake peered through his binoculars at the distant shimmering grey smudge that represented the fort.

'What can you make out?' he asked, handing the binoculars to Hassan.

The Arab adjusted the focus and studied the fort for a few minutes.

'I can see smoke from cooking fires and there may be a lorry, but it is too far for me to see more.'

'It doesn't look like a hive of activity.'

'I will go and observe. Stay here, Sergeant Blake. I will not arouse suspicion.'

Unfortunately Hassan was quite wrong about that...

Chapter 4 — First Blood

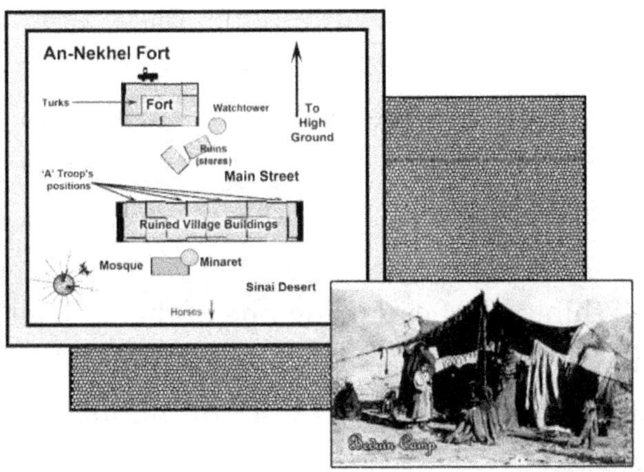

At first it appeared that An-Nekhel was deserted, but as he approached, Hassan's keen eyes picked out figures scurrying along the fort ramparts and more troops forming up in front of the wall beside the parked truck. The sinking sun was behind the patrol, which meant anyone in the fort was partially blinded and would have difficulty seeing any great distance while squinting towards the horizon.

A lone camel rider should have proved no threat to the An-Nekhel garrison. What was he going to do — hide a bomb under his dishdasha? But the Turks saw things differently. Hassan was still three hundred yards from An-Nekhel when a Maxim machinegun spluttered lead towards him. Slugs slammed into the road in spiteful, gouts of grit.

Hassan didn't wait to see if the shots were intended simply as a warning. He turned his camel and lumbered back the way he'd come. Sergeant Blake scanned the fort ramparts for an indication of the garrison's manpower. From the distance he was unable to make a precise estimate, but he was sure it was no more than a half- company — maybe fifty men.

'Well that answers one question,' Blake announced when Hassan returned.

'Fine, but what are we gonna do about 'em, Sarge?' Joe Dalrymple asked.

'I reckon it'd be handy to find out who they are and what they're up to.'

'Are you thinking of capturing one of them?' Callan asked.

Blake nodded.

'You have noticed they probably outnumber us five-to-one, haven't you?'

'Wouldn't be a fair fight with anything less,' Blake grinned, 'but I think we might rely on stealth and rat-cunning.'

'A' Troop was on a tight schedule. They couldn't stay in their present position for more than a day or their water supply would become dangerously low. So their window of opportunity was only for the coming night. They made plans that relied on the assumption that the garrison thought they'd chased away a single Arab and wouldn't be expecting trouble. And that would have indeed been the case if Hassan had been the only Arab prowling around An-Nekhel.

*

The patrol camped in a dry wadi. Sergeant Blake had rostered his men to keep an eye on the fort, but as darkness fell, no Turkish soldiers felt inclined to venture out. They waited until midnight before making a move.

January day temperatures may have been mild, but the nights were bitterly cold and everyone rugged up as best they could. When the men complained Hassan assured them they'd feel even worse on a blistering summer's day.

Lance Corporal Slim Blievers suggested they muffle the horses' hooves, but they didn't have sufficient material for the job, so they made a wide berth around the fort to approach under the protection of the village's ruined walls. Blake ordered the patrol to dismount and they walked for the last mile, before halting about one hundred yards short of the buildings. The march took longer than expected. They arrived an hour before dawn.

The village was simply a row of one and two storey terrace homes that were now crumbling and roofless. A mosque stood beside the village and gave the best cover for 'A' troop as they advanced. Leaving Col Grimly and Clarrie Monroe to tend the horses the remaining eleven men crept towards An-Nekhel. Hassan led his camel as the Anzacs had no idea how to control it. The moon had set by then and the night was black as pitch. The biggest danger so far was tripping over a rock, stepping on a snake or stumbling into a gully.

They reached the mosque wall without incident. Hassan urged the camel to sit using the reins and riding crop and the beast responded to its master without protest. Blake gave his orders by hand signals which the troopers could just make out, but they were prearranged anyway. He ordered his men to unsling their rifles and fix bayonets.

Callan and Hassan moved forward while the others positioned themselves inside the village ruins. There were several balconies and rubble heaps they used as ramparts while taking cover behind the walls. Hassan led the way to the crumbling outhouses between the fort and the village. The walls protected dozens of supply crates and ammunition boxes. They were just able to make out crates of rifles, ammunition, shells, bombs and dynamite. Flour sacks and other provisions were stacked right next to the ordnance.

Callan's heart was in his mouth. However, he was surprised to find he was less terrified than he'd been back home staring down a king-brown snake rearing only feet in front of him — especially when the nearest pitchfork was leaning against a fence fifty yards away.

In that case he froze and the snake lost interest before slithering away. This time he froze when Hassan stopped suddenly, placing his finger to his lips. The night was still and Callan thought he heard his heart thumping. Next he was *sure* he heard the crunch of feet on gravel and the muffled whispers of approaching men.

Two guards passed as Hassam and Callan pressed against the nearest wall. The Turkish sentries were no more than shadows, but then they stopped only feet from Hassan and Callan. Suddenly a match flared and both men lit cigarettes from the single flame. The match seemed to illuminate the whole area, but the guards' night-vision was temporarily destroyed by the sudden flash of light.

Get-in-get-out-quick was Sergeant Blake's instruction and Hassan obeyed it to the letter. He drew his scimitar, darted forward and drove the blade into the nearest sentry's back. The light was so poor that Hassan misjudged his aim. The sword skidded off the Turk's back-pack webbing. Hassan staggered forward under his own momentum while his intended victim dodged aside.

Callan saw at once things were not right. The Turks recovered quickly and pounced onto Hassan. Suddenly there was just a jumble of seething shadows and muffled grunts. Perhaps it was best that the light was so poor, otherwise Callan might have had reservations. As it was the struggling figures lost much of their humanity in the darkness.

Callan rushed to the rescue and, before he had time to think, he levelled his rifle and drove the bayonet into the nearest Turk's kidneys. Again almost instinctively, he twisted his rifle and dragged the blade free, dripping with blood that looked as black as the night sky.

Meanwhile Hassan and the other Turk sentry wrestled at Callan's feet. His training paid off. Without a second's delay he smashed his rifle butt into the Turk's skull. The man grunted and slumped over Hassan.

'Get him off me,' Hassan hissed as Callan stood gasping for breath.

Callan helped Hassan to his feet and they checked the Turks for a pulse. One lay dead in a pool of blood, but Callan had only stunned the other.

'This one will have to do.' Hassan whispered. 'If Sergeant Blake wants more prisoners, he can come and get them himself.'

They took an arm each and dragged the Turk back to the patrol's position.

'Good work,' Sergeant Blake said softly. 'Let's not push our luck. It's time to shoot through.'

'Hang on, Sarge,' Callan said. 'There's a pile of gear down there. I mean all sorts of stuff the Turks need — including dynamite.'

'Are you thinking what I think you're thinking..?'

'Yeah, Sarge, there's time before dawn.'

'You men stay put and cover us,' Blake said. 'Show me, Mac.'

'I will come too,' Hassan said.

Blake eyed him curiously. No one volunteered unless they absolutely had to.

'You will need to identify what is in the boxes. The writing will most likely be in Arabic,' Hassan said with a shrug.

'Good thinking, c'mon — you blokes keep your eyes peeled.'

It took only seconds to return to the stockpiles. The crates were stacked in neat piles, so there was no need to shift anything, but they needed fuse wire. Hassan indeed turned out to be useful and identified a box that contained pyrotechnic fuse blasting caps and fuse-wire. Breaking open the crates quietly was the biggest problem, but a well placed — still blood-stained — bayonet did the job.

As Hassan had no training in explosives, Blake told him to unwind the fuse-wire and take it back as far as he could towards 'A' Troop's position — behind the wall if possible. Callan opened another crate containing dynamite sticks. Blake rammed the fuse-wire into the detonator and crimped it in place with his teeth. He then jammed the blasting cap into the dynamite.

'One will do,' Blake said. 'We'll stuff it in with the rest and she'll go off like my missus when I come 'ome from the pub.'

Callan hadn't thought of Blake having a family, but now was not the time for reflection. It was time to scarper — they'd hung around too long as it was. Blake and Callan heard the crunch of boots as two more Turkish guards approached. One of them tripped over their dead comrade and life heated up considerably for Callan and the patrol.

The guards yelled the alarm at the top of their lungs. Even then 'A' troop might have got away with it if the Turks thought the dead and missing guards were the victims of a random Bedouin raid, but impulsive Lance Corporal Blievers ordered his men to open fire and that pretty well gave the game away.

Blake and Callan raised their rifles and fired. The two Turks dropped in a hail of lead, but their comrades had been alerted and instantly manned the fort ramparts and started returning fire. Bullets smashed into the village ruins spraying dust, brick shards and stone chips in lethal gouts of shrapnel.

'C'mon, Mac,' Blake bellowed above the constant tattoo of gunfire.

They dashed to the village as random bullets zinged overhead or splatted into the dirt at their feet. The fuse-wire guided them in the right direction. Blake and Callan reached the wall and ducked behind a portal although the door had long since rotted away or been used as firewood.

'Corporal!' Blake bellowed. 'Prepare to evacuate. Send someone to bring in the horses.'

'No need, Sarge,' Blievers replied, 'Col and Clarrie heard the shots and brought the horses straight up. They're by the outer wall now.'

'Good job. You and Mac here keep the Turks heads down. Grab that prisoner and get him on a spare horse. Everyone else, mount up.'

Callan scrambled up the rubble until he reached a spot close to Slim Blievers where he could fire at the fort. The rest of the patrol wasted no time struggling through gaps in the wall and mounting up. Col Grimly and Clarrie Monroe had done a sterling job controlling so many horses with just two halters. The Turk was still groggy and offered no resistance when he was bundled onto a spare mount, guarded on either side by Bluey Sturgis and Trev Warren.

Maybe Callan's night-vision had adjusted, but he was sure he could see more clearly and picked a target on the fort rampart. He squeezed the trigger and saw the Turks head jerk and disappear for view. Slim Blievers must have felt the same, because he dropped another man.

Nope, Callan, dawn is breaking. C'mon, Sarge we need to be outa here.

'Right,' Blake yelled, striking a match. 'This isn't how I planned it, but it'll have to do.'

The fuse wire spluttered into an intense burst of flame and acrid smoke.

'Get going!' Blake yelled and ran for his horse. Callan and Slim were only seconds behind. They took the reins from Col and mounted up as the patrol galloped away.

'What if they get to the fuse before she blows?' Callan cried.

'Too bad! Get going,' Blake yelled over his shoulder.

'Are you game, Mac?' Slim asked as he settled into the saddle.

'Game for what..?'

'Keeping their heads down. Follow me.'

Slim cantered along the village wall and around the corner into what had been An-Nekhel's main street. Callan and Flash-Jack were only yards behind. Using his feet to guide his horse, Slim urged it into a gallop and levelled his rifle and fired at the fort. Callan marvelled at how Slim operated the bolt action from his bouncing saddle, and managed to fire all of the remaining rounds in his magazine. Callan had removed his bayonet which hindered rifle-fire on horseback, but still only managed one shot before

Flash-Jack jumped over the sizzling fuse-wire and dashed past the fort. There was no point in further shooting so both riders expertly slung their weapons across their backs.

It was unlikely they hit anyone, but Slim's plan worked as there was a brief pause when the Turks ducked for cover, holding their fire. But brief was all it was. Just as Callan and Slim cleared An-Nekhel the Turks gathered their wits and with the first glimpse of dawn at their backs, it was light enough for them to see the fleeing horsemen. Worst still the Turks dragged the Maxim gun into action and soon it was spluttering red-hot death.

The two riders galloped alongside each other, but they were only fifty yards clear of the fort when a burst of lead hammered into Slim's waler. The horse died instantly, tumbling forward pitching Slim headlong into the desert. Luckily he landed close to his horse, which acted as a shield. More rounds slammed into the animal, splattering flesh and blood all over Slim.

'Oh, shit,' Callan said through gritted teeth.

Turning in the saddle he saw Slim lying beside his mount. Callan knew he was still alive, but he appeared to be wounded. There was nothing for it, Callan hauled on the reins and turned Flash-Jack around. Slim dragged himself clear of his dead horse.

'Get back!' he yelled. 'Save yourself, Mac. My leg's all shot to pieces.'

He ducked again as more bullets zinged past, but Callan kept coming. Slim saw what Callan was up to and just as he reached his fallen comrade, he held out his arm. Slim was in agony as he lurched onto his good leg, grabbed Callan's arm and flung himself over Flash-Jack's back behind the saddle.

One of the reasons walers were so popular with Anzac cavalry was their toughness. Flash-Jack not only bore two riders without complaint, but also endured two bullet grazes that nicked his rump, drawing blood, but did not slow him.

But Callan and Slim were sitting ducks without a chance...and then the dynamite blew! The first stick detonated with an ear-splitting crack followed micro-seconds later by the rest of the explosives — dynamite, bombs, ammunition all went up together, blasting the Turks from the fort ramparts. Bullets detonated and cracked in all directions like lethal fireworks. Masonry and other debris erupted hundreds of feet into the air and clattered to earth for a quarter of a mile. The flour bags went up like a desert simoom, caking Callan and Slim ghostly white.

The shock wave whooshed over Slim and Callan like a gigantic thump across their backs. Yet Flash-Jack didn't miss a step, but cantered clear of the devastation as the remnants of the explosion plunged to earth in their wake. 'A' troop halted a mile beyond An-Nekhel and turned to see the fireball engulf the village accompanied by a billowing pall of smoke snaking heavenwards. Blake ordered the patrol to wait when he saw Callan and Slim silhouetted against the first dawn rays on the eastern horizon. Callan was unable to read Sergeant Blake's mood when they rode up. His tone was cool, but not totally frosty.

'And just what do you two think you were up to?' he asked in a flat voice.

'I thought we needed to stop the Turks discovering the fuse before it blew, Sarge,' Slim reported. 'I ordered Mac to follow me.'

'Yes and I'm sure Mac didn't need any encouragement,' Blake suggested

This attempt by Slim to get Callan off the hook wasn't missed by Blake or the others, but there was a more urgent matter to attend to — Slim's leg.

Joe Dalrymple was the unit medico. He examined the wound and declared it was in bad shape. The best he could do was splint it and stem any bleeding. Anything else would have to wait until they returned to 4th Brigade HQ.

The sun was fully above the horizon when Joe felt he'd done all he could for Slim and the troopers managed to get him into his saddle. The Turkish prisoner was regaining his senses and looked on with a sullen mixture of bewilderment, apprehension and hostility. Hassan's watchful eye followed his every move with a look suggesting he'd butcher the Turk without a second thought.

Just as the patrol prepared to move on Bill Jones called to Blake.

'You'd better come a see this, Sarge,' he said calmly.

All eyes turned to the fort which was still shrouded by smoke. The Turkish truck rattled out of the haze. It had been protected from the explosion by the fort. As it drew closer the Aussies saw that it was full of armed Turkish soldiers.

Chapter 5 — Friend or Foe?

'Better get ready to shoo 'em off,' Sergeant Blake said with calm confidence, which was justified because the truck only held a few more men than 'A' Troop. Blake knew his soldiers would make short work of any exposed targets, and the Turks had thus far shown they were indifferent marksmen. They didn't however appear to be concerned about being exposed sitting in the back of the truck.

Once again the Anzacs acted as mounted infantry. Col and Clarrie handled the horses while the others lay behind what little cover was available. Each man loaded a magazine, pulled the bolt back and slammed a slug into the breech.

As the truck rattled along the rutted track an arm poked through the cabin's side window. A white flag then flapped in the wind. The arm waved vigorously ensuring it was seen.

'Hold your fire,' Blake ordered as the truck lurched to a halt a hundred yards ahead of 'A' Troop.

A Turkish officer stepped from the truck running-board and walked cautiously towards the Australians. Sergeant Blake rose to meet him. Still holding the flag above his head, the Turk stopped a few yards short of Blake.

'We must talk,' the officer said stiffly in heavily accented English.

'What about?' Blake said, all tough and businesslike.

'A truce.'

'And why would I care about a truce? We seem to have given you a good hammering. You don't have many men left.'

'You are correct,' the officer conceded, 'and some of our survivors are wounded, but I think we need one another right now.'

'I don't see how...'

Hassan nudged Blake's arm and pointed towards An-Nekhel. About fifty Bedouin camel riders stood in a line abreast just outside town. They remained stationary and showed no signs of advancing for the moment.

'I am Lieutenant Davran Cerci,' the Turk introduced. 'I commanded two platoons to guard the An-Nekhel outpost, but that is no longer possible — or necessary now you have blown everything up. The blast killed half my men.'

'Yeah, well sorry about that,' Blake said wryly, 'but there is a war on, you know. I'm Sergeant Blake.'

Lieutenant Cerci shrugged.

'What is done is Allah's will. We have a bigger trouble now. Those tribesmen have been watching the fort for days. They pounced the moment you left. They killed more of my men and butchered the wounded. This...' he indicated the truck, '...is all that is left of my unit.'

'That was quick.'

'It was over in minutes, we were lucky to get away.'

'You're gonna have to surrender, you know,' Blake said.

Cerci shrugged again.

'If you insist,' he said. 'I am not prepared to die for some mistaken notion of honour.'

'Wise decision,' Blake agreed. 'Bring your men in and we'll sort out what to do.'

Whether the truck was going to help or be a liability was problematic. It was a sturdy Locomolile general service lorry with twenty men crammed into the tray and cabin. The canvas sides had been rolled up revealing that several Turks were indeed wounded — a couple seriously. Whether the machine would endure the rugged track back to the canal was uncertain as was its range, although the Turks carried four spare eighteen-litre petrol flimsies.

Blake ordered Cerci to instruct his men to lay their weapons in the truck.

'What about the Bedouin?' Cerci protested.

'If you need to shoot them, I'll let you know,' Blake said. 'You'll forgive me if I don't quite trust you just yet,' he added laconically.

The Turks obeyed, especially when Hassan barked a few sharp commands. Slim Blievers was loaded onto the truck while three of the Turks who turned out to be capable riders mounted the spare walers. The truck was only marginally less congested because the Australians put their spare gear into the back as well. Cerci and another Turk sat beside the driver. Everyone mounted and Blake ordered them to move off.

'Hassan and Shorty scout ahead. Mac and Trev, you ride rearguard and keep an eye on that lot behind. Let me know if you see anything fishy.'

Slim bore his wounds stoically enough, as did the Turks although there was an odd groan as the truck bumped over a rock or into a pothole. The convoy of walers, truck and Hassan's camel set off westwards, while Callan and Trevor Warren waited for the Bedouin to move, which they did shortly afterwards.

'You reckon we can outrun those camels?' Callan asked.

'Too right, those ruddy things are designed by a committee,' Slim replied. 'They'll probably trip over their own front feet if they want to gallop.'

'I reckon they're designed for this sort of country,' Callan suggested doubtfully, 'We'd better not let them get too close.'

As it turned out the camels' speed wasn't an issue. Callan and Trevor played a game of chicken as the Bedouin approached. The Arabs carried an assortment of rifles ranging from ancient jezails to modern German bolt-action Mausers. When they thought they were within effective range, several Bedouin levelled their rifles and fired.

'Well at least we know their intentions,' Callan commented as bullets zinged past uncomfortably close by.

His words fell on deaf ears because Trevor was already heading away from trouble and Callan wisely followed. The Bedouin took up the chase, but at a leisurely speed. It appeared they knew how to pace themselves and their camels.

Once Callan and Trevor cleared the open plain and entered hilly terrain, they felt less vulnerable. The pursuing Arabs had to bunch up when they reached the pass. Boulders and spindly scrub lined the dusty road which was little more than two lines of tyre-tracks.

'It's time to give 'em a taste of their own medicine,' Callan suggested, with unexpected enthusiasm. In fact he may have been taking to warfare rather too casually in some people's opinion. As yet the impact of shooting someone or killing a man with his bayonet hadn't sunk in. Perhaps it never would. Right then he was in the business of fighting the enemy and he focused on that.

'I'm game,' Trevor agreed.

They dismounted and perched behind the largest rock around. While Trevor held the walers, Callan aimed his rifle back along the trail. Initially the Bedouin were hidden by the sloping ground that framed the curved valley. When the tribesmen finally appeared they were no more than two hundred yards away, which was dangerously close as they outnumbered Callan and Trevor by over twenty-to-one.

Callan held his nerve and fired.

An Arab dropped from his saddle as the shot echoed through the valley.

Callan fired again.

Another Arab fell.

The rifle cracked again.

This time a camel slumped to its chest, pitching its rider to the ground. The impact was profound. The Bedouin scattered to the sides and many retreated until they were safely out of sight.

'You can stop showing off now,' Trevor said. 'It's time to go.'

He got no argument from Callan and the two riders mounted up and galloped away. The Arabs were much more circumspect after that. They sent scouts ahead who kept well concealed until they thought the trail was clear.

'You reckon we can get up the ridge-line?' Trevor asked as they slowed their horses to a walking pace. 'We'd see 'em from a hell of a way off up there.'

So Callan and Trevor parted company and rode to the high ground on either side of the road. The walers scrambled up the terrain although it was by no means easy going, but that was the nature of the stoic beasts. By riding along the ridge-line both Anzacs were able to keep the Bedouin and their own patrol in sight. 'A' Troop and the Turks were now at least two miles ahead. Although the high ground made tactical sense from an observational point of view, the Arabs were not inclined to leave the road. Callan could only assume the camels were reluctant to lumber up the slope, but he didn't really know.

He heard rifle fire popping as Trevor fired from the opposite ridge. The range was extreme and it was unlikely Trevor hit anyone, but it kept the Arabs at bay. By late afternoon Callan signalled to Trevor to head back to the road and report to Sergeant Blake.

When they caught up, the patrol had reached the oasis where they'd learnt of the Turks at An-Nekhel. There was no sign of the old patriarch and his nomadic family, who'd probably just moved on. Nevertheless Blake was on full alert as everyone had heard the sporadic gunfire behind them. The Turks' lorry was parked across the track for maximum cover. They'd set up camp.

Billies boiled over camel-dung fires while the men tucked into tins of bully-beef. The Turks had managed to take a sack of flour and a crate of dried fruit before the Bedouin overran their position. Blake and Lieutenant Cerci arranged to divide the rations. There were no complaints as it looked that everyone would at least get a balanced diet for supper for a change. The Turks baked fruit-filled unleavened bread similar to damper, which everyone agreed was pretty tasty when eaten hot.

Callan made his report, suggesting Blake post lookouts on the high ground before dark.

'Good idea,' Blake agreed. 'Clarrie and Shorty get up on the right ridge. Ces and Bill, you take the left. Watch out the bastards don't try to outflank us along the high ground.'

Ces Robinson returned to camp just after nightfall.

'The Arabs have dossed down for the night, Sarge,' he said. 'They're about a mile down the track.'

'I wonder if they'll try anything tonight,' Blake said to no one in particular.

'Darkness won't stop them if they're so inclined,' Lieutenant Cerci said while Hassan nodded in agreement.

'OK, arm your fellows, Lieutenant. We'll secure our perimeter — a quarter of the men on each shift. I want sentries across the track and up to both ridge-lines.'

Once the men were in position and the remainder tried to get some sleep, Callan checked to see how Slim Blievers was getting along. He was feverish and his leg looked messy. Joe Dalrymple had bathed and redressed the wound, but knew Slim needed urgent medical attention if his leg was to be saved. The wounded Turks varied from mild to critical and Joe was doing his best for them as well.

Callan returned to the meagre fire and poured himself a cuppa.

'You know, Sarge,' he reflected. 'Why don't we sneak back to those Arabs and lob a couple of bombs into their camp. That'd sort 'em out.'

'Aren't you just the little firebrand, Mac?' Blake replied with a smile. 'You haven't forgotten they seriously outnumber us, have you?'

'No, Sarge, but we'd have the element of surprise.'

'We're not at war with the Bedouin, Mac,' Blake said with remarkable sympathy. 'We can't just go stomping all over their country blazing away whenever we feel like it. They're probably just trying to protect what they believe to be theirs.'

'Aren't the Bedouin nomads? They don't really have a country — and they shot Slim and killed all those Turks.'

'You care about the Turks?'

'Not really, but I care about Slim. He's one of our mates.'

'True and I've got a feeling we're going to need all the mates we can get before this show is over, but haven't you done enough killing for one day? Hassan told me you saved his life when you bayoneted that Turk sentry. How do you feel about having drawn your first blood, Mac?'

It was then that Callan realised he hadn't given the matter a second thought.

'Blow me down, Sarge it doesn't bother me at all. How the flamin' heck can that be? I mean it's not like I was a punchy sort of bloke back home.'

'Natural born killer, eh?' Blake grinned wryly. 'Some blokes take to it straight off while others heave their guts up and others go bonkers. I've seen 'em all. It looks like you've got the knack. I reckon that's going to be a great advantage when it comes to staying alive around here.'

It was a tense night, but the patrol wasn't bothered during the hours of darkness. There was a false alarm when someone fired at a prowling jackal, but otherwise the night passed peacefully. At dawn Bluey Sturgis, who'd been rostered to guard one of the ridge-lines, returned to camp.

'The Arabs have gone, Sarge,' he reported. 'Not a sign of the buggers. They must have shoved off 'ome.'

'We can only hope,' Blake said uncertainly. 'Mac, I'm appointing you acting lance-corporal. Bring in the piquets and we'll get going straight after breakfast.'

Blake ordered all the Turks to return their rifles and ammunition to the truck, and with a collective sigh of relief, the convoy set off to the west once more. They had a reasonable chance of reaching the Suez Canal by nightfall, but if not they'd be close enough to expect protection from the numerous British and Indian units patrolling the area to deter marauding nomads and Turks alike.

The main problem was the risk of the truck's radiator overheating as it trundled along in low gear. Hassan explained there would be no chance of the truck making it in summer, but so far, so good...

The morning passed and then around noon, gunfire erupted from the high ground either side of the track. Col Grimly tumbled from his saddle as a slug smashed his left shoulder. Another bullet slammed into the truck's windscreen, leaving a neat hole and crystallising the pane into a mosaic glass veil.

The shot hit the driver straight through his heart, killing him instantly. He slumped over the wheel as blood pumped straight from his aorta onto the cabin floor, drenching the foot pedals. Before Lieutenant Cerci could react the truck veered off the track, struck a pothole and tipped onto its side.

Men and equipment tumbled onto the desert. Two were hit as they scurried for cover behind the overturned lorry.

'Take cover!' Blake ordered, although exactly where was going to pose a problem. 'It's those bloody Arabs for sure. Somehow they got around us.'

That shouldn't have been surprising — it was their home-turf after all, such turf as there was. The surrounding country was flat and bare for two hundred yards on all sides until the rising terrain where the attackers lay. The Bedouin had chosen their spot well. A bullet hit Blake's waler smack in its forehead. The animal dropped where it stood, forcing Blake to jump clear and dash behind the truck in a hail of bullets chewing up dirt in his wake.

The patrol dived for cover where they could. Clarrie Monroe and Ces Robison took charge of the horses while the others returned fire.

'Sergeant Blake...' Cerci bellowed above the roar of gunfire.

'Yes, Lieutenant, now would be a good time to arm your men!'

Chapter 6 — Flight or Fight

Slugs slammed into the truck with metallic clunks. Most of the patrol had found some cover although the horses back along the trail, hoping to keep them clear of rifle-range. Unfortunately the Arabs anticipated that and about a dozen mounted men had moved behind the patrol and now blocked the escape path.

Col and Clarrie were forced back to the lorry after a burst of rifle fire from the camel riders. Fortunately none of the walers were hit. In fact it looked like the Bedouin were purposefully avoiding hitting the animals. That made sense, because the most likely reason for the attack was to kill all the soldiers and capture their horses which were a valuable commodity in the Sinai Desert.

The patrol was well and truly pinned down. Their ammunition was limited, but more importantly, so was their water supply. Whenever one of the Aussie sharpshooters fired, a volley of bullets zinged back in return.

'They can't keep this up all day,' Callan remarked as more slugs thwacked into the truck.

'Neither can we,' Blake remarked. 'I wonder how much ammo they've got.'

'Plenty,' Cerci said. 'You didn't blow up all our stores at An-Nekhel.'

'You reckon we can charge 'em down, Sarge?' Callan suggested.

'If we had lances, sabres and pistols, yes,' Blake said, 'but we've only got our rifles to shoot from on horseback and nothing to scrap with once we got among them. We're mounted infantry remember, not the ruddy Light Brigade.'

Yeah and look what happened to them!

'Tell you what, Sarge,' Callan said. 'I've got an idea...'

'...I take you're volunteering,' Blake said after Callan had explained.

Callan nodded.

'You know it's probably suicide.'

'I *know* it's *probably* suicide, but lying here waiting to be shot or die of thirst is *certainly* suicide.'

'Good luck then,' Blake said handing Callan his service revolver before giving his orders once the Turks were fully armed.

'Wait for my order,' he yelled so everyone could hear. 'Pick out targets where you think they lie and keep their bloody heads down.'

Callan checked his magazine was full and slung the rifle over his shoulder. He tucked the pistol into his belt and mounted up. Without a second's hesitation Callan drew the reins tight, half-stood in the saddle and nudged his heels into Flash-Jack's ribs. A gentle tap was all it required.

Flash-Jack knew the drill. With only a few strides, he bounded into a full gallop. As Callan rode ahead, the patrol and Turks opened up with a constant crackle of gunfire. Callan had no idea whether the Arabs fired back or towards him, so he just crouched in the saddle and hoped for the best.

Immediately he reached the Bedouin position two camels lumbered towards him — one on either side. The riders carried curved Arabian scimitars that could decapitate a man with a single well-aimed swipe. Callan drew Sergeant Blake's pistol, but knew it was virtually useless beyond point-blank range so he waited. It took nerves of steel, yet Callan was so focused he had no time for fear.

As the first Arab reached Callan's right flank, he raised his scimitar and swung with all his strength. Callan predicted the blow and ducked. He was so close he stuck the barrel into the Arab's ribs and fired. There was no time to examine what damage had been done. Callan aimed to his left and fired before the second Arab could attack. At such close range the bullet smashed the Arab's face pulverising his head to mush.

Callan rode on by without a backward glance, but about ten other tribesmen took up the chase. They fired intermittently from the backs of their lumbering beasts, but the shots went wide.

Flash-Jack's chances of out-running the Bedouin camels depended on some variables which raced through Callan's mind. In a sprint most horses would probably beat most camels but it depended on:

The terrain — luckily the ground was firm under-hoof.

There'd be no chance on sand.

Were camels better at long distances?

If so would the Arabs abandon or keep up the chase?

How far away was help anyway?

Was there any help at all?

Callan's plan was pretty much to jump on Flash-Jack's back and ride like hell for help, so it was best not to think about any shortcomings or pit-falls now. And Jack-Flash was doing a pretty good job of it too. Callan had a mere four-hundred yard start on the Bedouin and while he'd slowed Flash-Jack to a loping canter, the camels weren't closing the gap.

But they hadn't fallen back either.

So it looked like it was going to be a case of endurance. Callan knew Flash-Jack could keep up their pace all day if need be, but he'd need to stop for water eventually. The problem was the camels didn't. They could last for days without a drink.

After a couple of miles the status quo remained unchanged and Callan reckoned he had a pretty good chance of making it to the canal. Then he saw a smudge on the horizon ahead which grew into a dust cloud. Next he picked dark dots shimmer through the haze. It was only moments before Callan identified them as more camel-riders.

He was riding straight into another group of Bedouin!

Callan brought Flash-Jack to a halt. To his dismay, he saw not only were the Bedouin ahead coming straight towards him, as they drew closer he estimated there must be at least fifty of them. There was no way through that bunch, so Callan turned to see the Bedouin closing in from behind. There was nowhere to go.

What were the odds of barging through ten riders and make it back to the patrol? What was the point, Sergeant Blake and his men were doomed anyway. But better off to make a last stand with your mates and perish out here all alone.

'OK, chum,' Callan whispered in Flash-Jack's ear, 'are you up for one more push.'

The horse gave a snort which could have meant just about anything, but responded with a bound. Ignoring the new camel-riders, Callan urged Flash-Jack into a full gallop back towards the ten Bedouin who'd been chasing him. He drew Sergeant Blake's revolver. There were four rounds left in the cylinder chambers.

Callan thought he heard triumphant shrieks of delight from the oncoming Arabs as they urged their camels forward. Maybe if he hit them at full tilt he had a chance. Callan was so close now he could make out black eyes glaring hatred through their shemaghs.

Only seconds before Callan reached the Bedouin they faltered, stopped and turned their camels. Suddenly the Arabs were all cantering away. In the time it took the Bedouin to turn around Flash-Jack overtook them and Callan found himself galloping alongside his enemies. Why the blazes had they turned around? A couple of Bedouin glared at him and it looked as if they were trying to surround or herd him in the direction they were going.

Blow this for a lark, Callan thought but then did he see the venom in their eyes replaced with uncertainty or even fear?

Callan reined Flash-Jack to a trot when one of the Bedouin aimed his rifle. The shot whizzed past inches from Callan's ear. The Arabs raced on however, leaving Callan in their dust.

I dunno what that was all about, but that's one problem sorted out.

When he turned he saw the other camel-riders were almost upon him. Flash-Jack may have been a redoubtable animal, but he was tiring and unlikely to outrun the oncoming camelry. Callan's shoulders hunched in resignation as he raised the Webley revolver.

Well four of you jokers are going with me...

And then he heard a bugle call.

What the blue blazes...

The oncoming riders were now close enough for Callan to realise they weren't Arabs at all. They wore turbans instead of shemaghs and the leading riders carried regimental banners aloft as they rode line abreast with military precision. Neither were their faces covered. All the men sported magnificent beards and moustaches and were dressed in British military khaki. Then Callan realised who they were and they weren't Turks. He'd seen them before in their white parade-ground uniforms. They belong to the Bikaner Camel Corps from India.

The bugle sounded once more and the formation thundered to a halt only yards from Callan. Their leader walked his beast forward until he was next to Callan who had to crane his neck to look the man in the eye.

'Good day to you, young sahib,' the Camel Corps commander greeted with a lilting accent Callan remembered from Colombo. 'Allow me to introduce myself. I am Risaldar Gafur Dhawan at your service. Were those rascals bothering you?'

'And I'm glad to see you, sir,' Callan replied. He had no idea where a risaldar fitted into the military pecking order, but when in doubt calling someone sir was a good rule-of-thumb. 'Acting Lance-Corporal McAlister of the 4th Australian Brigade, sir.'

He threw a snappy salute just for good measure, which the Risaldar Dhawan responded in smart fashion as he eyed Callan with mild interest.

'I'm part of a reconnaissance patrol, sir. My sergeant and our blokes along with some Turkish prisoners were ambushed by more of those chaps you scared off. They're pinned down and in big trouble back along this track to the east.'

'Indeed,' Dhawan said urbanely, 'then we had better go and see what we can do to help our Anzac colleagues. Do you think your horse will keep up, Lance Corporal?'

Although not yet in general use, it seemed the Anzac acronym was creeping into some quarters of the Imperial military parlance.

'He's an Aussie waler, sir,' Callan replied, eyeing the camel corps with a wry grin. 'As Mr Paterson would say — he'll be there when he's wanted at the end.'

*

Flash-Jack was as good as Callan's word and kept up although he was the last to reach 'A' Troop and the Turks. When the Bikaner Camel Corps arrived, the Bedouin smartly retreated with a few harmless parting shots. Risaldar Dhawan decided not to give chase as the Arabs weren't a military threat and he saw there were more pressing matters at hand.

One of the Turks had been killed while Shorty Malone was wounded and lost two fingers on his left hand, putting him permanently out of action. So in three days 'A' Troop had lost as many men. Everyone pitched in to push the truck upright again, but it was a write-off. The radiator was riddled with bullet holes and all the tyres were punctured.

'It looks like we will be travelling slowly to HQ, Sergeant Blake,' Dhawan remarked.

'Dunno if the wounded will make it, sir,' Blake replied.

'We will do our very best to see they arrive alive.'

Blake had fought with Indian troops in South Africa and respected their tenacity and professionalism. This occasion was to be no exception. Several sowars rigged slings between their camels to carry those too badly hurt to walk or ride. They seemed to hold no animosity towards the Turks, treating their wounded enemies with the same care and attention as the Anzacs. Nearly everyone else rode double and then walked for fifteen minutes every half-hour to rest the horses.

It was well after dark when they finally boarded the ferry across the Suez Canal. Risaldar Dhawan took charge of the prisoners while the wounded were taken by train to Cairo. It was too late to continue so 'A' Troop camped beside the canal once more and returned to Mena Camp the following day.

When they arrived they kept busy ensuring the walers were fed, watered, groomed and settled for the night. One of the Light Horse Brigade vets treated the animals' cuts and bruises and reported there were no serious injuries and all the horses would be fit to resume duty after a few days rest.

It was well past midnight before 'A' Troop turned in. Each exhausted man collapsed onto their camp-stretchers and fell asleep instantly. But the army doesn't sleep and it seemed Callan's head had barely hit the pillow when Sergeant Blake shook him awake.

'Shake a leg, Mac you've been summoned to the inner sanctum,' Blake declared, rather too cheerfully in Callan's opinion.

When does the bastard sleep?

'C'mon, Sarge I've just put my head down.'

'Tell that to Major McGlinn, I'm sure he'll be happy for you to keep him waiting. I'm sure he has got nothing better to do than wait at your convenience.'

Since joining the AIF Callan seemed to have to shave every morning and he felt decidedly scruffy and unwashed when he faced the brigade major. He did his best to compensate with a drill-book salute while standing stiffly to attention.

'At ease, Lance Corporal McAlister,' Major McGlinn responded. 'Colonel Monash will see you directly.'

Indeed the brigade commander didn't keep Callan waiting long. Colonel Monash was a punctual man. Within minutes Callan was ushered into the colonel's office, which was surprisingly well appointed for a partitioned tent. Apparently Colonel Monash liked his comfort and made sure he had all he needed. Once again Callan snapped to attention and saluted.

'Ah, McAlister,' Monash greeted with warmth, 'do stand easy, my boy. Sergeant Blake has been telling me of your exploits in the desert. It seems you've proven quite the bold cavalier under fire.'

'Just doing my duty, sir,' Callan replied stoutly.

'Indeed you were,' Monash grinned again. 'It is my policy that duty diligently and bravely performed should be rewarded. I have decided — and Sergeant Blake concurs — you are to be mentioned in despatches and promoted to the rank of corporal to replace Lance Corporal Blievers.'

'I'm young and inexperienced, sir.'

'Ninety percent of the men in my brigade are young and inexperienced, McAlister. I have to select those with outstanding leadership qualities and I don't have much time to do it. I believe men who perform courageously in action will inspire their mates. I'm counting on chaps like you.'

Monash sensed the uncertainty in Callan's eyes.

'This is no time for false modesty, McAlister. I'm sure you're up to the job.'

'Thank you, sir. I'll do my best not to let you down.'

'That is all I ask. Good morning to you, young man.'

Callan took it that he'd been dismissed so he saluted once more and smartly marched into Major McGlinn's section of the command tent where Sergeant Blake stood waiting.

'Congratulations, Corporal,' McGlinn said, handing Callan a pair of double chevrons. 'Sew these on straight away and Sergeant Blake will explain your new duties.'

Callan's head was still spinning as he and Blake saluted and left the HQ tent.

Chapter 7 — Heartbreak and Havoc

Slim Blievers, Col Grimly and Shorty Malone were doing as well as could be expected, but for all three their war was over. The brigade surgeon was confident he could save Slim's leg, although he'd always walk with a limp in the future. Col's shoulder would heal, but it was unlikely he'd have full movement of his left arm while Shorty's lost fingers prevented any further active service.

After they'd recovered in Cairo, the three men were to be shipped home.

All around the routine of Mena Camp bustled on. NCOs kept men busy with military drill, domestic duties and didn't neglect recreational football and cricket matches — anything to keep the men busy and out of mischief. The Anzacs may have been slack by stiff-necked Tommie standards, but they were generally cheerful and ready to do their duty when needed. Colonel Monash recognised this quality and valued it above formal military protocol.

Robert's battalion had arrived and Callan took every chance to catch up with his brother although that often proved difficult in the maelstrom of camp life. Henrietta had given birth to a healthy baby boy she'd named George. Robert was content with the choice. George was a no-nonsense name and if it was good enough for the king, it was good enough for Robert's son.

Callan began stitching his stripes to his battle dress jacket until Bill Jones said he was making a dog's breakfast of it and took over. 'A' Troop all ribbed Callan about his promotion, but seemed genuinely pleased and agreed unanimously that it was well deserved.

During the morning Hassan joined the cheerful group for tea.

'Congratulations, Corporal McAlister,' he said rather formally. 'It is well earned. You have saved two lives including mine.'

'Just doing my job I reckon, Hassan. You'd have done the same for me. I know my mates would.'

Hassan shrugged.

'Nevertheless I owe you a life debt, which is a matter of honour.'

'The way this war is going, I'm sure you'll have a chance to repay it.'

'I will bear that in mind, young hero, but I think Allah has ordained otherwise,' Hassan replied enigmatically.

'You know something we don't..?'

'I am sure Sergeant Blake will supply all the relevant details in due course.'

Hassan shook Callan's hand solemnly and left reiterating his pledge that should Callan needed help he'd be there. Sergeant Blake turned up shortly after Hassan left and he did not look a happy man.

'Gather the men, Mac,' he ordered curtly.

'We've been disbanded,' Blake announced once 'A' Troop had assembled.

'Blow me down,' Ces Robinson declared. 'That has to be the shortest unit in history.'

'Apparently we've served our purpose. Major McGlinn informs me the intelligence team have gathered plenty of useful information from the Turks we captured. Those blokes weren't even Turks as such. They'd been conscripted from all over the place and didn't feel any particular loyalty to the Ottoman Empire.'

'You think they're all like that, Sarge?' Callan asked.

'I wouldn't count on it, Mac. We just got lucky.'

'Slim, Col and Shorty mightn't agree with you.'

'At least they're getting out of this alive.'

'What about us?' Trevor Warren asked.

'We're assigned to Lieutenant Bert Collins' 3rd platoon, 'C' company in Lieutenant Colonel Cannan's 15th battalion.'

Parting with Flash-Jack broke Callan's heart, but at least the waler was assigned to a farm-lad from Moree who'd grown up with horses and treated them kindly.

'Come back and visit him anytime,' the lad said. 'You'll see I'm looking after him just fine.'

'Thanks, I know you will,' Callan said. 'He does like carrots and apples if you can ever scrounge them.'

'I'll remember that.'

Callan couldn't bear to hang around the horse lines any longer, so he left in case he started blubbering.

Lieutenant Bert Collins turned out to be a rather timid individual who left his sergeants to manage their sections. The platoon commander may have lacked confidence, but was sensible enough to trust routine duties to his NCOs. So after a brief introduction, 'A' Troop who'd now become 'B' Section saw little of Lieutenant Collins.

That afternoon 'B' Section felt they needed a night in town to drown their sorrows. Callan who wasn't a drinker went along anyway because he enjoyed the company of his mates and hoped it would take his mind off losing Flash-Jack. As it was Good Friday, Sergeant Blake had no objections to granting them all leave for the Easter weekend.

A continual stream of military traffic flowed between Mena and town. The men cadged a lift on a passing lorry, which saved a long walk. Cairo was stifling, dense, noisy and smelt of petrol fumes, burning incense, sweaty humanity and cooking spices. The narrow streets were impossibly crowded with hawkers, market stalls, donkeys, urchins, beggars, prostitutes and conmen all wanting a slice of the tourist-soldiers' pie.

Often it was impossible to find a spot in the bars and cafes which were crammed with Tommies, Anzacs and Indians. Scuffles and arguments were common, making Callan wonder if the troops were actually having a good time. Many — the majority in fact — were drunk on wine and beer of dubious vintage and provenance. Street girls were doing a roaring trade, but Callan had been warned of ever-prevalent STDs. Having being brought up in the country where opportunities were rare, sex was something he had yet to encounter. In truth, although he was interested, he wasn't sure how to go about it anyway, so best to leave well enough alone for the time being.

Eventually they came to a steamy sector of town called Haret el Wasser. Amid the brothels and seedy bars they found a table in a small restaurant which served Greek and local Egyptian brews along with hot food. Most of the Anzacs had been brought up on a bland diet of unseasoned meat and vegetables and found the spice-laden fare challenging. Callan however enjoyed the tastes immensely, but found himself drinking beer to cool his throat.

'Where d'you s'pose the buggers'll send us next?' Bill Preston slurred after quaffing several strong ales.

'I dunno,' Clarrie Monroe replied in an equally unsteady tone. 'Maybe we'll just hang around this ruddy desert and get done-in by flies, mossies and stroppy camels.'

'I heard from a bloke who knows a bloke what heard a bloke who works with one of Colonel Monash's clerks that we're headin' for Constantinople,' Ces Robinson added.

'What's there?' Callan asked.

'Ruddy lot of flamin' Turks as far as I can gather,' Ces commented.

The conversation went back and forth as the men drank more and the tobacco smoke drifted in a dense cloud inches above their heads. Callan became vaguely aware of the boisterous atmosphere around him growing louder, more animated and agitated. No one really knows how the fight that became known as the Battle of Wazzir started. Some said it was a general dissatisfaction with the price and quality of booze and women, but Callan recalled that Bluey Sturgis didn't help matters.

The cafe sported a small stage where a percussion band belted out a beat while belly-dancers gyrated provocatively, peeling veils from their costumes until nothing was left. Everyone enjoyed the show, cheering and clapping along with a fair share of ribald cat-calls. It was Callan's first foray into an adult venue and he wasn't sure what to make of it, although he didn't mind watching a bevy of naked females swaying close by.

The night progressed well until sometime around midnight Bluey suddenly leapt from his chair sending it clattering into infuriated bystanders. Bluey's attention was firmly focused on a fez-capped Egyptian seated alone in a corner close by. The hapless local was drinking coffee and hastily writing in a note book on his lap.

Blue pounced and ripped the pad from the Arab's hand.

'Caught ya, you flamin' stinkin' nigger spy,' Bluey roared staring at the writing which of course he couldn't understand. 'I saw you sneaking around our table listening to things that don't concern you.'

Even then there was a chance to save the situation, but Bluey was beyond rational behaviour. Maybe the grief of losing his horse was a factor or he was simple a bad drunk. Bluey smacked the poor fellow on the side of his head, sending the fez flying across the table and that was pretty well that. The bar erupted into mayhem. Suddenly everyone was throwing punches — Arabs, Aussies, Kiwis and Tommies all joined the fray although the Indians discreetly made themselves scarce.

Tables toppled over and a chair crashed through the cafe window, spraying passers-by with glass shards. More enraged soldiers joined the melee. In minutes the brawl was carried into the street and quickly spread in all directions. The fight escalated to a full-scale riot. Men smashed shop-fronts, looting indiscriminately and beating up anyone who stood in their way. Terrified shop-keepers, cafe-owners, waiters and street-girls all dashed for cover. Several brothels and bars were set alight and soon it looked like the entire length of Haret el Wasser was ablaze.

Meanwhile Callan was doing all he could just to fend off blows from all sides — and not just from Arabs, but anyone who wanted to throw a punch. Callan's head spun and his vision blurred as he was knocked across a table and slammed onto the mosaic floor. The fall jarred him senseless and he blacked out.

Then a dark-robed figure hauled Callan to his feet.

'You must come with me at once,' the man said in a familiar voice.

Hassan to the rescue!

'You must come away,' he hissed urgently in Callan's befuddled ear.

Callan was in no condition to argue, allowing himself to be lead to the back of the cafe and into a back alley. Somehow Hassan had gathered the rest of B Section who were helping Bluey who'd received a well deserved clout that had knocked him senseless.

'Come,' Hassan hissed through clenched teeth. 'There is big trouble brewing and you do not want to be involved.'

Soon the nine men were lost in a labyrinth of alleys barely wide enough to walk in single-file. Joe Dalrymple and Trevor draped Bluey's arms over their shoulders, half-dragging their semi-comatose comrade along. It seemed as if the riot had spread beyond Haret el Wasser and all of Cairo was now in uproar. It wasn't long before MPs' whistles shrieked all over town.

'You must dodge the military police,' Hassan advised and received no argument from Callan and his mates.

As they reached the outskirts of town they dodged a squadron of mounted Tommie Yeomanry galloping to restore order in Cairo. They were followed by a Lancashire Territorial unit and the MPs. Once the horsemen had thundered by, Callan's band-of-brothers sheepishly skulked back to camp. Bluey recovered along the way and was subjected to teasing and jibes from his mates.

'Thanks, Hassan, you saved our bacon,' Callan said. 'How did you know where to find us?'

Hassan winced at the mention of bacon. He was touchy about certain things Callan could not understand.

'I have kept an eye on you since you came to Cairo. Haret el Wasser is a really bad area and should be avoided in my opinion. I feared trouble was brewing. There is much dissatisfaction and resentment between the Tommies, Anzacs and townspeople. It is best just to stay clear of such a situation. Is it not right to protect your comrades-in-arms?'

'Too right, you're true-blue,' Callan said pumping Hassan's hand.

'True-blue..?' Hassan said hesitantly.

'Sure, you know — fair-dinkum, bonza, grouse, a ripper bloke...'

Hassan simply smiled and shook his head. He'd been led to understand Australians spoke English, but possibly that wasn't so.

'By the way,' Hassan added, 'the man Bluey struck was indeed a spy. I took his notebook which is a list of British Imperial and Anzac troop numbers and units. Please take this to Colonel Monash's HQ.'

'Thanks Hassan,' Callan said taking the notebook. 'Pity the rotter got away.'

'Who says he got away?' Hassan grinned, patting the knife tucked into his waist-sash.

It took most of the night to return to Mena Camp, but Hassan's timely warning meant 'B' Section had made their getaway before the worst trouble flared. Later accusations of looting, rape, vandalism, knifing and bashings were rife and undoubtedly justifiable. The locals demanded several hundred pounds in compensation and a large delegation arrived at Mena Camp on Easter Sunday just after church parade.

'Don't these rascals know it's Easter Sunday,' General Birdwood was reported to have said and wasn't particularly pleased when his aides informed him they were Muslims and didn't give a hoot for Easter. It was business as usual for them. Whether the general was furious at the Egyptians for disturbing his Easter Sunday, or the men under his command for upsetting the locals, was unclear.

Colonel Monash was more sanguine and saw the Anzacs readiness for a scrap as a positive sign when they came to face their enemy.

Divisional commanders parcelled the outraged town delegates piecemeal to the brigade commanders who then delegated the problem to their battalion commanders and so on down the line. It was a classic divide-and-conquer strategy, hoping that the Egyptians would simply give up and go away. By the time the aggrieved brothel pimps and bar owners reached company level most had indeed abandoned their protests, but Major McGlinn organised a whip-around to placate the locals before sending them back to Cairo.

'Your first leave for months,' Sergeant Blake addressed his men incredulously, 'and you start a flamin' war and burn half the town to the ground.'

That was a gross exaggeration, but Blake hadn't been there and didn't want to trivialise the riot. As they were uncertain whether Bluey *hadn't* actually started the whole sorry business, Callan and his mates kept quiet, taking an ear-bashing from Blake in silence. Indeed Blake's assessment was probably true. Tens of thousands of young men cooped up in camp with only one sinful testosterone-relieving outlet was a recipe for trouble.

'What about the notebook?' Bluey asked. 'Hassan said it was fair-dinkum.'

'Yes very commendable, I'm sure. Colonel Monash is most appreciative, but wants you to save your agro for the Hun in future,' Blake said as a dismissal.

Fortunately for Anglo-Egyptian relations the Anzacs broke camp only days later. The brigade boarded trains to Port Said where a flotilla awaited to transport them across the Mediterranean Sea. Rumours abounded where they were to land. Marseilles was a hot favourite, but after reorganising and extra training on an island that Callan had never heard of, they set sail once more.

On 25 April the first Anzac battalions stormed ashore on the Gallipoli Peninsula. Although they missed their landing point, they still made good headway up impossibly steep terrain. However they stirred up a Turkish hornets' nest, which Callan along with 'B' Section and Colonel Monash's entire brigade marched straight into the following day.

Part 2 — Seafarers 1914-1916

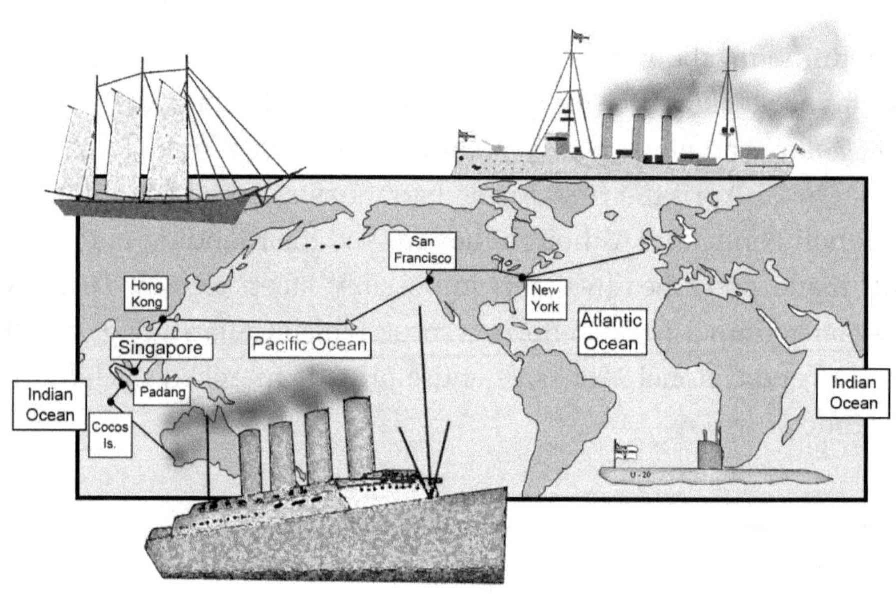

Chapter 8 — Second Last Man Standing

Harefield Manor Hospital, Middlesex — March 1916

Alone Australian officer paced along the hallway leading from the wards. He introduced himself and asked the nursing staff for directions.

'Good morning, Captain Blake,' a ward sister replied cheerfully. 'I trust you are well this bleak morning we proudly call spring.'

'In top form, thank you, Sister,' John Blake replied with a smile. 'You may not believe it, but we get frost in New South Wales too. How is Lieutenant McAlister today?'

'He is young and therefore impossibly impatient. I fear his convalescence will take some considerable time. He seems so melancholy most of the time and often suffers nightmares.'

'He's reliving the horrors. They don't spare any of us. Callan's the last of his mates who joined up back in fourteen. They're all either dead or so seriously wounded they were shipped back to Australia. He should be dead too with the amount of shrapnel he took on board. He was hit while dragging a wounded digger to safety. Saved the fellow's life and nearly lost his own in the bargain. And it wasn't the first time by a long chalk. He deserved his field commission I can tell you.'

'You admire him, don't you?' the ward sister observed.

'Yes, I recruited him, you know. He was a bit young and only turned eighteen in the Gallipoli trenches, but he's matured into a fine soldier.'

'Then, I'm pleased to inform you Surgeon Major Finsbury-Jones is confident he has removed every scrap of metal from your Lieutenant McAlister.'

'But when will he be up and about again?'

'These things take time, Captain Blake. The surgical team has done all it can. Now we must be patient.'

'I don't think patience is one of Callan's strong suits. But, maybe I have something that will cheer him up,' Blake said, tapping the side of his attaché case.

Four seriously wounded officers lay in neatly made beds in a small annex to the main ward. A young nurse in a crisp, starched uniform fussed over Callan as Blake entered. They helped Callan to sit up before she served him a cup of tea.

'How're you feeling today?' Blake asked. 'Apart from being white as a ghost, you don't *look* too bad to me.'

'Blow me down, Archie, you're a sight for sore eyes,' Callan replied softly, shaking Blake's extended hand. 'It's good to see you again, but I don't think there's a part of me that doesn't hurt. What are you doing here anyway? I might be half-dead, but I thought the brigade was still in Egypt.'

'They are, but I don't think we'll be there long. It's all hush-hush, but I reckon we'll be redeploying to the western front within months.'

'Did General Monash tell you personally?' Callan asked slyly as he distrusted rumours entirely after hearing so many in the Gallipoli trenches.

'I'm on his staff now. He ordered me to courier despatches for Lord Kitchener and Field Marshal Haig. He also granted me leave — the first I had since I can remember, I might add,' Blake said. 'I thought I'd drop by and see how you were getting along. It's time for you to get those legs moving and shake out those aches and pains. Fancy a hobble around the grounds?'

'It's ruddy freezing out there.'

Blake didn't insist, although he sensed an uncharacteristic resigned indolence had descended on his friend and comrade. Blake was uncertain whether cold weather was an excuse or Callan was just too weary to try and push himself.

Just two days before the Anzac withdrawal from Gallipoli, Callan had been seriously wounded and evacuated to Lemnos. Because of his severe injuries, he was transferred via Malta to Harefield Manor Hospital in Middlesex. Callan had made it through eight months of the most bitter and intense fighting imaginable, which whittled the original 'B' Section away to nothing.

SERGEANT JOHN BLAKE (OC) (FIELD COMMISSION)

LANCE CORPORAL SLIM BLIEVERS (2 IC) (WIA —

REPATRIATED TO AUSTRALIA

PRIVATES: JOSEPH DALRYMPLE (KIA)

BILL JONES (KIA)

COL GRIMLY (WIA — REPATRIATED TO AUSTRALIA)

Callan McAlister (Field Commission — WIA — Status Undetermined)

Shorty Malone (WIA — Repatriated to Australia)

Clarrie Monroe (Deceased — Pneumonia)

Bill Preston (MIA — possible POW)

Ces Robinson (WIA — repatriated to Australia)

Bluey Sturgis (KIA)

Trevor Warren (Deceased — cholera)

There were replacements of course, but they were raw recruits and many only lasted days in the trenches — some only lasted hours. Sergeant Blake was promoted to company commander, while Callan replaced Lieutenant Collins who died from typhoid during the fly-ridden summer months.

After leading what seemed like a charmed life, Callan's luck finally ran out when he'd been riddled with shrapnel.

'Righto,' Blake said looking through the window and the frosty landscape beyond. 'You're probably right, it's pretty miserable outside. But this should cheer you up — you've been awarded a gong — the DSM.'

Callan raised his eyebrows.

'What for — being the last man standing, well second last man standing counting you?'

'Something like that. You get the gong because I've already got one.' Blake grinned, presenting Callan with a package containing the medal, blue and white ribbon and a citation describing how he risked his life time and again.

'Nice trinket and well earned,' Blake said, 'but I think you'll be more interested in this.'

Blake delved into his case and produced a letter from Robert. Callan ripped it open and eagerly read that his brother was well and enjoying the break from fighting. After a short respite on Lemnos, Robert was back in Egypt awaiting further orders which, as Blake had suggested, would be deployment to the Western Front. Callan was pleased to hear his brother had been promoted to battalion sergeant-major. Robert wished Callan a speedy recovery and urged him to write back soon.

'He's sounds pretty cheerful about going to France,' Callan remarked. 'You'd think he'd be sick of the whole business after fighting Johnny Turk for eight ruddy months. Robert landed in the first wave on 25th April, you know. '

'He probably reckons anything will be an improvement,' Blake replied dryly.

'The Tommies don't seem to be finding it so easy from what I gather.'

'Kitchener and Haig are old school,' Blake said diplomatically. 'They still think they're fighting niggers in the colonies according to some people. I don't think they've quite latched onto the fact that we're fighting a modern war in the 20th Century.'

'Yeah, Arabs and Fuzzy-Wuzzies don't have machine guns and howitzers, do they?'

'Those do appear to be two concepts the high command has yet to appreciate.'

'You and I could see that when we were lowly foot-sloggers, Archie,' Callan said. 'Why the devil can't those ruddy generals get the picture?'

Of course Blake had no answer other than mule-headed, rearward-thinking stupidity.

'Like the bright sparks who thought it would be a good idea for us to clamber all over the Dardanelles for John Turk's target-practice,' Callan added.

'Actually it wasn't a bad idea,' Blake countered, 'just badly planned and executed. The battalion and brigade commanders did what they could, but their hands were tied by Division and Corp level incompetency.'

'And it was the companies and platoons that copped a hiding. General Monash did what he could, but if he'd complained they'd simply have replaced him with a yes-man, I suppose.'

Blake nodded.

Winston Churchill who initially broached the Dardanelles idea fell on his sword. Although Gallipoli the outcome wasn't his fault, the First Sea Lord resigned from cabinet to command a battalion on the Western Front.

'Ifs...' Callan went on sadly. '...If we'd landed a week earlier before General von Sanders could rally the Turks...if Colonel Mustafa Kemal Atatürk hadn't been such a brilliant commander...if we'd landed at the right place...if our artillery had be better co-ordinated when we went over the top...if the Suvla Bay offensive hadn't been cocked up by a bunch of Tommie Generals squabbling over who was top-dog instead of getting on with the job...if we had more spotter planes...I mean the "ifs" go on and on.'

In truth the Gallipoli campaign had tied up ten Turkish infantry divisions, an artillery brigade and many support units.

This mighty army would have otherwise been free to fight the Russians and relieve German forces on the Eastern Front. Tragically over forty-thousand British, French and Anzac soldiers died to achieve what could only be described as a diversion, but over twice that many Turks were killed.

'We seriously under-estimated Johnny Turk, Callan,' Blake sighed. 'They weren't like Lieutenant Cerci's mob of misfits, were they?'

Callan merely nodded.

'Anyway, forget that for a bit,' Blake said, 'I've kept the best for last. Here's something else that'll *really* cheer you up. This lot arrived in Egypt before I left. From what you told me in the trenches, I think you've been waiting for these.'

Blake once more rummaged in his attaché-case and pulled out a bundle of correspondence all addressed to Callan care of the 4th Brigade.

'These have been chasing you around for months and have been misdirected several times,' Blake said. 'Now that I'm on the General Staff, I hear about things like this.'

Blake handed Callan the other envelopes. Callan looked at the first letter of the bundle that Blake had arranged neatly in chronological order. Callan smiled for the first time in months when he recognised the neat hand-writing.

'I'll go and grab a cuppa and leave you to that lot for a while,' Blake said.

But Callan hardly noticed as Blake left the ward...

My dearest Callan

You must think I'm an utter beast not writing for so long. It broke my heart when I finally received all your mail. I know you will forgive me when I relate our voyage from Australia. In truth I can barely believe what has happened...

Darling Harbour, Sydney Cove — October 1914

Colonel D'vere-Brown led Ivy and her mother, Meredith, aboard the Norwegian freighter, *SS Runhild Halvorsen* bound for London's Tilbury Docks via the Indian Ocean, Suez Canal, Mediterranean, Gibraltar and then the Bay of Biscay, English Channel to the Thames estuary. The ship's commander was a crusty veteran who'd spent thirty years at sea. Captain Pål Johannessen was a daunting figure who smelled of fresh tobacco with just a hint of stale whisky.

Colonel D'vere-Brown was in a hurry. He'd been recalled to England to form his battalion from local yeomanry and territorial reservists. He needed to train them and get them to the front before the whole show was over. He proudly wore campaign ribbons from the Boer War and the fifty-five day Peking siege during the

Boxer Rebellion. He wouldn't have minded a few more gongs and perhaps a DSO into the bargain.

Unfortunately shipping was restricted due to German U-boats and battle-cruisers playing havoc with allied vessels. The choice was either to run the gauntlet across the Indian Ocean to Suez or take a long detour across the Pacific around Cape Horn. However, time and stormy weather aside, German warships still lurked in the Atlantic.

Meredith D'vere-Brown's maid, Alice, may have been a simple girl, but she was aware of the dangers and promptly gave notice. She'd been seduced by a shady Sydney-sider who spirited her away to the town's burgeoning bohemian quarter in Kings Cross. Unfortunately she fell under the influence of up-and-coming drug and vice queen, Kate Lee. NSW Police records indicate she was in and out of trouble after that, so perhaps she might have been better served taking her chances aboard *SS Runhild Halvorsen*.

'Where will I find another maid at such short notice?' Meredith lamented.

'Do not fret, Mama,' Ivy soothed. 'I am sure we can dress and undress ourselves just for once. I will be your maid for the voyage. It will be fun and such an adventure — two girls sticking together.'

Meredith smiled and hugged her daughter.

'Thank you,' she said, 'you're such a kind and sensible girl. I would be lost without you.'

'I know you are made of sterner stuff than those silly socialites, Mama,' Ivy replied with her most beguiling smile. 'Papa has often told me how you stood beside him reloading his revolvers in front of blood-thirsty hordes of Boxers storming the Peking Legation and even taking a few pot-shots yourself.'

Ivy's mother smiled.

'Yes my darling, we do rather take for granted other people doing tasks we can quite adequately perform ourselves.'

Norway was technically neutral and Captain Johannessen stood to make a fortune from his cargo of top-grade merino wool, Tasmanian apples and Huon pine timber if he docked at Tilbury before the New Year. Johannessen was prepared to take the gamble and steam for Suez. At first Johannessen refused to take the colonel and his family. In German eyes they were enemy nationals and therefore contraband. To make matters worse by carrying military personnel — even if it was only one man — *SS Runhild Halvorsen* could be consider a troop ship and fair game. But greed was a great leveller after Colonel D'vere-Brown offered to pay top-dollar for his family's passage.

The *SS Runhild Halvorsen* left Sydney a fortnight before the Anzac convoy cruised out of Port Melbourne. After berthing at Hobart's Constitution Dock to load the Tasmanian cargo, they set sail once more and within days, steamed briskly into the Indian Ocean. For Ivy the voyage proved a great adventure. The only other passengers were a Norwegian family who were delighted when Ivy started to learn their language. She was quite a gifted linguist and soon managed basic sentences.

Ivy was delighted to see dolphins gambolling across the ship's bow and thrilled when she spied pods of humpback whales on their annual southerly migration back to their Antarctic feeding grounds. She also marvelled at the sinister killer-whale packs which stalked the humpbacks ready to pounce on any stragglers. Fortunately she didn't see any attacks or witness the Albany whaling fleets as they took advantage of the pods streaming right into their harpoon gun-sights.

Captain Johannessen hove to for minor technical repairs in the engine room. All the passengers were thrilled when sharks circled the ship ripping into jetsam tossed from the galley.

Ivy was of course a great favourite with the crew who didn't get to see nearly as many females as they would have liked. Meredith D'vere-Brown was a diligent chaperone, but the sailors all acted impeccably.

With the repairs complete and the engines running smoothly once more, *SS Runhild Halvorsen* steamed north-west for Colombo. But early one morning the passengers and crew were awakened by an unbelievably loud blast, followed quickly by another. The ship's hull rocked as if struck by a tidal wave, which was what Ivy initially thought. She hurriedly dressed and rushed to the open deck. Soon she was joined by others who scanned the horizon.

The sea was calm and there was no sign of inclement weather. Everyone exchanged puzzled glances. Suddenly the ocean erupted in a mighty explosion only yards away. The sound echoed through Ivy's skull and for moments she was deafened. Hundreds of gallons of sea-water spewed skywards, spraying the deck and drenching the screaming crew and passengers.

And then they saw the grim, grey shape of a warship only a mile away. Its three stacks belched black smoke as the ship steamed straight towards them at full speed. A German flag billowed from the warship's bridge mast and prow. After another salvo churned the ocean just ahead of SS *Runhild Halvorsen* bow, Captain Johannessen got the message and telegraphed the engine room to stop his ship.

Crewmen raced helter-skelter across the Norwegian freighter's decks. Ivy had no idea what they were about, but it seemed they all had assigned positions when under attack. A sailor rushed past and urged the passengers to go below, but they ignored him as if transfixed by what they were seeing.

'Good Lord, it's a Hun cruiser,' Colonel D'vere-Brown said.

And it wasn't just any cruiser, it was the Dresden Class *SMS Emden,* which had terrorised the Indian Ocean and Far East since the war began. Not only had the warship captured and sunk many thousands of tons of shipping, its crew had also carried out a daring raid at Penang Harbour on the West Malayan coast.

As SS *Runhild Halvorsen* sloshed to a stop and wallowed in the gentle tropical swell, *Emden* loomed majestically alongside only a hundred yards away. Ivy heard orders being bellowed from a loud hailer, but they were in German and Norwegian, so she understood very little.

In moments a cutter was lowered from *Emden's* deck to the ocean. A sailor started the inboard motor and soon the boat chugged towards the Norwegian freighter. The cutter was crammed with German sailors and marines commanded by a dashingly handsome young officer. As SS *Runhild Halvorsen's* crew rushed to heave a boarding ladder over the side, a sailor ushered all passengers back to their cabins.

While Ivy and her parents waited, German boots clanked along the gangways and ladders. There were urgent shouts and the sound of gunfire followed by an eerie silence. The ship was so still, Ivy was sure she heard waves lapping against the hull.

After about half-an-hour the cabin door crashed open. A handsome German naval officer stood silhouetted in the hatchway.

Meredith screamed, but the officer stood stiffly and unflinching.

'I say,' Colonel D'vere-Brown challenged. 'Don't you blighters knock? You're scaring my family.'

'Then I do apologise sincerely,' the officer said, clicking his heels and saluting. He spoke well with only a mild Teutonic accent. 'Permit me to introduce myself. I am *Kapitän-Leutnant* Hellmuth von Mücke, executive officer aboard *Emden*.'

'What do you want with us?' the colonel blustered. 'We are innocent passengers.'

'Unfortunately I do not think that is quite correct,' von Mücke replied urbanely.

'What do you mean? This is a neutral ship.'

'Indeed, but you are not, are you Colonel D'vere-Brown.'

'How the devil did you know that?'

'*Ja*, you are listed on the passenger manifest as "Mr D'vere-Brown", are you not?' von Mücke ginned slyly. 'Captain Johannessen is a pragmatic man, but a little nervous right now.'

Ivy had no idea what the German officer meant.

'You see,' von Mücke continued, 'the ship's manifest states your destination is Bergen, but after inspecting of the cargo I became curious.'

'What is so special about the cargo?' Ivy asked.

'Apples and wool, I understand, but why does Norway need more timber, fräulein?' von Mücke said.

'Huon Pine is a very special wood according to the stevedore I spoke to on Hobart wharf.'

'That may be true, but I discovered little of that wood is actually Huon Pine. The remainder is construction hardwood. So I asked myself where there was a shortage of such timber for construction and England seemed like a logical answer.'

Ivy stared at him. He seemed remarkably well informed for a simple seaman.

'But that does not matter. It did not take long to discover the truth. We fired a few warning shots into the air and examined the purser's files. After that the crew was more than willing to disclose your true destination — Tilbury Dock on the Thames, if I am not mistaken.'

'So what does this have to do with us?' Ivy asked.

'Once I knew the ship was not bound for a neutral port, I explained to Captain Johannessen I would have to impound the cargo or sink his vessel. The good captain offered you up in exchange, Colonel D'vere-Brown if we grant *Runhild Halvorsen* safe passage to Bergen.'

'If he goes to Bergen,' D'vere-Brown sneered, but von Mücke was undismayed.

'Oh we shall radio our u-boats in the channel to ensure Captain Johannessen does not lose his way. But, you must come with us as a prisoner-of-war, Colonel.'

'Be damned!' D'vere-Brown stormed. 'That blaggard, Johannessen. I am not even in uniform yet.'

'Precisely, Colonel — not *yet*. But I understand you intend to be in service very shortly and I consider it my duty to stop you doing so.'

'And if I refuse..?'

'Oh, that is not an option, *Mein Herr*. My marines will see you come one way or another.'

'I will not leave my family. Their safety is paramount at this time.'

'Then they will come too,' von Mücke said evenly. 'Gather your belongings. You have five minutes.'

Chapter 9 — Steam Gives Way to Sail

There was no shortage of willing hands to help Ivy and her mother on the rather undignified descent to the *Emden's* cutter. Ankle-length dresses and petticoats weren't really the most practical attire for sailing in tropical waters. Ivy needn't have worried about her mother, who was full of surprises.

'I can manage quite nicely, thank you,' she said with acidic haughtiness built of *noblesse-oblige,* which put the sailors in their place even if they didn't understand English.

Once aboard, Colonel D'vere-Brown helped his wife and daughter to a central bench while German sailors stowed their luggage. Captain Johannessen wisely stayed out of sight on his bridge fearing — justifiably — that the colonel would throttle him given the chance. Colonel D'vere-Brown accepted the Germans as enemies, but in his eyes the Norwegian sailor's betrayal was unforgiveable.

Once again Ivy's mother showed her grit as she clambered up the boarding ladder to *Emden's* main deck where *Fregatten-Kapitän* Karl von Müller met them with a puzzled expression. *Emden's* commander nodded occasionally as his executive officer explained what had occurred on board *Runhild Halvorsen*.

'*Willkomen Oberst und miene damen,*' von Müller said, clicking his heels and touching the peak of his cap before returning to his duties.

Excerpts from Ivy D'vere-Brown's journal written whenever she could:

Dear Diary — 6 November 1914

The Emden is not a pretty vessel or in any way majestic. Its three funnels seem too far forward in my opinion & the bow, although undoubtedly purpose-built, does not show the sleek lines of modern-day warships. The treacherous Boche have rigged a forth dummy-funnel to trick shipping into thinking she is not Emden at all. But she bristles with guns. I have been told by Lieutenant von Mücke there are ten four-inch guns pointing fore & aft and amidships. You notice I have picked up some nautical terms whilst aboard.

Thankfully Captain von Müller has partitioned a small area for Mama & me to conduct our toilette. The Curse-of-Eve is something I can only confide to you, dear diary, but men are fortunate to be able to be so base & casual about their personal needs.

We have been aboard for three days, but now I hear we are sailing for the Cocos Islands which are an Australian territory I believe. I do not know the purpose of this venture, only that Captain von Müller is dissatisfied with the shipping Emden has intercepted since releasing Runhild Halvorsen & its treacherous commander.

Papa frets awfully by the impotence of being a POW. Mama & I try to comfort him, but to no avail. The German crew are courteous & I believe generally doing all they can to make us comfortable. I understand Captain von Müller is known for being a daring warrior, but he is also chivalrous & has tried to spare as many innocent civilian lives as possible.

I must admit, dear diary, that I find Lieutenant von Mücke a most dashing officer & could perhaps easily fall a little in love with him had we not been at war. But then I still dream of dear Callan McAlister, my sweet wild colonial boy. I wonder if we shall ever meet again.

Talking of sweet boys, we have been assigned a young rating named Wendall, who speaks excellent English with a delightful accent. He is very attentive & I am vain enough to believe he is making starry eyes at me. Papa says he has simply been posted to spy on us & see we don't get into mischief, so we must be ever vigilant.

Dear Diary — 9 November 1914

We are all up early, it must be 5 am, yet here in the tropics the cool mornings are blissful. We have arrived at Direction Island, in the Cocos Archipelago. It is so isolated smack in the middle of the Indian Ocean between Australia and Ceylon. We have anchored in a lagoon which is indeed an idyllic tropical haven.

I see from the deck that Lieutenant von Mücke is taking a party ashore in two boats towed by a little steam-launch. There must be thirty or forty men. Wendall tells me a wireless station is on this lovely & lonely atoll. I fear the Boche intend to destroy the station & will undoubtedly find other monkey business to attend to.

I see the boats have reached a jetty. It seems deserted. There is only one other vessel moored close by. It looks like a schooner or a yacht to me, but I am no expert on ship design.

9 am.

I must leave you now, dear diary. There is the most ghastly hullabaloo from above decks. The ship's claxon is wailing, which I think is a signal for the landing party to return. I must discover what is afoot...

Ivy quickly dumped her diary into her waterproof satchel, which she slung over her shoulder. She donned her broad-brimmed hat, opened the cabin hatchway and strode onto the main deck. Sailors ran all around her, urgently yet in good order they deployed to their action stations throughout the ship.

Ivy felt *Emden's* boilers being stoked into life as black smoke belched from the three true smoke-stacks. *Emden* swung violently on its mooring line as the bollard-chains clanked to lift the massive anchor. She had no time to consider what was afoot. Wendall arrived in moments, announcing that she and her mother were to accompany him.

'Where to?' Meredith challenged.

'I am to take you ashore in the pinnace,' Wendall explained. 'You are in danger aboard. An enemy cruiser approaches. The *Fregatten-Kapitän* will go to fight it. We have tried to contact *Kapitän-Leutnant* von Mücke, but he is still ashore. *Emden* will sail without him and his men.'

'What about Papa?' Ivy wailed.

'He must stay aboard. He is a POW and must take his chances. You are non-combatants and Captain von Müller wishes you to be taken out of harm's way.'

'I will not leave my husband,' Ivy's mother declared stoutly.

Wendall didn't hesitate. He grabbed Meredith, flung her kicking over his shoulder, carried her to the awaiting boat and plonked her aboard. Ivy scurried after them retrieving her mother's parasol that had fallen onto the deck. Otherwise Ivy felt utterly helpless.

'Don't worry,' the colonel called, glad to see his family being taken to safety just as a naval battle appeared likely to erupt.

Ivy eyed him suspiciously. He sounded altogether too nonchalant about the prospect of being shelled by a mystery warship that had boiled over the horizon with guns bristling. He'd also calmly permitted Wendall to man-handle his wife without any objection. Something was on the colonel's mind.

The pinnace was lowered and cast off unceremoniously. Captain von Müller was apparently only prepared to spare one rating – Wendall – whose job was to sail to the wharf. But Colonel D'vere-Brown's plan was simple and effective. Once the pinnace was clear of *Emden's* stern and the ship's crew raced to their duties, Ivy was appalled to see her father climb over the transom rail and without hesitation – leap overboard!

Colonel D'vere-Brown splashed into the ocean only yards behind the *Emden's* screws that churned white water in the ship's wake as its engines surged to full power. The colonel disappeared in the maelstrom. Luckily *Emden* had gained enough speed to give Ivy's father some seaway. Instead of being sucked under the cruiser's stern, he bobbed to the surface just clear of the prop vortexes.

'Quickly, we must get Papa aboard,' Ivy yelled to Wendall. 'There are sharks in the water.'

As he had yet to hoist the pinnace's single sail, Wendall reacted by frantically turning the boat with its oars. Meredith nudged beside him on the central bench, took one oar and they rowed surprisingly well in unison.

The Indian Ocean surrounding the Cocos Islands was indeed shark infested, but most were fairly benign reef-sharks and there certainly were no signs of grey fins slicing through the waves. Colonel D'vere-Brown was not a strong swimmer and, fully dressed, was in more danger of drowning than becoming shark-bait. With Wendall's help, Ivy managed to haul her father aboard.

After coughing up a pint of sea water, Colonel D'vere-Brown recovered and lay panting in the pinnace's bilge.

'And just what do you think you're up to, my darling?' Meredith challenged although not unkindly.

'I knew you'd miss me,' he replied with his most charming smile

'You could have easily been killed.'

'Perish the thought,' he replied glancing seawards. 'Looks like I'm better off than on the *Emden.*'

The German cruiser now steamed at full speed. Its forward 4" guns blazed into life to challenge the mysterious enemy. Explosive shells belched towards the distant warship. Great gouts of foam bracketed the oncoming cruiser before *Emden* scored two direct hits. The roar of the shells blasting from the red-hot barrels and whistling away was mind-numbing. The attacking ship replied with a salvo. Its guns opened up and within seconds jets of water exploded either side of *Emden's* hull. More shells followed.

Lieutenant von Mücke's steam launch now towed the cutters back across the lagoon, but the landing party was too slow and *Emden* didn't wait.

'We think it is *HMAS Sydney,*' Wendall said. 'The *Fregatten-Kapitän* thought she was over two hundred miles away, but it appears he was mistaken and she was closer.'

The wireless station operators had managed to transmit a distress message before *Emden's* radio crew emitted jamming signals. *HMS Monitor* had responded and judging by the signal-strength she was at least two hundred miles away, which gave *Emden* maybe ten hour's grace before *Monitor* could steam at full speed to Cocos.

HMAS Sydney however was much closer. She was on convoy duty, escorting the same fleet that carried Callan to war. *Sydney* left the convoy, heading straight for Direction Island.

'The landing party has been abandoned,' Wendall said. 'Look they are turning back to shore.'

'Well we don't want to run into them, do we?' Colonel D'vere-Brown suggested slyly. He was already plotting how to dodge von Mücke's men and somehow get word to the Australians who might find a way to return him to England.

Unfortunately Wendall had read the colonel's mind. He drew an ugly Mauser 'broom-handle' automatic pistol from his jacket pocket.

'I am sorry, *Herr Oberst,*' he said steadfastly. 'I may be a lowly sailor, but you are still a prisoner-of-war. Do not do anything foolish or try to overpower me. There are ten shots in this magazine. I will get you with one of them and...' he waved the barrel towards Ivy and her mother, '...we do not want innocent casualties, do we?'

Colonel D'vere-Brown saw the risk of his family becoming collateral damage in a scuffle, so he submitted to Wendall's orders. The colonel hoisted the sail at gun-point while Wendall handled the tiller. Under sail it was only a short voyage past the anchored three-mast yacht to the Direction Island wharf. Lieutenant von Mücke had just moored his craft and met the new-comers with several armed sailors. All the men were stripped to their breeches and vests and sensibly wore pith helmets. Von Mücke however looked impeccable in his crisp white tropic uniform.

It was early summer and the tropical wet-season build up was oppressive. Colonel and Mrs D'vere were bare-headed. While the dainty parasol Ivy had salvaged was helpful, it wasn't very practical. With famed Teutonic efficiency the sailors raided the radio station they'd come to destroy and found headgear for Ivy's parents.

For the following hour the landing-party watched the sea battle unfold only miles from shore. *HMAS Sydney* had only been launched the previous year, so she was modern and in pristine condition. *Emden* was only eight years older, which was still pretty new in warship turns. Both vessels had similar top-speeds with *Sydney* having a slight edge. It was the guns that made the difference — *Emden* had more, but *Sydney's* were bigger. And when it came to naval bombardments, size mattered.

The mood of the wireless station operators and islanders ashore was quite festive considering they'd just been invaded. Darcy Farrant, the station superintendent, had told von Mücke that the Kaiser had awarded the Iron Cross to many of *Emden's* crew, including the lieutenant, in honour of their successful raid on Penang harbour. Ironically an enemy wireless station supplied *Emden's* first news from home.

Up until *Emden's* departure von Mücke and his team had been the model of propriety and military correctness, but now the atmosphere grew edgy. The Germans rounded up all the locals they found and confiscated their weapons which only amounted to a few shotguns. They were still permitted to stand on building roofs and watch the battle at sea.

For the next hour the landing-party witnessed the two cruisers slug it out. It slowly became apparent that the big guns were likely to prevail and *Emden* was copping the worst of it. As *Emden's* pounding continued, Lieutenant von Mücke was left with a singular dilemma. With only the steam launch and three small boats at their disposal, it looked as if the landing-party could be marooned if *Emden* failed to return.

'It doesn't look too good,' Colonel D'vere-Brown said smugly. 'Even if Captain von Müller manages to give *Sydney* the slip, she'll have to find a bolt-hole for repairs.'

Lieutenant von Mücke glared at him.

Oh, Papa, please do not goad him. Lieutenant von Mücke may be dishy, but I am sure he might be quite ruthless if driven to it.

'We do not know the outcome,' von Mücke replied icily. 'As you see both ships have now sailed beyond the horizon.'

'I bet you a quid *Sydney* comes out on top,' the colonel challenged.

'Very well,' von Mücke replied confidently and even took another side bet with one of the Cocos wireless operators.

The Germans may have come to regret doing such a good job of wrecking the wireless station. They'd baled up the operators before trashing the transmitters, toppling the aerials and cutting underwater cables to Africa, Asia and Australia. Now they were left with no means of communicating with *Emden* and no way of knowing how the battle had developed.

After the cruisers disappeared, the Germans took over Direction Island and hoisted their ensign from a flag pole which had once flown the Australian national banner. The D'vere-Brown family were left with no other option than to sit in the shade of some palms and await developments. Despite the humidity, the colonel's linen suit soon dried in the tropical heat.

One of the station wives brought them cool drinks and fresh fruit. She was a friendly woman and eager to hear news from Australia, so she made herself comfortable and chatted to Ivy and her mother just like old chums.

By noon von Mücke reached a decision and informed Colonel D'vere-Brown who was still feeling cocky.

'Looks like you'll be the POW now, Lieutenant,' he said.

'Perhaps...and...perhaps not,' the German replied enigmatically. 'We are once more going to sea, *Mein Herr*.'

'Oh and how do you plan to do that with one steam tug and a couple of small boats?'

'Do you see that yacht *Ayesha* anchored in the lagoon?'

Colonel D'vere-Brown nodded.

'I have commandeered that vessel in the Kaiser's name. Welcome aboard, *Herr Orberstleutnant!*'

Chapter 10 — On the Run

I vy stared in disbelief.

'It's not very big to go out on the open ocean,' she said doubtfully.

'Someone sailed it across the open ocean to reach here, *Fräulein*,' von Mücke replied cheerfully. 'In any case, it will not concern you, *Fräulein*. There is no need to inconvenience you or your mother further. You will both remain here in the care of *Herr* Farrant. You will be perfectly safe and I am certain arrangements can be made for your return to the mainland in due course.'

'I will not leave Papa,' Ivy declared, 'and you can't make me!'

Von Mücke shook his head wearily.

'In fact I can,' he replied, 'but I would prefer to avoid any unpleasantness, so if you insist you may accompany your father, but I will make no allowances for you during what I think will be arduous times ahead.'

'And the same goes for me,' Meredith affirmed stoutly.

'I rather thought it would,' von Mücke sighed with a resigned voice.

Ayesha was a three-mast schooner that belonged to the Clunies-Ross family who'd taken over the Cocos Islands way back in the 19th Century. Somewhere along the line Queen Victoria had granted possession of the archipelago to the Clunies-Ross family and they'd ruled the place as an enlightened dictatorship ever since. The system seemed to be working so far and the inhabitants, who were mostly Malayan, European or Chinese, appeared to be getting along fine.

Mind you the current *Tuan* of Cocos, John Sydney, could be a bit testy if you didn't tow the party line, so no one on Direction Island objected when von Mücke decided to pinch his personal yacht. Lieutenant von Mücke negotiated with Superintendant Darcy Farrant for half the island supplies which he paid for — along with his gambling debts to Colonel D'vere-Brown and the wireless operator — with gold sovereigns from a money-belt around his waist, but that pretty well cleaned out his cash supply.

'Isn't Mr Farrant's over-eagerness to collaborate with the Boche a trifle unseemly, Papa,' Ivy declared from her teenage moral high-ground.

'Do not judge the superintendant too harshly, my dear,' her father replied. 'He is well aware that Lieutenant von Mücke can take anything he wants as spoils of war. This way he will receive at least some reparation and still have plenty left in his store-house to last the island community for months. The Germans are well behaved now, but Mr Farrant undoubtedly wants them on their way as soon as possible just in case trouble starts.'

When Farrant's wife heard that Ivy and her mother were to be taken aboard *Ayesha,* she immediately bustled them to her bungalow. After rummaging through her bedroom duchess, she filled a muslin bag with spare underwear, basic toiletries and other ladies' essentials that would be unavailable on their voyage to wherever they might be heading.

'Now, Mrs D'vere-Brown and Ivy, it's time to be practical,' Mrs Farrant announced with authority. 'You'll have no need of stays or button boots, so come with me and we'll see you're more aptly attired for the tropics.'

Ivy and her mother possessed broad-brimmed hats and cool, cotton shifts so Mrs Farrant only needed to supply a pair of sandals and rubber plimsolls for them both.

'There are some linen strips in the bag for your monthlies,' Mrs Farrant explained. 'I have no idea how long you will be at sea, so you may have to wash them out. Wear the plimsolls aboard and the sandals ashore and you should be fine.'

Ivy was secretly relieved to be rid of her corset, which may have shown her slim waist and perky young breasts to great advantage, but was uncomfortable and restricting when it came to moving around heaving decks in heavy seas. Whatever Ivy's mother thought about the idea of doing her laundry was unclear. She simply smiled stoically and no doubt wished she'd been accompanied by a lady's maid. Dressing herself was one thing, but washing soiled linen...?

'Do not worry, Mama,' Ivy reassured her mother as she was becoming accustomed to. 'I am sure I can do a little scrubbing without ruining my lily-white hands.'

'Now off you go,' Mrs Farrant said, kissing them both as they parted. 'You're plucky lasses both. God speed and keep you safe.'

Dear Diary — 10th November 1914

Now we are aboard the yacht Ayesha & the adventure begins, I have time to put pencil to paper once more. Lt. von Mücke (who I shall refer to as Lt vM for brevity from now on) ordered his crew to set sail last night. He is worried that we will be discovered by Australian warships — oh, bravo to our brave colonial boys if that should be so!

[Ivy seemed to have forgotten that Australia had been an independent nation since the beginning of the century]

Mama & I are squeezed into a tiny alcove at the stern where the yacht pitches so. At least the Boche sailors have erected a screen, so we are afforded some token privacy, but I fear Mama is somewhat distressed by our primitive situation. Lt vM simply shrugs & gives us an infuriating 'I told you so' look.

The Boche are crowded onto the deck —
10 Officers and petty-officers and 40 sailors.
Apparently Ayesha only needed 5 or 6 men to
crew her. Now 50 are aboard as well as
Mama, Papa & me.

Lt vM has organised his steam boat to
tow Ayesha beyond the reefs, which he assures
me, are treacherous.

The indefatigable lieutenant darts from
mast to bow calling for his men at the tiller to
steer port or starboard as needed to clear the
reefs. We have Emden's two cutters in tow & a
brace of tiny jollyboats strapped to the deck.

Lt vM frets that we will not clear the reef
before dark & risk being dashed against the
coral. Would not that put a flea in his ear &
scotch his plans, but I doubt the cutters will
hold us all. The thought of swimming back

ashore through shark-infested waters does not appeal to me.

Dear Diary — 11th November 1914

It is with mixed feelings that I report we have made it into the open Indian Ocean. Once clear of the reefs Lt vM called his steamboat crew aboard Ayesha then abandoned the trusty vessel to her lonesome fate which will most likely never be revealed to us.

Say what you will of them, the Boche are well organised. They have quickly organised themselves into teams — one for sail-making, another for rope-splicing, cooking and so forth.

Ayesha's hull is in poor shape & Lt vM is concerned that it may not hold. The vessel leaks abominably & the ship's pumps are out of order. Men are busy making repairs.

Dear Diary — 12th November 1914

Oh my, I have such a wicked secret to confide. No one else must know but you, my dearest clandestine journal. I must confess those young sailors have quite turned my head & taken my breath away. Their uniforms are in such disrepair, they must go about their duties with barely a stitch on.

I declare I find their manly countenance most pleasing, although darling Mama does not know which way to look.

Dear Diary — 13th November 1914

The heat is simply beastly for there is no sign of rain even though the afternoon clouds boil into great thunderheads, but subside at night before they can refresh us with a downpour. God bless darling Mrs Farrant for insisting we abandon our stays & heavy shoes. (Note to Paris Fashion Houses — Girdles have no place in the tropics!)

To add to our woes the water cans the crew filled before setting sail are tainted & must be emptied before being scoured clean. We have a store of seltzer-water aboard, but Lt vM is determined to save that in case we must abandon Ayesha. It will be all that is available to quench our thirst should we be forced to board the cutters. On a positive note, the pumps have been repaired & Lt vM reports the hull is now quite dry if not perfectly so.

Dear Diary — 14th November 1914

These past two days have been almost unbearable...

Ayesha pitched violently in the six-foot swells that pounded her fragile planks sending spray over the gunwales making it impossible for anyone aboard to stay dry. It was a blessing in a way, relieving the fair-skinned Germans from the blistering heat, but salt caked their muscular torsos.

Fortunately Ivy and her parents had found their sea-legs and didn't suffer any nausea. Even so Ivy dozed through the night, but barely slept for long.

So far there was no sight of land or other shipping. Many of the German sailors had never served on a sailing vessel before and it was left to a handful of ex-fishermen and tall-ship veterans to show them the ropes. Colonel D'vere-Brown bunked down aft with the officers and was able to regularly check on his family.

Ivy and her mother used the last of their sewing equipment to stitch the sailors' clothing which rapidly fell to tatters in the sun and salt-spray. From their position astern Ivy and her mother often idled away their time watching *Emden's* cutters dragging behind the *Ayesha*. The small vessels pitched wildly in the swell and looked as if they would capsize at any moment.

As she watched, Ivy noticed one of the cutters glide down a particularly large wave and hurtle towards the *Ayesha's* transom. Suddenly von Mücke dashed to the stern with several crewmen armed with poles. The lieutenant bellowed frantic orders that Ivy didn't understand, but was in no doubt about the urgency.

The cutter slammed into Ayesha's gunwales with a thud that shuddered throughout the boat.

'He's worried the cutter will puncture our side,' Colonel D'vere-Brown explained calmly at Ivy's side. '*Ayesha* is in poor shape — her hull is paper-thin, the rigging is fraying apart and the sails are almost in tatters. She will not bear even the slightest punishment. Von Mücke fears she'll break up.'

'You are of great comfort, Papa,' Ivy replied with a thin smile.

'It's okay. We can always take to the cutters...'

Or not!

As Colonel D'vere-Brown spoke, von Mücke took a machete from one of his sailors and slashed the tow-rope. The cutter drifted aside, carried away by yet another monster swell.

'Papa, there is not enough room for us all in the remaining cutter and those two tiny dinghies.'

'It seems our gallant lieutenant fears the cutters smashing the hull more than our chances should we be forced to abandon ship.'

Von Mücke's apprehension was well founded. The cutter had indeed punctured *Ayesha's* stern and the only thing stopping water pouring in was their forward speed. As *Ayesha* sank between each wave, sea sloshed through the fracture below the main deck. Carpenters raced to cannibalise parts of the ship's upper structure to block the breach.

The second cutter was abandoned shortly afterwards when it looked as if would also ram *Ayesha*.

'Now we can only hope it is not literally a case of "sink or swim",' Colonel D'vere-Brown commented dryly.

'It was necessary,' von Mücke replied in almost a whisper.

But that night the weather broke. Storms had reared into the stratosphere all afternoon and finally poured earthwards with a blaze of lightning bolts. *Ayesha* pitched right into the centre of one such storm. Torrential rain hammered onto the deck with such brutal force it was impossible to hear the lightning cracks and rolling thunder about the din of the deluge. Soon the deck was awash with knee-deep water.

Lieutenant von Mücke bellowed orders above the roar all around him. Somehow his men understood, rushing to their duties. A team of axe-wielding sailors smashed drainage vents in the gunwales allowing water to wash overboard. Ivy fretted that it was a terrible waste of fresh water until she saw other crewmen rigging canvas sheets right across the deck. Yet more men rigged ingenious pipes and aqueducts made of canvas, wood or any available materials. Thus water was siphoned from the collection sheets to the storage tanks which were now spotlessly clean.

During the entire time the Germans struggled to replenish their water supply and simultaneously prevent *Ayesha* being swamped, waves mercilessly hammered the long-suffering craft while severe wind-gusts threatened to rip the sails to shreds. Von Mücke ordered all sails to be furled while he manned the helm to hold the bow into wind.

Just as the men stowed the last sails lightning flashed continuously almost blinding everyone aboard. Then, to Ivy's dismay the masts caught fire. A luminous glow spread to enshroud the spars and rigging as well. The aura shimmered intensely, showing no sign of diminishing and was accompanied by an acrid burning smell.

'Dear God,' Ivy whispered. 'The ship is ablaze and we're doomed.'

'Fear not, *Fraulein* Ivy,' Wendall said with a confident smile.

He'd virtually been her constant companion throughout the voyage.

'The ship is safe,' he explained as rainwater streamed down his cheeks. 'It is electricity from the lightning. You call it *St Elmo's fire*. It will disappear when the storm passes.'

The ship is safe, now there is optimism if ever I heard it, Ivy thought.

Yet when the storm and electric glow finally abated and stars blinked to life between the clouds, *Ayesha* remained intact and her water supply was fully stocked.

The storm season had indeed set in. Most of the following nights were accompanied by a drenching.

Dear Diary — 23th November 1914

We have been at sea for almost a fortnight & finally we have sighted land which Lt vM believes to be part the Dutch East Indies which consist of thousands of islands. He believes we have reached Sumatra & now plans to navigate close to shore, hopefully reaching the neutral Dutch port of Padang.

Our noble skipper spends much time precariously aloft or clinging to the bowsprit ever alert for treacherous reefs which could well be our undoing. Now we must negotiate reefs &

islands, Ayesha lies at anchor during darkness when sailing is too hazardous.

Twice the crew been called to arms — beat to quarters I believe the nautical term to be — when smoke was spied on the horizon. I'm sure Lt vM is a bold captain, but what exactly two machine guns & a dozen rifles can do against a cruiser's mighty guns is a mystery to me.

Finally making landfall may be a relief, but on a less happy note, I fear Wendall is in a pickle...

During the ten day voyage, the sailors ate well enough using the stores they'd commandeered from Direction Island. There was an ample supply of bully beef, canned vegetables and fruit along with bottled lime juice to ensure the crew's health.

After their evening meal and once the evening storms subsided, the crew generally gathered around the deck and sang their favourite songs. Ivy particularly enjoyed listening to the music because the crew had many fine voices, which helped take her mind away from the war — if only temporarily.

Unfortunately romantic, balmy tropical nights had quite turned young Wendall's head. Two nights before their first landfall, Ivy found herself lingering on the transom, yet again unable to sleep. Wendall had become something of a stalker, which wasn't particularly hard on such a small vessel. His shipmates had noticed his lovelorn state and ribbed him mercilessly.

Finally Wendall could endure his passion no longer and took the opportunity to pounce. Other than the watch-keepers, the crew had all bedded down and, having learnt to grab rest whenever they could, were soon asleep. Wendall embraced Ivy from behind, muttering a torrent of Teutonic endearments with the intention of stealing (literally) a kiss.

How on earth the love-blind fool thought he was going to get away with it was anyone's guess. Ivy spun around, kneed him in the groin before wriggling free and squealing for help. Lieutenant Schmidt, the officer of the watch rushed to the scene followed by von Mücke and Ivy's parents.

Schmidt bellowed at Wendall in German, ordering him to be placed under arrest. Two burly sailors escorted Wendall away. The lad was crippled with pain and groaned miserably. Schmidt continued his tirade which Ivy couldn't understand, but was reasonably certain meant something like — *I don't care how sore your balls are — I'll deal with you later!*

'Goodness me, Ivy,' her mother said as she placed her arm around her daughters shoulder. 'Where did a young lady learn to kick a man so?'

'Instinct I suspect, Mama,' Ivy replied.

'My apologies, *Fraulein*,' von Mücke offered with a curt salute. 'That was inexcusable behaviour for a German sailor and will be dealt with severely. You are not hurt?'

'No, Lieutenant,' Ivy said. 'Please do not be too harsh on poor Wendall. I'm sure he meant no harm.'

'How I deal with my crew is not your concern, *Fraulein*. But it has convinced me you and your mother will be put ashore when we dock at Padang. My crew and I do not need any...distractions.'

'That will be most satisfactory, Lieutenant. Mama, Papa and I will have no trouble finding passage to Singapore or Hong Kong.'

'Once again you misunderstand me, *Fraulein*,' von Mücke sighed wearily. '*Herr Oberst* D'vere-Brown is *still* a prisoner of war.'

Chapter 11 — Padang

'**O**f all the pig-headed, stubborn, boorish....' Ivy blustered, but found herself lost for words. 'After all you've done for him, Papa.'

'What have I done?' Colonel D'vere-Brown asked mildly.

'You pitched in to collect rainwater and lugged equipment for the carpenters and helped anywhere you could.'

'Self preservation. I didn't want *Ayesha* to sink around us any more than the Germans.'

'Well I feel like giving Lieutenant Smarty-Pants von Mücke a great fat kick in the backside.'

'Remind me to steer clear of you when you're in a kicking mood.'

They both laughed and Ivy hugged her father.

The following day a Dutch destroyer von Mücke identified as the *Lynx,* steamed out of Padang Harbour to investigate the oncoming yacht. After prowling around, *Lynx* despatched a motorboat to convey *Ayesha's* commander to the warship. Von Mücke now donned his uniform which he'd kept as clean as possible, while commanding *Ayesha* barefooted and dressed only in shorts and singlet.

After an hour he returned to *Ayesha* in a dark mood.

'Something troubling you, Lieutenant von Mücke?' Colonel D'vere-Brown asked blandly.

'The Dutch are idiots! *Bauern idioten!* They threaten to impound my ship and intern the crew.'

'Ah, so I understand that would now make you the POW, sir.'

'They will not — cannot — do so. We are a warship with the right to enter and leave a neutral port, which is precisely what we shall do.'

'*Emden* is a warship, lieutenant,' Ivy's father insisted. 'Surely you cannot class *Ayesha* as a battle cruiser?'

'*Emden was* a warship,' von Mücke spat. 'She was so badly damaged *Fregatten-Kapitän* Karl von Müller was forced to scuttle her. *Emden's* crew has been taken prisoner. *Ayesha* is all that is left and we will never surrender!'

Technically von Mücke was correct, but *Lynx's* commander doubted the authenticity of *Ayesha's* warship status. He insisted that *Lynx* escort *Ayesha* into port where he would telegraph the Dutch colonial authorities in Batavia for clarification.

Padang was much larger than Ivy had imagined. She'd expected a sleepy fishing village, but Padang Harbour was deep enough for ocean-going freighters and about a half-a-dozen were docked at various piers.

To Ivy's dismay *Ayesha* manoeuvred around several German steamers moored in the neutral port. Lieutenant von Mücke ordered the German naval ensign hoisted up the main mast and transom flag pole just to show the Dutch he meant business. Sailors lined the decks of the German ships and cheered when they realised *Ayesha* was crewed by their countrymen. Many threw presents of cigarettes, biscuits, chocolate and, most welcome of all, toothbrushes to *Ayesha's* crew who'd managed with only a mouthwash of seawater for a month.

Whereas Ivy and her mother had depleted their sewing kit sharing their needles and thread with German sailors, they were not prepared to pass their toothbrushes around.

Von Mücke sent his 2IC, Lieutenant Schmidt ashore to contact the German legation and organise resupplying *Ayesha*. A flotilla of bumboats already surrounded the schooner with their occupants babbling all at once to attract attention. Bananas, coconuts, pineapples and other tropical fruit were common produce, but clothing, footwear, hats, gold trinkets, souvenirs and an abundance of whores were also on offer. Although produce was ludicrously cheap, von Mücke's resources were strictly limited so he'd appreciate government help.

Schmidt returned after several hours. He rode in a steam barge which towed *Ayesha's* dinghy. A short, solitary figure boarded the schooner with Lieutenant Schmidt. He was dressed in a crushed linen suit, high collar, tie, Panama hat and polished shoes protected by spats. He looked particularly uncomfortable under the equatorial sun and raised a parasol before formally greeting von Mücke.

'Who is he?' Ivy asked Wendall who'd rejoined the crew after a severe reprimand and a formal apology to Ivy, which she accepted with lady-like grace.

'He is what they call a "neutrality officer". His job is to sort out problems with different combatant nations when they're in Dutch territory. Our captain does not like him because he is Belgian who he feels are a rather inferior race.'

'I don't think he should air his prejudices right now. The Belgian is holding all the cards.'

It turned out that the neutrality officer spoke French, Dutch, Flemish and German fluently as well as being solidly competent in English. The discussion swayed back and forth for some time, but eventually the neutrality officer confessed he must defer to his superiors in Batavia and *Ayesha* was to remain in port until then. Von Mücke vehemently objected, but there was little else he could do right then.

'Very well,' he declared in English. '*Frau* D'vere-Brown, you and your daughter will gather your belongings and allow this gentleman to escort you ashore.'

Ivy snatched the two muslin tie-bags and her satchel which held all they possessed, but that was as far as they went.

'We will not leave without Papa,' Ivy announced.

'We have been through this before, *Fraulein*,' von Mücke heaved yet another frustrated sigh. 'Your father will stay aboard as a POW.'

To make his point, Lieutenant von Mücke drew his pistol and levelled it at Colonel D'vere-Brown. Undaunted Ivy marched in front of her father and stood defiantly facing von Mücke.

'Papa comes with us,' she challenged. 'We will leave *Ayesha* together or you will have to shoot me first.'

'Don't tempt me, *Fraulein*,' von Mücke snarled between clenched teeth.

'And I shall follow right behind them,' Meredith said. 'So you will have to kill me too if you choose to shoot my husband in the back.'

Ivy began moving towards the boarding ramp between Ayesha and the Dutch steamboat, shoving her father along and shielding him as they inched backwards. Meredith linked arms with Ivy, adding to the colonel's protective wall. Colonel D'vere-

Brown smiled. He was so proud of his family's courage, but he dared not risk their lives further. If he was to remain a POW then so be it. At least his girls would be safe. He was about to relent as he noticed the tension mount in von Mücke's eyes and his finger tighten on the trigger of his gun.

Fortunately the neutrality officer intervened.

'May I suggest you reconsider, Lieutenant,' the diminutive man said unsteadily in English so everyone could understand. 'It may be disadvantageous for you to take any rash action. In truth the Dutch Government is more sympathetic to the King George than the Kaiser at present. It is no secret that all of Holland's armed forces have been mobilised to her border in case of German invasion. I do not think Batavia will view your position favourably should you harm a British officer while on Dutch territory.'

'I do not care what Batavia thinks,' von Mücke growled.

'That might be unwise,' the neutrality officer warned, 'I believe if it came to a fight between your vessel and our destroyer *Lynx*, the outcome would not be in your favour.'

'That would be a blatant act of war!'

'Not if you violated Dutch neutrality. It would merely be police work.'

Dear Diary — 24ᵗʰ November 1914

How can I express the thrill and terror of leaving Ayesha of which I had grown so strangely fond? I cannot explain it, but sea &

wind battered she might have been, she bore us stoutly to Padang.

I can hardly believe that our noble captain Lt vM held a cocked pistol aimed for my very heart as we inched towards the gangplank, which was our conduit to freedom & safety. Lt vM's expression revealed only torment and doubt.

But as we turned to step from Ayesha's deck with Brave Mama protecting Papa's back, I glanced over my shoulder and saw Lt vM shake his head before lowering his pistol & returning it to its holster. He could have ordered his men to over-power us, which would have been easily done. Yet Lt vM relented. Could it be he secretly harboured a soft spot in his heart for my family & me?

Then the strangest event occurred. While the neutrality officer looked on with smug relief,

Ayesha's crew raised a cheer in unison. They had no desire to see Papa shot or any harm come to Mama & me, for Papa had been a favourite on board, always chipping in & helping where he could.

The last person I spied as our steamboat chugged for shore was the forlorn, hapless Wendall with a look of abject misery on his countenance. I waved & blew a kiss to him.

Papa made much of us on the trip to the pier. He kissed Mama & me, telling us we were such brave girls, but should not be so reckless in future. He is normally so reserved in public, but right then he didn't care. The neutrality office (whose name we never discovered, simply addressing him a 'monsieur', which Belgians do not mind even though they are *vexed to be confused with Frenchmen) looked particularly pleased with himself.*

We were greeted on the docks by a British factor who arranged our accommodation. The hotel was not to the Ritz's standard, but beggars cannot be choosers & we were all treated to a most welcome bath & fresh attire...

Once Colonel D'vere-Brown and his family were safely ashore there was a host of administrative details for him to attend to. The factor whose name was Archibald Burton advanced the family some local cash for Ivy and her mother to prowl the markets for wardrobe replenishments. Burton represented the interests of several British companies involved in rubber production, gold mining and, most lucrative of all, the spice trade. He was the closest anyone came to a formal British presence in Padang.

Ivy found the crushed Oriental pandemonium, stifling heat and humidity accompanied by the combined smell of humanity, peanut oil, garlic and diesel petrol almost overwhelming, but exhilarating and exotic at the same time.

Ivy thought the tropical downpours aboard *Ayesha* were phenomenal enough, but they seemed even more intense on dry land. As December approached, afternoon thunder clouds swelled upwards as if ignited by a clockwork timer. The D'vere-Brown family quickly adapted and completed any outdoor activity by noon. Afternoons were reserved for lounging in a shady veranda enjoying an aperitif gazing at the cumulonimbus spectacle and awaiting the evening deluge. Although Ivy had not turned eighteen, Colonel D'vere thought it was time to introduce Ivy to a pre-dinner cocktail.

'A daily G-and-T will do Ivy no harm,' he declared when his wife looked concerned. 'Indeed it is proven to deter malaria.'

Indeed tonic-water did contain a minute quantity of quinine, but as a proven malaria-prophylactic Colonel D'vere-Brown's claim was stretching it pretty thin. You'd have to be a hopeless drunk for the remedy to be successful, by which time cirrhosis of the liver would probably claim you long before malaria.

'What will become of Lieutenant von Mücke and his crew, Papa?' Ivy asked, sipping her drink, which she found bitter, but refreshing.

Ayesha was just visible through the cargo ships docked at the jetty.

'Who knows?' the colonel replied. 'I've heard the telegraph wires are running hot between here and Batavia, but no one seems prepared to make a decision. The Dutch don't really want to stir up a Boche hornets' nest, nor do they wish to offend the allies. So they're rather between a rock and a hard place. The Batavian governor is sitting on his hands — probably wisely — and hoping the problem will just go away.'

And go away it did.

Ivy occasionally noticed von Mücke around the port, but he was preoccupied and ventured no more than a curt nod in her direction. Other than Lieutenant Schmidt, who organised resupplying *Ayesha,* the German sailors remained on board.

Then on 14 December, *Ayesha* weighed anchor and sailed out of Padang harbour. No one tried to stop her.

'Papa, surely they don't tend to sail *Ayesha* back to Germany?' Ivy declared.

'I don't think so,' Colonel D'vere-Brown said. 'I believe Lieutenant von Mücke plans to rendezvous with one of the German freighters at sea and he'll abandon *Ayesha*.'

'Just like the steam tug when we left Cocos. Is it not heartbreaking to think of our dear little schooner set adrift on the open Indian Ocean and left to her fate?'

'War is filled with heartbreak, Ivy,' her father replied softly.

What befell Lieutenant von Mücke and his men was to become one of the greatest escape stories in 20th Century history and firmly established the gallant band as modern-day legends.

Colonel D'vere-Brown's military position allowed him certain privileges, but also responsibilities. Ivy's father was desperately keen to return to England to reform and train his regiment for deployment to the Western Front. But communications to and from Padang were sporadic and unreliable.

Dear Diary — 24th December 1914

Christmas in the tropics! How I miss the cold dark evenings, log fires, hot chocolate & beautiful carol singing at Midnight Mass.

But we will make the best of it I am sure & I

have made some wonderful discoveries since we were kidnapped by the Emden.

While Papa paces our hotel veranda like a caged lion, I have come to enjoy the closeness I now share with Mama.

All I remember as an infant & young girl is being in the care of nannies most of the time. I was really only with Mama at specified times during the day. Dearest Mama always seemed so distant & graceful yet such a gentle person, but never an intimate friend. Papa used to read my bedtime stories & I feel I share a special bond with him. I know I missed him dreadfully when he was away on duty.

I discovered Mama to be resourceful, cheerful & above all calmly serene. I have learnt so much of Mama & Papa's adventures in China when I was a mere toddler. Sadly, I *remember very little other than misty glimpses of my early childhood flashing through my mind.*

Christmas and New Year were an interesting cultural hotchpotch. Padang's population was predominantly Muslim, but Roman Catholic and Dutch Orthodox churches had claimed their share of converts, although the latter Christian persuasion were a dour lot and not prone to enjoying themselves. Luckily the Chinese were always in the mood for a celebration and livened things up with some spectacular fireworks.

It was February before the cogs-of-power eventually clunked into action.

'I've just received a message from Singapore via Batavia,' Archie Burton, the British factor, announced one morning six weeks after *Ayesha* had set sail. 'The Royal Navy is sending a ship for you, Colonel.'

The following morning a British torpedo destroyer steamed into Padang. A sub-lieutenant in a crisp dress white uniform found the colonel and presented him with orders to sail to Singapore immediately. The young officer, who Ivy thought was not much older than her, explained that the colonel would then be transported to England by the quickest means possible.

Colonel D'vere-Brown insisted his wife and Ivy accompany him. The destroyer commander raised no objection as it was only a short voyage and then the colonel's womenfolk would be someone else's problem.

Ivy had proven she was a feisty enough miss, but she was inwardly relieved they were sailing aboard a Royal Navy warship.

She'd heard that pirates and slavers swarmed around Indonesia, especially the Malacca Strait. On several occasions the destroyer fired bursts from the twin bridge-mounted Lewis guns to shoo away suspicious motor-powered sampans.

Padang to Singapore is less than three hundred miles as the crow flies, but over four times that distance by sea around Sumatra. When Ivy suggested it was shame they couldn't take an overland route, the destroyer commander pointed out that would be fine if the way was not barred by mountains, impenetrable jungle, rivers swollen to torrents by monsoonal rain, salt-water-croc infested mangrove swamps, deadly snakes, malaria-bearing mosquitoes, head-hunting savages and the occasional Sumatran tiger.

'The sea option it is then,' Ivy conceded.

'A wise choice indeed, Miss D'vere-Brown,' the commander replied urbanely. 'We will make a steady fifteen knots and have you safely disembarking by tomorrow evening.'

The destroyer commander was as good as his word and the D'vere-Brown family stepped ashore at Singapore's Keppel Harbour where they were met by Lieutenant Colonel E V Martin, commander of the 5th Indian Light Infantry Regiment, which along with two artillery and engineering companies was the total force defending Singapore. All other units had been shipped off to shed their blood dutifully in France.

Deep in the bosom of British Far Eastern colonialism Ivy might have felt secure at last. The *Ayesha* incident was safely behind her and she never expected to hear of Lieutenant von Mücke again, but Ivy and her family's association with the *Emden* had not yet finished.

Chapter 12 — Mutiny!

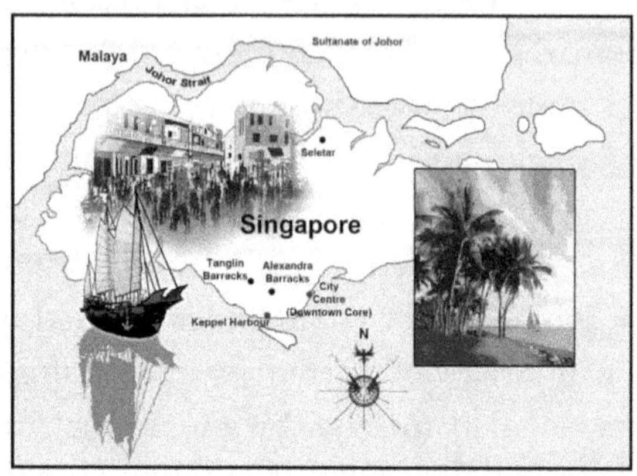

Ivy took an instant dislike to Colonel Martin. He was pompous and spoke in clipped clauses rather than sentences which she found affected and irritating. She never discovered what the 'E V' stood for in Colonel Martin's name and nor did she trouble to find out. Martin addressed her father as 'D'vere-Brown' in an overtly condescending tone, completely ignoring Ivy and her mother as mere females and therefore beneath consideration let alone meaningful conversation.

Ivy conceded that Colonel Martin had provided a comfortable bungalow for their accommodation. It stood next door to the colonel's own home close to Alexandra Barracks between Keppel Harbour and the main Singapore business district. Ivy loved the tropical residence with its sweeping lawns, majestic trees and colourful, fragrant gardens. She wasn't so keen to know that cobras and even deadlier kraits were common and often slithered inside. The house staff kept a pair of mongooses to deal with the lethal intruders.

After leaving the D'vere-Browns a few days to settle in, Colonel Martin invited the family to dinner for Chinese New Year on Sunday 14 February. Ivy was reluctant to go, but her mother chided her for being crass and she would attend graciously no matter how much she sulked and pouted beforehand.

The evening proved as unpleasant as Ivy had anticipated. They were accompanied by Major and Mrs Cotton, who were pleasant enough company. Major Cotton was Martin's 2IC and there was obvious friction between the two men. In fact there was friction between everyone and Lieutenant Colonel Martin! She'd heard his subordinate officers wouldn't even speak to their CO directly, but preferred to communicate by correspondence.

The meal was excellent, yet Martin found fault in every course. Whether it was the way it was cooked or served, he complained about some aspect of the dish. Ivy found the belligerent colonel spoiled what should have otherwise been a very pleasant evening. His blustering didn't help.

'Damn niggers — can't trust 'em, what, D'vere-Brown?' Martin addressed Ivy's father, ignoring the others around his table.

'My only experience with native troops was during the Peking siege, where I found them trustworthy and they behaved admirably,' Ivy's father replied guardedly.

'Chinks — tarred with the same brush. No chink police or militia left in town tonight because of their heathen New Year debauchery.'

That was true enough. The viceroy deemed the threat from Germany to be so slight that he released the Chinese military units to celebrate New Year and return to duty on Tuesday, the day after the festival officially ended.

'Damn heathens,' Martin continued. 'Got nothing but an unruly mob of Muslims in my regiment — spend half their day bums up and heads down pointing to Mecca. Damn waste of time, what? Can't put a stop to it though — hands tied, you see.'

'Surely their duties here allow for periods of prayer?' Colonel D'vere-Brown suggested mildly.

'Can't be too careful — there are more than three hundred Boche jack-tars interned in Tanglin Barracks, not three miles away,' Martin said. 'Don't trust 'em one bit.'

'German sailors,' Ivy said. 'How did they wind up here?'

'Shipmates of yours, my dear,' Martin replied showing the first sign of geniality. 'From the *Emden,* you see. Some were shipped to Malta, some to Australia — rest wound up here.'

But that was as friendly as Colonel Martin got before returning to his rant about the condition of his troops. The 5th Bengal Light Infantry was indeed manned entirely by Rajput Muslim sepoys and NCOs with only a handful of British officers. Since the Mutiny in 1857, Indian units were normally manned by a mixture of religious beliefs to reduce the chance of secular solidarity and possible insurrection. It was a system that had worked well to date.

Rumours had simmered since the outbreak of war that many Muslims were sympathetic to the Turks and felt their allegiance was more with Constantinople than London. As one of the 5th Light Infantry's primary tasks was to guard the German POWs, Martin was right to be concerned about collaboration with the prisoners, especially as German spies were rife in the colony.

However the 5th Light Infantry was due for rotation to Hong Kong, although that piece of information had not been relayed to the sepoys. They thought they were destined for the Western Front's carnage. Rumours that the Germans had developed a secret electrical death-ray weapon that could annihilate everything within a five mile radius didn't help matters. No one knew who had started that particular story, but the Germans certainly used enormous railway-borne artillery cannons. They were known as *Gamma-Gerät* and could fire one-hundred-and fifty-pound HE shells seven miles with great accuracy. Such formidable weapons must surely give anyone second thoughts about rushing into combat.

Fortunately for Ivy the Chinese residents decided to light up Singapore with fireworks displays, so the diners moved out to the gardens to view the show. Afterwards Colonel D'vere-Brown escorted his family to their bungalow, promising to attend a regimental parade the following morning.

The parade was just a parade to Ivy. She'd seen many of them and didn't mind the spectacle and stirring marching music, but generally she was ambivalent. Once the ceremony was over, Ivy and her mother returned to the bungalow for lunch while Colonel D'vere-Brown rode to Keppel Harbour to arrange the family's passage to England via Hong Kong. After lunch there was pretty well nothing else to do. Ivy soon became bored...

Dear Diary — 17th February 1915

I must relate the extraordinary events of the past three days. I cannot believe that treachery & bloodthirsty cruelty could abound so foully in this idyllic colony...

Singapore pretty well closed down on Sunday 14 February both because of the Christian weekend and Chinese New Year holidays. Ivy was blowed if she'd hang around the bungalow while her mother took a nap and her father was off goodness knew where. Ivy had bought a colourful sarong from the market. The garment was sumptuously elegant and felt divinely comfortable, so she was keen to be seen wearing it about town.

She quickly rounded up Kwok Ze Yu, a twelve year old Singaporean Chinese lad who made himself useful around the barracks for pocket money.

'I will pay you five Singapore dollars if you take me for a ride,' Ivy offered.

'You no chaperon,' Ze Yu protested. 'I get into plenty number ten big trouble.'

'I promise I won't tell.'

Ze Yu stilled looked sceptical.

'All right, ten dollars, you little rascal and I'll pay for afternoon tea.'

Every man has his price. Ze Yu was the son of a fisherman who caught enough to feed his family, but there was little cash left over. To supplement the family income, Ze Yu operated a pedal-powered trishaw which was Singapore's favourite means of transport, although motor cars were already clogging the city streets and were especially favoured by colonial officials.

'We go chop-chop quick,' Ze Yu urged. 'Before anyone see. Where Missy Ivy want to go?'

'I'd like to pay a visit to Tanglin Barracks.'

'Nothing there, Missy Ivy,' Ze Yu protested. 'Just prison men.'

'I want to say hello to some old shipmates as Colonel Martin so aptly put it,' Ivy replied mischievously.

Ze Yu merely shrugged — one destination was just as good as another — although he preferred the more colourful areas like Geylang Road and Bugis Street. Ze Yu was a street kid. He ran errands for cash and helped around the port whenever there was an opportunity of a gratuity. He carried messages and mysterious packages for the Triad gangs when they needed an inconspicuous courier to operate under the police force's nose. At twelve he possessed a heap of city smarts and figured Ivy couldn't come to any harm at Tanglin Barracks.

He didn't mind pedalling Ivy around. She was petite, pleasant, friendly and genuinely interested in everything around her.

Tanglin Barracks consisted of several large high roofed buildings surrounding a vast grassed area where, to Ivy's surprise, the German POWs were playing cricket. The guards were mainly British members of the Singapore Volunteer Corps assisted by men from the Johor Military Force supplied by Sultan Ibrahim from just across the Strait on the Malayan mainland.

The guards didn't object when Ivy told them she'd been aboard the *Emden,* especially when several prisoners recognised her and waved cheerfully. A number of the POWs spoke fluent English and were eager to hear news about their comrades with Lieutenant von Mücke's shore party. The senior POW, *Oberleutnant* Jules Lauterbach, had been *Emden's* navigation officer and seemed especially attentive when it came to talk of escape.

The POWs and guards enjoyed a relaxed relationship and soon Ivy was seated in a canvas chair, sharing tea from tin cups with Lauterbach and about a dozen other English speaking sailors.

She poured a cup for Ze Yu into which he added as much sugar and condensed milk as he could. He found a shady spot and waited by his trishaw.

At which time gunfire rattled through the Tanglin Barracks and pandemonium broke out.

Ivy leapt to her feet and turned towards the main gate in dismay. A horde of sepoys charged along Tanglin Road straight for the barracks. A volley exploded from the sepoy ranks, enveloping them in smoke as the stench of cordite wafted into the Barracks parade ground. Two guards dropped where they stood. One man groaned only to be shot again while the other lay still.

'What's happening?' Ivy cried as Lauterbach grabbed her arm, dragging her towards one of the buildings.

'I believe the 5th Light Infantry Muslims have mutinied,' Lauterbach said. 'It's been coming for a month now — perhaps much longer. They are dissatisfied. Quickly bring the boy too.'

As sepoys poured through the gates, they butchered any guards they came across, but left the POWs unharmed, except one unfortunate sailor who simply got in the way of a stray bullet, which killed him instantly. The attack was over in moments. A handful of guards had no chance against a hundred mutineers.

Lauterbach guided Ivy and Ze Yu into one of the barracks dormitories. Several sailors followed. Without a word as the gunfire reached a crescendo before abating, the sailors pushed two camp beds aside, lifted a rattan mat to reveal a cavity below.

'Get down there,' Lauterbach ordered. '*Schnell!* Don't make a sound.'

Ivy was too shocked to object. Ze Yu followed her without hesitation. They were enveloped by total darkness as the Germans replaced the rug and beds just as twenty sepoys barged into the dormitory. Ivy heard muffled voices in a heated debate above her, but couldn't make out any of it. Men were yelling in several languages, none of which was English.

Then as quickly as the shouting had erupted, there was silence. Moments that seemed an eternity passed before a beam of light streaked into Ivy and Ze Yu's hiding place. As her eyes adjusted, Ivy saw a tunnel leading from the pit they occupied. It was just wide enough for a man to crawl through. This wasn't just a handy storage area.

Lauterbach reached down and lifted Ivy back into the dormitory. Ze Yu quickly followed.

'Have they gone?' Ivy whispered.

'*Ya Fraulein*, you are safe — for the moment.'

'Handy thing that this hole just happened to be here..?'

Lauterbach eyed her sheepishly.

'Don't worry. I won't tell anyone — especially not Colonel Martin.'

'I think our escape tunnel may have become redundant, *Fraulein*. I do believe another opportunity has presented itself.'

Ivy was appalled when she returned to the parade ground. At least a dozen men lay dead. The Germans had lined them in a neat row, but the bodies still sent shudders through her.

'Those poor souls,' she lamented, 'what did they do to deserve this?'

'Wrong place at the wrong time,' Lauterbach remarked under his breath. 'The sepoys told us they'd killed two other British officers at Alexandra Barracks.'

Ivy noticed that although a number of rifles lay on the ground, the German POWs had not joined the mutineers who'd taken the Barracks Maxim machineguns and left. The sepoys had tried to recruit the Germans, claiming they were allies in view of the Turks being Muslims too. But the POWs weren't buying it. Mutiny was a capital offence in the Imperial German Navy, just as it was anywhere else. There was only one penalty for treason and none of the sailors wished to be associated with it and end up swinging from a rope or facing a firing squad.

Attempting to escape was a legitimate act of war. Your enemy isn't going to execute you if you're recaptured, but throwing in your lot with traitors who'd just murdered a dozen British servicemen was plain lunacy.

'But now, *Fraulein*, much as I find your company charming, I urge you and your young companion to seek safety. I regret I will be unable to escort you further.'

'I quite understand *Herr Oberleutnant*. You wish to take advantage of this chance to be elsewhere.'

'Quite,' Lauterbach replied with just the trace of a smile.

'Ze Yu, will you please take me back to Colonel Martin's bungalow?' Ivy said as she took her seat on the trishaw. 'I think it will be a good place to discover what is afoot and I must be at dear Mama's side during this crisis.'

Ivy glanced over her shoulder as Ze Yu pedalled as fast as he could along Tanglin Road towards Alexandra barracks. Lauterbach and about forty men followed purposefully until they veered south east towards Keppel Harbour and a possible berth out of Singapore. Ivy was surprised how many POWS remained behind at Tanglin Barracks. Ivy assumed Lauterbach had only asked for volunteers unless the others were planning a different escape path.

Ivy watched with mixed feelings as the Germans disappeared into the cluttered labyrinths of shanties. She admired their bravery and courtesy, but they were the enemy after all.

If they must be recaptured all well and good, but please don't let them be hurt in the process.

Ivy and Ze Yu had more immediate problems right about then. The sepoys were on foot and were looting along the way which slowed them down. Ze Yu was pedalling at such a pace he soon caught up with the mutineers!

Chapter 13 — Singapore Siege

Ze Yu squeezed the brakes with all his might, causing the trishaw to skid yet barely slow at all. Ivy lurched forward as they slammed into the last two mutineers who were caught completely off guard. The sepoys barrelled into their comrades ahead giving Ze Yu a split-second to swerve sideward and dash down a side street, scattering rubbish, dogs, cats and chickens in every direction. People were noticeably absent, wisely taking cover inside their homes.

A few sepoys gave chase, but fortunately they hadn't recognised Ivy as European. Perhaps the sarong had fooled them. Ivy didn't know it but the mutineers were on a British killing-spree and had already murdered several British civilians and wounded a Chinese couple who were just too slow to get out of the way.

Finally, when the sepoys saw they weren't gaining on Ze Yu's trishaw they abandoned the pursuit. By that time Ivy and Ze Yu were close to Colonel Martin's bungalow. When they reached the garden wall, Ivy and Ze Yu scrambled over with the help of vines and shrubbery. Ivy didn't give a thought to what poisonous snakes might be lurking there.

Smack! Smack!

Two bullets slammed into the brick work, ricocheting in oblivion. Ivy knew instantly the shots had come from Colonel Martin's bungalow as gun-smoke drifted through the windows.

'Don't shoot, Colonel Martin!' she screamed. 'It's me — IVY D'VERE-BROWN!'

'Quickly, get inside,' Ivy's mother called.

Ivy and Ze Yu dashed across the lawn just as mutinous sepoys barged through the compound main gate only thirty yards away. The rebels levelled their rifles and aimed straight at the two running fugitives. At that range, trained soldiers could hardly miss. Suddenly Colonel Martin was standing on the veranda. He held a Webley pistol in each hand and blazed away without hesitation. Ivy's mother fired a .303 rifle through a window pane smashed to jagged shards.

Three Sepoys fell while the others retreated to the protection of the garden wall. Say what you will about Colonel Martin as he stood in the open blowing the smoke from his pistol barrels — the man was no coward.

Ivy and Ze Yu dashed through the open door. Colonel Martin stepped inside behind them and slammed the door closed while Ivy embraced her mother.

'Darling!' Meredith sobbed. 'I have been frantic — wherever have you been?'

'I'm fine, Mama,' Ivy soothed. 'Ze Yu has taken good care of me.'

Her mother would have scolded her more, but Ivy turned to Colonel Martin with information she was sure he'd want to hear.

'The sepoys have raided Tanglin Barracks, Colonel,' she said. 'They have killed the guards and run off. I think they're going to Keppel Harbour.'

'*I* think some of them have come here,' Colonel Martin said. 'I estimate there are between fifty and a hundred mutineers at the gate.'

All the colonel's bluster and pretention had disappeared as he calmly assessed their position. One of the Malay States Volunteer riflemen had brought news of the breakout from Alexandra Barracks just before the sepoys attacked.

Ivy looked around appalled. There were only three junior officers and Mrs Cotton in the bungalow. They did seem well armed though. The bungalow front room was strewn with rifles and service revolvers. The colonel had an ample supply of ammunition as well. Martin's rare meeting with his officers was to plan the regiment's removal to Hong Kong. Mrs Cotton kept Meredith company while their husbands were busy at Keppel Harbour.

'Here Ivy, take a revolver,' Meredith said. 'I'll show you how to fire and load. It isn't hard — goodness me, men can manage it.'

'Young man, can you load a rifle?' Colonel Martin addressed Ze Yu.

The boy nodded.

'Good lad. Reload from that ammunition box whenever I hand you an empty weapon.'

Ze Yu nodded again.

The sepoys gathered their nerve and rushed the bungalow. Colonel Martin and his officers blasted a lethal volley, while Ivy's mother kept up a steady rate of fire. She smoothly squeezed the trigger, operating the bold action with practised ease. Ivy took aim, holding the revolver with both hands. She pulled the trigger and shrieked as the recoil toppled her backwards.

'Are you hurt, miss?' one of the officers asked.

'No, I am quite well sir,' Ivy replied. 'I have not fired a gun before and I must get used to it. Thank you for your concern.'

After that Ivy remembered firing and reloading the revolver all afternoon until the sepoys retired once more. Luckily gun smoke was so thick she had no idea if she actually hit anyone. How she would have reacted to killing a fellow human being — however much they deserved it — was something she didn't really wish to ponder right then.

'How long do you think we can hold them off?' Ivy asked.

'So far, so good,' Colonel Martin replied enigmatically.

Colonel Martin had ordered his household staff to run for safety as it was unlikely the sepoys would target native Singaporeans. During the lull Ivy and her mother brewed tea and passed cups to Ze Yu and the officers.

'I have no idea how we coped before tea,' Meredith commented.

'Probably drank more rum,' Colonel Martin replied and actually grinned as he sipped his tea.

But the bungalow's defenders were granted a temporary reprieve. A company of Malay Straits Volunteers had heard the gunfire and turned up to man the garden perimeter, effectively stalling the sepoy attacks. For the present at least...

'They're coming again,' the officer commanding the volunteer riflemen called from just inside the gate.

Colonel Martin raced to the officer's position and saw a group of sepoys about equal in strength to the bungalow defenders. The sepoys stopped short of the wall and their leader advanced under a flag of truce. Martin strode forward to meet him. After a brief discussion the sepoy returned to his men and they dispersed in seconds.

'Chap said he wanted to join us,' Martin snapped as he entered the bungalow. 'Said they ain't mutineers. Can't trust 'em though.'

'Extra guns wouldn't go astray,' one of the officers ventured.

'Our force is sufficient. Fellow said only 'A' wing of Alexandra Barracks has mutinied — maybe four hundred rascals at best. Others didn't try to stop 'em though. Now they're split into groups. We'll mop 'em up soon enough. I told those fellows to make themselves scarce until this is all over and then we'll sort it out.'

But no sooner had the 'loyal' sepoys vanished than other mutineers took up positions around the bungalow and started pelting the compound with a steady hail of bullets. The defenders sought cover and returned fire as the siege slid into a desultory stalemate.

*

Colonel Martin might have felt secure, but that wasn't the case at Keppel Harbour, which was where Ivy's father found himself as a terrified constable cycled down Pasir Panjang Road with news of the mutiny.

'They're heading this way,' the policeman reported.

'How many?' the colonel demanded, instinctively taking command.

'At least a hundred. They shot at a car full of people.'

Ivy's father might have taken command, but of what? There was probably a half-platoon of troops from mixed units all carrying out non-related tasks. It looked as if they would break ranks and flee as the sepoys came into view. The mutineers hesitated while an animated discussion ensued about what to do next. Colonel D'vere-Brown took advantage of the breather.

'Stand fast,' he ordered. 'Form on me. I am now your temporary commanding officer.'

Years of service had shown the colonel that troops will perform the most amazing deeds if well led. D'vere-Brown instantly rallied twenty troops. All they required was a reliable definite leader and precise orders they understood...and Colonel Martin had unwittingly handed them a life-line.

Over the weekend the 5th Bengal Light Infantry had been transporting weapons to the wharf awaiting shipment to Hong Kong. Five fully laden lorries stood on the quayside brimming with rifles and ammunition.

'Break open that case,' D'vere-Brown ordered, indicating a box of 303 rifles.

He also directed two men to open as many ammunition cases as they could. Each man quickly loaded a five-shot magazine, clipping it into place in front of the rifle trigger guard.

Meanwhile the mutineers must have felt enough men had arrived and poured onto the dock. At first they were cautious, but they were thirsty for British blood. The fact that the soldiers on the wharf were mainly Sikhs and Singaporean volunteers, appeared to have escaped the sepoys' notice.

'Take cover behind the lorries,' D'vere-Brown yelled. 'Wait for my order.'

The mutineers looked to one another for support and seemed uncertain, until suddenly someone screamed what could only be described as a war cry and they surged forward.

They were thirty yards from D'vere-Brown's men, who held their nerve admirably.

'Fire!' the colonel bellowed.

Twenty rifles spat red-hot lead into the mutineers.

Men fell while others tumbled over the bodies in the tight-packed group.

'Fire!'

Another volley sprayed death into the insurgent ranks.

'Fire!'

It was all over. The sepoys turned and bolted back along Pasir Panjang Road.

'Hold your fire,' D'vere-Brown said in a hushed voice as he surveyed the carnage. A dozen bodies lay still while an equal number writhed in agony only feet from where he stood. It was then that he realised he hadn't even armed himself.

'Well done, men,' he called.

'What now, sahib?' one of the Sikhs asked.

'We form up as a unit. Arm ourselves with as much ammunition as we can carry, then we'll go and do some damn soldiering. Those fellows are going to regret they started this. Do you think someone can find me a loaded revolver?'

Leaving a five-man squad to guard the arms trucks, Colonel D'vere-Brown, pistol in hand, led the remaining troops back to the Martin bungalow. They passed a stalled car with the bodies of three men and a woman sprawled around the machine. Its engine was riddled with bullet holes. Were these the unfortunate souls the policeman had seen, or where they more innocent victims?

D'vere-Brown simply shook his head and marched on. There was nothing he could do for the dead — his job was to protect the living. As the troops drew closer to Colonel Martin's home, they heard the crackle of rifles. Fortunately there was no hint of machinegun chatter.

Ordering his men to halt, D'vere-Brown advanced cautiously. As he peeked around a building he saw the mutineers deployed behind upturned carts, motor vehicles, walls and buildings, peppering away at the bungalow where his family was on the receiving end.

The colonel gathered his men, forming them in a column of three ranks.

'Right, lads,' he instructed. 'We march up behind those blighters, fire a volley and then double time to the bungalow gates. I'll be right ahead of you, so those chaps defending the place don't take us for mutineers.'

The men stepped forward confidently in good order. The sepoys were so preoccupied with the bungalow that they didn't see or hear the oncoming danger.

'Halt!'

Thirty well-drilled boots crunched to a stop.

'Present...Fire!'

The sepoys had just enough time to turn and face the blast of lead.

'Forward at the double...March!'

Colonel D'vere-Brown didn't wait to examine the butcher's bill, but led his men into the bungalow compound before the smoke cleared and the sepoys could recover.

'Hold your fire...Stand fast...reinforcements!' one of the defending officers bellowed much to D'vere-Brown's relief.

Colonel Martin greeted him enthusiastically.

'By Jove well met, D'vere-Brown. Looks like you gave those scoundrels a taste of their own medicine. What's the situation at Keppel Harbour?'

'Under control, Colonel. I have men guarding the arms trucks while we drove the main bulk of rebels back here. We passed several murdered victims...innocent civilians have been slaughtered. What do you propose to do?'

'Better hold on here until reinforcements arrive,' Martin said.

Although both colonels were equal in rank, no one would dispute Martin's authority to take overall command. So far he was handling the crisis well enough. It appeared that the main rebel force surrounded Martin's bungalow and it was best to keep them occupied there, rather than have them rampaging through the colony. He suspected other units would already be mobilised to quell the uprising, which indeed proved to be the case.

Colonel D'vere-Brown was now free to attend his family. Ivy wisely omitted her adventures at Tanglin Barracks, while her mother was discreet enough not spill the beans.

The mutineers continued the siege all night. Although there was little to eat, the defenders had enough water and dug a latrine in a garden bed at the rear of the bungalow. It was soon putrid, but would serve until morning. Ivy and her parents had little to do through the night as the soldiers had the bungalow defences well organised. Ivy took opportunity to relax and brew tea.

'War does smell ghastly,' Meredith observed. 'I fail to see why men favour it so.'

'Most of these chaps would be unemployed if it wasn't for the military,' Colonel D'vere-Brown replied.

He was so infuriatingly reasonable at times.

'Colonel Martin seems to enjoy fighting, his experience must count,' Ivy observed.

'Major Cotton informed me Martin has never seen active service,' Ivy's father said. 'Maybe that's why he's so difficult to get along with. He's just spoiling for a good scrap.'

'What a pity,' Ivy sighed. 'The colonel should be leading his men into action, not fighting against them?'

'I believe Colonel Martin could have averted this crisis had he shown more empathy towards his men and not alienated his officers.'

'I must say he didn't seem very sympathetic to his troop's religion,' Ivy said.

'That's the trouble with an empire,' D'vere-Brown said. 'The people you conquer may seem primitive and hold views you think foolish — but they are their views and beating them over the head isn't going to change them overnight. I daresay this empire is going to come back and haunt us in the future.'

'What makes you say that, papa?'

'No empire lasts forever — not the Chinese, Romans, Greeks, Ottoman or whatever. Ours is in decline. There are independence movements everywhere especially on the subcontinent. Sooner or later all the empire's colonies will be independent.'

'That's not a bad thing, is it?'

'There is enormous wealth in possessing colonies for their raw materials and trade, but there is a huge expense involved. Just think how much it costs to keep our colonial armed forces. The trouble is we'll leave a political vacuum and just how the newly independent countries deal with that is anyone's guess.'

'Some native people here think they're more English than the English,' Ivy's mother ventured. 'They may be unwilling to stay in the colonies if the British leave. They consider themselves British subjects and entitled to immigrate en masse to England rather than be governed by people they feel are inferior to them or incapable of the task. I wonder if anyone has thought of that.'

'Right now I don't think anyone is thinking past getting through this war with Germany,' Colonel D'vere-Brown sighed.

Chapter 14 — Home Run

The siege continued all night, but with so many defenders now in position around Colonel Martin's bungalow, the mutineers were hard pressed to do much damage. By the same token no one was prepared to venture far in the darkness. Chinese New Year meant a waxing new moon, so the night was pitch-black other than cooking fires and distant electric lights from the city centre.

But it was really all over for the sepoys. Royal Marines from *HMS Cadmus* were already ashore and, joined by British artillery men, local militia and police, began mopping up Keppel Harbour. By morning they'd reached Alexandra barracks and routed the mutineers, who fled in every direction. Many rebels were rounded up or killed over the next two days before two Japanese cruisers accompanied by French and Russian warships arrived to quell the last vestiges of resistance.

Mutineers were not the only fugitives and many German POWs were recaptured, although *Oberleutnant* Lauterbach slipped through the cordon and escaped to China.

As soon as it was safe, Ivy insisted on taking Ze Yu home with a couple of Royal marines as escort. Ze Yu's family lived on a fishing boat in a jumbled marina not far from Keppel Harbour. His parents hugged their son with open relief to see Ze Yu safely.

'Thank you, Ze Yu,' Ivy said, bending forward to kiss him on the cheek. 'I will never forget how helpful you have been.'

'Any time you're in Singapore, Missy Ivy,' the boy replied. 'You visit Ze Yu.'

Ivy promised she would and waved goodbye.

At first the extent of the danger still posed by the mutiny was unknown and some British citizens chose to be evacuated to the Malayan mainland or, in the D'vere-Browns' case, to Hong Kong. The Colonel saw no need to remain in Singapore and took the opportunity to get his family back on track for England.

*

Ivy sailed with her family on a US steamer from Hong Kong to San Francisco. From there they boarded the trans-continental railroad to New York where Colonel D'vere-Brown had arranged for funds to be deposited in a Wall Street bank.

Dear Diary — 1ˢᵗ May 2015

I have been less than diligent in my journal keeping, but my sojourn across North America was so exhilarating, I hardly thought to put pen to paper. The sheer vastness and magnificence of this continent is simply breathtaking. For once our journey has been uneventful other than the wonders we behold at every turn. I have sketched many scenes and hope to complete the painting for posterity when we reach England.

Sailing from Hong Kong was tedious, but adequate after our previous onboard accommodation, which I hope I have described well enough in my previous missives.

Papa is now in such a rush and has booked our passage ahead so there will be the least chance of further delays.

San Francisco is just a wonderful, bustling metropolis that still reflects the brash and — dare I say bawdy — character of the gold rush days. Yet Sacramento, the Californian state capital is more serene even though I believe it was just as wild during the forty-niners' gold stampede. Oil-rigs are to be seen on nearly every property, which are sadly the ugliest of structures.

Words cannot describe the grandeur of crossing the Rocky Mountains. The peaks are still heavy with snow as it is yet early spring and the maples and birch trees still conceal their gorgeous foliage amid the flowing aspens. I have spied quite a number of majestic bald eagles which the Americans so pride as their national emblem, yet are prepared to slaughter if they are considered a threat to livestock.

As we pass the endless plains that spread on forever, I cannot help but regret the passing of the vast buffalo herds that once grazed as far as the eye can see. Now the grasslands accommodate domestic cattle or have been tamed by a farmer's plough.

Of the noble American Plains Indians, only handfuls remain. A few sad, forlorn-looking families have erected tepees close to the railway depots, hoping to sell trinkets to passengers while the locomotives are replenished with water, coal and firewood. Many of these once noble savages appear to be rather under the influence of alcoholic beverages.

I've noticed the railway employees and passengers treat the Indians poorly by insulting them or simply ignoring their plight. I remember seeing Aboriginal people suffering similar abuse on occasions during my visit to Australia.

The cowboys in their broad-brimmed Stetson hats, denim dungarees, embossed wedge-heel boots and tasselled leather chaps are a fine sight as they herd great droves of cattle. Here in the north they are more like our own Herefords, with not a long horn in sight.

In fact cowboys are in the minority as most railway — or railroad as the Americans say — towns are filled with men in bowler hats and serge suits while women dress in smart sensible skirts and bonnets, if not exactly in the latest Parisian mode.

But now we have left the Wild West behind and arrived at the industrial might of the Great Lakes cities. How dark and colourless the smoke-filled sky has become compared with the clear azure heavens of the Utah and Wyoming. Now our view through New York State is much marred by collieries and slag-heaps.

Yet here we are finally in New York. Mama and I have barely a moment to view the grandeur of Central Park, savour a beefsteak at Delmonico's in Lower Manhattan or enjoy a spot of 5ᵗʰ Avenue window-shopping before Papa has whisked us away in a taxi-cab. Here at the East River Dock our majestic ocean liner awaits to convey us to Liverpool in the utmost luxury...Our ship is Cunard Line's pride and joy and what an enormous, awe-inspiring vessel the *Royal Mail Ship Lusitania* has proven to be...

'Oh, Papa isn't she the most handsome ship ever?' Ivy gushed as she craned her neck skywards to encompass the entire spectacle from wharf to the four mountainous smoke stacks.

'Not just majestic, she holds a Blue Riband for record Atlantic crossings and is the fastest ship afloat today. She's known as *the Greyhound of the Sea*.'

Although the quayside buzzed with excitement as passengers boarded *Lusitania,* the ship was by no means fully booked, which is why Colonel D'vere-Brown was able to obtain tickets at such short notice.

After inspecting their palatial cabins, Ivy was keen to explore.

'It will take me the entire voyage to see all the ship,' she commented in awe as they took tea in one of the many lounges. 'There is so much room. It's almost as if the boat is only half full.'

'Perhaps this will explain why,' Meredith said, handing Ivy a copy of the morning edition of *The New York Times*.

Below an advertisement announcing *Lusitania's* departure was a stark warning from the German Embassy which had been posted in every large circulation periodical across American.

NOTICE!

Travellers intending to
embark on the Atlantic voyage
are reminded that a state of
war exists between Germany
and her allies and Great Britain
and her allies; that the zone of
war includes the waters adjacent
to the British Isles; that
in accordance with formal notice
given by the Imperial German Government,
vessels flying the flag of Great Britain, or of
any of her allies are liable to
destruction in those waters and
that travellers sailing in the war zone
on ships of Great Britain or her
allies do so at their own risk.

IMPERIAL GERMAN EMBASSY

Washington DC 22 April 1915

'I suppose that would put some people off,' Colonel D'vere-Brown observed, 'I mean that is the longest sentence I've ever read.'

'Obviously you haven't read *Robinson Crusoe* or *Gulliver's Travels* then, Papa,' Ivy declared. 'In any event I doubt if any Boche warship would be big or fast enough to tackle *RMS Lusitania*!'

Thus, under the expert eye of her master, William Turner, one of Cunard's most notable and highly-awarded captains, *RMS Lusitania* nudged clear of the wharf aided by a tug flotilla. As they glided gently past Liberty Island, it seemed to Ivy that the burnished green copper statue was bidding them farewell with the torch extending from her right arm.

Once safely clear of Staten Island to starboard and Brooklyn to port, the harbour pilot disembarked, leaving *Lusitania* to steam out to sea at full speed. After the *SS Runhild Halvorsen, Ayesha,* the British destroyer and finally a tramp steamer across the Pacific Ocean, *Lusitania* was sheer opulence and Ivy intended to make the most of every moment. She was also rubbing shoulders with many Canadian, American as well as British rich-and-famous families and individuals.

Fine dining — at the captain's table on occasion — sumptuous buffet breakfasts, high teas and leisurely strolls around the promenade deck, attentive officers, deck games, after-supper dances almost on a grand ball scale were all elements of the whirlwind life aboard for young Ivy. She flirted with a couple of the sons of wealthy American magnates, but nothing that aspired to a shipboard romance. As much as anything, Ivy simply enjoyed relaxing with her sketchpad and paints.

A week sped past in the blink of an eye. Nevertheless Ivy was thrilled when Ireland's west coast smudged the horizon. Captain

Turner steered *Lusitania* on a southerly course ten miles at seaward of County Cork in preparation to navigate around Southern Ireland into the Irish Sea and on to Liverpool. During the morning Captain Turner announced the crew would be carrying out a safety drill and all the lifeboats were swung out on their davits. Ivy noticed that curiously they were not stowed afterwards.

'Papa, why have they not replaced the lifeboats?' Ivy asked during lunch.

'I cannot say,' he replied honestly.

'Perhaps now we are clear of open waters they will keep them out for cleaning when we dock at Liverpool,' Meredith suggested. 'My, isn't this tomato and basil soup delicious?'

'Maybe a precaution,' the colonel suggested ominously. 'We are now in the exclusion zone.'

'You'd think we'd have a warship escort,' Ivy said.

'Yes, you would,' Colonel D'vere-Brown replied. 'Perhaps none is available, or none that could keep up with us. In any event, as we know *Lusitania* can out-run any ship in the Boche navy.'

After another sumptuous lunch, Ivy occupied herself with her paints on the upper deck while her parents took one last stroll. But she wasn't there long. Dank patchy fog started to intermittently envelope *Lusitania's* upper decks. Ivy felt the ship slow after travelling at full speed until then. Just after two o'clock, Ivy packed her paints and paper into her satchel.

I do believe it is time for a cuppa and one of those delicious éclairs...

Crunch! Blam! Boom!

All three sounds slammed into Ivy's eardrums simultaneously. The entire massive juggernaut lurched sideways, tossing her to the deck. Ivy scrambled to her feet, dazed and confused, grabbing anything to prevent her tumbling over again.

Within seconds another explosion blasted from the bowels of the hull, although Ivy had no way of telling what further damage had been done. This explosion was far greater than the first torpedo impact causing untold destruction below decks. Almost immediately *Lusitania* listed to starboard before her bow slowly pitched forward. Flames belched from passages and hatchways. Ivy heard terrified screams as people were engulfed in flames or overcome by oily fumes.

Suddenly passengers raced around Ivy, many screaming hysterically as crewmen struggled to release the lifeboats from their derricks. The port lifeboats proved useless as they'd swung inwards when the deck heeled over. On the starboard side another equal vexing challenge faced those trying to board the boats. They now leant so far out that clambering aboard was so hazardous, many people failed to grasp the lifeboats, lost their grip and plunged into the icy ocean over sixty feet below.

My God, they're abandoning ship...it's only been seconds...where are Mama and Papa..?

Steaming boldly off the Irish coast had of course put *Lusitania* squarely in British territorial waters. This made *Lusitania* fair game in the view of *Kapitän-Leutnant* Walther Schwieger, commanding the German submarine *U-20*. The U-boat had stumbled on *Lusitania* by sheer chance as there was no way she could match the giant liner's speed.

Schwieger ordered a single torpedo to be fired which slammed into *Lusitania* just below the bridge. Whether the second explosion was caused by the ship's fuel supply or contraband munitions rumoured to be carried in the hold was later hotly debated. Right then the point was academic as the mighty *Lusitania* was undoubtedly sinking. Soon other sounds were heard — the gush of exploding boilers, crashing superstructure and most of all, the forlorn creaking groans of the mighty ship as if she somehow felt the agony of her demise.

Ivy could barely keep her footing as the deck tilted forward and people started slipping towards the bow. Crewmen urgently hammered at the brakes to release as many lifeboats as possible, but pitifully few reached the ocean.

Pandemonium erupted as passengers struggled through hatches and doorways, slipping over one another as the ship canted even further. Many unfortunates slipped backwards down the ladders and stairwell they just clambered up. As they fell others were knocked down with them. A cacophony of screams and curses filled Ivy's ears like one continuous wail of despair. The pandemonium was deafening.

A woman with a baby and two small children screamed hysterically as she struggled to reach a lifeboat.

'Give me the baby,' Ivy cried. 'Hold onto your children — don't let go.'

The sobbing woman obeyed. Clutching the baby, Ivy took one of the children's hands so the four of them formed a chain. Then laboriously, inch by inch, they edged towards a life boat. Crewmen scooped the women and children up and placed them in the lifeboat.

'Get aboard, miss,' a sailor shouted.

'No, I'll help some of the others,' Ivy replied.

The sailor didn't argue — he was preoccupied enough. He tossed a life jacket to Ivy.

'Then put that on, miss,' he advised. 'We ain't waitin' and she's goin' down — fast!'

Indeed it was only Captain Turner's instant realisation that his ship was doomed that any lives were saved at all. He gave the order to abandon ship at once and his men sprang to action. After the *Titanic* disaster three years earlier, *Lusitania* carried enough lifeboats for all passengers and crew, but she sank so quickly only half a dozen of those escape-vessels were lowered successfully. Worst still it was almost impossible to board the lifeboats amid the chaos and panic. Many passengers and crew simply jumped overboard. Some died on impact, not realising how far the water was below the tilted hull. Hitting the water wearing a life jacket achieved the same vertebrae-crushing result as jumping from a sky-scraper onto a concrete pavement.

Where are Mama and Papa..?

There was no more time to speculate. Again Ivy felt the deck sliding beneath her feet. Already the ship was a third under water and the deck was tilted at almost twenty degrees, making any sort of footing impossible. People lost their grip and tumbled down the sloping deck. Some crashed into superstructure and either bounced clear or lay wedged with no chance of rescue. Others splashed into the sea, either to swim away or disappear completely, failing to re-emerge.

Ivy lost her grip on the railing she'd been clutching. Her feet slipped from under her and she slithered downwards. The deck was massive and the sheer distance Ivy travelled was staggering. She reached the wheelhouse in seconds and slammed into a figure, clinging to a hatchway latch before the sea swamped it. The impact knocked him over and both Ivy and he sank into the swirling sea.

The bitter cold hit her like a million pin-pricks. Whereas the balmy waters of the Indian Ocean had been a refreshing relief, the North Atlantic was fearsomely hostile. Ivy's life jacket held her head above the surface. She cast around desperately for a lifeboat or raft, but all she saw were bobbing heads amongst tons of flotsam made up of deck chairs, tables, other furniture, wooden fittings and countless other unidentifiable objects.

Ivy's next sensation was someone spluttering to the surface. To her surprise Captain Turner floated in his lifejacket right beside her.

'You must swim away, Miss,' he said, commendably calmly in Ivy's opinion. 'The ship will suck you under if it sinks completely. I do believe the bow now rests on the seabed, but that does not mean the hull will not roll over.'

He did not wait for a reply, but swam to warn others to move clear. As she struggled with as much speed as possible with the cumbersome lifejacket acting as a drogue, Ivy noticed Captain Turner did not swim away. He paddled purposefully back and forth urging anyone close to the ship to swim away.

He would still be on board if I hadn't knocked him into the sea...I wonder if he planned to go down with the ship...

But there was no time for Ivy to reflect further. As each of *Lusitania's* immense smoke stacks slipped below the water surface, millions of gallons of water streamed into their gaping maws. Flotsam, screaming people were washed into the cavernous tubes. As each funnel disappeared, more victims were dragged to their deaths.

As the final chimney sank, Ivy felt herself being pulled towards the vortex. She was aware that others were to share her fate as three or four surged to certain death. Yet the *Lusitania* gave up her dead. A sudden eruption from the ship's boilers blasted a jet of steam upwards through the funnel. Fortunately the sea temperature cooled the blast which spewed Ivy and the others clear of the funnel, dropping them into the ocean astern of *Lusitania.*

From that moment the ship seemed to melt into the sea. The gargantuan aft section reared high before descending almost sedately. Ivy saw *Lusitania's* four massive propellers slide out of sight before the hull disappeared altogether.

For a moment Ivy felt a shroud of silence envelop her, which lasted for several minutes as she recovered from the shock of the disaster. And then, almost imperceptibly she began to hear a myriad of sounds — human voices now replaced the mechanical, grinding protests of *Lusitania* as she surrendered to the deep.

Groans, screams, sighs, gasps, prayers and curses filled Ivy's ears. Calls for help surrounded her. Cries from terrified people, drowning people, freezing people, hopeless people...dying people...

Mama, Papa, where are you?

Chapter 15 — A Safe Haven?

After the first mind-numbing shock, Ivy stopped thinking about the water temperature. Her head was spinning as she tried to gather her bearings and make some sense of this madness. How could this have happened? She'd been sailing on the biggest, fastest ocean liner afloat. How could something so immense have sunk to the ocean floor so quickly?

Ivy was unaware of time, but *Lusitania* sank just eighteen minutes after the torpedo struck.

As she floated her body no longer felt particularly cold, more like numbness, but when her teeth began to chatter, she knew she had to try and warm up. The only thing she could think of was to keep moving. This was difficult in a bulky lifejacket with her satchel strapped across her back and acting as a sea anchor. All this meant expending extra energy, but Ivy had no other choice.

The crew had assembled a number of collapsible boats and managed to get them to sea although some were swamped by overloading or sucked into oblivion by whirlpools caused as *Lusitania* sank. Worst of all were lethal vortexes formed as water had poured down the funnels.

As she swam randomly, possibly in circles, she encountered other survivors.

'Quickly,' she called to anyone she came across. 'Get together with anyone you find and form a huddle. Link your arms and legs. Keep as close as possible to share body heat. Put children in the centre.'

Dear me, wealthy privileged people can be so hopeless when it comes to looking after themselves. Self reliance has been bred out of them by servants.

Ivy had no medical or even first-aid training, but it just seemed common sense to her. She remembered as a child how warm and comfortable she'd felt when she'd snuggled into her father's arms while he read her bedtime stories by Lewis Carroll, Rudyard Kipling, Edith Nesbit or Mary Sherwood...

Goodness me, my mind is wandering. Pull yourself together, Ivy! Don't go to sleep...don't even get drowsy... Mama, Papa, where are you?

So for the next two hours Ivy splashed, kicked, sang and yes, even swore, although her profanity repertoire was pitifully inadequate for the occasion. She lost count of the survivors she herded into groups, yet rather than joining one of those life-preserving huddles, she swam on to organise others, hoping beyond hope that she would finally bump into her parents.

But even her spirits were daunted when she started to find men women and children in lifejackets who'd survived the initial horror, only to slide in hypothermic comas and finally the numbing blackness of death.

She became aware of one lifeboat about a hundred yards away. Slowly she willed herself towards the floating sanctuary, but once she was close enough to make out details, she saw the boat was hopelessly overcrowded. Dozens of survivors clung to lines around the boat, but there was simply no more room onboard. Those in the water begged to be hoisted from the sea, but where were they going to fit?

'Take my place,' she heard a man call.

Papa!

She recognised his voice as he dropped into the water and helped two children upwards to fill his spot. As he did so, others tried to push him aside and clamber aboard. After a tussle the children finally made safety, but Colonel D'vere-Brown lost his grip on the line during the struggle and disappeared. He wasn't wearing a lifejacket. Ivy paddled to the where she'd last seen him, but he didn't re-surface.

'Papa!' she screamed.

She cast around, but her visibility was limited by the lifeboat and the ocean swell that slapped into her face. Ivy sensed she wept, but salt spray washed away her tears of frustration, profound sadness and desolation.

Wreckage floated everywhere, including empty lifejackets. Ivy gathered a few together and made a makeshift raft, but staying afloat wasn't her paramount problem. Her own jacket and buoyant painting satchel were more than enough to keep her head above water. Sea temperature would be the critical factor.

The survivors still in the water should all have died within five minutes except for a global phenomenon, which raised the water temperature in the Eastern Atlantic. For some sound geographical reason the Gulf Stream spews warm seawater from the Mexican coast northwards along America's Eastern Seaboard. Here it forms the North Atlantic Drift, which wends its way leisurely across to Europe warming the surrounding ocean by a few degrees. That doesn't mean you can slosh around in the

Atlantic indefinitely, but rather death from hypothermia is insidious rather than instantaneous.

Nevertheless, after two hours in the water, Ivy became delirious. She still heard the wailing sounds of dying and desperate survivors, but her senses were dimming by the moment. The water chill-factor eventually lowered her body core temperature to a point where she no longer thought coherently and her body shook uncontrollably. It only needed a degree or two more before she lost consciousness and drifted into oblivion.

Ivy was unaware that a motley fleet of fishing ketches, private yachts, tugs, Galway hookers, in fact anything afloat along the southern Irish coast had taken to sea. Finally the first of this assorted armada reached the disaster area and started rescuing survivors.

'Sure, sweet Jasis, this is jest a wee slip o' a lassie,' Ivy heard a voice that was almost a whisper. 'Bless me there's nothin' to keep out the cold.'

'Gently, me darlin' boys, lift her gently.'

Ivy was unaware of the arms that reached for her and lifted her from the sea. She didn't feel the wooden deck as she was laid there and covered with blankets. She was still insensible when a mug of tea was held to her lips and she sipped the steaming, sugar-laced liquid. She was exhausted beyond endurance and slumped into unconsciousness.

*

'I thought we'd lost her.'
Ivy heard the voice, but it was miles away.

'It was touch and go, doctor,' a woman's voice responded, 'but her temperature and pulse have returned to normal. I think she will stabilise now.'

'Mama...Papa...where are you..?' Ivy whispered.

'Now don't you fret, sweetie,' the woman replied. 'You sleep a while and everything will be fine.'

Everything will be fine...oh well that's all right then...of course it won't be fine...Papa has drowned and Mama might be too...God what did we do to you to deserve this...Where were you when we needed you?

But sleep is what she did...to a point. She drifted in and out of awareness while reliving the hell of *Lusitania*'s end. She recalled the terrified screaming most of all, but oddly heard low voices in the back ground. Although she couldn't make out what was said, she was sure she heard a man's German accent.

It was daylight when Ivy sat bolt upright. She was in a narrow cot shrouded by blissfully white sheets and woollen blankets. Her wet clothes had vanished and she wore a simple, comfortable nightgown. She looked about to see she was in a crowded room with several other women asleep on mattresses while another two shared a double bed. Miraculously, Ivy's painting satchel had survived and had been placed under her cot. A man stood close by holding blankets, towels and clean sheets.

'Please do not over-exert yourself, *fraulein,*' the German-accented man said softly. 'You have suffered a great trauma.'

'Yes, thanks to you Boche villains,' Ivy hissed. 'If you think you have captured me, well you are very much mistaken!'

In confusion, Ivy rose and stumbled to the door, almost tripping over the other sleepers. She lurched into a corridor. Mattresses lined the floor with barely enough room for Ivy to get by. She almost collided with a woman dressed in a crisply starched nurse's livery.

'Young lady, do think it wise to be abroad?' the nurse asked severely.

'Better than being held prisoner by the Boche. Where am I anyway?' Ivy demanded.

'Why the Queen's Hotel, Queenstown, County Cork and you are certainly not a prisoner.'

'But there are Germans here...'

'Germans? Why perish the thought, darlin' girl. We're safely in Ireland.'

'But I heard a German voice.'

'Oh bless you, little miss. That would be Mr Humbert. He owns the hotel.'

'A German owns this hotel?'

'Don't fret now, bless you, sweet girl. Mr Humbert is a naturalised British citizen now, and a thorough gentleman. He has availed his entire establishment for the survivors' use.'

Ivy may have still been unconvinced, but she was suddenly aware of more pressing matters to concern her.

'Can you show me the bathroom, please? I need to use the lavatory.'

'Ah, Jesus be praised, it's always a good sign when our natural bodily functions get back to normal,' the nurses said cheerfully. 'At the end of the hall, do you need assistance?'

'You are very kind, but I can manage, thank you,' Ivy replied.

She had no desire for help to perform that particular task.

Ivy was hungry and after freshening up, Mr Humbert escorted her to the hotel dining room where she found a spot at a long table with about a dozen other bedraggled survivors. She tucked into a bowl of mutton stew accompanied by soda bread with a Spanish orange for desert, all washed down with sweet, milky tea.

Once she'd eaten some solid food, Ivy dressed in her now dry clothes. Her shoes were still damp, but it was time to find her parents. Ivy pulled herself together and set about discovering her parents' fate.

'Does anyone know where other survivors are?' Ivy asked, only to receive blank stares in reply. Her fellow passengers were mostly in shock and many were so confused they were still unable to believe the disaster.

'People have been taken to the hospital, other hotels, churches and private homes,' Mr Humbert said.

'I must go to each location. Mama and Papa may be at one of those places.'

'Permit me to accompany you, *fraulein*. I will get you an overcoat and bonnet. We do not want you catching your death of cold after enduring so much.'

As they left the hotel, Mr Humbert stopped Ivy, held her shoulders gently and looked straight into her eyes.

'I must tell you, *fraulein*, there are not only survivors, but many...many bodies too. They lie in the town hall and along the quayside. I do not wish to distress you further than necessary, but you may also have to look there. Are you prepared for that?'

Ivy paused before nodding. She thought she'd seen her father drown when he sacrificed his spot in the lifeboat, but could she be sure? His hair had dropped over his brow and one dark suited, moustached man could be confused with another. Salt water had been splashing Ivy's face after all. Whatever the outcome, she still had to discover what had happened to her parents.

Ivy spent all Saturday afternoon visiting where survivors were housed. Many places including the hospital had already made lists of those people they were sheltering, and people in private homes were able to speak for themselves, but no one had heard of Colonel D'vere-Brown or his wife. Once they'd called everywhere Mr Humbert knew of, he once again reminded Ivy of a task she was reluctant to face.

'We now go to the town hall and the docks, *fraulein.*'

They reached the wharf first. Ivy was appalled at the number of bodies laid in neat rows. They were hundreds of them all covered with shrouds which Ivy would have to lift one at a time — hundreds of dead men, women and children.

She gasped as she revealed each face. Some looked peaceful, some terrified, some merely puzzled, but they were all pale and cold.

'I do not know if I can continue, Mr Humbert,' Ivy said after examining over twenty bodies. 'I fear I am unable to gaze into another pair of lifeless eyes.'

'Then it is fortunate that you don't have to and neither do I, thank God.'

Ivy's father stood only yards away. He of course had been on the same torturous mission as Ivy. She flew into his arms, hugging him until he gasped for breath, but he didn't care.

'If the sea didn't get me, you'll squeeze the life of me,' the colonel said as he tried to laugh.

'I do not care, Papa. I will never let you go. I thought I saw you give up you place on a lifeboat. I saw you sink. I thought you drowned.'

'Yes, I slipped under the boat, but managed to come back up on the other side. Your mother threw me her lifejacket and I hung onto a towline. Nearly froze to death though.'

'I think I did too...but...Mama...where is Mama?'

'She's...'

'She's not dead...please, papa, tell me she is not dead.'

'No, your mother is fine, Ivy, a bit shaken up, but that's only natural, don't you think?'

'Where is she? I cannot see her.'

'Don't worry. I called Liam to take her to Crosshaven. Maeve will see she's comfortable. She wanted to stay and look for you, but I insisted she went.'

Liam and Maeve O'Donoghue were the housekeeper and gardener who managed the D'vere-Brown holiday cottage when the colonel and his family were away.

'There is a telephone at the Queen's Hotel...'

'Oh Papa this is Mr Humbert. He has been so kind. I spent last night at his hotel.'

As the two men shook hands, Colonel D'vere-Brown thanked Mr Humbert warmly for caring for Ivy. If he was puzzled by the hotelier's accent, he didn't mention it.

Once they'd been connected to the cottage, Ivy was delighted to hear her mother, who sobbed with relief and joy. Finally Colonel D'vere-Brown wrested the earpiece from Ivy to ask Liam to bring the trap into Queenstown. That done he once more relinquished the phone to Ivy. She chattered with her mother until a solemn policeman demanded the receiver for official business.

Mr Humbert collected Ivy's paint satchel and insisted she keep the overcoat. She thanked him for his kindness, kissing him on the cheek as she said goodbye.

'Can you believe it, Papa? My journal and most of my artwork has survived since Australia!'

'A miracle indeed...and an even bigger miracle is that *we* survived all the way from Australia.'

It was only a two mile boat trip from Queenstown Wharf to Crosshaven Harbour, but about four times as far overland and even then they still had to use a ferry across the Lee River to Monkstown where they waited for Liam.

'I'm sure someone would have taken us by boat, Ivy.'

'Papa I do not mind waiting for Liam in the slightest. In fact it will be some time before I wish to set foot aboard any floating vessel...if ever.'

'Fair enough, but now you are safe and sound with nothing to worry about.'

'Oh, I will worry, Papa. I will worry for the rest of my life every time I think of all those poor lost souls. I will never forget and I will never forgive the Boche. If only there is something I can do to make them pay for what they did.'

'I doubt the government will give you a rifle and send you into the trenches.'

'Perhaps not, Papa, but I will think of some way to do my bit and I do not mean knitting socks for soldiers.'

'Soldiers need socks...'

'Don't make fun of me, Papa...I will do something purposeful.'

In time Liam arrived in a two-wheel canopied trap pulled by an elderly horse which was in no hurry. After a snack of oats, carrots, an apple and water, the horse made its leisurely way back along unsealed roads and tracks. It was past midnight when they arrived at Crosshaven where Meredith D'vere-Brown waited for them.

Part Three — Emerald Isle 1916

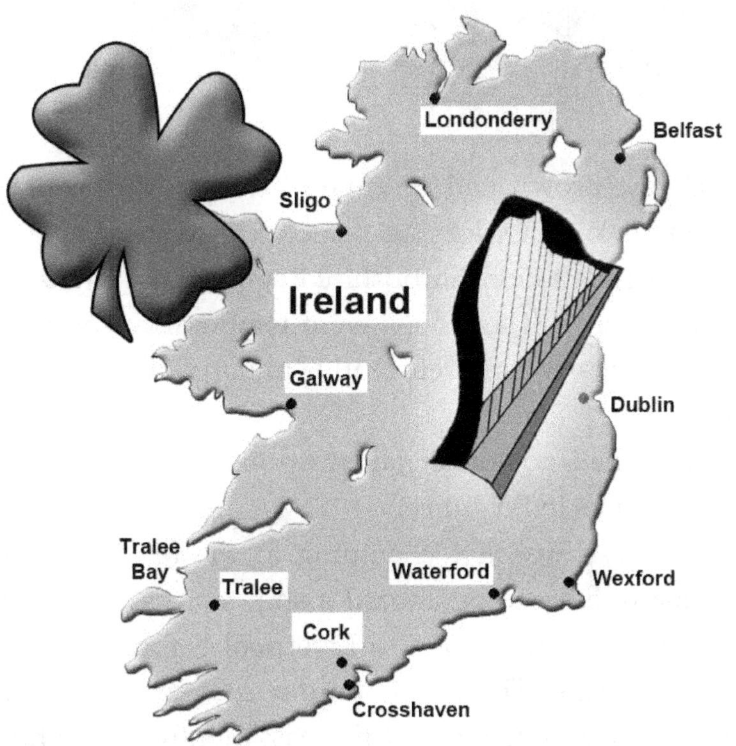

Chapter 16 — Irish Sojourn

Colonel D'vere-Brown had no time to dwell. After contacting the London War Office, he was recalled to England to command the 11th Battalion, Shropshire Regiment, which had been formed in his absence. The troops were temporarily commanded by the brigade major and currently undergoing training on Salisbury Plain.

The colonel had no sooner taken up his post, when the 11th was shipped to Ypres in Belgium.

Meanwhile Ivy was left champing at the bit. She and her mother did finally have to go aboard a ship to cross the Irish Sea from Kingstown Dock in Dublin to Liverpool before returning to their Shropshire home. The idyllic border country was a far cry from the hurly-burly excitement of the past months and while Ivy relaxed readily enough, she still yearned for some meaningful employment to help defeat the Boche.

The first letters arrived from her father. Initially they seemed optimistic yet guarded and rather artificially 'stiff-upper-lippish'. There were of course personal passages for Ivy's mother, as well as descriptions of trench-life, which seemed to dwell more on moral and personal hygiene than fighting the enemy.

And then Ivy remembered her promise to Callan McAlister — a promise she had so far failed to keep. She had no idea where he was. She understood Australian troops served in the Middle East or the Dardanelles where the Gallipoli Campaign was grinding into its fifth hellish month.

She wrote to her father, but he was unable to enlighten her, suggesting she simply address her letters to 4th Infantry Brigade Australian Imperial Force HQ, Alexandria. From there they could be redirected to wherever Callan might be stationed. So she wrote once a week, outlining her adventures...

*

Callan had just finished the letters and was about to re-read them when Archie Blake returned. Callan replaced his mail neatly in the envelopes and stacked them in chronological order.

'Can you believe it, Archie,' Callan cried. 'No wonder she didn't write. It's a miracle she's alive. Listen...'

'I know...'

'You know...how? I've only just read them myself.'

'Remember I'm a staff officer now,' Blake said with a grin. 'When I discovered that lot, it didn't take a genius to work out who'd written them. So I telephoned around when I got to London. It wasn't long before I contacted the young lady in question...'

'You've spoken to Ivy?'

'Yes, in fact I believe she's on her way...'

But he didn't have time to finish because Ivy had just entered the ward. Of course she hugged Callan which made his wounds ache, but he didn't complain until she finally released him.

'I came immediately Captain Blake contacted me, dearest Callan. I have just arrived from the railway station by taxicab,' Ivy cried. 'Oh, you poor, dear boy. Captain Blake told me all about how brave you were and how you were wounded. Well you will jolly well come home with me until you are better...'

'I'm not sure I shouldn't be getting back to duty...' Callan ventured without any great enthusiasm.

'Nonsense, you are in no shape to go fighting the Boche...Is that not correct, Captain Blake?'

'Absolutely, young lady.'

'You see, Mama and I will take care of you. Papa is coming home on leave and we shall all go to Crosshaven and forget this wretched war for a few weeks. We have not been back since the *Lusitania* went down.'

Callan stared at John Blake who merely shrugged.

'I will not take no for an answer,' Ivy declared. 'I have studied first aid and trained as a nurse's aide at Wolverhampton Hospital, so I know what is good for you, Callan McAlister.'

'I see no difficulty,' Blake offered. 'Look, like I said this is need-to-know, so keep it under your hat, Callan — and you, miss. The battalion — in fact the entire brigade will deploy to Blighty shortly. We're going to reorganise, re-equip and retrain for Europe. It looks like we'll be initially stationed somewhere on Salisbury Plain. Nothing will happen until after Easter at least, so you go to Ireland with Miss D'vere-Brown. I'll know where to find you when it's time for your recall.'

'I'll need papers and travel authorisation.'

'Leave that to me, I'm a staff officer remember. I'll also arrange for your back-pay in Pommy notes. Nice to see you didn't gamble it away in two-up games.'

'I'll be here to pick you up first thing tomorrow,' Ivy said. 'I trust that will be acceptable, Captain Blake. I do hope we shall become firm friends. Please call me Ivy.'

'I can think of nothing that would please me more, if you will call me Archie,' Blake answered gallantly.

Ivy usually got her way when at her charming best and Callan wasn't going to argue either. Other than a few days off on Lemnos, he had been constantly on duty for over a year.

*

Callan loved Ireland. The green — Ivy called it verdant — landscape, quaint villages, friendly people who spoke with accents he could barely understand all enchanted him. Yet the tranquillity was a facade shielding a groundswell of discontent and latent revolution. Ivy explained that Ireland's history hadn't been as serene as the countryside might suggest.

She proudly took Callan's arm as they waited at the platform. He was a dashing sight in his freshly cleaned uniform, medal ribbons and emu-plumed slouch hat.

They'd taken the ferry from Holyhead to Kingstown before catching a train to Cork where Liam O'Donoghue met them in a magnificent 1912 Vauxhall A12 3.5 litre Laurence Pomeroy tourer. Liam had polished the car so not a speck of dust marred the paintwork.

'Liam, this is my dear Australian friend, Lieutenant Callan McAlister. He is a true hero from Gallipoli.'

'Honoured to be sure, sor,' Liam said, touching the peak of his cloth cap.

He hesitated when Callan offered his hand. The hired help didn't expect familiarity from the mistress' houseguests. But Liam grinned when Callan took his hand and shook it firmly.

'I'm pleased to meet you, Liam. What a truly brilliant vehicle,' Callan declared.

'It's a long way from our pony-trap. I didn't know you owned a car,' Ivy said.

'Sure 'tis on loan from Lord Delaney himself, Miss Ivy. His Lordship's chauffeur and most of his men have gone to the war, so I have done a deal with the darlin' man, so I have.'

Lord Delaney was a local magistrate who owned an estate in western County Cork and was a longstanding friend of the D'vere-Brown family. Callan thought it odd that Irishmen would serve in the British army, especially after Ivy had explained the country's political history. Yet many Irish units fought valiantly for the British Empire. Westminster had passed laws for Irish self rule, but not all Irishmen favoured the change. Implementation of Home Rule was delayed for fear of civil war, especially in Ulster. Callan guessed Ireland was complicated.

'I take his lordship around and look after the car. In exchange I can drive it whenever he doesn't need it. It will be handy with the colonel staying for a week or two, so it will. '

'Nice deal,' Callan observed, while Ivy was already scheming how she'd sweet-talk Liam into teaching her to drive the car. He was a push-over where Ivy was concerned.

Callan enjoyed riding in a luxury automobile which was a far cry from the horse and sulky back on the farm. After a pleasant drive they arrived at Crosshaven. The small town was exactly how

Callan imagined English villages to be, although he'd have met a cold reception had he mention the word, 'English'.

Maeve and Ivy's mother greeted them warmly. Callan thought his status as a commissioned officer now made him a more appropriate companion for Ivy than a private soldier, but English people were hard to read. They could be so infuriatingly snobby at times and genuinely friendly at others. Callan resolved to simply take them as they came and didn't intend to change his behaviour for anyone whatever their wealth or privilege.

Maeve mothered Callan unashamedly. She had three boys who'd left home to crew fishing trawlers in search of the silver darlings across North Atlantic fishing grounds as far as the Grand Banks off Newfoundland. It was hazardous work and Maeve prayed to the Holy Trinity, Blessed Virgin and myriad saints as only a good Irishwoman can for her sons' safe return. Meanwhile she welcomed the chance to mother another young man.

Maeve and Liam also had four daughters, two of whom were married and had moved to Cork to continue their sacred duty of producing new Catholics every year. The remaining twin girls were in service at Lord Delaney's manor.

'I think we shall find mufti for you, Master Callan,' Maeve declared. 'One of my boys is about your size and you'll not want to go about in your uniform.'

Callan may have felt Maeve simply wanted to keep his uniform clean until he returned to duty, which was indeed the case. However she also knew that a British uniform would not be favourably received by all Irishmen who may not be able to make the distinction between an Aussie Digger and a Tommie. Not that it would make much difference to the local IRB members who judged anyone fighting for Britain to be fighting against Ireland.

Yet not all Irishmen supported independence. 180,000 men had joined Irish regiments which were part of the British Army. The Ulster Volunteers had formed to oppose any movement to separate Ireland from Britain. As Ivy said — Ireland was complicated.

But none of this affected Callan and Ivy, who were enjoying the mild early spring of 1916. Crosshaven was a delightful village with quaint teahouses and sufficient pubs even for Irishmen. Sumptuous fry-up breakfasts, buffet-lunches, morning and afternoon teas, hearty suppers, tennis and croquet games were all the order of the day. Liam often drove Ivy and Callan to scenic locations for picnics and country strolls. They often fished for mackerel off the town jetty. When out of sight of judgemental eyes, Ivy took the Vauxhall's steering wheel and, after a shaky start, began to master the machine.

Callan's recovery was remarkable. Good food, a comfortable bed, milder weather, exercise and Ivy's delightful company all contributed to his speedy convalescence. The only problem with his return to good health was it made him eminently available to return to duty which was inevitable after Easter.

They often lunched with Lord Delaney who'd fought in the Zulu wars, Sudan and South Africa. The O'Donoghue twins openly admired Callan, smiling coquettishly whenever they met him. Lord Delaney was a widower and may have been a crusty old devil, but Ivy soon had him eating out of the palm of her hand. Callan thought she could charm the Kaiser himself, if she put her mind to it.

Callan liked Lord Delaney's down-to-earth manner and the fact that he recognised Lord Kitchener and Field Marshal Haig for the blithering idiots they were.

'Still think they're fighting bally fuzzy-wuzzies,' his lordship complained. 'Don't the damn fools know the Boche have machine-guns and artillery, what?'

Callan remembered Archie Blake had come to the same conclusion.

Local folk agreed *'pretty-as-picture'* Ivy D'vere-Brown and the bold hero from Gallipoli made as handsome a young couple as they'd ever seen. Although Ivy's mother thought the blossoming relationship was a harmless flirtation, Colonel D'vere-Brown was less sanguine when he arrived at the beginning of April.

Liam and Maeve's three boys, Alby, Kieran and Peadar, had returned from a successful fishing voyage off Labrador with their pockets a-jingle with spring wages. They took to Callan instantly. He wasn't stuck up like some of those Tommie toffs, and while he wasn't a true drinking man, he could hold a pint or two of their favourite tipple, Guinness.

On the Monday afternoon following Palm Sunday, the O'Donoghue lads invited Callan to join them for a meal of steamed mussels, soda bread and a few pints at Kennefick's Hotel. The pub was one of their prime watering holes. Local musicians dropped in regularly and it was great atmosphere for singing and dancing. The boys had heard Callan play and suggested he bring his harmonica, which was one of the few surviving items from his original kit. Ivy wanted to join them, but the O'Donoghue boys and her father declared it a lads' night out.

'Now don't you be bringing Mister Callan home any the worse for wear,' Maeve admonished.

The boys answered with a dutiful 'Yes, Ma,' although they didn't look particularly sincere about it.

After the boys left Mrs D'vere-Brown ordered afternoon tea.

'I see you have grown fond of young McAlister, Ivy,' the colonel observed.

'Yes, Papa,' Ivy replied blushing. 'I believe we have become close friends.'

'Just friends..?

'Papa, what are you suggesting? Callan has always acted like a perfect gentleman.'

'Undoubtedly, but how do you see this "friendship" proceeding?'

'I haven't given it any thought. With the war and Callan returning to General Monash's brigade at any time, I am taking one day at a time.'

'You are eighteen. A young woman...and...young women are...romantic.'

'Do you imagine my head is filled with nothing other than starry-eyed frivolities, Papa?'

'Do you not think of romance, darling?' Ivy's mother asked coyly. She had avoided broaching the idea of match-making for Ivy, but perhaps now was the time.

'Why, Mama, I do not think this is a proper topic of conversation.'

'Quite the contrary,' Colonel D'vere-Brown said. 'You have reached an age when you should soon consider marriage.'

'Marriage!'

'Why yes,' Meredith said. 'You surely do not wish to remain an old maid your entire life. Your papa and I were wed when I was your age.'

'I do believe I have a little time left,' Ivy smiled. 'Callan is sweet...'

Colonel D'vere-Brown wasn't going to permit Ivy's mind wandering down that particular amorous path.

'Young McAlister is a nice enough chap, but he just won't do, you know.'

Ivy stared at her father.

'He has no title, no lineage, no property and no prospects in society...'

'Papa, the McAlister farm is half the size of Shropshire!'

'Precisely...he is a farm boy. We will not permit you sailing off to the antipodean colonies on a romantic notion. We shall find a suitable suitor for you in good time. There are several eminently eligible young officers in my battalion — all with excellent pedigrees and good prospects.'

Good prospects of being dead next week if life-expectancy in the trenches is what we are led to believe, Papa. And pedigree — does he think he's breeding dogs?

'I am certain you will find any one of them an admirable husband.'

In a pig's eye, Papa, I will choose who I marry!

Ivy knew there was no use arguing with her father. She loved him dearly. He was brave and considerate, but could be infuriatingly pompous at times. She certainly wasn't going to settle for some chinless, dim-witted 'right-honourable' or baronet just because he'd inherited a snobby title. But the conversation did further stimulate her interest in Callan, who she was indeed coming to think of as more than a pal.

'I hope you don't hold any of these fanciful suffragist ideas either, Ivy,' Colonel D'vere-Brown added.

'That is something I may consider, Papa,' Ivy replied sweetly, 'but as my majority is yet three years hence, I believe the point to be irrelevant for now.'

'Yes, you would do well to remember that, my dear.'

*

Meanwhile Callan and the O'Donoghue boys arrived at Kennefick's Hotel...

Chapter 17 — Trouble Brewing

Monday night — 18th April 1916

nd initially things went well. Callan soon developed a taste for Guinness stout which went well with mussels steamed in seawater with chives, parsley and a dash of beer. Four local lads arrived with a banjo, fiddle, bodhrán and button accordion. After a little encouragement from the O'Donoghue boys, Callan joined in on harmonica, while the crowd sang along.

Australia not only abounded with Irish ex-convicts. Tens of thousands of free Irish immigrants had fled starvation during the 19th Century potato famines, sailing to Australia to try their luck at the Ballarat, Sofala, Kalgoorlie and Palmer River gold fields. They'd brought traditional folk tunes with them, so Callan was familiar with their music. Being of Scottish descent, he'd learnt similar songs from his parents and grandparents.

The Irish players in turn loved Callan's recitals of Banjo Paterson and Henry Lawson poems, which they quickly put to music. With a log fire blazing, good food and drink accompanied by the bar-crowd in fine voice, who could ask for a better evening's entertainment?

So when the rowdy bunch became instantly silent, the only sound was Callan's harmonica. It took a few seconds before he realised he was now a solo act and lowered the harp from his lips.

A tall man Callan judged to be in his mid-twenties strode to the bar accompanied by four other tough looking characters.

'Blimey, who's that joker?' Callan muttered to Alby O'Donoghue.

'Swate Jasus, but 'tis the big fellow himself so it is,' Alby replied in an awed whisper.

'Well I can see he's tall and he sure can wreck a party, but who is he?'

'Michael Collins. The fellas with him are the Kent brothers — local Fenian lads from Castlelyons, just east of Cork '

'You may not all know me, but you know Thomas, Richard, David and William here,' Collins announced in a voice just loud enough to be heard without shouting. 'We're all good republicans. The brotherhood needs your help.'

For such a young man, Collins knew how to command attention. He was an up-and-coming IRB firebrand whose roles included financier and arms procurer. He'd recently returned from England and was now based in Dublin. His minders were well-known County Cork hard-nosed home rule radicals. Collins didn't beat about the bush. He didn't have time.

'Lads, I'm down from Dublin for just tonight, but the *Cause* needs men — fightin' men and I know there is no shortage in the southwest...'

A rousing cheer rose from the drinkers of course...

'Any man who can be spared,' Collins continued, 'make your way to Dublin. Make contact with the IRB representatives. They won't be hard to find, just ask around.'

'What's this all about?' demanded a voice from the crowd.

'I must keep that secret for now, but believe me your help will be of great value to Ireland. Now I must go, UVF spies are everywhere, but the drinks are on the IRB!'

Another roar went up when Collins took a wad from his coat pocket and passed twenty-five pounds to the bartender before leaving as mysteriously as he'd appeared.

'What was that all about?' Callan said to Alby.

'Trouble...'

But that was all Alby had time to say, because he was so right.

Michael Collins was on a whirlwind IRB recruitment drive, touring Ireland by truck, car and railway train. As a relative newcomer, initially he travelled unnoticed, but his luck couldn't last and he soon came to the authorities' attention. As Collins had said, numerous UVF spies kept surveillance throughout the country. They had no idea what Collins was up to, but they knew he was looking for men, and a large body of bellicose IRB radicals meant civil unrest and possible widespread strike action.

But Michael Collins and the other IRB leaders had bigger plans in mind.

Police and military were on the lookout for Collins and his cronies. They were only one step behind him, but that was enough time for Collins to fade into the night leaving the bar full of revellers just as two Black Marias screeched to a halt in front of Kennefick's Hotel. Twenty of County Cork's finest piled out of the police trucks and stormed into Kennefick's with truncheons swinging.

'Time to skedaddle,' Peadar O'Donoghue yelled, ducking as a policeman took a swipe at him.

Peadar barged into the cop's midriff, knocking him over as the brawl erupted. Patrons and musicians instinctively came out punching as the police crashed into them. One drinker smashed a porter bottle against the bar, converting it into a nasty weapon, but he was silenced when a police baton cracked the side of his skull, dropping him unconscious to the slate floor.

Women screamed, men cursed and struggled with uniformed officers, all punching, kicking, gouging and biting in the cramped bar-room. Peadar grabbed Callan by the scruff of his neck and pushed his way to a door leading to the back-yard privy. Alby and Kieran were right behind them, fending off blows as they rushed from the hotel. Once through the back door they ran smack into a police squad stationed beside the privy to intercept possible fugitives.

'You're nicked, me fine wee fellas,' an officer bearing sergeant's chevrons declared with undisguised glee.

'We was just having a drink...' Kieran protested.

'An' a feed...' Alby confirmed.

'An' some music...' Peadar added.

Callan kept quiet. All around him drinkers darted for freedom. As it took three or four policemen to restrain a single struggling patron, there were simply too many for the police to deal with. Callan and his companions were bundled into one of the Black Marias. They soon found themselves crammed into Crosshaven watch-house with only four other erstwhile revellers who the police had managed to apprehend.

Callan and the O'Donoghues languished in their cell until midnight when the police sergeant opened the cell door.

'You first,' he ordered pointing to Callan, apparently for no other reason than he was closest.

Callan was escorted to a bare room furnished with a kitchen table and four chairs. To Callan's surprise Colonel D'vere-Brown and Lord Delaney were present along with a young man who sat at the table dressed in a Royal Navy lieutenant-commander's uniform.

'Please be seated,' the RN officer said in a quiet, courteous voice.

'What's going on, sir?' Callan asked as he took his seat.

'I was rather hoping you could tell me, Callan,' the Colonel D'vere-Brown replied. 'Allow me to introduce Lieutenant-Commander James Matthews. He has driven over from naval HQ at Queenstown Dock.'

'Why is the Royal Navy interested in a pub fight — not even that? We were just having a pint and a sing-along when the police burst in and started knocking everyone around.'

'Colonel D'vere-Brown has filled me in on your background. It is your companions I am interested in,' Lieutenant-Commander Matthews said.

'The O'Donoghues haven't done anything wrong. Like I said we were just having a night out.'

'Oh, we shall talk to them all in good time for sure, but right now I'd like you tell me what happened from the time you arrived at Kennefick's.'

So Callan explained and Matthews became very attentive when he mentioned Michael Collins and the Kent brothers.

'You have no idea who Collins is, do you?' Matthews said.

'No sir, but I reckon everyone else in the pub did,' Callan replied. 'And they knew the other fellows too. There was a lot of hand shaking and back-slapping when they came in.'

'I'm sure you're right. I wonder why he wanted men to go to Dublin.'

'He wouldn't say and I don't know whether anyone was interested.'

'Oh, they're interested all right. Thank you, Lieutenant McAlister. You have been very helpful. You're free to go.'

'What about Alby, Kieran, and Peadar?'

'I'll have a quick chat with them and then I'm sure I'll be able send them home.'

Lord Delaney remained with Matthews to question the others. Maeve and Liam waited nervously outside the police station.

'The boys will be fine,' Callan assured them. 'The police are only interested in that Collins bloke and he didn't even talk to us.'

'Why is the navy interested in an Irishman, Colonel?' Callan asked as they walked to the cottage under brilliant full moonlight.

'Have you heard of the Secret Service Bureau, Callan?'

'No, sir. We didn't get a lot of up-to-date gossip in the Gallipoli trenches.'

'The Admiralty thought it up, so there are a bunch of naval types involved. Right now they're concerned about Irish insurgents and terrorists disrupting the war effort. Michael Collins is an IRB rising star and so a person of interest. He is one of the IRB's procuring officers and Lord Delaney has heard rumours that a shipment of weapons is expected from Germany any time now.'

'You mean the IRB is planning a rebellion?'

'Matthews and his Secret Service chums think so.'

*

Ivy and her mother waited in the cottage front room. They'd brewed tea and both gave Callan a, *you-have-some-explaining–to-do-young man* look.

'What?'

'Callan, how could you be so silly?' Ivy chided.

'Bar-room brawling is not acceptable behaviour,' Meredith added primly.

'Exactly,' Ivy continued primly.

'It wasn't a brawl,' Callan said defensively, 'it was a police raid...'

'Oh, well that makes it all right then.'

'Tell them, sir.'

'You're on your own, my boy,' Colonel D'vere-Brown grinned. 'It's late and I'm for bed. Come, Meredith we'll leave our bold hero of the Dardanelles to fend for himself.'

Ivy stood only a few feet from Callan after her parents left. The fire had subsided to vermillion embers but its warmth still filled the room.

'What am I to do with you?' Ivy sighed.

She stepped forward, placed her arms around his neck and kissed him. Callan was taken by surprise as her lips pressed firmly to his. She lingered for a moment before drawing back slightly.

'Why, darling Callan,' she whispered. 'I do believe you have not been kissed before.'

'Not a lot of kissing to be had in the Gallipoli trenches' he replied.

He realised he often used the expression 'Gallipoli trenches' nowadays as if his entire life's experiences had happened in the past year, so he added, 'Nor on a New South Wales farm.'

'Do you think of the war often and your lost chums?' Ivy asked, sensing his melancholia. 'Archie Blake says you have bad dreams and I've heard you cry out at night.'

'It comes and goes, but the feeling never goes away entirely. You'd think I'd be relieved that I've made it so far, but it's more a dread of how many times I've come so close to dying. I hope I haven't lost my nerve. I don't want anyone like Lydia Fallon giving me white feathers again.'

'There is no danger of that.'

She kissed him again and was pleased to receive a far more positive response.

'You must think me awfully forward and brazen,' Ivy said at last.

'I don't really have anyone to compare you with, but you don't hear me complaining. I could get used to this.'

'Well, indeed I would like you to do so, but I fear Papa will have something to say about that.'

'I understand he doesn't approve of his daughter keeping company beneath her station with a common farm boy.'

'I fear so. Not that *I* think of you in that light.'

'He left us alone by the fire. Now it if that won't encourage romance, nothing will.'

'He believes I'm really angry with you, so I think he is teasing you. Anyway he knows I cannot come to much harm under his roof.'

'We Anzacs are a wily lot and it is a full moon tonight,' Callan grinned, taking her in his arms again.

'Why sir, do you wish to have your wicked way with me?'

'Nothing would please me more, but we'd best retire to our...separate...beds. But on the way home tonight your dad asked

— well more like ordered — me to accompany him tomorrow. He's volunteered to help Lord Delaney and the police investigate any IRB funny business in the area.'

That was true enough and, while Callan had seen farm beasts mating, he wasn't entirely sure what having his wicked way entailed. He also knew that Ivy was simply being bold and flirtatious and would never allow either of them to act improperly.

'Back in uniform again..?' she asked.

'No, but Lord Delaney wants me to take a gun. The colonel offered me one of his service revolvers, but I prefer a rifle. I don't think his lordship will consider it a very officer-like weapon, but I can hit the ace out of a playing card with a rifle at three hundred yards. Pistols are just for waving around and making a noise.'

'You're not expecting trouble, are you?'

'I doubt it, but best to be prepared. C'mon one more kiss goodnight and we'd better turn in. Lord Delaney wants us up bright and early.'

Callan went to bed contentedly knowing Ivy was a warm-hearted girl who genuinely felt for him and enjoyed being kissed. That night he slept soundly and, for the first time in months, wasn't haunted by nightmares.

Tuesday — 19ᵗʰ April 1916

The following day Liam chauffeured Lord Delany, accompanied by Colonel D'vere-Brown and Callan to local republican hot-spots — churches, public houses, private dwellings and common land. Four constables riding in a police car escorted the Vauxhall. Liam's sons had been released and wisely signed on as crewmen to the first herring trawler sailing for the Labrador Coast on the evening tide.

The general reaction to Lord Delaney's enquiries left Callan with the impression trouble was brewing, but there was no concrete evidence. Most folk were suspicious and tight-lipped in the presence of an English magistrate and his policemen. Even the Kent boys were unforthcoming. All four men were at Bawnard House, their family home in Castlelyons. They denied they'd had any dealing with Michael Collins other than a passing acquaintance — and where's the harm that, sor me darlin', I ask you?

'We've heard rumours of an arms shipment being smuggled into County Cork,' Lord Delaney challenged.

'There are always rumours, milord,' fifty-year-old Thomas Kent stated civilly enough. 'This is Ireland — we thrive on rumours, stout, jigs, laments, the silver darlings and spuds.'

Thomas's three brothers backed him up saying their appearance at Kennefick's with Collins was purely coincidental. Lord Delaney didn't believe them for a moment, but with no hard evidence he let it slide. His lordship was justified in his misgivings because Thomas had recently done a two month stretch after a RIC raid discovered him in possession of illegal weapons. In their defence though, the Kent brothers were still in County Cork and hadn't gone to Dublin with Michael Collins.

Wednesday 20th April 1916

On Wednesday, Lieutenant-Commander Matthews left messages at Crosshaven and Lord Delany's manor house saying he'd received positive information that the Norwegian freighter *Aud-Norge* was off the west coast of Ireland with a suspected cargo of contraband arms and ammunition. All available naval craft were at sea to intercept *Aud-Norge* but had so far failed to find it.

The deal had been brokered by British philanthropist and home rule sympathiser, Sir Roger Casement, who was either in Germany or Norway wheeling and dealing in treachery. Matthew's Secret Service colleagues thought the Germans wanted to slip Sir Roger into Ireland to help distribute the rifles to IRB troublemakers.

Thursday 21st April 1916

Lord Delaney telephoned the Crosshaven cottage half way through the morning and he was in fine form.

'Get your fellow O'Donoghue to drive you and young McAlister over here to pick me up,' his lordship said. 'I've got constables on the way. We're heading for the west coast. Bring weapons and spare ammunition.'

Chapter 18 – Gun-Runner

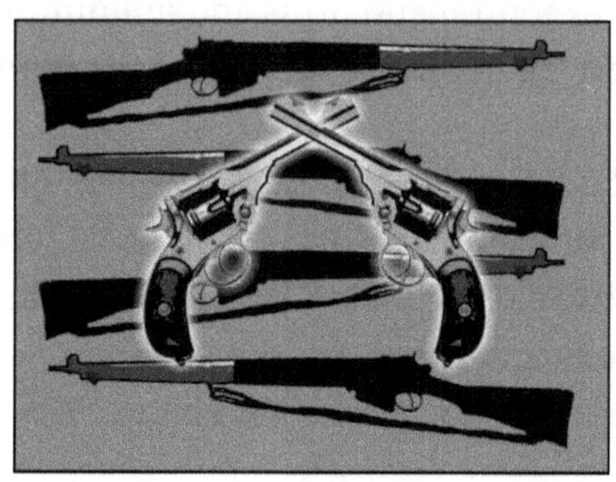

All Cork and Kerry County police units were on high alert. Car and foot patrols now scoured the beaches, countryside and byways. The previous evening fishermen reported a suspicious vessel close to Tralee Bay where a small craft had come ashore somewhere along Banna Strand. The intelligence was mixed from a single person aboard to half-a-dozen. The local constabularies took no chances and moved in strength.

The Vauxhall pulled up at Tralee police station by mid-morning. An inspector and three sergeants co-ordinated the search, but had so far come up empty-handed.

'We have covered the coast, my lord,' the inspector said. 'My men have reached Tralee Bay which we think is the most likely landing place for a dinghy or currach.'

'Take us there,' Lord Delaney said. 'I'd want to see first-hand.'

So a convoy of police vehicles and the Vauxhall sped along County Kerry's high-hedged country lanes to the coast. When they could drive no further the policemen proceeded on foot, leaving Liam to guard their transport.

'What's that ahead?' Callan asked as they trekked along Banna Strand, the open beach pounded by Tralee Bay surf.

He'd sighted a black smudge several hundred yards away at the water's edge. The party raced forward and discovered an overturned dingy. Three paddles lay abandoned just beyond the high-water line. Two constables quickly righted the dinghy revealing U-19 stencilled on the gunwales.

'Now that is interesting, what do you make of that, my lord?' the inspector asked.

'Boche sub-marine if I'm on the mark, 'Lord Delaney suggested.

'All right, you men spread out and look for signs or tracks,' the inspector ordered. 'Stay alert!'

It didn't take long to find footprints leading inland to woods nearby. Several paths led through the trees and undergrowth so the searchers broke into small groups to cover them all. After a mile of hard slogging, the terrain rose. They'd reached McKenna's Fort, an ancient Celtic ring fort now much overgrown so it looked just like any other hill.

As Callan topped the hill crest he heard the distant popping of two gun shots. He and the policemen dropped flat on the ground. The first bullets had already zoomed harmlessly past, but another two rounds slammed into the turf right beside Callan. He heard the reports a second later. The shooters lay on the hilltop on the far side of the fort.

Ruddy hell! Here I am in peaceful Ireland being shot at. I might just as well be back in the flaming trenches!

Callan levelled his rifle and took careful aim. He'd found that at close range firing as quickly as possible to keep enemy heads down before lobbing a Mills bomb into them was a good tactic.

However, at a distance, slow accurate shooting worked best. Before he could squeeze the trigger the policemen opened up, blazing away indiscriminately. Turf and rocks sprayed up as the bullets slammed home, but hitting no one before the two snipers disappeared behind the rise.

'After them!' the inspector yelled and twenty officers charged down into the fort centre before scrambling up the far side. Others ran around the rim, which although longer, was easier going and took about the same time.

Callan saw no point in joining the chase. Also he'd spotted something the others missed in the excitement. Just the hint of a shape lay half-hidden by a gorse coppice, which might easily be mistaken for just another shadow. Nine months of peering through periscopes from sniping lookouts had taught Callan to pay attention to details.

'Colonel, Lord Delaney, there's something half way down the hill inside the fort.'

'Something?' Lord Delaney replied.

He was a man who liked to be fully informed and 'something' was insufficient intelligence in his opinion.

'Dunno, my lord, but I'm going to investigate.'

The inspector and his officers had all gone in hot pursuit of the ambushers, so Callan, the colonel and Lord Delaney were the only three left. Callan checked his rifle although he knew it was ready with a full magazine while the other two men cocked their Webley service revolvers.

The fort had fallen almost to silence other than occasional distant gunfire, bird calls and the crunch of heather underfoot. As they drew closer to the coppice, they heard a low groan of what could only be someone in pain. The shapes Callan had first spotted turned out to be a pair of booted feet.

A middle-aged man lay between the thorny gorse bushes and looked in pretty bad shape. His clothes were torn, ragged and soaking wet. He shivered violently although his face was drenched in sweat dripping through a few days dark stubble. When Callan and Colonel D'vere-Brown lifted him clear of the brambles, Lord Delaney studied the prone figure for a few minutes with a puzzled look.

'Damn my eyes, this is Sir Roger Casement,' Lord Delany exclaimed

'You know him?' the colonel asked.

'I ought to. Bally chap was forever prowling around Westminster petitioning for one thing or another. Asquith and his damned liberals were always fobbing him off from the Commons to the Lords for us to deal with. To his credit, he did fine work in Africa and South America, but the wretched fellow turned traitor. Used to have a fine beard, so I didn't recognise the blighter at first.'

That was true. Although Sir Roger Casement was born in County Antrim, he'd served with distinction in the British Foreign Office. He was knighted for his philanthropic work to improve the conditions of native workers in the Belgian Congo and Peru. Lately he tarnished his reputation by taking up the Irish cause while looking to Germany for support. Not only did Casement want Germany to arm the IRB, but he also tried to recruit an 'Irish Brigade' from Irish POWs held by the Germans and Turks, but with little success in either endeavour.

Delaney knelt beside Casement who was breathing shallowly. 'Casement, can you hear me, old boy?'

At first Sir Roger didn't respond, but after a moment nodded slightly. Callan saw in Casement's eyes that he recognised Lord Delaney.

'What happened to you man?'

'Boat capsized in the surf...damn great wave knocked us clean over...' Casement replied in barely a whisper, verging on delirium. 'No one here to meet us...'

'Us — who was with you, man?'

'Monteith...Bailey...they dragged me under cover...I told them warn MacNeill...too weak to go on, you see...'

'I bet those two jokers were the one's shooting at us, but who's MacNeill?' Callan asked.

'Eoin MacNeill is a Sinn Féin heavy-weight and the IRB's chief-of-staff,' Colonel D'vere-Brown said.

'Warn O'Neill about what, for God's sake, Casement?' Lord Delaney demanded.

'The uprising...can't get enough guns or men...call it off...'

Casement's voice trailed away and he lapsed into unconsciousness. He probably didn't mean to expose his two co-conspirators, but Sir Roger was sick beyond reason.

'Blimey, that's what that Collins joker was after — rebel recruits!' Callan declared. 'Sir Roger's in deep trouble, isn't he? I mean he's gun-running for the rebels.'

'If he survives I expect they'll hang him for treason,' Delaney said evenly. 'See if you can round up some of those bobbies, McAlister. We need to get Casement to hospital quickly. It looks like he's contracted some sort of fever and is suffering from exposure.'

'What's the point if they're just going to hang him anyway?' Callan commented.

Lord Delaney glared at Callan and told him to get cracking with less of the smart-arsed antipodean back-chat, thank you.

Callan caught up with the inspector and a couple of his men on their way back to McKenna's Fort. They were out of breath and empty-handed.

'The blighters got away,' the inspector panted, 'but they won't get far with my lads after them.'

'Their names are Monteith and Bailey. That should help track them down,' Callan said.

'How the blazes do you know that?'

'There's a third man and Lord Delaney thinks he's the ringleader. You'd better come and look, Inspector.'

Their work was done after the police took over, so Liam chauffeured them back, dropping Lord Delaney at his manor house before returning to the cottage.

'Thank goodness, you will be here for Easter,' Meredith said after her husband had explained Sir Roger's capture.

Callan was looking forward to some serious quality-time with Ivy, who fussed greatly when she learnt he'd been shot at. But it wasn't to be. No sooner had they settled down for afternoon tea when the telephone rang.

'Lord Delaney is on the line, sir,' Maeve said. 'He wishes to speak to you, Colonel.'

'D'vere-Brown,' Delaney's voice crackled through the earpiece. 'I'm not well pleased with this Casement business. Not well pleased at all. I shall take the train up to Dublin on Saturday morning. I'd like you to come along and bring that wise-cracking Anzac with you.'

'Surely the authorities in Dublin can handle it, my lord. I understand Brigadier Lowe has men in the area.'

'Quite so, D'vere-Brown, but I wish to be present. I have a feeling Dublin will need as many of His Majesty's magistrates as we can find.'

There was no point in arguing, Lord Delany wasn't really asking anyway. He was a peer of the realm and expected the king's officers to do what he damn well told them.

'It is simply not fair, Papa,' Ivy wailed. 'I was so looking forward to spending our Easter break together.'

'Why don't we all go to Dublin?' Meredith suggested reasonably. 'I'm sure Ivy would love to show Callan around. It is such a beautiful city.''

As there was no specific threat at the time and Dublin was probably as safe as Cork anyway, Colonel D'vere-Brown didn't object. He knew Ivy would complain endlessly if he refused, so anything for a quiet life.

Liam was despatched to buy the rail tickets at Cork station for Saturday's train. Ivy and Callan went along for the ride. Meanwhile the colonel rang Lord Delaney with some trepidation explaining his plans. Rather than be peeved, his lordship was delighted and invited them all to stay at his Dublin townhouse in a well-to-do area close to Trinity College.

Good Friday was a dreary twenty-four hours in Ireland. The country literally stopped. The faithful obediently herded their large families to church where they were subjected to *Stations of the Cross* in which Christ's passion was depicted in graphic detail on fourteen iconic plaques to be piously acknowledged by all. And there was no levity afterwards. All the pubs were closed, and it was no meat for supper.

The D'vere-Brown family were back-sliding Anglicans, but took Callan to a C-of-E chapel in Cork for a mercifully short morning service. Liam drove them home where Maeve served them lunch of fishcakes, fried eggs and potatoes with a vegetable salad from the cottage-garden.

Callan reckoned it tasted pretty good and Maeve had made a slap-up job of it.

After lunch Maeve and Liam completed their ecclesiastical duty at nearby St Brigid's Catholic Church. Meanwhile Ivy and Callan walked along the coast where she pointed out to sea where the *Lusitania* sank. He asked her about the ordeal, but she was reluctant to speak of it, so he didn't push her. He held her hand and she seemed to appreciate the gesture.

On Easter Saturday Liam drove the D'vere-Brown family, Callan and Lord Delaney to Cork station. It was a bit of a squeeze with their luggage, but everyone fitted in somehow and it was only a short journey. Once he'd dropped his passengers, Liam was released from duty and planned to spend the Easter weekend with Maeve and their daughters.

To Callan's surprise Lieutenant-Commander Matthews waited on the platform with two armed sailors to see them off. He saluted crisply before being introduced to Ivy and her mother.

'I have good news for you, my lord,' he addressed Lord Delaney. 'Our sloop, *HMS Blue Bell* intercepted the *Aud-Norge* yesterday. She wasn't a Norwegian cargo ship at all, but a Boche armed freighter with a German crew who surrendered straight away, but scuttled the ship while under escort to Queenstown.'

'By Jove, what was she carrying, Matthews?'

'Munitions as expected, my lord — rifles, machine guns, ammunitions and explosives, so it looks like the Irish conspirators will now go without. I'd say Sir Roger Casement was right to be concerned.'

'There is no longer danger of trouble then?' Ivy said, clapping her hands.

'I don't think there was ever any great risk of that, my dear,' Delaney replied. 'The Irish are such a dysfunctional bunch. So we shall enjoy a peaceful Dublin sojourn over Easter.'

Callan enjoyed the scenic steam-locomotive trip to Dublin. The emerald-hued country-side was ever-mesmerising even if the weather could be appalling to keep it so. They caught a cab from Kingsbridge Station to Lord Delaney's stylish Georgian terrace house. A housemaid and cook were in attendance as well as a butler who walked with a distinct limp.

'It must be grand being a lord,' Callan whispered to Ivy. 'You've got all these people running around after you.'

She giggled, remembering her father wanted to marry her off to some peer or another. Maybe it wouldn't be all bad, but she was blowed if she'd let someone tell her who she'd marry. Had things been different, she'd set her sights squarely on Callan McAlister, but he had a war to fight first and would sadly return to it shortly.

I'll make my own choice all in good time, so there Papa.

If Dublin was in turmoil there was no sign of it. Ivy and Callan walked arm-in-arm to Temple Bar and strolled along the Liffey riverbank. The entire party dined at a pub that evening. There were many soldiers in uniform on leave from the front who mixed cordially with other Dublin citizens. Dublin was indeed a 'fair city' as suggested in *Molly Malone,* one of Callan's favourite tunes, which he often played on his harmonica.

Callan noticed a large number of un-escorted women roamed the streets and frequented bars. Many were much the worse for wear and wantonly solicited passers-by.

'Aren't they looking for trouble?' Callan asked as a group of young women staggered by on what looked like a pub-crawl.

'Separation women, I daresay — damned hussies, what?' Lord Delaney replied with a contemptuous snort. 'Bally government pays 'em a pension while their husbands, brothers and fathers are overseas at the front. Sadly many of these silly little fillies ain't spending the money wisely.'

On Easter Sunday Lord Delaney gave his staff the day off. Before she left to visit her family, his cook packed a sumptuous hamper accompanied by several bottles of claret, of which his lordship was particularly fond. Colonel D'vere-Brown didn't mind either.

'There is cold meat, cheese, eggs and fruit in the pantry should you feel peckish at suppertime, my lord. I baked this morning so the bread is fresh,' Cook said.

'Capital, Cook,' Lord Delany beamed. 'I am sure we shall manage famously and be well contented.'

Lord Delaney led Callan and the D'vere-Browns a short distance along Grafton Street to St Stephen's Green for a picnic lunch and a stroll in the park. Many townsfolk and uniformed soldiers accompanied by their families and sweethearts also enjoyed the leisure time. And there was more to come on Easter Monday, which was a bank holiday. Vacations were sparse in 1916, so everyone was making the most of their time off.

So Easter Sunday passed uneventfully. With Dublin in high, holiday spirits, everyone, including Ivy and Callan, was having a wonderful time...

Chapter 19 — Easter Rising

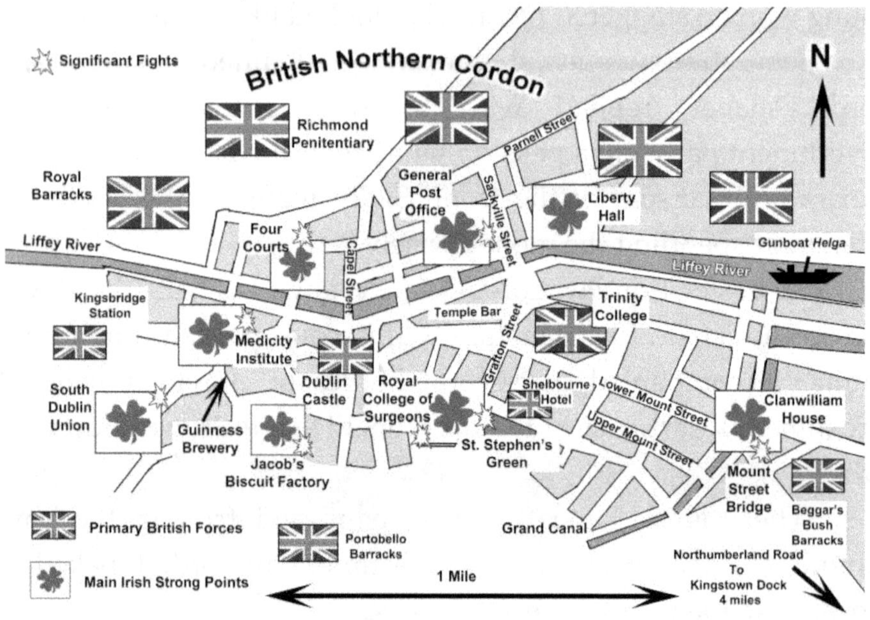

Easter Monday — 24 April 1916

Callan awoke refreshed and content on Monday morning. He looked forward to another pleasant day strolling around Dublin with Ivy as his guide. Meredith even suggested the young people might prefer to spend the day exploring the city together. What the colonel thought was hard to judge, but he said nothing.

After a leisurely breakfast, Ivy and Callan set off towards the Liffey River Bridge on Sackville Street. Callan carried a Dublin United Tramways route map and a timetable because he fancied a visit to the Guinness Brewery later that afternoon. Dublin was a compact city where most people walked or rode bicycles, but the tram was another cheap means of transport if your feet got tired.

'Do you know there was a huge strike about three years ago,' Ivy said in the role as tour-guide. 'The ITGWU caused a terrible kafuffle that lasted for months. Dublin came to a standstill. Only the Guinness employees stayed at work.'

'Sensible blokes,' Callan grinned.

Towards noon they ambled across the Bridge into Sackville Street. Ivy suggested lunch at the Hotel Metropole next to the post office while they admired Nelson's Pillar, which stood majestically right in the centre of the street.

A lazy, public holiday atmosphere pervaded through central Dublin with few people about. So it came as a surprise when Callan and Ivy were overtaken by a column of men and women marching purposefully along the Liffey bank from Liberty Hall, the ITGWU and IRB headquarters. The company were in motley outfits, but many wore green uniforms with slouch hats much like Callan's Diggers' headgear. They were also armed with an assortment of weapons, ranging from Mauser rifles, single shot Martini carbines and pistols to fowling pieces, machetes, 17th Century civil-war pikes and even pitch forks.

The men stomped into Sackville Street and halted in front of the GPO building which was about half way along the street. On the command of a fine-moustachioed middle-aged fellow with a receding hairline, the column faced left — in reasonably good order Callan thought. Passers-by consisting predominantly of separation women quickly gathered and stopped to see the show. Many of the spectators yelled abuse at the men.

'What the blazes is going on?' Callan asked.

'Oh, it's just the Fenians flexing their muscles again. They march around all the time, but no one takes them seriously.'

Like many people Ivy didn't distinguish between Sinn Féin and the IRB, although the former was a very small political group with quite a moderate attitude regarding Home Rule and favoured a harmonious relationship with Great Britain.

'Hey, I recognise that Mick Collins bloke up there in front,' Callan declared. 'I wonder what he's up to.'

He didn't have long to wait to find out.

'Charge!' the moustachioed fellow bawled and the entire company rushed for the post office entrance.

The post office guards had no chance and were immediately over-run. Callan and Ivy could only stare helplessly as within minutes rifle butts smashed through the windows. They heard bellowing and screams from inside moments before a group of people — presumably customers and employees — were bundled out of the front door and told to be on their way.

Rousing cheers came from the post office as a crowd gathered in Sackville Street. Hundreds of rather shady denizens emerged from the dreary Georgian tenements they occupied to see what the commotion was all about. Other faces appeared at windows from the buildings opposite the post office.

'Sure by Jasus, what's the racket,' one particularly slattern shrieked from a second-story window.

'On the job was youse, dearie?' others yelled from below.

'Nothing wrong with earning a few bob with my man off to war.'

The ribald banter went back and forth until the conversation returned to the matter at hand.

'Some of them IRB scoundrels have taken over the post office,' someone opined. 'Looks like they'll rob the place.'

'They'll do no such thing,' the second-storey woman wailed. 'Not my bleedin' separation money anyway.'

Many other women felt likewise. Whatever the IRB was up to, it obviously didn't meet the ladies' approval. By then several hundred women had joined the crowd and were about to storm the post office in their outrage. A barrage of expletives howled forth, causing Ivy to blush. Ivy had spent time with servicemen, but they always watched their tongues when she was within earshot, so the obscenities — as her mother called them — seemed even more venomous coming from women's mouths.

Several soldiers on leave were swept along with the throng, while a handful of policemen looked on impotently with no hope of controlling the crowd. They were saved by a troop of patrolling lancers who were drawn to the commotion and cantered down Sackville Street. The clatter of hoof-beats scattered the crowd, but alerted the IRB members inside the post office.

A volley of gunfire spat from the broken windows as the lancers rushed past. A couple of the horses stumbled, pitching their riders onto the cobblestones before tumbling into the base of Nelson's Pillar. The lancers tried to control their frightened mounts, but the horses continued along Sackville Street leaving their riders to stumble away with little dignity followed by jeers from the crowd. More ominously three men and their horses lay dead on the street. It was not that the separation women supported the IRB particularly, but neither were they over-fond of British soldiers pushing their weight around on the fair streets of Dublin.

'Crikey, what are they playing at?' Callan said. 'They've killed those troopers.'

'I think that is the general idea,' Ivy replied. 'Look...'

As the crowd reassembled a lone figure appeared on the post office steps. He was a pleasing looking fellow, but with a slightly cross-eyed stare. Ivy and Callan moved with the mob to hear what he had to say. He held a rolled paper in one hand, raising it high for all to see.

'Fellow Irishmen and women this is a momentous occasion,' the fellow announced, somewhat pompously in Callan's opinion. 'Today the Irish Republic is born. The first shots for freedom have been fired!'

'Ruddy hell,' Callan said under his breath, 'the blighters have started a rebellion.'

'I Patrick Pearse, Commander-in-Chief of the Irish Citizen Army,' the announcer continued with grandiose flair, 'do hereby proclaim the Provisional Government of the Irish Republic for the people of Ireland...'

The crowd fell silent as Pearse read the declaration aloud.

'Irishmen and Irishwomen...' he began reading for several minutes, much of which sounded like political gobbledegook to Callan, but the meaning was clear enough — we're going to govern ourselves and we're prepared to shed blood for the right to do so. Pearse then read the names of the seven men who'd signed the proclamation: Thomas Clarke, Seán MacDermott, Thomas MacDonagh, Éamon Ceannt, James Connolly, Joseph Plunkett and finishing with his own name. These were the true revolutionary power-brokers. Callan noticed Eoin MacNeill was not included. Sir Roger Casement thought he led the independence push, but appeared to be only its figurehead.

Blimey, did poor old Sir Rog have the wrong end of the stick or what?

What reception Pearse expected was unclear, but the crowd's feeling was distinctly mixed. Everyone paused when a green banner painted with a yellow harp flapped up the post office flagstaff bearing the words:

Irish
Republic

Seconds later a green-white-orange tri-colour rose beneath the first flag, which didn't fill the crowd with awe either. In fact the mob was distracted with a more personal motivation.

'We want our money,' one harridan squawked from the street and was instantly joined by others until the noise made Callan's head ache.

The separation women charged the post office once more and would have probably been successful had it not been for a few courageous rebels who stood guard on the steps and fired a volley over the oncoming heads. The women turned and darted for cover, tripping over and trampling some of their fellows as they scrambled away.

After several attempts the women gave up, especially when someone smashed a shop window. By chance it was a sweet shop and jars of confection were soon pillaged with glee. About then the last vestige of order and dignity vanished as the crowd went on a looting spree, which the police were powerless to control. Store fronts along the street soon fell victim to systematic pilfering. Others joined the separation women and soon Sackville Street was bedlam.

Ivy clung to Callan as she stared horrified at the disaster unfolding before her. But amid the confusion and raucous bellowing, Callan noticed armed men and women leaving the post office to enter surrounding buildings. Moments later they appeared on roof tops and upper-storey windows.

They've posted sentries and snipers!

Small groups armed with rifles and pistols also formed at the Liffey River end of Sackville Street. Callan saw they weren't looters, but determined and disciplined rebels. These units, numbering between five and fifteen members, took off across the river and disappeared to the south, east and west.

'Sorry Ivy, but lunch will have to wait. We'd better get back and tell your dad and Lord Delaney,' Callan said, guiding her towards the Sackville Street Bridge. 'These blighters have just declared war!'

Away from the post office the City became ominously quiet. It seemed that everything had stopped. The trams were abandoned and townsfolk had cleared the streets, anticipating danger. As they reached the southern Liffey bank, Ivy and Callan heard gunfire ahead from St Stephen's Green and to their right around Dublin Castle, the seat of British government.

'Are they storming the castle?' Ivy asked.

'Sounds like it, but what the dickens is going on at the Green?'

When they passed Trinity College, they saw the gates were locked and the defences manned by uniformed youths who Callan later discovered were military cadets. He tried to discover their situation, but a nervous voice told him to go away before someone shot him. Trinity College was important psychologically and a central strong point, but the ICA had passed it by or simply not got to it yet.

Callan and Ivy ran the rest of the way, arriving at Lord Delaney's townhouse panting for breath. The colonel and Delaney were already in the street. Both men were armed and gazed towards St Stephen's Green where the gunfire was intensifying.

'Papa, it was terrible,' Ivy wailed rushing into her father's protective arms.

'They've taken over the GPO,' Callan gasped.

'Who have, McAlister?' Delaney demanded tersely.

He wanted intelligence delivered much more coherently from an Imperial officer.

'Looks like the ICA have made its move, my lord...'

Callan told Delaney and the colonel what he knew with Ivy filling in some local knowledge and remembering the names of all the proclamation signatories.

'Parcel of rogues if ever there was,' Delaney grunted.

'I saw Michael Collins with them too. They're all in the post office now. They're in strong company strength, my lord — about a hundred and fifty men and women.'

'And it looks like other units are attacking selected targets around town,' Delaney replied. 'Inside everyone. I'll contact the Royal Barracks and see what they know.'

And not a moment too soon! Rebels spotted them and a volley of shots from St Stephen's Green zinged into the brickwork as Lord Delaney slammed the door shut.

'Cheeky rascals,' Delaney said, although it seemed to Callan that he was rather enjoying the excitement. Maybe life as a lord was just plain boring and not so desirable after all.

It took Delaney an hour to contact the military authorities. The ICA had obviously cut some above-head telephone lines while the GPO exchange was certainly unavailable. But Lord Delaney was one of four thousand Dubliners who subscribed to the automatic exchange at Crown Alley, which although close to the GPO, had not been captured or destroyed.

Finally Delaney contacted Curragh Camp about thirty-five miles to the southwest. It was the largest military base in Ireland commanded by Brigadier William Lowe. After listening for a few moments, Delaney replaced the receiver.

'Righto, General Lowe has been informed of the situation and is preparing to bring his force here by train tonight. He's asked me to gather as much information as possible and meet him at Kingsbridge Station. He expects to organise his men and arrive before midnight. Damned if half the garrison hasn't gone to the Easter races and it'll take all afternoon to round them up.'

The holiday mood had spread to the military, it seemed

'I'd like you to come with me, D'vere-Brown. One more experienced military head won't do any harm, what?'

The colonel nodded. He was of little use where he was.

'What would you like me to do, sir?' Callan addressed the colonel who technically was his commanding officer for the time being.

'You my boy, are about to become an exploring officer,' D'vere-Brown said. 'I know you're a stranger to Dublin, but it's a small area and you can read a map. Make notes and try to contact Royal Barracks by tomorrow afternoon or the following day. That should give you time to have a good look around.'

'Papa, are you asking Callan to be a spy?'

The stigma of spying being ungentlemanly still lingered in Edwardian Britain, and Ivy's opinion was no exception.

'Call it reconnaissance if you like the sound of that better, Ivy,' Callan said cheerfully. 'It's what I did in the Sinai Desert before going to Gallipoli, only then I rode a fine waler. His name was Flash-Jack,' he added absently.

'Quite so,' Lord Delaney said, 'but a bicycle must suffice this time. Take one from the garden shed and bring a pistol with you.'

Lord Delaney spread out Callan's street map, explaining he wanted Callan to reconnoitre Sackville Street again before heading east along the Liffey bank to the Grand Canal then follow it west to the Guinness brewery and finally cut across town to the Royal Barracks.

'That should give you a good idea what's going on south of the river,' Delaney said. 'Better stay in mufti too and maybe those rebel scallywags won't be tempted to take a pot-shot at you. If you can't get through, use this house as your command centre and try to make contact by phone. Carry your pay-book for identification, so our chaps won't shoot you either.'

'I was issued with dog-tags at Gallipoli, my lord.'

'Ah yes, new fangled idea that came in last year, did it not? Damned clever really.'

No one mentioned what would happen if the ICA caught him out of uniform, but as Callan had told Ivy — Anzacs are wily fellows — so he didn't plan on being captured.

'What about me?' Ivy demanded.

'You will stay here where it is safe,' Meredith said resolutely.

'Absolutely, my dear,' the colonel agreed. 'And you must do the same. You have seen enough danger in this war to last a lifetime.'

'Yes, my darling,' Meredith replied dutifully without the slightest notion of obeying him.

Cook had prepared lunch for Meredith, Lord Delaney and the colonel. So, after the two men departed in haste, Callan and Ivy polished off their share.

*

Lord Delaney and Colonel D'vere-Brown set off on foot, deeming it the least conspicuous mode of travel. They passed Marble Bar and travelled parallel to the Liffey River towards Dublin Castle, a hugely imposing edifice symbolising Great Britain's might and right to rule Ireland or anywhere else she chose for that matter. As they approached, gunfire spluttered and they dived behind an abandoned costermonger barrow.

'The bounders have taken the castle,' Delaney hissed through clenched teeth, rubbing his bruised hip and wondering whether he was getting too old for this sort of high adventure.

'No, my lord,' D'vere-Brown replied, 'those shots came from our right. Over there.'

'City Hall, by Jove! The scoundrels!'

Sure enough after a few minutes, the two men noticed a desultory exchange of fire between the castle and City Hall across the road.

'We'd better find out what's going on...' Colonel D'vere-Brown suggested.

'A bloody war — that's what's going on, man,' Delaney said.

'No, this isn't a war — not yet.'

The colonel recalled the Belgian trenches with men mown down in thousands as they stumbled through knee high mud on suicide charges into machine guns just to satisfy some General's morning whim. So far there had been no more gunfire than accidental discharges in his battalion lines.

'It looks like our fellows are holding out in the castle. If we can get under the main gate there is plenty of cover,' D'vere-Brown said.

'But, we'll be fired on from both sides, dammit.'

'We'll have to take the chance they're not very good shots.'

'This is madness, man.'

'Yes, isn't it, my lord?' the colonel beamed.

'Damn your eyes, D'vere-Brown.'

But Lord Delaney grinned as he scrambled to his feet and, with the colonel hot on his heels, made a dash for the castle gates. The great game was on and he was part of it. Rifles and pistols opened up from City Hall. Bullets ricocheted from the paving stones, spraying masonry into dust. Both men heard rounds buzzing past their ears like a swarm of enraged wasps...

Chapter 20 — The Exploring Officer

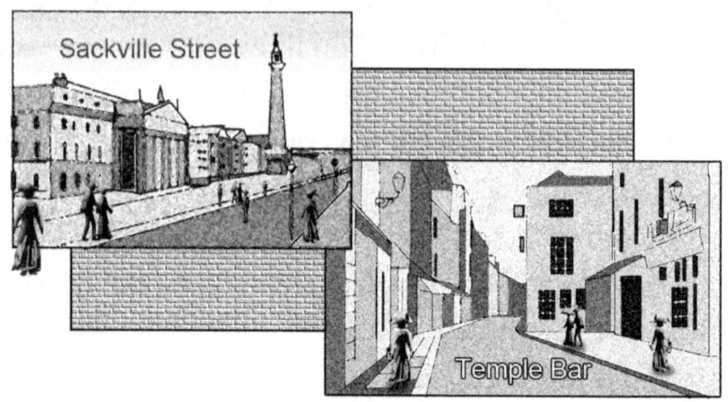

Ivy begged Callan to let her go with him, but he refused, saying he would sneak up to the GPO and hang around for a while then return to the townhouse. He explained he'd be better prepared for Lord Delaney's task the next morning after a night's rest.

'I don't know whether any of us will sleep at all,' Meredith said. 'That gunfire hasn't ceased at all. I hope Humphrey and Lord Delaney are safe.'

It was the first time Callan had heard Colonel D'vere-Brown referred to by his Christian name.

Callan set out on foot as the afternoon shadows lengthened. He left the bike, judging it a hindrance on such a short trip. Nothing much had changed other than British troops had erected barricades at the north end of Sackville Street. It was hard to judge the soldiers' strength or identify their unit. By the erratic nature of their gunfire towards the GPO and surrounding roof-tops, Callan estimated they were no larger than a squad — maybe a dozen men. They'd mounted a Lewis gun behind their barricade of sandbags, broken carts and assorted debris. The gun peppered sporadically preventing ICA men over-running their position.

Sackville Street was in shambles. All the shop front doors and windows were broken while fires raged within many buildings. Smoke and flames licked outwards into the street. Both looters and occupants had abandoned their homes and businesses, wisely making themselves scarce. There was no sign of the constabulary to discourage looting.

But other people were about. If fact, there was a lot of movement in and out of the GPO. Men and women on foot or riding bikes, who Callan took to be messengers or couriers, hurried in all directions risking a hail of bullets if they were spotted by the soldiers guarding northern Sackville Street. During the evening a group of women edged along the pavement using doorways and alleyways for protection. Callan was aware of the Cumann na mBan, but uncertain what role they played. The women made it to the GPO safely and vanished inside.

After a few hours observation, Callan gathered the impression that the situation had stabilised to a stand-off. Later that evening rain began falling although it seemed unlikely to douse the fires along Sackville Street. Callan noticed glowing smudges along the city skyline, indicating other fires raged.

Time to stop being a hero and nip back for a cup of cocoa and a toasted sandwich.

Ivy made a great fuss of Callan when he returned to Lord Delaney's house. She instructed him to take off his wet clothes while Cook and the housemaid, Vivienne, boiled kettles for a bath and to launder his clothes. Lord Delaney's butler, Mr O'Rourke, took Callan's suit away for pressing. This wasn't strictly in a butler's job description, but in a small household O'Rourke doubled as valet.

Ivy reported St Stephen's Green was occupied by an ICA company and they'd dug in, although their positions were clearly visible from the upstairs windows.

Cook lamented the fact that the shops were closed, but estimated she had eggs, bacon, sausages and vegetables to last several days. It was unlikely that any of the produce and milk drays would make their rounds and risk become ICA targets. Meredith suggested Cook didn't send Vivienne to any market stalls, judging it to be too dangerous. Flour was plentiful, so there'd be no shortage of freshly baked bread.

'We'll manage,' Meredith said, but Cook was a perfectionist and remained unconvinced.

Although the telephone remained functional, no word came from the colonel or Lord Delaney.

*

Tuesday — 25th April 1916

Ivy, her mother and the household staff, spent a restless night listening to gunfire, which was mostly distant, but occasionally sounded close by. Callan, on the other hand, slept well. He had a snug bed, a goodnight kiss from Ivy and no one was actually shooting at him, so compared to Gallipoli and the Sinai he wasn't particularly concerned.

He'd have slept in, but for the hullabaloo that awoke him before dawn. Ivy stood beside his bed, which was a pleasant surprise, but she roughly shook him.

'Callan, come and look. The street is full of rioters!'

'You'd better get, Mr O'Rourke,' Callan said pulling the drapes aside and peering out as the roar of screaming voices grew to a crescendo.

'He's already up and dressed.'

Sure enough a mob had infested the street, raiding houses wherever they saw an easy opportunity. The crowd once again consisted mainly of separation women who'd decided to broaden their looting horizons to include the affluent dwellings around St Stephen's Green. They smashed windows and broke through doors, knocking the owners senseless if they resisted. The street lights were out, but a three-quarter moon illuminated the street. Also many looters carried torches and paraffin lamps.

There was still no sign of the DMP. Callan was unaware at the time that the lord lieutenant, Baron Ivor Wimborne had declared martial law from his vice-regal lodge in Phoenix Park. The police had stood down, leaving law and order to the military, whose priorities didn't include looters right then.

'Mr O'Rourke, get any remaining weapons, please,' Callan said.

'His lordship has two shotguns, sir.'

'They'll do, get them and my rifle — and as many cartridges as you can find. Quickly, we only have minutes to spare.'

Callan dressed quickly. He had no wish to tackle an inflamed mob in his pyjamas and slippers.

The entire household had gathered in the parlour. Meredith took Callan's rifle while Ivy handled the service pistol. Callan knew they were both able to handle the weapons after hearing about the Singapore mutiny. Cook was armed with a meat clever and looked ready to use it.

'Mr O'Rourke, take one shotgun and guard the back door with Cook in case they try to break in. Vivienne, be a brave girl and lock all the windows and doors and close the drapes. I don't want that lot to see inside. Mrs D'vere-Brown — Ivy, watch from the front windows. You've got loaded weapons, be ready to use them.'

'What about you?' Ivy asked in barely a whisper.

'I'm going to see if I can deter that rabble.'

'Alone..?'

'I've got this,' he said patting the shotgun barrel, 'and I've got you and your mother ready to back me up.'

Callan stuffed spare cartridges into his freshly pressed coat pocket and strode to the front door. Only a narrow wrought-iron fenced garden stood between him and the street mob who were already wrenching open the front gate when Callan stepped onto the threshold.

'Stop right there!' he challenged the half-dozen slatterns who barged through the gate.

He'd yelled at full voice, but was barely heard above the roaring looters. He fired a single barrel into the air, which abruptly stopped everyone. Before the mob recovered, Callan broke the shot gun, ejected the spent round and reloaded so he still had two shots to deal with the mob.

'No one's coming in here, so bugger off!' he cried.

'Bugger off yerself,' came the reply.

'Is it worth getting your guts blown in half?'

'Ha, youse wouldn't shoot ladies, now would youse?'

'Maybe not, but as I am yet to see a lady out here, it doesn't matter does it?'

'Cheeky one ain't you, me wee darlin'?' one of the bolder women said slyly, advancing as she spoke.

'One more step...'

She took one more step, followed by her cronies.

Callan shot her in the leg.

'Sweet Jasus,' the woman wailed as she fell backwards. 'Sweet bleedin' Jasus, Holy Mother and all the saints, the whipper-snapper shot me.'

While she complained Callan once again took the opportunity to reload the discharged barrel. It was still smoking as he rammed the shot home and snapped the breech-block closed.

The wounded woman bellowed and wept while her associates looked on malevolently.

'Stop whining,' Callan yelled. 'I aimed aside, so you only copped a few pellets. That was a warning. You've had two, you'll get no more. Now get off this property and if anyone dares to so much as put a toe inside the gate again, I promise I will blow their heads off.'

The crowd froze.

'You think I'm joking? Well, come and try me!'

And that would have worked for everyone close by, who were edging away to find easier picking and hauling the injured woman with them. But there were other groups who converged on the scene eager for loot. They hadn't heard Callan's warning or seen the woman wounded, so it looked like Callan would have to make good his threat and use the shotgun to kill.

Yet just as the mob turned truly dangerous, a volley of gunfire rang out with bullets zinging only inches above head-height. The crowd took the hint and bolted towards the Liffey River. Callan gazed back to St Stephen's Green to see half-a-dozen women marching towards him. They were armed with rifles and dressed in an assortment of military gear. Their leader was a striking, but severe looking woman in an immaculately tailored green uniform, Sam Browne belt, jodhpurs, putties, polished boots and an elaborately feathered slouch hat. She carried a Webley service revolver.

The group halted in front of the garden gate. While the other women fanned out, keeping a lookout, the leader stared at Callan curiously.

'Top of the mornin' to you, sir,' she greeted civilly enough.

'Dunno that it's working out so well. I've been rudely awakened. It's starting to rain again. Then that lot turned up and I haven't had breakfast yet.'

'The shooting around town didn't disturb you then?'

'I...I'm a sound sleeper,' Callan replied. He was about to say he was used to it, but didn't want to give away his military status.

'I saw what happened,' the woman continued. 'Not afraid to shoot women, I see.'

'It is not my choice to make war on women. I warned her...and I notice you're armed and in uniform, which is likely to invite a few bullets in your direction.'

'Well said — I despise looters.'

She conveniently forgot the ICA had commandeered merchants' trucks, carts and private automobiles when they constructed their barricade around St Stephen's Green. One civilian was killed when he refused to give up his vehicle without a fight.

'I am Constance, Countess Markievicz of the Cumann na mBan. We have occupied St Stephen's Green and the Shelbourne Hotel over there.'

'So I see. I'm Callan McAlister from New South Wales.'

Callan thought it best not to mention his military status until he saw how the land lay.

'Australia is a long way off. What are you doing here?'

'Holidays...I'm a friend of the family.'

'I know this is Lord Delaney's townhouse. You have some high-priced acquaintances, Mr McAlister.'

She should know. Constance was a well-to-do London-born County Sligo lass who'd married a Polish count. She joined the Dublin artistic set and was constantly campaigning for one humanitarian cause after another. Although he disapproved of their leftist antics, Lord Delaney was an eager patron of Dublin theatre and knew the countess quite well. However Count Markievicz wearied of Dublin's avant-garde bohemians and left for Poland three years ago, never to return.

'A friend of a friend of the family actually.'

'Are you in the armed forces?'

'Not right now — this isn't my fight.'

'I think I shall have to take you to Commandant Mallin for questioning.'

'Who's Commandant Mallin?'

'OC of the ICA contingent at St Stephen's Green. We have a large force and secured the area.'

'Large enough..?'

'We have only met nuisance resistance so far.'

'Like I said, I'm an Australian and it's not my fight, so good luck with everything, Countess. It has been a pleasure meeting you, but I choose to stay right here where it's safe. I'm not going to see Commandant Mallin.'

'Unfortunately you have no choice,' she said, meeting his stare with steely eyes while pointing her revolver inches from his nose. 'You will come with me now — move.'

Callan shrugged.

That's what I get for trying to protect Lord Delaney's posh townhouse. No good deed goes unpunished, eh?

He felt in no immediate danger, so leaving the shotgun propped against the front door pillar, he joined the countess just as British and Irish Auxiliary troops moved cautiously towards St Stephen's Green from the Liffey banks.

Dublin's military situation had changed remarkably overnight. British and Irish loyalist units arrived at Dublin from every available military base. General Lowe reached Kingsbridge Station around midnight. His first order was to deploy units in a cordon around Dublin's CBD. Lowe soon heard St Stephen's Green had been barricaded by rebels, so he dispatched part of the cordon to go and sort them out.

It was still pre-dawn when Callan and the countess picked their way past the upturned street traders' drays, trucks, park furniture, produce baskets and private cars which had been commandeered to construct the defences. About two hundred men, women and teenagers busily reinforced the barricade or swung pickaxes and shovels digging trenches around the park perimeter.

It seemed to Callan the majority of the garrison was very young, even by his standard. Many rebels were barely in their teens. Callan was marched to meet Commandant Michael Mallin, a no-nonsense forty-two year old fellow who sported a bushy military moustache. Indeed he'd served in the British Army on India's Northwest Frontier for fourteen years before returning to Ireland.

'What have we here, Countess?' Mallin demanded.

'I'm not sure, Commandant. His name is Callan McAlister and he claims to be an innocent bystander, but he is handy with a shotgun and not afraid to blast separation scrubbers with it.'

'I just nicked her...'

'You haven't said a bad word about him yet, Countess,' Mallin grinned, turning to Callan. 'So explain yourself, young fellow and don't play games with me. If I catch you lying, I'll let Countess Markievicz shoot you for pure enjoyment of it.'

Callan knew if he started lying he'd soon be caught out, although he still played the neutrality card.

'Just in the wrong place at the wrong time, Commandant Mallin. I'm an Anzac from General Monash's fourth Australian Brigade. I was wounded at Gallipoli and I'm on leave until the brigade is redeployed. As I told the countess here, I know Lord Delaney through a friend I met in Australia.'

'Which makes you on England's side.'

'It doesn't make me on anyone's side. I live half way around the world and I don't know anything about Ireland except I like the scenery and Guinness.'

'Fair call, but what am I to do with you?'

'It won't matter. The authorities will send troops to flush you out and they'll probably send more from England. Your position is rubbish. You're surrounded by high buildings, why didn't you occupy them?'

'I don't have enough men,' Mallin admitted.

'The British do and you're in a killing ground down here. Those trenches are useless. They need to be four times as deep. Believe me — I know all about trenches.'

To prove Callan correct, a machine gun opened up from the top storey of the Shelbourne Hotel on the corner of Kildare Street just across the road from St Stephen's Green. The rebels were unaware that Royal Irish Regiment troops had stealthily infiltrated the Shelbourne in small groups throughout the night. These troops laid low ready to strike when reinforcements arrived. Now rifles joined the firing as troops moved into position on other roof-tops and upper windows.

Worse still RIR soldiers were forming their own barricades to cordon off streets leading from St Stephen's Green, cutting them off from the north. Callan estimated it wouldn't take long before the rebel stronghold was surrounded.

He dived behind the biggest truck he saw and crawled between the wheels. Four bodies already lay dead on St Stephen's Green as rain and bullets continue to pour onto the rebel position.

Chapter 21 — St Stephen's Green

Ivy paced the room in frustration and despair. By the time she'd reached the front door, Callan had already disappeared. Soon gunfire erupted in earnest. After daybreak British troops were visible in the morning drizzle. The men were cautious, but advanced down Grafton Street with grim determination.

'What are we to do, Mama?' Ivy wailed. 'We must go and discover what has become of dear Callan.'

'That would be most unwise, darling,' Meredith admonished. 'He seems quite able to take care of himself and it looks like half the British Army has arrived to rescue him from the clutches of that harridan.'

'You know who she is, Mama?'

'I got a glimpse of her from the front window and I've indeed heard of her. She's the Countess Markievicz, with quite a reputation as a good-time girl among the arty types in town. His lordship is quite smitten with her I believe, but she's rather involved with Irish nationalism, which makes her dangerous.'

'Well, I think it's time to rescue my Callan from her evil intentions.'

'Your Callan..?' Meredith said with a smile.

'Our Callan then,' Ivy said.

'Quite so, darling although you may rest assured the Countess has no time for evil intentions right now.'

Despite her mother's sensible advice, Ivy was having none of it. At the first opportunity while Meredith completed her morning toilette, Ivy pulled a shawl over her shoulders, gathered an umbrella and stepped into the.

Although troops were stationed in alleyways alert for roof-top snipers, no one stopped her as she strode resolutely towards St Stephen's Green. Other women were also about, but Ivy had no idea of their purpose. A British barricade stood across Grafton Street, but as she approached it, a strong hand gripped her shoulder — gently but firmly.

Ivy gasped and spun around.

'Mr O'Rourke!'

'Yes, miss, I saw you slip away and thought it prudent to follow if you'll forgive my boldness.'

'Have you come to force me back?'

'That rather depends on what you have in mind, miss.'

'I don't quite know what I intend, Mr O'Rourke, but you must not put yourself in jeopardy.'

'I served with his lordship in Africa, miss, so danger isn't new to me. His lordship offered me this job when I was invalided out of the army after a dervish bullet shattered my leg. His lordship knew the pension would hardly feed a family of six.'

'He's not the old curmudgeon he pretends to be, is he Mr O'Rourke?'

'Indeed not, miss. My boys have all moved to America and Australia and my daughters are married. My wife, God rest her, has passed on, so now I am content in his lordship's household. Cook and Vivienne, God love them, really do all the hard work.'

O'Rourke cleared his throat.

'I do apologise, miss, I seem to be rambling.'

'Not at all, Mr O'Rourke, but what is to done about poor Callan?'

'If you'd permit me to suggest, miss, we will not be allowed past the barricade and we need a better look at the Green.'

Two major buildings stood around the St Stephen's Green. One was the Shelbourne Hotel on the north east corner, which the British controlled and commanded a view over most of the green. The other was the Royal College of Surgeons on the western side and it looked as if some rebels were inside, but there were a number of other high rise buildings which neither side had yet taken advantage of.

'If you'd come this way, miss. I have an idea.'

O'Rourke escorted Ivy to an alley that led behind the Shelbourne Hotel and the stylish Georgian terraces fronting the green. Most properties included small high-walled back gardens much like Lord Delaney's townhouse. Ivy was dressed in a long dress and dainty button-boots, while O'Rourke's lame leg made it impossible to scale the walls, so they tried several gates until one yielded. The terrace back door was unlocked.

The property was divided into tenement flats, so a common staircase led to the top storey. A couple of curious residents peeked through their doors, but they were nervous and didn't challenge Ivy or O'Rourke as they climbed the stairs. The butler was in considerable pain when they reached a step-ladder leading to the loft, but he managed to climb the final stage. The loft was empty with a gable window overlooking St Stephen's Green.

'Let's take a look, miss,' O'Rourke suggested.

Their view was clear enough. To their left machinegun bullets sprayed from the Shelbourne Hotel onto St Stephen's Green whenever a target presented itself. A dozen casualties littered the lawn, but it was difficult to tell if they were dead or wounded. Ivy stared for several minutes before sighting Countess Markievicz strutting from one cover point to another, taunting the gunners. There was no mistaking her as a woman, which seemed to deter the marksmen although some rounds spat into the ground close by.

'There is that infernal hussy,' Ivy whispered. 'Callan must be somewhere close by.'

'If Lieutenant McAlister is smart, he'll be keeping his head down, under one of those lorries, miss,' O'Rourke said. 'And he strikes me as a smart young fellow indeed.'

'We have to get in there and find him,' Ivy declared with a resolve she had no idea how to achieve.

'Is that prudent, miss?'

'No, but I've just thought of something that might work. We'll need Mama's help. It is all about perception and expectation.'

*

'You can't stay here, Commandant,' Callan yelled from below the truck. 'They're ripping your people to shreds.'

Mallin now lay next to him after crawling from one cover point to another, encouraging his men. It wasn't particularly successful, because every time he moved into the open, he drew a hail of bullets towards wherever he headed.

Callan had now been under fire for over an hour, but was content to stay put. The Turks had bombarded the Anzac line intermittently for hours and even days, so he'd learnt to be patient once he'd found a reasonably secure position.

Keep your head down, Callan old chap. Wait for an opportunity.

'We're pinned down,' Mallin conceded.

'How long do you think it'll take 'em to get artillery and bombs over here?'

'We hold the College of Surgeons. It's a sturdy building. I don't know about artillery, but it'll stop machinegun fire.'

'I'd start getting all your people inside, if I were you. The Green is untenable. You'll all be slaughtered by lunchtime if you stay here — not to mention the rain. If the British don't kill you, pneumonia will.'

'You stay here,' Mallin ordered.

'Yeah right, Commandant. Just where the blue-blazes do you think I'd go?'

And right about then there was a lull in the bullet-ridden onslaught. Callan crawled forward far enough to peek from under the truck along Grafton Street. He couldn't believe his eyes.

The British barricade was partly cleared to let a small procession through. Meredith D'vere-Brown led the way followed by Ivy and O'Rourke pulling a two-wheel costermonger's dray. Cook and Vivienne brought up the rear. All the women wore white pinafores with large red crosses roughly stitched to them. O'Rourke wore a white dust-coat which also bore a red cross, although Callan couldn't see it at the time.

'We have come to take your wounded to safety!' Meredith called in an uncharacteristically forthright manner.

Callan didn't need to think twice before seizing his chance.

'I'll take care of your worst casualties, Commandant Mallin,' he said. 'I think we have an unofficial truce. It's like a stunned silence. I've seen this a few times at Gallipoli, but it won't last long. Get everyone including your walking wounded to the College — or anywhere else — while you still have the option.'

As the medical party approached, Callan rose to his feet, arms spread and hoping the soldiers wouldn't shoot.

'Would you like a hand, ladies?' he said cheerfully.

Ivy wanted to rush forward and squeeze him, but Callan raised his finger in warning.

'Here, I'll make a way through the barricade,' he said, pulling crates and produce baskets aside, making just enough room from the cart to pass through.

'Put this on, Callan,' Meredith said, taking a red-cross arm band from her apron pocket.

As Ivy had predicted it was all about perception and expectation. Look the part and people will believe you. No one was going to fire on red-cross Samaritans and live with their consciences. The cart held half a dozen wounded. Countess Markievicz selected four youths and two young women who were all in dire straits. She eyed Callan suspiciously and at first he thought she'd insist he remain her prisoner. She was however too busy urging her walking wounded towards the College so she let it slide.

With the weight of six people aboard, it took all Callan and O'Rourke's strength to haul the dray clear of the barricades. Cook and Vivienne pushed from behind, while Meredith and Ivy did their best to comfort the wounded rebels.

Only seconds later British machineguns began peppering St Stephen's Green once more. Most ICA elements had retreated to the College of Surgeons haven, but a few were too slow and mown down mercilessly. The fight for St Stephen's Green may have been over, but the fight for the College of Surgeons was just beginning.

Once the dray reached the British barricade, Callan was relieved to see a brace of Army ambulances parked in Grafton Street out of the firing-line. A captain bearing doctor's insignia on his lapels greeted them.

'Jolly good show,' he said rather too jovially in Ivy's opinion. 'We'll take care of these prisoners from here.'

'They're badly wounded,' Ivy challenged.

'Yes, I thought they were, I am a doctor and have a nose for these things,' he replied, thinking it a tremendous joke. 'Not to worry, we'll take 'em to the Rotunda Hospital and look after them there.'

It was handy that unwounded ICA prisoners were also held at the Rotunda Hospital courtyard not far from the GPO, even if they were left out in the rain. Ivy felt a tinge of guilt leaving the rebels to their fate, but they needed more than basic first aid to pull through, so she'd have to be satisfied knowing she'd done the best she could.

O'Rourke guided everyone back to Lord Delaney's house as quickly as possible. They'd pulled off a brazen heist to save Callan and possibly six other young people. Now was the time to lie low with a hot cup of tea.

*

'Why, Mister O'Rourke, I thought I'd just faint,' Vivienne declared when they were safely inside. 'I was scared half to death.'

'You are a very brave girl,' O'Rourke said gently. 'It'll be an adventure to tell your grandchildren.'

'But will I be a hero or a villain, sir.'

'Depending on which side wins, do you mean?'

'Yes, sir.'

'It won't matter, we saved lives today and that is what counts. I am very proud of you. Now go and help Cook. I'm sure Lieutenant McAlister, Madam and Miss Ivy will appreciate some freshly baked scones with their tea.'

The household had become more intimate after working as a team. Cook and Vivienne had been quick to provide white smocks and aprons for Meredith and Ivy who in turn used their embroidery skills to stitch the red crosses. O'Rourke borrowed Lord Delaney's tropical smoking jacket that had made its way back from Africa. Finding an abandoned dray was easy enough while the rest was bluff and bravado.

They'd been lucky of course. Callan was still in the front line. There would have been no chance of finding him if Countess Markievicz had spirited him away into the College of Surgeons. But they're rescued him and hopefully six young people would live to tell the tale. No one involved was making a judgement call on who was right or wrong or, as Vivienne put it, who were the heroes and villains. They all had mixed feelings, so better stay as a loyal team and try the best you can.

Callan wasn't sure what his next move should be. He got off to a pretty slow start following Lord Delaney's orders, but he'd gathered some useful intelligence from his short time in the enemy camp. His biggest quandary was still whether to wear his uniform or go in mufti.

And then the phone rang.

O'Rourke answered the call and listened for a few seconds.

'It is for you madam,' he said.

'The colonel..?'

O'Rourke smiled and handed the ear-piece.

'Darling, we were so worried. Are you safe?'

'I'm fine. We had a little excitement passing Dublin Castle and a few other rebel strongholds, but we reached General Lowe's headquarters in the end. His lordship is feeling a bit sad and sorry for himself, though.'

'What happened, is he all right?'

'A bullet nicked his backside. Just a flesh wound and there is no sign of infection, but it hurts like billy-o. What about you?'

'Actually we have had an exciting morning, but I'll let Callan tell you all about it.'

'Callan, what's he doing there? He's supposed to be scouting the east side.'

'Oh, he hasn't been wasting his time, darling.'

She handed the phone to Callan.

'G'day sir. I'm glad you made it to HQ in one piece.'

'Thanks, Callan old man. Other than individual snipers and saboteurs, the rebels have concentrated up at four strong-points in west Dublin: the Medicity Centre, Jacob's Biscuit Factory, South Dublin Union building, south of the Liffey and the Four Courts in the north. They're contained, but it'll be the devil's own job prising 'em out. But what's this I hear about you?'

'Yes, sorry about that sir, but I sort of got captured by this countess...'

'You got captured by a woman?'

'It's not as bad as it sounds. I escaped pretty quickly. Countess Markievicz is part of Commandant Michael Mallin's company which took St Stephen's Green. They made a right botch-up of it, sir and our lads have them bottled up in the College of Surgeons on the west side of the green. They're pinned down by machinegun emplacements with nowhere to go. If you can get some artillery pieces or mortars down here, we could blast them out in no time.'

'I'll pass that onto General Lowe. I'm hesitant to blow up some of these beautiful city buildings, but the general has no such qualms.'

'Mallin had about two hundred people, but he's taken heavy casualties. Many of them are just teenagers.'

'Not like you then, Callan.'

'No sir. Some of them can barely fire their guns and there are about thirty women with them.'

'Fine Callan, but I'm afraid we have a large number of raw recruits in our own ranks. Do you know there were barely four hundred troops in the city when this trouble flared? We now have ten times that number and we're cordoning off the inner city.'

'Is that enough, sir?'

'Should be, but don't worry. The Sherwood Foresters, an assortment of North County units, are sailing from Liverpool and should arrive at Kingstown tonight. I'd like you to grab a bike and ride over there to meet them. It's only about five miles so you should have no trouble getting there this afternoon. Find their senior officer and guide them through town. You should know your way around by now and a little local knowledge is better than none.'

'Yessir. Is there any particular location you'd like them to go to.'

'Tell their commander to contact General Lowe's HQ as soon as he reaches the city. There is a Signals Corps unit down there already, but they're having trouble establishing communications.'

'Yessir.'

'Right, I must go now. Give my love to Ivy. Good luck.'

The colonel hung up.

'He didn't have time for chit-chat,' Callan said, replacing the receiver.

'I'm pleased you didn't mention how you got away,' Meredith said with a smiled.

'I thought I'd leave that to you girls. The colonel has given me another job to do.'

Chapter 22 — Reinforcements

Getting around Dublin was a lot easier said than done. Certainly RIR and British troops now occupied numerous barricades throughout the city and had pretty well cordoned off both north and south banks of the Liffey. Most barricades were manned by sections or platoons and many were supported by at least one machinegun. But rebels also manned their own barricades and sniped from roof-tops. Cycling through the city, Callan was just as likely to run into either, who'd both shoot first and ask questions later.

Often spiteful shoot-outs erupted between rebels and soldiers, yet many civilians were out and about. Men and women stood gossiping in doorways, while others peered through front parlour windows. Even if he looked the part, Callan avoided speaking to anyone who'd pick him as an outsider, but whether that was good or bad, he really didn't know.

Dressed in mufti, Callan found himself waving a white handkerchief and his dog-tags whenever he approached a British position. Once he'd identified himself he still received sullen looks from the soldiers who were suspicious of spies whoever they were spying for.

'There's a nest of rebels around Boland's Bakery and Clanwilliam House. A local lad thinks they're Eamon de Valera's fellas,' a nervous young RIR lieutenant informed Callan. 'We thought they'd over-run Beggars Bush Barracks, but they seem content to hold several buildings along the Grand Canal. Yesterday the buggers shot up a company of Gorgeous Wrecks in Northumberland Road on their way back from parade. There were heavy casualties.'

The Gorgeous Wrecks were Irish home guard loyalists who wore arm bands on their uniform sleeve which read 'Georgious Rex', signifying their support for the King. They were a common sight marching through Dublin's streets and were looked on with affection by unionists and separatists alike. It was unlikely their weapons were even loaded, but they were just in the wrong place at the wrong time when de Velera's men mistook them for British regulars and opened fire.

'Okay, but I'd better take a look before I head down to Kingstown Dock,' Callan said, checking his map.

'Good luck to you then,' the lieutenant said, 'but shouldn't you be in uniform?'

'Thanks, mate, but if I'm going to poke around where I'm not wanted, I'm better off in disguise.'

Callan skirted past Boland's Bakery and crossed the Grand Canal at Lower Baggot Street Bridge. A few artillery pieces were now in action and shells occasionally whistled over to crump into a distant building and explode. Callan followed the canal to the Mount Street Bridge. He saw armed men moving furtively amid the luxury semi-detached houses in that particularly affluent suburb around Northumberland Road. Beggars Bush Barracks was situated on the east side of the street where the Gorgeous Wrecks were stationed and now tended their wounded.

Cartloads of sandbags arrived from side-streets and rebels began constructing barricades and fortifying windows and doorways. Callan had no idea where the sandbags came from, but both sides appeared to have an endless supply.

There was no fighting at the time he passed the barracks now safely held by a handful of British and RIR troops. Estimating rebel numbers proved problematic. Callan thought that whatever their strength, a small number of marksmen in strategic positions including Clanwilliam House, Boland's Bakery and a schoolhouse next to Mount Street Bridge along with several buildings fronting Northumberland Road, could hold off an army marching from the south.

Callan reached Kingstown without incident. He stopped to eat a sandwich Cook had prepared along with a knapsack full of tasty consumables including a bottle of Guinness. He chatted to a few passers-by who were intrigued by his accent. The arriving troops were no secret and most people seemed to welcome the prospect. Obviously not all Dubliners supported the uprising.

Soldiers milled around the dockside waiting for the troopship which wasn't due until late that night. A squad from Arklow was keen to see the ship arrive, hoping to cadge a couple of Lewis guns. Trouble was brewing down south and they wanted extra fire-power.

Callan made himself known to a starchy captain commanding the Signals corps unit. The captain was not impressed with Callan's intelligence and promptly told him to make himself scarce.

'Now look, old boy,' the captain said with one of those infuriatingly condescending home-counties accents. 'We can handle a bunch of bog-trotters and I don't much care for His Majesty's officers skulking around in mufti. It's just not on, but I suppose as you're a colonial, you don't know any better.'

'I have my orders from Colonel D'vere-Brown, the 11th Shropshire Battalion's CO,' Callan replied sharply. 'And I intent to ruddy well carry them out.'

'Duly noted, but we can handle things quite adequately, thank you. I have telephone and telegraph communication with General Lowe's HQ. We did actually manage that all by ourselves. And do address a superior officer as "sir".'

'When I meet one, I'm sure I will.'

Callan left the captain spluttering threats of insubordination and court marshal, but he'd have to do better than that to intimidate an Anzac veteran.

With nothing better to do, Callan poked around and discovered some disused sacking in one of the warehouses. He found a quiet corner, piled the sacks into a bed and promptly went to sleep. He was woken by a sentry who prodded a bayonet at his chest.

'Oi, whatya abart, yer cheeky bugger,' a private soldier challenged. 'Yer can't doss around 'ere.'

'I'm waiting for the troopship from Liverpool.'

'Who are yer? Yer don't sound English. I reckon yer one of them Fenians lookin' fer trouble.'

'I'm Lieutenant Callan McAlister from General Monash's 4th Anzac Brigade. Now stop prodding me with that flaming bayonet and take a look at my dog-tags and pay-book.'

'Sorry, sir,' the private said, snapping to attention after he examined Callan's credentials. 'But as yer ain't in uniform, I have to be careful.'

'Quite right, what's your name, private?'

'Arthur Billings, sir.'

'Good, Billings, because I'll need your help. As you rightly observed I'm in mufti. I was on leave when the uprising started and now I'm an exploring officer. I'm here to provide intelligence and guide the reinforcements into Dublin.'

'*SS Patriot's* due to dock soon, sir. She's steamin' into Dublin Bay right now.'

'Then let's go and meet her. We need to steer clear of that poncey captain too.'

'You mean Mr Bainbridge-Smyth, sir. 'E's a bit of an acquired taste if you don't mind me sayin' so, sir.'

'I won't tell if you don't.'

The disembarkation was a shambles. It took Callan only a second to recognise the men were raw recruits. It wasn't so long ago he'd been one. The Sherwood Foresters formed a huge brigade, often referred to as *Robin Hoods* or simply *Foresters*. There were currently thirty-three battalions from North Mid-Land regiments who were fighting in all theatres of the war. But most of the troops deployed to Ireland were mere fresh-faced lads, some of whom thought they'd come to France. Many hadn't finished basic training and some had never even fired their rifles.

No senior officers were evident, while the subalterns and captains had little idea how to organise their platoons and companies. Finally Billings tracked down Captain Frederick Dietrichsen, one of the battalion adjutants and introduced Callan. Dietrichsen seemed genuinely interested in Callan's information, but right then he was overwhelmed with logistical problems which no one seemed able to solve.

'Beggin' yer pardon, sir,' Billings said. 'I better get back to my own officer. Mr Bainbridge-Smyth don't like his men wanderin' off.'

'Too right, Billings. We can't have you getting into strife. Thanks for your help. I'll stick with Captain Dietrichsen until we get to Dublin.'

As the night progressed Callan helped Dietrichsen organise his men. Finally battalions were sorted and allocated assembling areas. Callan was dismayed to find they only carried rations for two days. They had brought no Lewis guns, which some embarkation officer in Liverpool had considered an unnecessary burden. To make matters worse the brigade did not have a single mills bomb or long-handled grenade between them and many of their ammunition boxes were marked with bullets incompatible with their rifles.

'You'd better set the useful ammo aside,' Callan told Dietrichsen, 'and issue your men with as much as will go round.

Callan and Dietrichsen worked through the night until they'd done all they could to have the brigade ready to march. During that time Dietrichsen found an opportunity to introduce Callan to his battalion CO, Colonel Fane.

'Funny you know,' Dietrichsen said during a tea break. 'I sent my family to Dublin. I didn't want to risk 'em with Zeppelins bombing Nottingham. Now they seem to be in the middle of a war-zone. Maybe I'll catch up with them when the shooting stops.'

'They don't know you're coming then?' Callan replied.

'I don't see how. We didn't know ourselves until Monday night.'

*

The Sherwood Forest Brigade officers were a peculiar bunch of public-school chums who'd as little idea about going to war as their troops. Just after dawn brigade OC, Colonel Maconchy, battalion commanders including, Colonel Taylor, Colonel Fane and Colonel Oates — the only regular army senior officer in the battalion — and all his officers retired to a nearby yacht club for breakfast, leaving their men to bully beef, biscuits and tea. Callan and Dietrichsen joined the officers as Colonel Maconchy outlined their orders from General Lowe.

'Colonel Fane and Colonel Oates, you will advance your 2/7th and 2/8th Battalions to the east along Merrion and Northumberland Roads to Trinity College,' Maconchy said, stabbing a wall map with his swagger-stick. 'I will lead the 2/5th and 2/6th Derbyshire battalions and Colonel Taylor's South Staffordshire Regiment to the west and concentrate on the South Dublin Union. Our orders are to take any rebel positions. We will not by-pass a single building harbouring any rebels, is that clear?'

A lot of head nodding and yessiring followed.

'Every rebel must be killed or taken prisoner,' Maconchy reiterated. 'Captain Bainbridge-Smyth and his team will accompany the Nottingham Foresters as signals and intelligence officer.'

'Dunno about the "intelligence" bit,' Callan muttered to Dietrichsen.

'Do you have anything to add, Lieutenant McAlister?' Maconchy said acidly. 'I'm sure we'd all be so much more enlightened by some home-spun wisdom from the dominions.'

'I can't speak for the western route, sir,' Callan replied, all business and ignoring the colonel's sarcasm. 'But, I passed the Bolin's Bakery arca yesterday and I advise extreme caution. From what I could gather the rebel strength is small, but they're well fortified and can shoot straight.'

'Two battalions should be able to handle a handful on undisciplined men,' Maconchy replied.

'Northumberland Road is wide at the Grand Canal, Colonel,' Callan insisted. 'You have no armour or artillery support and no machineguns or hand-bombs.'

'Thank you, Lieutenant, I am well aware of our situation. That will be all. I think you'll find the Sherwood Foresters know their business. I doubt these rebels will take kindly to disciplined musketry and cold steel.'

After a leisurely breakfast the column formed and began their march to the capital. Initially there was an almost festive atmosphere as the troops tramped along in two columns of four, spreading across the entire road. Cheering Dubliners lined the pavement, shop fronts and windows. Everyone had a union jack to wave around enthusiastically. Considering Brigadier Lowe's orders were to advance on Dublin at all speed, the brigade was in no great hurry. Colonel Fane led the 2/7th Battalion while Colonel Oates followed with the 2/8th Battalion.

Although they had no logistic support all the Sherwood Foresters were weighed down with full kit, rifles, bayonets and some ammunition, but the weather had cleared to a fine spring day and the men marched in reasonable comfort.

Callan cycled ahead with a team of uniformed scouts. They met no resistance all morning. Around lunchtime Callan rode back to the column and was surprised to see the troops straggled along the road enjoying a smoko. Even stranger was the sight of Captain Dietrichsen embracing a young woman with several children milling around.

'What's going on, Billings?' Callan asked as he approached Captain Bainbridge-Smyth's signals unit which led the brigade. 'Are ladies throwing themselves at us now?'

'Rum thing, ain't it sir? That's Mr Dietrichsen's missus and kids. He sent 'er over 'ere to stay safe and blow me down, 'ere she is in the crowd.'

'She must have heard which regiments were disembarking. Word gets around.'

'Aye, sir.'

'Which means the rebels will know all about us too.'

Bainbridge-Smyth took a message from one of his telegraphers.

'Time to move,' he bellowed without deferring to Colonel Fane. 'Orders from HQ to move on Dublin post haste.'

What the colonel thought was hard to read, but the column was soon marching again. Dietrichsen bade his family goodbye, promising to reunite as soon as the rebels were put back in their place.

Bainbridge-Smyth rode in a commandeered truck which also carried his wireless and telecommunications gear. Before long, Colonel Maconchy led the rest of the brigade westwards to cut Morehampton and Sanford Roads while Dietrichsen's company led the other two battalions along Merrion Road which eventually turned into Northumberland Road only five hundred yards from Beggar's Bush Barracks.

It was about two-thirty in the afternoon and all was quiet. There'd been no sign of rebels all day and there was no sign of them now. The Sherwood Foresters approached Mount Street Bridge leading over Grand Canal. Clanwilliam House stood dead ahead.

'Come lads,' Dietrichsen called, waving his service revolver high. 'Smarten up. Let's put on a good show for the Irish.'

Dietrichsen took pride in the fact that his company led the battalion.

'Shouldn't we scout out the lay of the land..?' Callan suggested.

'Nonsense,' Bainbridge-Smyth cut in. He'd left the truck to join the head of the column. 'You can see there is no one around.'

So the Sherwood Foresters marched on. Only yards from the bridge a storm of lead slammed into the troops. A bullet pierced Dietrichsen's chest. He sank to his knees with a puzzled expression before toppling over cracking his head on the cobblestones. A dozen other men slumped to the ground. Some remained still while others screamed in agony.

'Get down!' Bainbridge-Smyth bellowed, dashing behind the wireless truck.

'No!' Callan cried. 'Move back — withdraw five hundred yards.'

But it was too late. The Sherwood Foresters all dived for the ground, not for cover. More bullets homed in on the prostrate figures. Half a dozen bucked as they were hit. Shots came from Clanwilliam House and buildings either side of Northumberland Road.

Callan acted instinctively. He raced to the nearest house and smashed through a bay window facing the street. It was a sturdy structure, but Callan's blood was up and he crashed through anyway. Two men holding rifles aimed towards the street turned to him in astonishment.

'Good lad, come to join the fun, have youse?' one of the snipers called, mistaking Callan for a rebel as he wasn't wearing a British uniform. Callan pulled his pistol from his pocket and shot both men at point blank range. Fighting Turks at close quarters in trenches slippery and awash with blood had taught Callan not to hesitate for a second. Callan replaced his service revolver and grabbed one of the rebel's Mauser rifles. Spare magazines and a box of rounds sat on a coffee table along with two half finished teacups. He pocketed the spare ammo.

Someone made tea...

At that moment a middle-aged woman flung open the door and charged Callan with meat-cleaver. Callan swung the rifle butt into her face, knocking her senseless and dislodging several teeth.

'Sorry, missus,' Callan said. 'I don't like fighting women, but this flaming country makes it so damned hard to avoid.'

He turned back to the street in horror.

Chapter 23 — Mount Street Massacre

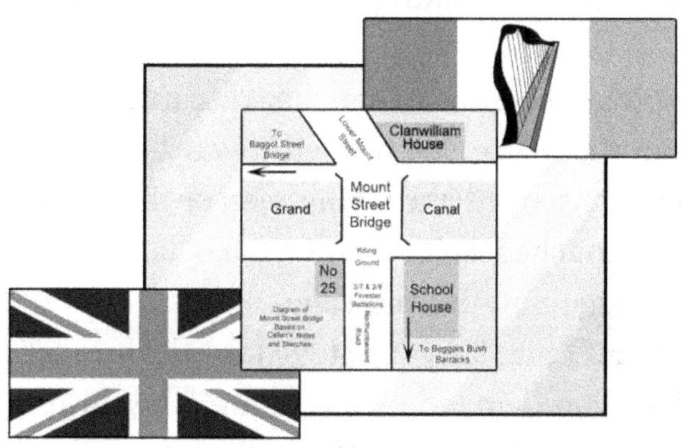

Callan looked out of the shattered window frame. The street was chaos. The Sherwood Foresters lay like an amorphous khaki blanket covering Northumberland Road. Men crawled over one another with no idea where to go. Captain Dietrichsen staggered to his feet, urging his men to seek shelter. He lasted only seconds before another bullet killed him instantly.

Some men saw a school-house close to the bridge and sought shelter there, but were cut down in the withering cross-fire from marksmen in the school, Clanwilliam House and one of the street-front buildings — number 25 Northumberland Road.

Callan leant from the bay window far enough to aim the Mauser rifle at the number 25 where rebels were firing into the Sherwood Foresters, lying only feet away. He shattered a glass pane, but didn't know whether he hit anyone.

Blimey what a bloody shambles. Why don't the dopey buggers withdraw and regroup.

That simply didn't appear to be an option for the Sherwood Foresters. Twenty men lay dead and many more had been wounded in ten minutes! Colonel Fane had established his command post a hundred yards back, but as yet had not arrived at the firing line. Callan couldn't stand the slaughter and stupidity any longer.

He emptied the rifle magazine, discarded the weapon and bounded from the house. He headed towards the communications truck, jumping over dead and dying men or those just too scared to move. Callan crouched behind the truck's tailgate just as Billings handed Bainbridge-Smyth a message.

'It's from HQ, sir. They insist we take the bridge!'

'Why?' Callan demanded 'There are other bridges only a few hundred yards away. We can outflank them.'

'Just the sort of yellow talk I'd expect from a bloody colonial,' Bainbridge-Smyth sneered. 'Billings, relay this message to all section commanders and a copy to Colonel Fane. Take the bridge by frontal assault. Smoke out those rats.'

'They'll be slaughtered. You're murdering them!' Callan screamed in Bainbridge-Smyth's ear above the roar of rifle-fire.

'You coward,' the captain snarled. 'No wonder Gallipoli was such a fiasco.'

Callan felt like slugging the sanctimonious prig.

'Men from this brigade fought in the Dardanelles too, you know. Where were you? In some cushy billet at home is my guess.'

It was hopeless, whether Bainbridge-Smyth was the ranking officer or not, nervous junior officers gathered around looking for guidance. The Signals Corps captain started barking orders, assigning targets for each platoon. When an officer blew his whistle, a section leapt to their feet and charged. Men stormed the bridge to reach Clanwilliam House, the school, and number twenty-five. They were all cut down within a matter of yards.

I've got to stop this. We need bombs and fire-power or we'll all be dead before nightfall.

'Billings, get a message to HQ requesting artillery support or a machine gun and grenades at least,' Callan ordered.

'You will do no such thing, Billings,' Bainbridge-Smyth countered. 'McAlister I might remind you I command this signals unit. Interfere once more and I will have you court-martialled.'

Callan turned, looking for another source of help. He spotted the gate to Beggar's Bush Barracks. It was as good a place to start as any. He heard Bainbridge-Smyth's disparaging jeers as he raced away. Once again he waved his pay-book and dog-tags as he ran under the arch leading to the Barracks' parade ground. The gate had been open since the Sherwood Foresters arrival.

He was met by a delegation of Gorgeous Wrecks with puzzled expressions on their faces.

'Lieutenant McAlister — 4th Brigade, AIF.'

The men snapped to attention in good order.

'What's in your armoury?' Callan asked.

'Lee-Enfield bolt action rifles, sir,' one elderly NCO replied.

'Field-guns?'

'No, sir.'

'What about Lewis guns or mills bombs?'

The NCO shook his head.

'Do you have phone contact with General Lowe's HQ?'

'Yessir.'

'Right, we need to get some fire support up here urgently, before the battalions are wiped out.'

The NCO spent some time on the telephone, before assuring Callan that HQ promised to hunt up something and get it to Mount Street Bridge ASAP.

'It's the best we can do,' Callan sighed. 'You don't happen to have a lieutenant's uniform anywhere?'

To Callan's surprise the Gorgeous Wrecks found a spare uniform belonging to one of their officers who was away on leave. The jacket and pants fitted reasonably well although the hat was a size too large, so Callan padded the rim with newspapers.

'I'd better get back and see what I can do to minimise the slaughter,' Callan said, tightening his puttees. 'You men keep nagging HQ on that telephone, okay.'

Callan left the barracks to find Colonel Fane and explained that he'd urgently requested heavy weapon's support.

'Good man,' Fane said. 'Where's that wretched signals unit?'

'Almost on the bridge, sir.'

'I need it here at my command post.'

'Captain Bainbridge-Smyth is using it as a barricade at the moment, sir. I think he's frightened of getting into the driver's cabin. The windscreen has been shot to smithereens. He's sort of taken over the forward units.'

'Has he, by Jove? We'll see about that.'

'Do you want me to order him back, sir?'

Callan would have taken great delight in sticking it to that poncey Pommy.

'No, I'll do it myself,' Fane said. 'I must see what's going on anyway.'

So hugging the splendid townhouse walls, Callan, Colonel Fane and his staff officers edged towards the Mount Street Bridge. Bainbridge-Smyth still cowered behind his truck while urging others to charge to their deaths. The captain didn't look too pleased to see Callan had returned. He wasn't overjoyed by the colonel's arrival either.

'I was going to have this man charged with desertion,' Bainbridge-Smyth whined to Fane. 'McAlister thinks he can just pop in and out of action as the fancy strikes him. At least he looks more like a soldier now.'

Fane ignored him.

'We have to get those men under cover,' Fane declared, but how that was to be achieved was anyone's guess. The Foresters had by now found protection in doorways and behind garden walls. Those close to the school house had suffered the worst. After receiving deadly fire from number 25, they leapt over the school wall only to receive more lethal volleys from within the school building. Some men had reached safety, aided by householders who risked their lives to drag the wounded through their front doors into their parlours.

'There aren't that many rebels, sir,' Callan assessed, noting the muzzle flashes, 'but they hit one of our blokes every time and we can't get a shot back at them. We must out-flank them.'

'Yes, yes, McAlister, I can see that for myself. Captain, contact HQ and tell them we propose to bypass Mount Street and cross at the Baggot Street Bridge and attack from the west. I've already posted a platoon at Baggot Street and they report it is clear of rebels.'

Bainbridge-Smyth dictated a message to Billings, but Lowe's reply was a flat denial. They were to take their objectives by frontal attack only. Fane asked for clarification and got it in no uncertain terms — no detours, Mount Street Bridge, the school-house and Clanwilliam House are all to be taken by frontal attack!

Dear God, we're led by fools — it's Gallipoli all over again.

Callan could only watch in horror as platoon after platoon formed, waiting for their officers' whistles before charging. And once again, charge they did. One entire company attempted to reach the school house, but enfilading fire from number 25 and Clanwilliam House ripped them to pieces. Another platoon tried to storm the bridge with the same tragic results. The Foresters may have been inexperienced, but they certainly didn't lack courage. They charged like the forlorn hopes of Wellington's armies during the Napoleonic Wars. And they died like forlorn hopes.

The Foresters had only been in combat for two hours and had already suffered over a hundred casualties with the majority of the battalion's officers either dead or wounded. Shortly afterwards Colonel Fane was shot in the arm and replaced by Colonel Oates. Oates also brought his 2/8th battalion into the fight. Battalion commanders may have changed, but the situation didn't until two incidents occurred.

The first was the appearance of four nurses dressed in crisply starched red-cross livery, caps and capes. Each woman carried a Gladstone bag of medical equipment and dressings. The leading nurse strode forward with her arm raised, glaring at the schoolhouse, number 25 and Clanwilliam House. She said nothing, but her body language declared that if any of you rogues shoot, you'll answer to me and you won't like that one little bit.

As they reached Callan's position, they were right in the firing line.

'Nurse, get back!' he yelled. 'You're in great danger.'

The leading nurse stopped and glared at Callan, oblivious of the bullets whistling around her.

'Lieutenant, I do you the courtesy of addressing you correctly. I expect you to reciprocate.'

Callan stared at her blankly.

'We are all qualified ward sisters.'

'The rebels will shoot you, sister.'

'They will do no such thing. I will not permit it. Now excuse me, Lieutenant, but my colleagues and I have work to do.'

Callan looked on in disbelief as the sisters went quickly and efficiently into triage mode. They dressed wounds and administered laudanum and directed those walking wounded to break cover and help their critically hurt comrades to the rear. Dubliners left the safety of their luxury residences and helped other men into their houses to be treated within.

The rebels did not fire a single shot at the nurses, civilian helpers or the wounded they treated, but they still took pot-shots at any other targets that might present themselves. So the Mount Street Bridge hosted a ludicrous situation where four steely-nerved nurses and random courageous on-lookers helped wounded men to safety while a gun-battle raged around them. It reminded Callan of the stunt Ivy and her mother had pulled to extricate him from Countess Markievicz and Commandant Mallin's clutches at St. Stephen's Green.

Many of the wounded Foresters had reached shelter by the time the next event occurred around five o'clock. Several buckets of Mk 12 'hairbrush' bombs arrived along with a Lewis gun, but the battle was far from over.

Colonel Oates assigned his companies their objectives. As a supernumerary officer, Callan joined the men advancing towards number 25, while another company edged towards the schoolhouse. The Lewis gun opened up, spraying Clanwilliam House and keeping the snipers' heads down.

Callan picked up a rifle with its bayonet fixed — there were plenty lying around the street. He joined the men giving covering fire as a squad darted up the stone steps leading to number 25.

Shots blazed from within and several men stumbled and fell, dropping their hairbrush bombs. Callan dashed forward, grabbed a bomb and pulled the safety-catch. The fuse spluttered to life as Callan lobbed the grenade towards number 25's front door.

The bomb exploded, yet the door remained intact, but it gave other soldiers time to place more bombs on the doorstep. Everyone ducked for cover as the bombs exploded, if not simultaneously, then close enough for their collective force to blast the door open. Callan picked up another bomb, ignited the fuse and pitched it inside.

Flame and shrapnel belched through the doorway and the troops charged in with guns blazing. Smoke and dust filled the hall leading to a staircase where a single figure stood dazed and disorientated. Half a dozen Foresters were now inside number 25 all firing at once. They riddled the rebel with lead, killing him instantly. The staircase was on fire and had been weakened by Callan's grenade blast. As the dead rebel collapsed so did the stairs, crashing into a fiery heap at the soldiers' feet.

'Drag him clear,' an officer cried. 'We'll need to identify him later.'

Number 25 was on fire and too badly damaged to investigate further, but it looked as if the single rebel was the only one inside. Surely there were more judging by the fire-power they poured into the 2/7th Battalion.

'Looks like the other blighters did a bunk when we tossed the bombs in,' the officer said. 'Time to move, our chaps at the school-house might need help.'

Callan and his companions reached the school-house without further casualties. Having silenced the cross-fire from number 25, the British Lewis gun now concentrated on Clanwilliam House, peppering the upper windows so the rebels could no longer get any clear shots into Northumberland Street without the risk of being killed.

Men stormed the school-house, but the rebels had also abandoned the position, leaving the bodies of an unarmed man and a woman. A local man who'd ventured out said they were the caretaker and his wife, who like so many others, were just in the wrong place at the wrong time.

Familiar story, Callan thought.

So as the shadows lengthened, the Foresters turned their attention to Clanwilliam House. Callan tagged along as men hugged the bridge walls to reach the building. They hurled more bombs through the shattered windows. Soon fire spread through Clanwilliam House.

During the night with the blaze illuminating the scene, Foresters broke into Clanwilliam House and tackled the rebels hand-to-hand. While some units stayed to mop up Clanwilliam House as it burned through the night, others fought bitter street battles, clearing buildings one-by-one on their relentless advance into central Dublin.

For Callan it was a blur. He fought until he was exhausted. Just after midnight Colonel Maconchy sent reinforcements to relive the 2/7th and 2/8th Battalions.

Right boys, I've done my bit. I'm no use to anyone in the state I am now. It's time to leg it back to Lord Delaney's place, get into my own uniform and report to Ivy's dad, wherever he might be.

Finding his way back to St Stephen's Green was tricky through the labyrinth of narrow roads without street lights, all of which were out in the area. He ran into several British units and one rebel group. After a brief gunfight he ducked into a laneway and finally reached Lord Delaney's townhouse just before dawn. St Stephen's Green was quiet, so Callan assumed British units were waiting for daylight to continue peppering away at the Countess and Mallin's dwindling force holed up at the College of Surgeons.

Callan rang the bell and moments later O'Rourke opened the door.

'Forgive me for saying so, but you look like hell, sir,' O'Rourke observed.

'You should see it from my side,' Callan grinned.

Ivy clattered down the stairs and flung her arms around him.

'Callan, my darling boy, I have been frantic with worry. We have heard wireless reports and all sorts of terrible rumours. There has been gunfire everywhere — and now artillery is blowing everything up.'

'Unfortunately the rumours are not exaggerated,' Callan said. 'There has been a blood-bath at the Mount Street Bridge...God I need a hot bath and a soft bed...'

Chapter 24 — Street Fighter

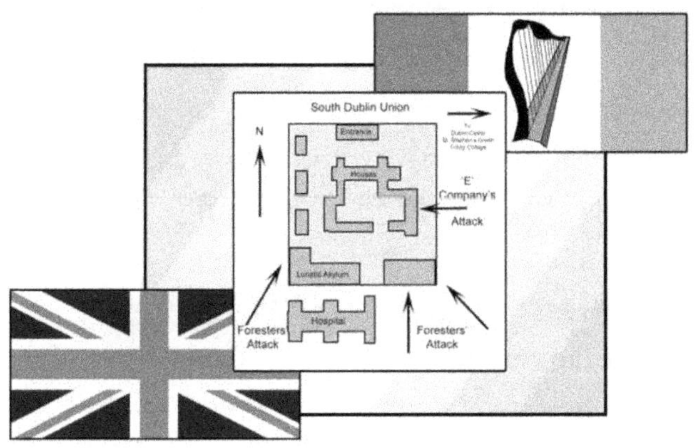

Thursday — 27th April 1916

Callan slept until noon. He awoke refreshed and ready to tackle whatever came his way. A hot bath, steaming cocoa, toasted cheese sandwich and of course Ivy's kiss goodnight before he went to bed made a world of difference. The distant rumble of artillery confirmed Ivy's observation that everything was being blown up. Callan learned that a British gunboat, *Helga,* had steamed up the Liffey and bombarded Eamon de Valera's positions around Boland's Bakery, although there were no reports that it had done any significant damage.

Shells from *Helga* and other artillery pieces also pounded central Dublin and the GPO in particular. Virtually every building in Sackville Street was smouldering or fully ablaze while the GPO was being slowly pulverised.

'Have you heard from your dad?' Callan asked as he woofed down sausages Cook had prepared for lunch.

'He rang yesterday and seems safe enough on Brigadier Lowe's staff,' Ivy replied.

'Things have quietened down here as well.'

'Fighting around St Stephen's Green has slackened off. The rebels are bottled up in the College of Surgeons.'

'If the troops are smart, they'll play a waiting game without taking too many risks. Mind you the Army didn't look so smart on the Mount Street Bridge. Frontal Assault! What was Brigadier Lowe thinking?'

'Do not distress yourself, dear,' Meredith said. 'I am sure you won't be called on again and you are quite safe here.'

'This wretched war seems to have a way of following me around,' Callan said. 'Blimey, it was exactly a year ago yesterday when I first arrived at Anzac Cove.'

Ivy's growing affection for the young Australian did not go unnoticed. Meredith D'vere-Brown watched her daughter fall in love. Her feelings had become mixed. Whereas she agreed with her husband that an advantageous match for Ivy was desirable, she also wished her daughter to have a happy marriage. Of course if she did eventually choose Callan then he would undoubtedly whisk her away to the antipodes, which had to be discouraged at all cost.

Well, he'd have to survive the war first, which may have been a heartless way of looking at things, but it was the savage reality of the times in which they lived — and died.

Colonel D'vere-Brown rang shortly after midday. He spoke briefly to Meredith before she handed the ear-piece to Callan.

'I'm pleased you're back in touch,' the colonel began, 'I believe you've been playing the hero over at Mount Street.'

'I don't know about that, sir. Trying to stay alive is more like it.'

'Quite so, quite so, but I've got an irate signals captain here who wants to charge you with insubordination among other things...'

'Not that pompous ass Bainbridge-Smyth?'

'Don't say another word, Callan. I don't think you realise how serious this is. I'm at the Castle for a while, get over here right away.'

'But sir...Colonel Fane was there...'

'Well he's not here now, he's wounded. So shift yourself, Callan. That's an order.'

'Yes, sir.'

Callan slammed the earpiece back onto its hook.

'I don't believe it,' he sighed. 'I'm on a charge.'

O'Rourke had pressed Callan's uniform, so at least he looked the part when he left Lord Delaney's townhouse, pistol in its polished leather holster and rifle with fixed bayonet slung over his shoulder. Callan chose to wear his peaked cap rather than slouch-hat which was similar to those worn by some ICA members. His single lieutenant's pip glistened on his epaulets while his DCM ribbon marked him as a soldier of experience and distinction.

I'll show that drongo, Captain-Flaming-Bain-Flaming-Bridge-Flaming-Smyth!

Callan reached Dublin Castle safely. The streets now bristled with British and RIR troops who were well supported with Lewis guns, light artillery and long range shelling from *Helga*. Even tanks had reached the battlefield and were doing serious property damage. Their crews showed scant regard for the historic value of the buildings they systematically destroyed either with explosive shells or using the tanks as battering-rams. A company of the 2/8th

Foresters lounged around the Castle forecourt, keeping an eye on City Hall, but it was all quiet over the road.

The rebels were now bottled up in several strong-points and would have to be ferreted out. However the streets of Dublin were not entirely safe as individual snipers randomly picked off targets.

Lord Delaney had attached himself to Brigadier Lowe's staff just to stay in the thick of things. Meanwhile Colonel D'vere-Brown was appointed chief of liaison and communication between the Castle, Royal Barracks and wherever else the brigadier chose to make his HQ. Elements of the Foresters had marched to the Castle during the morning and Captain Bainbridge-Smyth's signals unit came with them. D'vere-Brown had become the captain's temporary CO.

Bainbridge-Smyth had wasted no time before he complained about an upstart colonial know-it-all who'd made a nuisance of himself on the Mount Street Bridge. It only took the colonel a second to make the connection and rang around to see if he could locate Callan. The sooner this was sorted out the better.

Callan had barely walked through the Castle's imposing portal when Bainbridge-Smyth strutted towards him, leaving Billings to man the communication gear. The signal's truck was parked in the Castle's front courtyard, looking much the worse for wear, but still serviceable nevertheless.

'I've got you now, you jumped up little...'

Callan walked straight past Bainbridge-Smyth, jabbing his leg aside as he went, tripping the captain who tumbled onto the gravel driveway.

'What did you see, Billings?' Callan asked as he approached the truck.

'Why I do believe Mr Bainbridge-Smyth tripped, sir. I do 'ope he ain't 'urt 'imself or nuffin'.'

'Good man. Where's the colonel?'

'Inside wiv the section commanders, sir. There's a push on norf of the river.'

'You saw that, Billings!' Bainbridge-Smyth roared as he picked himself up.

'Yes sir. I saw you trip on the gravel. Nasty slippery stuff that gravel, sir. You could do yourself a mischief, so you could, sir. Do you need any 'elp, sir?'

'McAlister tripped me — deliberately.'

'Sorry, didn't see nuffin like that, sir.'

Bainbridge-Smyth would have pressed the matter, but right then the telegraph started clicking drawing Billing's attention to his duty.

'Message from Brigadier Lowe, sir. 'E's changed 'is mind and now wants all units to advance on the South Dublin Union and support Colonel Oates' men already in place there.'

'Take it to Colonel D'vere-Brown then, man,' Bainbridge-Smyth snapped. 'As for you...' he added turning to Callan, but the Australian had already gone inside.

There was no further opportunity for Bainbridge-Smyth to pursue his case as the company had its marching orders. Callan approached Colonel D'vere-Brown, snapped to attention and saluted.

'Lieutenant McAlister reporting for duty as ordered, sir.'

'Very good, McAlister. You will take command of 2nd platoon E Company. Their officer has been wounded.'

Billings was right behind Callan with Lowe's amended orders. Colonel D'vere-Brown scanned the document.

'E Company has been ordered to rejoin the battalion at the South Dublin Union,' D'vere-Brown said. 'Colonel Oates is in position with the remainder of the 2/8th. They arrived via roads parallel to the Grand Canal to storm the Union complex from the south. He requires E Company to protect his right flank, attacking the rebels from the east.'

Bainbridge-Smyth stormed into the brief area.

'That man...'

'Not now, captain,' D'vere-Brown said in a pained tone. 'We have our duty to do first.'

The South Dublin Union was a sprawling complex of offices, dormitories, storerooms, maternity hospital, warehouses, lanes, brick walls and workshops. In its time it had been a workhouse and the Irish Rebel 4th Battalion were now barricaded in the buildings. They'd boarded doors and windows and gouged loopholes through the brickwork.

While Colonel D'vere-Brown led the signals unit to Colonel Oakes' battalion headquarters, Callan assessed the situation and he didn't like what he saw. Intelligence reports suggested two hundred rebels defended the Union and they were well dug in. Rebel tri-colour flags flapped defiantly from the rooftops. It may have been a large number of men to prise out of the Union, but firstly the 2/8th had to get close enough to take them on.

Men from the main battalion could be glimpsed as they edged their way closer to the Union's southern walls. Heavy gunfire bellowed from the loopholes and the Foresters were having a hot time of it.

'Well, it's not going to get done by looking at it,' Callan remarked to the company commander standing beside him. 'We'll need pick-axes and bombs.'

'All arranged, old boy. Your platoon has been issued with both. Do you want to do the honours?' the captain said.

'Not especially, but if you insist.'

'I'll take the lead then.'

'I reckon there's plenty to go around. You go left and I'll take the right.'

The captain nodded and E Company crept towards the Union's east side. Whatever Brigadier Lowe might think, these men had learnt caution from their Mount Street Bridge experience. The Foresters hadn't been involved in street fighting before, but they were learning fast.

So began a harsh battle that lasted until nightfall. Callan's men reached a building and crouched below the window and loophole level. The rebels fired, but could not depress their rifle barrels steeply enough from the loopholes to hit the Foresters. Callan saw a barrel poking from a loophole. He grabbed it with one hand, yanking it forward while firing his service pistol through the narrow opening. A man screamed, giving Callan the satisfaction of knowing he'd hit someone.

The Foresters were safe enough crouched along the east wall, but they weren't doing much good either. Callan scampered beside the company captain.

'We can't get the bombs through the windows and the loopholes are too narrow.'

'Get two men on the pick-axes while the others discourage the Irish. You know what to do.'

'Yessir.'

Callan decided this officer was courageous and knew his stuff.

Four burly privates made short work of bludgeoning two holes in the brickwork. As the masonry crumbled rebels fired a volley from inside. Callan had anticipated that as it was exactly what he would have done, so he emptied his service revolver into the hole. Bullets zinged in both directions but the Foresters remained unscathed.

One of the solders ignited a bomb and rammed it into the hole, but the hairbrush grenades were cumbersome and bulky. It jammed in the breech, which would have been fine and just blown the hole bigger. Unfortunately a quick-witted rebel kicked the bomb outwards and it dropped onto the rubble pile left by the pick-axe men.

'Down! Flat!' Callan bellowed.

He felt the blast and thought his eardrum would burst as the bomb exploded. The men were covered in dust and bore a few cuts and scratches, but they'd all dived for cover in time and miraculously no one was seriously hurt. For a moment Callan's world was silent. Dazed and disoriented he was aware of the gunfire exchanged through the wall as sound slowly returning to normal. That is if he could consider being in the middle of a bloody gunfight normal.

'Who's got a bomb?' Callan yelled, reloading his revolver.

A soldier next to him handed him another bomb. Callan unslung his rifle, checked the bayonet was secure and handed the weapon to the soldier while explaining his plan.

'Okay, private. Are you up for this?'

The man nodded.

Callan handed him the rifle and wedged the grenade onto the bayonet. He stepped back from the wall and fired four rounds through the fissure. On the fourth shot one of the private's comrades primed the bomb. Callan fired the remaining two shots and the private rammed the bomb through the wall, shoving the rifle as far as its stock.

Seconds later a muffled roar blasted debris back through the hole that was now twice its original size. Before the rebels had time to recover, two more bombs tumbled inside and exploded. The opening was now big enough for men to squeeze though, bayonets pointing ahead.

Once inside the scene was mayhem. Four rebels crouched stunned and bewildered. The Foresters bayoneted them all and there was no quarter asked or given from then on. Men scrambled from room to room, out of doors that led to courtyards and alleys then into other buildings large and small. Rebels hid behind abandoned vehicles, sandbag barricades, in doorways, corridors, windows and anywhere else they could mount an ambush.

It was street-fighting at its most intense, harrowing and bloody. Callan literally bumped into one rebel and simple drove his pistol barrel into the man's gut and pulled the trigger. The rebel grunted and emitted a pitiful gurgling wheeze as he dropped. Callan moved on, he was back hand-to-hand with Johnny Turk scrambling through mud and blood in the Gallipoli trenches.

Dust and grit stung Callan's eyes and the stench of cordite filled his nostrils. The screams of dying men and savage war-cries filled his ears. His muscles strained to their limit and sweat drenched his uniform. Every sense was razor sharp.

Men came at him and men died without hesitation. Callan's only edge was months of unrelenting experience that had become instinct. His only thought was survival at all costs with no time for compassion or curiosity. Callan had learnt to kill men without compunction. It was the only thing that had kept him alive so far and it was the only thing that would keep him alive in the future.

The Foresters fought like veterans, and so did the rebels. Just as Callan and his men kicked in one more door and tossed a bomb through, the E Company commanded clambered over a mass of rubble towards him. His left arm was in a sling and his head bandaged, but he still carried his service revolver.

'How do you do, old boy?' the captain greeted.

'It's just the way to spend a sunny afternoon. Blow the idea of a quiet pint or walking a pretty girl in the park.'

'You'll get your chance then. We've been recalled. Colonel Oates has decided the rebels have been contained and it's not worth losing more men trying to winkle out the last of the buggers.'

'Too right. I'm with you, cobber,' Callan said, waving his men back. 'The Guinness Brewery is around here somewhere, isn't it?'

'Sorry old man, it's still in rebel hands.'

'Bugger, I'd kill for a drink.'

'You might get one. Rumour has it we're heading for Reilly's Fort.'

'What's so exciting about that?'

'It's a pub.'

Chapter 25 — Dublin Swan-Song

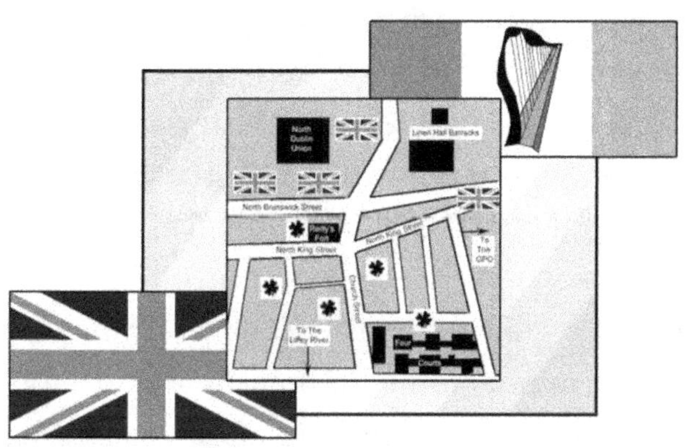

Friday — 28th April 1916

Callan's position as platoon commander didn't last long. Colonel Oates appointed a replacement from the Foresters' ranks, acknowledging Callan had been cited for gallantry under fire by the E company captain. By then all his bravery had evaporated and Callan just wanted to rest.

Unfortunately the British really knew little of the South Dublin Union's purpose other than it having been a workhouse and a haven for the city's impoverished. Those destitute individuals were housed in a facility for un-wed mothers, foundlings and orphans. There was also an insane asylum aptly named after Bedlam in London.

Both these buildings were badly damaged, resulting in high civilian casualties. Parts of this collateral damage were the asylum inmates who now roamed free either causing mischief or simply wandering aimlessly through the rubble. Callan spent a couple of hours rounding up those up he could catch and placing them in the care of medical staff who arrived from other hospitals, but it was like herding cats at times.

When he finally returned to the signals lorry, he discovered the Foresters were in the process of regrouping and encircling the South Dublin Union to contain the complex. Sections of the brigade were then ordered north across the Liffey to join the cordon on North King Street where one of the last major rebel concentrations was still fighting hard. The signal unit was to accompany those Foresters.

'You'd better stay with me, Callan,' Colonel D'vere-Brown suggested. 'You might come in handy and I don't want you running off getting into trouble again. Grab something to eat from the catering section and try and get some sleep if you can.'

'What about Captain Bainbridge-Smyth, sir?'

'That will have to wait. I think the good captain is too busy to worry about you right now.'

An hour before dawn, D'vere-Brown shook Callan awake.

'Come on young man, we're heading north of the river. Climb aboard the lorry. There's a new general in town.'

General Sir John 'Conky' Maxwell had been sent from England to take overall command of the Irish forces. Although he left operation command pretty much in Brigadier Lowe's hands, Maxwell made it clear the only acceptable outcome was the rebels' unconditional surrender.

Once they reached General Maxwell's HQ there was little for Callan to do. Lord Delaney greeted him warmly before returning to whatever busy-work he'd found to keep him occupied. Callan asked politely after his lordship's injured backside and wounded pride and was told curtly not to be cheeky.

Callan's official position was Colonel D'vere-Brown's courier, but with generals and colonels pouring into Dublin from all directions, they had ample messenger-boys of their own. Callan spent most of his time steering clear of Captain Bainbridge-Smyth. He toured the north cordon, reporting back to Colonel D'vere-Brown and Lord Delaney with any intelligence he thought might be useful.

Sackville Street blazed from one end to the other. The GPO was now well alight and the rebels were having a hot time of it. Some had braved a hail of bullets to move into a shop at 16 Moore Street leading off Sackville Street. The new location didn't offer much more cover, but at least it wasn't on fire. The tables had turned considerably and now rebel bodies littered the streets as the British and RIR troops mowed down anyone who came within their field of fire.

The most severe fighting now centred between North King Street and the Four Courts tenements along the Liffey Riverbank. If Callan expected a pint at Reilly's Fort, he was to be disappointed. Rebels vehemently defended the pub and any consumables on the premises were long gone, destroyed by bombs or artillery. The area was a labyrinth of laneways, brick walls and hidden passages where — just like the South Dublin Union — rebels lurked ready to ambush from every corner. Hand-to-hand fighting with fixed bayonets was the order of the day.

Saturday — 29th April 1916

By midnight the GPO roof collapsed, making the position virtually untenable, yet still a handful of defenders clung on, although most had now battered their way through brick walls to 16 Moore Street. It was clear to everyone the rebellion was in its death throes and it was only a matter of time before all the ICA strong-points fell. The British forces had bypassed many key rebel locations such as the College of Surgeons, Boland's Bakery, Jacobs Biscuit Factory, the Guinness brewery and South Dublin Union, leaving a token force on guard to wait for the rebels to grow hungry.

Yet the struggle around North King Street and the Four Courts remained bitter and bloody. And it was to take its toll on some Foresters who'd been in combat since their mauling at Mount Street Bridge. They'd been joined by Colonel Taylor's South Staffordshire Regiment who'd also seen stiff fighting.

Callan spent Friday night and early Saturday morning making himself useful, running errands, supporting units, helping evacuate wounded soldiers and any other tasks that cropped up. He and Billings laid telephone cables and changed a tyre when a bullet ripped into the signals lorry wheel.

At about three a.m. the truck was parked behind a barricade in North King Street. Troops were searching for rebels from house to house and usually meeting bloody resistance before breaking in, only to find their enemy had slipped away through a back entrance.

Messages still buzzed back and forth, keeping the Signals unit busy. Captain Bainbridge-Smyth darted around erratically, barking orders unpleasantly to the squad assigned to him. It seemed to Callan that the captain was even more jittery than usual. Many of his instructions confused the men and were petty, unnecessary, redundant or plain contradictory.

Bainbridge-Smyth's antics didn't help the men who were jumpy enough already. Everyone ran for cover as missiles clattered onto the cobblestones and brickwork. A bunch of street urchins took it upon themselves to chuck stones at the British troops. The children turned tail and ran when Callan gave chase, but he caught a straggler.

'Listen you dopey little bugger,' he yelled, cuffing the squirming boy around his ears. 'Clear off home before one of you gets shot. Those troops are trigger-happy enough without you making an easy target.'

'Me 'ome's been blown up, sor.'

'You live on North King Street? What's your name?'

'Fergal O'Donnell, sor. I did live here, but my 'ouse is on fire.'

'Where are your parents?'

'Dunno, sor.'

'They aren't with the rebels, are they, Fergal?

'Dunno, sor.'

'And you wouldn't tell me if they were, would you?'

'Dunno nothin' about that, sor.'

'What about a pal's place?'

'I could go to Sean's. Number 'undred and seventy-five. It's across the street just over there.'

The terrace windows were mostly darkened with their drapes drawn, illuminated only by the reflection of fires from other buildings, although faint glows flickered from a few windows. Electric power had been cut off almost universally throughout the inner city, so householders used paraffin lanterns or candles to see by.

'Right, get over there quick as you can, Fergal. It's no time of night for you to be running around. Stay indoors until this is all over.'

Callan released the kid, who bolted. It looked like he and his mates were prepared to take Callan's advice.

'Letting the enemy escape, eh McAlister?' Bainbridge-Smyth sneered from behind, levelling his service revolver and aiming at the boy.

Callan slammed his own pistol barrel against Bainbridge-Smyth's forearm, knocking it down as the captain fired. The shot ricocheted off the cobblestones without doing any damage.

'You've got to be joking,' Callan snarled. 'He's just a lad no more than twelve years old. You fancy the idea of making war on children, do you?'

'They're all rats, no matter what size!' Bainbridge-Smyth screamed. His face flushed crimson while he shook uncontrollably as he waved his pistol in Callan's face. '...and striking a superior officer is another charge I'll be bringing against you...'

Just then a volley of bullets sprayed the street. One soldier dropped with a bullet in his thigh while others ducked for cover, dragging their wounded comrade with them. No one saw where the shots came from, but suddenly Bainbridge-Smyth went berserk. Screaming for men to follow, he charged towards number 175. A squad-sized group of South Staffordshire men followed. They kicked down the front door and barged inside.

'Ruddy 'ell, sir,' Private Billings said, ''e's gone stark ravin' bonkers, so 'e 'as.'

'Trying to be a hero, I suppose,' Callan commented.

'Ain't 'is style, sir.'

'Now Billings, you're talking about your section commander.'

'Yes sir, dunno what came over me, sir.'

Both men exchanged grins, but only for second — shots echoed from number 175...

'Bring your rifle, Arthur,' Callan said, and the two men sprinted to the smashed doorway at number 175.

Other troops who'd crouched behind barricades suddenly advanced without orders and started barging into other houses all along North King Street, many of which had already been cleared by the South Staffs. Some men who weren't interested in taking more risks stayed under cover smoking and simply glanced at Callan and Billings with mild curiosity.

Three women sat weeping in the dim kitchen candle-light.

'Have mercy, sir,' one cried. 'Don't shoot us.'

'I'm not going to shoot anyone. What happened?'

'They took the men-folk and our two wee lads upstairs sir. Then there was shootin'.'

Callan led Billings to the stair-case. Several soldiers clattered down the steps. One man vomited as he rushed past. Some faces were ashen and another trooper wept. Callan recognised profound remorse when he saw it. Others simply showed indifference while one muttered, 'Serve the bog-trotting bastards right.'

An upstairs landing led to two bedrooms. Billings shoved the door open. Two men and a youth lay dead, crumpled over the bed or sprawled grotesquely on the floor. Blood spattered the wall-paper while the bedspread was drenched red. Callan saw no signs of weapons anywhere.

'Oh, shit! What have they done?'

'This way quick, sir,' Billings hissed.

Callan eased the second bedroom door open. Fergal and another boy who Callan presumed was his pal, Sean cowered in a corner. Captain Bainbridge-Smyth loomed before them, casting an ominous shadow over the terrified boys. He pointed his revolver only feet from them.

Callan placed his revolver barrel against Bainbridge-Smyth's temple.

'Lower your weapon, Captain,' Callan said between clenched teeth, 'or I swear I'll shoot you dead where you stand.'

'Oh, do shut up with your sanctimonious clap-trap, McAlister,' the captain sighed wearily. 'No one will miss this pair of stinking Paddy gutter-snipes.'

'You'll still be dead.'

Bainbridge-Smyth turned and glared at Callan.

'Three unarmed men were killed in the other room. I don't know what Colonel Taylor will make of that, but you'll never get away with murdering children.'

'This is war — people die!'

'It's over. We've beaten the rebels, there's just mopping up left.'

'Ha! You think this is over, do you? It's just the start and these two brats are the next rebel generation. Why not cull them now?'

'I daresay you might be right, but it's over for us. Now lower that gun and get out of here while you still can.'

Callan heard Billings' rifle bolt click a round into the breech. He sensed rather than saw Billings raise and aim the gun.

Oh, shit.

'I think you should do what Mr McAlister says, sir,' Billings said uncertainly — he was on seriously thin ice right then. 'Might be best all round, sir.'

Bainbridge-Smyth glared in fury, but after what seemed an age, he decided facing down a couple of gun-barrels was too much. He slowly holstered his service pistol, strode past Callan and thumped downstairs, leaving Callan and Billings with the two weeping boys.

'It's all right,' Callan said, 'no one's going to hurt you now. What happened?'

'They dragged us up 'ere, sor,' Fergal sobbed. 'They shot Sean's da and uncle Alan and cousin Patrick. They didn't do nothin', sor. They weren't Fenians and didn't 'ave no guns.'

'I believe you, Fergal. Let's get you downstairs.'

'Are me ma and Aunty Joyce and big sister Maureen dead, sor?' the other lad whispered.

'No, they're fine, Sean. Come on, let's dry those tears and show them what brave fellows you two are.'

After reuniting Sean and Fergal with the sobbing women, Callan went looking for Colonel Taylor, but Colonel D'vere-Brown intercepted him first.

'Callan, I told you keep out of trouble,' D'vere-Brown said. 'Bainbridge-Smyth wants to add assaulting a superior officer and mutiny to his string of charges. Can't you just leave the man alone? Apparently you've dragged Private Billings into the whole sorry mess as well.'

'He was going to kill two innocent boys. I couldn't let him do that. He'd already ordered three unarmed men gunned down. They're over there in number 175 if you want to take a look, sir.'

'I know. There have been other incidents along North King Street tonight.'

'More killings?'

'Yes, quite a number. It seems other South Staffordshire men snapped and took it out on whoever they found. Look, you're out of it from now on, Callan. It's nearly dawn. I want you...no...I'm ordering you to return to Lord Delaney's townhouse and wait there for me.'

'What about Captain Bainbridge-Smyth and these murders, sir?

'I don't know. It will be up to Colonel Taylor in the end I suppose. I'll do my best for you and Billings, but you both face serious charges.'

'Dammit, Colonel, is that why we're fighting? Is that what I spent eight wretched months in the Gallipoli trenches for — to watch British soldiers murdering innocent civilians?'

'It's complex, Callan. Now just this once — do what I tell you.'

Callan was unable to recall what followed. He left North King Street and walked towards the GPO. It was only ten minutes away. Yet somewhere along the way he sought shelter in a doorway. Sitting on the doorstep, Callan rested his head in his hands in despair. If anyone noticed him, they simply passed by. Eventually he slept because the sun was high when he recovered his reason and consciousness.

Unshaven, filthy and dishevelled he dragged himself to his feet and trudged towards Sackville Street. The once majestic thoroughfare was now a rubble-strewn shambles. Most houses including the besieged GPO were smouldering, gutted ruins. Artillery and random shells from *Helga* had carved huge swathes of destruction through central Dublin. Callan was vaguely aware that the guns around Sackville Street had fallen silent, but he couldn't care less.

He barely glanced when Cumann na mBan Nurse Elizabeth O'Farrell strode from the GPO right past him along Sackville Street. She held a letter with James Connolly's terms of surrender, referring to the rebels as the Irish Republican Army for the first time — the term IRA had been coined! Callan had reached Lord Delaney's home when Brigadier Lowe rejected Connolly's demands outright, insisting on unconditional surrender. While

Callan shrugged off his feral uniform and wallowed in another hot bath, Connolly, who was seriously wounded and with no other option, capitulated. Callan was enjoying one of Cook's hearty stews as word went out to all rebels, ordering them to lay down their weapons.

The battle for Dublin was over, but Callan's demons were just emerging. That evening he knelt on the floor beside Ivy who sat in Lord Delaney's favourite leather chair. He placed his head on her lap and wept for the first time since he'd enlisted in the AIF. Ivy had no idea what to say that might sooth his anguish, so she remained silent and let his grief run its course.

Part Four — Western Front 1916-1918

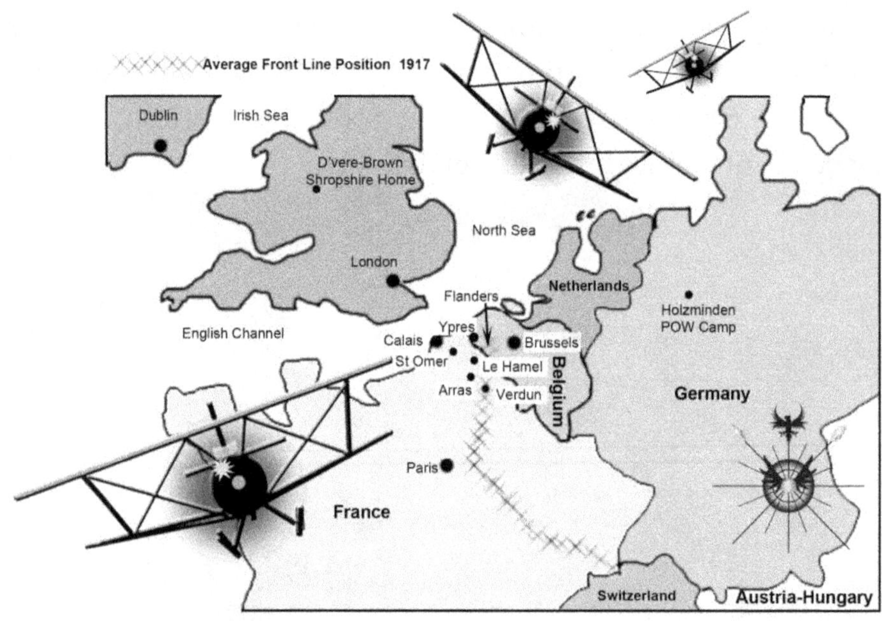

Chapter 26 — A Parting Shot

Sunday — 30th April 1916

'It's clean up time,' Lord Delaney declared at breakfast. 'Pockets of rebellion still lurk around the country and the army is deploying units to flush 'em out. General Maxwell has asked me to return to Cork and oversee the legal side of things there.'

'They have enough lawyers in Dublin, then?' Colonel D'vere-Brown observed blandly.

'I'm afraid it's out of civil hands now, old boy. Since martial law was declared, Dublin's miscreants are all to be tried by court martial.'

'What do you think will happen to them?' Callan asked, rather too sulkily in the Lord Delaney's opinion.

'Shoot a few of the ring-leaders, I daresay,' his lordship replied, rather too jovially in Callan's opinion. 'Gaol the rest and let the rank-and-file go home. I doubt if they'll cause much more trouble with their guns confiscated.'

'Then it will be best all round if we return to Crosshaven and at least enjoy what is left of your leave, darling,' Meredith said to her husband. 'You have but one week left and I should like to spend the time in peace and quiet.'

'It'll be a pleasant change,' Colonel D'vere-Brown agreed.

'Amen to that,' Callan sighed.

Callan was asleep when the colonel and Lord Delaney had returned around midnight. Although Delaney was resoundingly cheerful about the rebellion's demise, Colonel D'vere-Brown appeared more relieved than anything else. Meredith and Ivy shared that relief although Callan was less sanguine. Resignation was the most positive emotion he could muster right then.

'What's going to happen about the murders on North King Street, sir?' Callan asked.

'There will be an enquiry of course, but I doubt much will come of it. It'll be put down to a tragic circumstance in the heat of battle, I should imagine.'

'But I was there! I was a witness and so were Private Billings and the survivors of number 175. What's to be done about Captain Bainbridge-Smyth?'

'I have come to an arrangement with Colonel Taylor. Bainbridge-Smyth has agreed to drop his charges against you and Private Billings. You will not be called as a witness.'

Callan was speechless.

'Private Billing will be promoted to sergeant and transferred to Aldershot as a signals instructor.'

'You bought him off..?'

The colonel ignored him.

'Bainbridge-Smyth will return to the Signals Corps and be posted directly to the Western Front.'

'He'll get off scot-free.'

'You more than anyone, Callan, should know life in the trenches isn't getting off scot-free. And as for you...'

'What will happen to Callan?' Ivy interrupted.

'We still await instructions from the AIF. In the meantime Brigadier Lowe has been informed of your contribution at Mount Street and the South Dublin Union. He also appreciates the moral dilemma you face regarding the North King Street incidents. Subsequently in addition to endorsing Colonel Oates' citation for a military cross, he has given you a field promotion to first lieutenant.'

The colonel handed Callan a large envelope containing his epaulette 'twin-pips' and the official documentation.

'Congratulations!' Ivy declared flinging her arms around Callan's neck.

'So I'm being bought off too.'

'Call it what you like, but that *is* the way of it and I will not hear another word...'

'But, sir...'

'Not another word. War is a messy business as you well know, Callan. Things rarely go the way we'd like, but in this case the matter is closed. Do I make myself perfectly clear?'

Oh yes.

'Yessir.'

Callan knew when he was beaten and he grew to care less and less by the moment. Lord Delaney arranged for first class tickets to Cork for the following day while Meredith chose to visit one of the nearby aid-stations and do what she could to help.

'I'll come with you, Mama,' Ivy offered.

'No sweetheart, I'd like you to stay with Callan today. I think he would appreciate your company to take his mind off things.'

So Callan and Ivy spent Sunday afternoon strolling through South Dublin. Mr O'Rourke had done his best with Callan's uniform, which may not have been up to parade-ground spit-and-polish standards, but passed casual muster. The streets were strewn with wreckage and many buildings were reduced to devastated shells. Callan and Ivy helped Dubliners recover where they could, but most homeowners would have to wait for cranes, bulldozers and trucks before the serious cleanup could begin.

'Funny,' Callan said, 'just a week ago we were enjoying a family picnic on the green. Now look at the place and goodness knows how many people have been killed or injured.'

'Don't let it trouble you, Callan dear,' Ivy said squeezing his arm.

She smiled and was silent for a while as if considering her words carefully.

'I liked the way you said "family picnic" just now,' she said. 'Like you were one of our family.'

'I'm sorry if I was presumptuous.'

'No, not at all. I think it is sweet. It pleases me you feel that way.'

'Like a brother or a cousin..?'

'No, silly — definitely not like a brother. A cousin would be all right if you were a very distant one.'

She turned and kissed him right there in the public street and Callan had to admit he felt a lot better.

Monday — 1st May 1916

Callan wasn't sorry when he boarded the train at Kingsbridge Station bound for Cork. Dublin's fair city held no fond memories other than stolen moments with Ivy. He left a depressing mix of wreckage, misery, suffering and needless death. The tranquil green countryside showed no hint of rebellion as fertile meadows, picturesque towns and lush woodland rolled by. The fresh smell of spring was in the air, while Ivy held his hand all the way to Cork.

Liam met them in the Vauxhall and after dropping Lord Delaney at his manor, he drove the others to Crosshaven. Maeve prepared a seafood chowder supper and afterwards they sampled a fine port Lord Delaney had presented to Colonel D'vere-Brown.

Callan went to bed feeling mellow and secure. The horrors Dublin had branded into his conscious were dulled — at least temporarily. He wasn't sure how long he slept, but when he awoke he was aware of someone easing into the bed beside him.

'Wha..?'

'Sssh, Callan, darling. We do not want to wake Mama and Papa or what would they think?'

'Ivy, what are you doing here?'

'Why that must be clear, my dear boy,' she giggled. 'I couldn't sleep for thinking of you.'

Ivy wore a white night shift and nothing else. She took his hand and placed it on her breast.

'Does that feel nice to you? I know I like it.'

'Yes, it's sort of soft and firm at the same time,' he offered, which may not have been particularly romantic, but Ivy took it as a compliment nonetheless.

She kissed him with more ardour than ever before, while Callan was happy to reciprocate and let passion take its natural course. It would have too — with all the reckless inexperience of youth if the hallway telephone hadn't rung. The sound seemed amplified in the night stillness accompanied by Colonel D'vere-Brown's feet thumping on the floorboards as he hurried to answer the call.

'Keep quiet!' Callan hissed. 'We'll have to wait until the coast is clear.'

Minutes later, the colonel banged on Callan's bedroom door.

'Quick under the bed,' Callan whispered and Ivy just disappeared as her father entered the room.

'Sorry to wake you, but that was Lord Delaney on the telephone. He wants us to head over to Bawnard House in Castlelyons. Get dressed — uniform and side-arms.'

'Isn't that the Kent place? You know those coves who came into Kennefick's Hotel with Michael Collins. Didn't we check 'em out before going to Dublin?'

'Precisely, but RIC snitches have reported they're in possession of illegal weapons.'

'Not again — why us? Can't the RIC handle it?'

'Apparently they are sending constables, but His lordship wants a military presence and he trusts us after we were so helpful in Dublin. It's part of a general order from Queenstown HQ to round up Fenian suspects. No show without Punch, eh?'

Callan scrambled into his uniform and boots.

'God knows what this is all about, Ivy, but I don't like the sound of it. You stay here until it's safe to go back to your room.'

He kissed her lightly and left. Ivy went to the window to see the headlights pierce the night as the engine roared and the car sped into the distance at top speed. She turned and gasped to see her mother's silhouette in the doorway.

'Oh dear me, Ivy. You reckless, wanton child. What foolishness have you been up to?'

'Well none actually, Mama,' Ivy replied sheepishly. 'I suppose I was saved by the bell.'

'This is no joking matter, young lady. Oh Ivy, for such a sensible girl, you can be a scatter-brain at times. I fear I have given you far too much leeway with that young man.'

'I love him, Mama. He is honest, brave and handsome, what girl wouldn't want to give herself to him?'

'You will not be giving yourself to any man until you are respectably wed, my girl, so we'll hear no more of that licentious talk. As I have said before, your father and I will find a suitable match for you all in good time. And you will wed...intact.'

'And will my groom be..."intact"?'

'What men do as bachelors is of little account. It is how they behave after they marry that is import.'

'And if I don't love him — what then, Mama? You love Papa, am I not to have the same chance for happiness?'

'I grew to love your father because he is a decent man, but we were practically strangers on our wedding night.'

There was an awkward pause as Ivy sulked for a moment.

'Darling,' Meredith said eventually. 'Callan is a nice boy, but he is yet a boy.'

'I am his age.'

'Girls develop into women far sooner than boys become men. Callan has no prospects, no inheritance and no position.'

'His parents own land in New South Wales.'

'Yes Ivy, but they are farmers not estate owners with paying tenants. There is a world of difference.'

'I still love Callan, Mama. Nothing will change that.'

'I do not doubt it, but handsome and heroic as he might be, it is high time we sent your Lieutenant McAlister back to his Australians.'

'Are you going to tell Papa?'

'That very much depends on your future behaviour, Ivy.'

'You mean I am to be blackmailed.'

'That is precisely what I mean.'

Meredith kissed Ivy lightly on her forehead.

'Once Callan leaves, you will have no further communication with him. What started as a harmless flirtation has obviously grown into something far too dangerous. Trust me, Ivy — if you disobey me, I will tell your father and Callan's disgrace will be your fault. Now go back to bed and try not to get any more silly romantic notions in that pretty little head of yours.'

Ivy stormed off — it was probably the worst thing her mother could have chosen to say.

Tuesday — 2nd May 1916

Callan and the colonel arrived at Bawnard House around four just as the first shimmers of gold clipped the eastern sky. Two trucks were parked some distance from Bawnard House. Their army drivers stood around smoking while guarding two handcuffed prisoners who looked more like vagrants than dangerous Fenians. The trucks had transported armed RIC constables who stood in front of the house. They were led by a severe looking man in his late forties with warrant-officers' insignia on his sleeve denoting him a head constable.

'Colonel D'vere-Brown and Lieutenant McAlister — what is the situation?'

'Head Constable William Rowe from Fermoy Station,' the police officer announced, snapping to attention with a smart salute. 'The four Kent fellas are inside and I believe their mother is with 'em. Acting on information received, we have instructions to search the premises for illegal weapons. The Kent family are known Fenians with prior form. We also arrested two suspects on the way over here, sir.'

'Carry on, Head Constable. Lieutenant McAlister and I are here at Lord Delaney's request, but you appear to have the matter in hand.'

'Thank you, sir,' Rowe said, saluted and turned to issue orders to his men.

Bawnard House was a medium sized two-storey building and comfortable by Irish standards. Two bay windows projected either side of the front entrance. Head Constable Rowe deployed his men to form a cordon, although there weren't sufficient to encircle the entire building. Callan joined the constables beside Rowe allowing the men to span out a little further.

While Colonel D'vere-Brown commanded men at the front entrance, Callan accompanied Rowe around the house to within a few yards of the kitchen door. Rowe chose not to use the front door as there was no protection from ambush at the bay windows.

'Ahoy, inside,' he called. 'It's Head Constable Rowe with a contingent of RIC officers surrounding the house. I know youse Kent fellas are inside with your ma.'

Silence.

*Bad sign...*Callan was alert with his service pistol cocked and ready.

'Throw out your guns and ammo, there's me darlin' boys,' Rowe continued. 'You know I've always been square with youse. We don't want no trouble, do we lads? There's been enough shooting up in Dublin to last a lifetime.'

'Bugger off you Protestant arse-licker,' a muffled voice finally responded from one of the upstairs windows.

'Is that youse I hear, Dick,' Rowe replied. 'Come quietly and I'll do what I can to see you straight...'

'No surrender! We'll see men dead first.'

The window pane exploded into a million shards as a shotgun sprayed a fistful of pellets into Head Constable Rowe. At virtually point-blank range the blast smashed his skull to scarlet pulp. Standing only feet from Rowe, Callan ducked as blood, bone chips and gore splattered him from top to bottom. He fired several shots into the window, but couldn't see any results in the darkness.

Standing by the front door, Colonel D'vere-Brown heard the shots.

'Take cover!' he yelled.

Callan didn't need telling, he was already racing to nearby bushes for protection. A hail of bullets shattered the windows of Bawnard House when the constables opened up with everything they had. More lead belched from other windows. Colonel D'vere-Brown stood resolutely, emptying his revolver into the house, providing covering fire for the retreating constables. Only when all the RIC men were out of shotgun range did the colonel calmly step back to safety.

The constables were thinly spread, but they had Bawnard House covered from most angles in case the Kents decided to make a run for it. There was little chance of outflanking the defenders who might well be guarding the side windows.

'Don't take any unnecessary risks, men,' D'vere-Brown admonished. 'Containment is all we're interested in right now.'

And so began a three-hour shoot-out. As sunlight shifted the dawn shadows, Head Constable Rowe's virtually decapitated body was enough to discourage any rashness. No one was interested in storming the kitchen door, while there was no way of approaching the front door without risking enfilading fire from both bay windows. In the meantime a slow, but steady blaze of shotgun pellets along with occasional rifle shots spewed from Bawnard House. The RIC responded to each shot with a ragged volley, but with only thirty rounds apiece, the constables fired sparingly.

Around seven o'clock a detachment of Royal Fusiliers and military cadets arrived. There were now sufficient men to completely encircle Bawnard House.

The soldiers naturally looked to Colonel D'vere-Brown for leadership. Callan had to give him his due after Head Constable Rowe's grisly fate. The colonel stepped right in front of the building armed only with a speaking-trumpet supplied by one of the fusiliers.

'I am Colonel D'vere-Brown and I am here with a contingent of armed soldiers. The jig is up. Bawnard House is surrounded. There is no escape. Your situation is serious enough, so let's not make things worse. Throw out your guns.'

Once again the demand to surrender was met by silence, but after a few moments three shotguns and a rifle were tossed from the bay windows.

'That's it,' a voice called. 'We're out of ammo anyway.'

The front door creaked open and four men emerged. Three raised their hands, but the fourth appeared wounded and was helped by an old woman. For some reason one of the men was barefooted, while another was so jittery he shook violently as he hopped rather than walked from the house.

'I'm Constable Frank King, sor — been a copper round here since o-four. I know these fellas well,' one of the constables whispered to Callan. 'That's the whole Kent bunch. Thomas is the one with no shoes. The other sound fella is William. That's David with his ma, Mary — looks like he's been shot. The loony fella is Dick who ain't been right for a bit now.'

As if to confirm the constable's assessment, Richard Kent suddenly bolted to the back of Bawnard House screaming, 'They ain't going to hang me!'

He was right. A volley of shots from RIC and fusiliers brought him down with multiple wounds before he'd gone a few yards. Old Mary Kent wailed in despair. Leaving his brothers to help David, she ran to where Richard lay grievously wounded. Colonel D'vere-Brown, Callan, several fusiliers and Constable King stood over Richard to assess his condition, but he was shot to pieces and barely hanging on.

'Youse murderin' eejits,' Mary Kent wept. 'There was no need for this. Can't youse see Dick is soft in the head?'

'There was no need to blow Will Rowe's brains out, either,' King growled bitterly. 'But I'll go fetch Canon O'Leary just now. I think Dick will need him.'

It appeared the fusiliers had come prepared for a fight and brought a doctor with them. While Constable King went looking for a priest, the doctor examined Richard Kent and confirmed there was little to be done other than get the stricken fellow to hospital quickly.

As the doctor completed his diagnosis, Callan heard a scuffle from behind one of the garden walls. He discovered the constables had pushed Thomas, David and William against the brickwork and were reloading their rifles. The Kents looked worse for wear with cuts and bruising on their faces.

'It's the end for youse Fenian scum,' one constable snarled.

There was no mistaking the RIC's intention. Three executions by firing-squad were imminent, yet the fusiliers appeared unwilling to intervene. The Kent brothers stood tall, defiantly facing the constables who raised their rifles.

'I order you men stop right there,' Callan roared. 'Haven't you seen enough shooting for one day? Ground your rifles at once.'

The constables eyed Callan with open hostility.

'You don't order us about nothin', soldier boy,' one of the constables spat.

'Damn right I do. Ireland is under martial law, which makes me your boss. I'll shoot the first man who tries to harm these prisoners, do not think for a moment I won't. Is killing one another all you Irish know how to do?'

Callan wasn't precisely sure whether Ireland or just Dublin was under martial law, but neither did the constables it seemed. They lowered their rifles and sullenly handed the Kent brothers over to the fusiliers. The RIC gathered Will Rowe's body, boarded their trucks with their other two suspects and drove away, leaving the fusiliers to guard the prisoners and search Bawnard House. Ransack was more like it, but they discovered no more weapons.

The troops commandeered a horse and dray, which carried Richard and his mother while Thomas, William and David marched ahead under armed escort to Fermoy lockup.

'What a ruddy waste,' Callan sighed. 'There's no way the Kent brothers would have gone down for just four guns. Now they're in deep shit.'

'Their choice, Callan,' Colonel D'vere-Brown observed. 'Come on, I'll drive you back then I'd better call Lord Delaney. He'll want a full report.'

Chapter 27 — Wings

Callan was puzzled by Ivy's attitude towards him when he returned to Crosshaven. Colonel D'vere-Brown sang his praises, recounting how Callan had prevented further bloodshed, although Callan couldn't see the point if the Kent brothers were likely to be executed anyway.

Ivy appeared unimpressed as well. She congratulated him politely, but offered no embrace or even a peck on the cheek. She remained friendly, but distant, perhaps even aloof.

Callan realised the previous night's bedroom antics had something to do with her attitude, but he couldn't see where he'd gone wrong. Maybe she was having a counter-reaction in the cold light of day and now regretted last night's recklessness. He didn't know that Ivy was terrified her mother would spill the beans to the colonel, who'd blame Callan whatever the circumstances. Yes, she'd been silly and impatient, but there was no undoing that now and it wasn't as if Callan had complained at the time.

Ivy was in a spot.

On one hand she was bursting to tell Callan how much she still loved him, but not wanting to display any sign of intimacy which her mother could seize upon to expose her. Callan may not need her father's patronage once he returned to the AIF, but he certainly didn't want to make an enemy of a senior British officer.

Whether Ivy totally understood what physical love actually meant was problematic. Her mother had never broached the subject and she had no older sisters to turn to for advice. While her boarding school chums may have experimented a little, Ivy was still largely ignorant about the whole matter other than it gave her a deep sense of contentment and sublime dreaminess.

Oh, why does life have to be so beastly and complicated? Still three years to go before I'm twenty-one and even then as a woman, will I be truly free?

Fate intervened however. When her father returned to the Belgian front, Ivy would seize the chance to square her relationship with Callan. Unfortunately a letter arrived a few days before the colonel's departure, recalling Callan to active duty. The envelope contained Callan's orders, travel authorisation to Salisbury Plain and two blue arm patches issued to Anzacs who served at Gallipoli after the first landing. Men in the first wave wore red patches. There was also a cheerful letter from Archie Blake saying he'd been promoted to major and hoped Callan had enjoyed his leave peacefully by the Irish seaside.

Too right, I've had a ripper time thanks, Archie!

In the meantime Thomas Kent came before a tribunal chaired by Lord Delaney with a panel of army officers who had no choice but to sentence Thomas to death by firing squad. Richard had since died of his wounds, while David awaited trial and William was acquitted because he claimed to have been a reluctant bystander. His brothers backed William's story and declared Richard had shot Head Constable Rowe, but Tom was deemed the ring-leader and had to go.

Others who joined Thomas Kent in front of firing squads that May included the seven signatories of the Declaration of Independence, Michael Mallin and later Sir Roger Casement. Among those spared were Eamon de Valera, Countess Markievicz, David Kent and Michael Collins who were all to serve varying gaol terms.

Ivy bid Callan farewell with a chaste kiss, but didn't mention anything about writing. Perhaps she'd send a letter explaining how she felt once he arrived in England. He was sure she still cared for him, but perhaps it was best to let her make the first move, especially now they were apart. Even Callan knew long-range love-affairs were tricky and often unrewarding.

Liam drove Callan to the railway station. Neither man spoke during the short journey. As they shook hands firmly on the platform Liam said softly, 'Keep faith in Miss Ivy, Sir,' but his voice was drowned by a shrieking train whistle and the gush of steam from the locomotive. As he watched Callan board his assigned carriage, Liam was uncertain whether the young man had heard or not.

*

General Monash's HQ, Salisbury Plain — July 1916

'All right, Major Blake what is it that's so important?' recently promoted Major General John Monash asked.

The general spoke calmly, but as the new commander of the AIF 3rd Division and with a pedantic eye for planning, logistics and troop welfare, he was a busy man. His new 4th brigade major was not in the habit of bothering him unnecessarily.

'Lieutenant McAlister, sir.'

'And what precisely has our young hero from Dublin been up to?'

'Well nothing, sir. That's the problem. He's a competent platoon commander and I was thinking of giving him a full company, but I believe he's lost his edge.'

'Or his nerve..?'

'No sir. He doesn't shirk his duty, but he's going through the motions like a machine. It's as if he's lost interest.'

'Who hasn't the way this war keeps dragging on?'

'I agree, sir, but leading men into machinegun fire when you simply don't care can be a dangerous attitude. '

'Lieutenant Colonel D'vere-Brown from the Eleventh Shropshires thinks very highly of him as I recall. I'm sure you have that letter of commendation filed away safely, but I can't relieve my officers from duty simply because they're fed up.'

'Not at all, General. There are several excellent, capable lieutenants to take charge of McAlister's platoon. Unfortunately McAlister became fond of the colonel's daughter while in Ireland, but it seems the young lady's ardour has waned. McAlister hasn't heard from her since returning to the brigade. I think he needs a diversion to take his mind off what appears to be a lost love.'

'Leave in Soho perhaps..?'

Blake placed a message on Monash's desk.

'The Royal Flying Corps?'

'Yessir, the RFC is crying out for new aviators — unfortunately they're going through pilots at an alarming rate. The going survival time is about six weeks.'

'Do you think McAlister will respond to this?'

'I believe so, General. He's always up for new challenges. You have continually advocated co-ordinated operations between artillery, infantry, tanks, reserves, communication, supply, troop morale and now aviation.'

'You mean put one of our own into the RFC and hopefully he will survive long enough to teach 'em to liaise with us. Don't we already have Australians in the corps?'

'Under British squadron commanders — one more Anzac to white-ant 'em won't hurt and may be the opportunity McAlister is looking for.'

'I do not run this division for the convenience of subalterns, Major.'

'Indeed not sir, but you like to place men where they are most suited and I think sending McAlister to the RFC will be in all our best interests.'

'I have colonels to spare for that sort of analysis.'

'Exactly, sir, but they may be told what people want them to hear — and may be tempted to tell you what they think you want to hear. McAlister is nothing if not honest. He'll give a candid bottom-up appraisal. He will experience the problems first hand from an operational officer's perspective.'

'If he lives long enough. As you said, longevity is not something the RFC is noted for. Why else are they crying out for volunteers now?'

'And life in the trenches is a safe place, sir?'

'That is something I hope to alter. Headlong charges over open territory through barbed-wire into machinegun fire aren't going to win this war. We have to start thinking a lot harder and acting a lot smarter.'

'McAlister is a bright lad, General — and he's a survivor.'

'Very well, Major. Send our young hero to flying school. Now we have a parade to prepare for. His Majesty is due next week...Oh and Blake,' the general added as Blake turned to leave, 'keep track of McAlister will you. I'd like him to stay in touch and let us know what he's up to.'

'I take this is not social, sir. You want his assessment of the RCF's potential and limitations.'

'Exactly, I expect we shall be using the AFC, but it is early days yet and I want to know everything about the corps when it's needed.'

General Monash was correct that the Australian Flying Corps was in its infancy, but he was a far-thinking man ready to exploit any opportunity should it arise. Many high-command officers thought of aviation as no more than a courier service, which shot down the occasional observational balloon, but Monash had other ideas.

'Does that also mean an assessment of the blokes running the show?' Blake asked.

'Especially that.'

Callan didn't object when Blake told him he'd 'volunteered' for the RFC. He said goodbye to Robert who was now a platoon commander and happy to stay that way. Callan then packed his kit and missed King George V inspecting the Anzacs on Salisbury Plain. Callan wasn't particularly sorry about the parade, which he considered a waste of time. Thousands of men spending untold hours polishing their boots and pressing their uniforms just to stand around for hours waiting for a bunch of big-wigs to ride past didn't make any sense to him. Strangely, Monash, who seemed to be such a down-to-earth general, set great store in pomp and ceremony.

*

During ground-school at the School of Military Aeronautics Oxford campus, Callan learnt very little about aviation. None of the instructors bothered with the theory of flight, but insisted trainees could disassemble and rebuild a Lewis gun while blindfolded. As a decorated veteran, Callan impressed his fellow cadets in that respect. Whereas the Lewis gun was the main airborne weapon, Callan still thought it would have been more useful if someone had explained exactly how a plane stayed in the air and, more importantly — how he could keep it there.

Nevertheless after a month he was issued with flying helmet, goggles, gauntlets, severe weather clothing, boots and a couple of engineering text books. He was then packed off to Brooklands Aerodrome in Surrey where he joined other eager young men from all corners of the empire who'd been lured by the glamour and thrill of aviation. They were to discover there was very little glamour involved, but thrills aplenty.

Callan completed fifteen hours training in a temperamental pusher-prop Maurice Farman II Shorthorn. It was a pig to fly and known as 'Rumpety' because its engine vibrated so badly. Callan's initial airborne sensations were joy, fear, discomfort and intense concentration. After two hours dual circuit training and a particularly robust landing, Callan's Canadian instructor tapped him on the shoulder.

'I spent six months at the front, was shot down twice and yet survived. The last thing I want is you killing me, Callan, so off you go by yourself. Have a crack at some take-offs and landings and do try to say in one piece, buddy.'

That was the last dual flight for Callan. He flew thirteen more solo hours, watched three pilots die in accidents and a dozen more carted off to hospital in Hungry Lizzies. Just as he was getting used to the sheer exhilaration and accomplishment of flying by himself, Callan lost control once on landing when a freak cross-wind tipped his plane onto its wingtip. After the aircraft cart-wheeled spectacularly, Callan walked from the wreckage with only a few bruises and wounded pride.

'Don't worry, old fellow,' Callan's instructor said. 'Prangs are a rite-of-passage around here. Most fellas crash a Rumpety before they finish here, but I think I'll recommend you for higher training before you cause any more damage.'

Higher training, as the name suggested, was bigger and better and more enjoyable than Callan could have envisaged. He soon soloed in the Avro 504 bi-plane which was a delight after the ground-seeking Shorthorn. Previously Callan had not flown above two thousand feet or gone beyond sight of the aerodrome. The 504 climbed to eight thousand feet in ten minutes, rolled and looped with relative ease and was not prone to the instant stalls and subsequent spins of the Shorthorn.

Callan also mastered formation flight, navigation and aerial gunnery with a Lewis gun bolted to the top wing enabling the weapon to shoot over the prop using a lanyard attached to the trigger.

In November with sixty-five hours total flying experience and no aerodynamic theoretical knowledge whatsoever, Callan was presented with his wings. There was no graduation parade or ceremony, the squadron command simply handed the badge over, congratulated Callan and sent him back to war.

Callan sailed on a troop carrier belonging to the armada that crossed the Channel constantly to support the endless ravenous demands of war. Warships escorted the transport vessels alert for the ever present U-boat threat. St Omer, just a short drive from Calais, was the RFC HQ where Callan was assigned to a squadron somewhere south along the battled-scarred landscape that had once been picturesque, rural France.

'Goodness gracious, sir,' the orderly-room clerk declared as he processed Callan's paperwork. 'Someone is having a grand jest.'

'Just like this whole damned war,' Callan growled.

'Sorry, sir. It's just you've been assigned to Major Gene McAlister's auxiliary squadron. He's a Yank, you know.'

'I didn't know actually, but other than sharing a name, I am unaware we have anything in common.'

The harassed clerk didn't elaborate, but simply directed Callan to a truck, with orders to report to the Major on arrival.

'You leave in an hour, sir. Best grab a bacon sarnie and a cuppa at the Os' — dunno what's available en route.'

Taking the sergeant's advice, Callan also stuffed an apple, a tin of bully-beef and some biscuits into his pockets then filled his water canteen. Two enlisted men were already aboard the truck when Callan tossed his kit-bag into the back.

'Let me give you a 'and, sir,' one of the men said, proffering his arm.

'Thanks, I'm Lieutenant McAlister.'

'Yessir — 'eard there was a new occifer joinin' the squadron, you bein' the major's namesake an' all. I'm Charlie Patterson, armourer, and this is me mate Bill Simpson. 'E's an engine fitter. Back from leave we are, sir.'

'Pleased to meet you both, I'm sure I shall be relying on your skills for my life very shortly.'

'We do our very best to offer satisfaction, sir,' Simpson added cheerfully.

The driver arrived and checked all were on board.

'You can ride up front if you care to, sir,' he said.

'No thanks, I'd like to pick these blokes' brains and find out about the squadron.'

The driver saluted, cranked the truck's motor and they lurched away along a road that was little better than a dirt-track on the muddy side.

'So what's the squadron like?' Callan asked. 'They haven't even told me the number other than it's classed as auxiliary.'

'Oh, it don't 'ave no number sir,' Patterson explained. 'What wiv the RFC expandin' so quick, we ain't been given no designator yet. In fact we ain't actually wiv the RCF neiver, we're still with the GSC.'

'GSC?'

'Yes sir, the General Service Corps. We're a standby unit, but that don't mean we do much standin' by.'

'We plug 'oles like,' Simpson added. 'We go where there's a need.'

The two airmen explained Mac Squadron — as it was known until General Hugh Trenchard, officer commanding the RFC in France decided exactly where he wanted the squadron to fit into the system. One of Trenchard's reasons for keeping Mac Squadron as a separate unit was to use it as an independent combat proving ground for new aircraft types. Right then the squadron consisted of three flights:

- Fifteen brand new single-seat Sopwith Pup scouts (as fighter planes were known)
- Twenty equally new Bristol F.2. Fighter multi-roll twin-seat bi-planes
- Twelve Sopwith 1½ Strutters also used as bombers, ground-attack and reconnaissance work

The scouts not only clashed with the *Luftstreitkräfte* Fokkers in aerial dogfights, but acted as fighter escorts for the other planes during bombing raids. For such a newly formed unit the squadron had seen some action resulting in fuselages riddled with countless bullet holes, a dozen seriously wounded aircrew, but miraculously no deaths so far.

'We've got a lucky mascot see, sir,' Patterson said. 'Major Mac brought it over from the States. A squadron's gotta 'ave a mascot — stands to reason, don't it?'

'What sort of mascot?'

'That's a surprise, sir.'

'I can hardly wait.'

Callan was beginning to wonder whether the two airmen were entirely sane and what the rest of the squadron members were like.

Chapter 28 — McAlister's Squadron

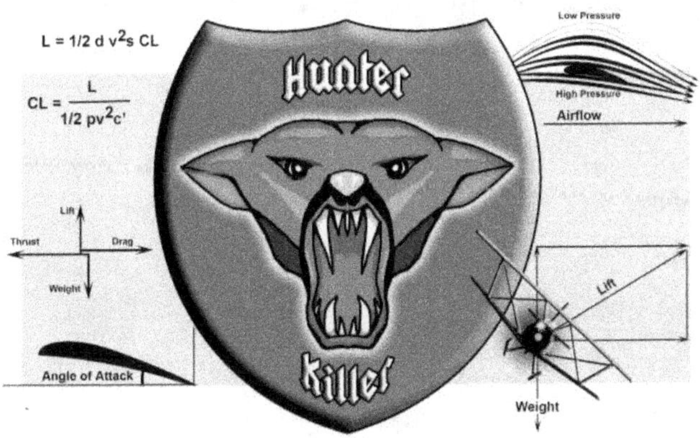

Mac Squadron HQ was situated in an abandoned farmhouse surrounded by tents and several barns now utilised as hangars or workshops. The planes were not lined in neat rows as Callan would have expected, but scattered randomly and many were hidden behind buildings and under trees.

'Makes the kites 'arder for the 'Un to see, dunnit sir?' Simpson explained. 'The Boche bastards likes to raid over the lines sometimes and cause mischief and the like.'

Each plane had a shield painted on the engine cowl depicting a snarling cat Callan took to be a panther. The squadron motto was also stencilled on the shields, with a brazen war-cry — Hunter-Killer!

Patterson and Simpson pointed to the Major's office. They checked with the orderly room staff and took Callan's kitbag to his assigned quarters.

The duty sergeant knocked on the CO's door.

'Replacement officer has arrived, sir,' he called.

'Show him in,' a muffled American voice replied.

Callan entered the spacious office to be confronted by a mountain lion, who challenged him with a snarl, arched back and bristling fur.

'Shit!'

'At ease, Claude,' the major drawled from his desk.

The beast obeyed and settled onto its haunches while eyeing Callan suspiciously. Meanwhile a tall man in his early forties rose and extended his hand.

'Howdy, partner,' he greeted with disarming familiarity. Senior officers usually addressed their underlings by their surnames. 'Don't worry, Claude ain't gonna bite.'

'That's very reassuring, sir,' Callan said uncertainly. 'I take it Claude is the squadron's lucky mascot Patterson and Simpson told me about and the inspiration for your fuselage design?'

'Sure is. My pa found him as a cub out in the New Mexico high country after his ma got shot by trappers,' Major McAlister grinned and nodded. 'Pa named the little mite after some bad-ass desperado called Claude Valentine he came up against back in the old days.'

He spoke with a relaxed western twang that put Callan immediately at ease.

'And you must be one of my kinfolk from down-under,' the major declared. 'Call me Gene in private and the mess. We fly-boys don't stand on ceremony — ain't got time for it.'

'Dunno about kin, sir...Gene. My guess is there are lots of McAlisters about.'

'Maybe, we'll chew the fat on that later. Meantime, what's your handle on aerody?'

Callan stared at him blankly.

'Language barrier, I guess,' Gene continued. 'Aerodynamics — I'll bet you ain't been told a darned thing.'

'No one seemed concerned about anything but engines, stretching wing fabric and Lewis guns at training school.'

'No sweat, I'll get one of the boys to give you the low-down. It's the first thing we normally do for new guys around here.'

Gene's attitude was like a breath of fresh air which reminded him of the Anzacs who respected those in authority only if they proved worthy, not as an automatic birthright. Callan discovered Gene's father, Sam McAlister had been a US Army scout during the frontier Indian wars. He'd had a passing acquaintance with a number of western legends including fellow scout Buffalo Bill Cody when they'd occasionally served together on the trail.

'I was brought up as a wrangler,' Gene explained. 'Practically born in the saddle. I remember Buffalo Bill stoppin' by our spread one time and recruited me for his Wild West show. I met up with Sam Cody when we toured Europe. Sam lived in England back then. He was the spittin' image of ol' Buffalo Bill and just as big a showman, but they weren't kin. Sam was into aviation in a big way, which started me off. My pa was always gettin' them two fellas mixed up. Shouldn't get 'em confused now, though. Sam killed hisself in an aero crash back in thirteen, but ol' Bill's still kicking on.'

Sharing the same name was not all the two men had in common. Callan and Gene chatted on about horses as they were both excellent riders. Callan explained about the walers and how he'd started the war as a private in the Sinai Desert. The squadron commander was in no particular hurry to do anything else. Gene had been shot down over no-man's land, but made it to safety, dragging a gun-shot leg. He now limped and used a cane.

'My combat flying days are over, I guess,' Gene reflected. 'I do training flights OK, but I dunno how I'll be back in the saddle out west when this shindig is over.'

Gene said a CO's job was mostly record-keeping anyway and a mass of paperwork demanded his attention, so Callan was dismissed and shown to his quarters by an orderly-room clerk.

Callan's tent-mate turned out to be a twenty year-old Kiwi lieutenant called Bruce Adamson who was also his theory-of-flight tutor. Bruce took his teaching duties seriously and had compiled comprehensive notes and diagrams explaining: lift, profile and induced drag, weigh and thrust equations, angle-of-attack, wing loading, camber and design, banking, skidding, stalling, streamlining, C-of-G and centre-of-pressure relationships, flight controls, wind, pressure and temperature effects and a host of other gems that opened Callan's eyes to the 'why' of aviation.

Callan learnt of Sir Isaac Newton and Thomas Bernoulli who were early movers-and-shakers in understanding the principles of flight.

'You won't learn it all in a day,' Bruce explained, 'but hopefully you'll live long enough for the facts to sink in. C'mon, that's enough for today — I'll show you how to get the kites started, then we'll grab a pint and I'll introduce you round.'

By early evening all the planes had returned and their pilots gathered around the bar in the officers' mess tent. Callan was first struck by how young they all were. Gene was the only pilot or observer older than twenty-five. Other specialist ground-crew officers like the equip-o, admin-o, transport and maintenance chiefs may have been in their thirties and forties, but the aircrew were all just kids.

Mac Squadron was a truly international affair including pilots and observers from all corners of the empire as well as several Yanks who'd been poached from the French *Lafayette Escadrille*. How Gene procured his skilled aviators remained a mystery, but bribing senior officers with vintage wine and classy French whores was a strong rumour. In any event no one asked questions, so no one was told lies.

Callan had heard aircrew could be aloof and unfriendly, but that didn't apply to Mac Squadron.

'Some blokes don't like to make friends,' Bruce said after his third pint. 'They're worried a chum might just get killed in the next dogfight. Mac's attitude is what-the-hell and likes everyone to get along fine.'

The following day, Callan received his baptism under fire...

*

Day One

Pre-dawn — breakfast and briefing — another ground assault was on, so Mac Squadron was ordered to destroy the German artillery spotter balloons. Ten Bristol Fighters were tasked to destroy the balloons with ten Pup escorts. They were shown their assigned sector co-ordinates and warned to be on the lookout for not only enemy scouts, but friendly planes that could be collision risks if they strayed off-course.

Dawn — planes armed and refuelled — ground-crew standing by to swing the props — take-off — watch out for Huns above and coming from the sun. Callan was Bruce's wing man and the formation's tail-end-Charlie.

Bruce and Callan were assigned two-seater Bristol Fighters with an observer-gunner to man the swivelling Lewis guns. It was Callan's first flight in a Bristol Fighter and his first flight into possible combat. Despite wanting his men to be friends, Gene didn't pair crews, but assigned pilots and observers ad hoc. He felt every man should be able to operate with any other person in the squadron. It also meant crews didn't form personal attachments and avoid the creation of 'good crews' and 'bad crews'.

The aerodrome was twenty miles behind the front and hopefully just beyond German artillery range so it took quarter of an hour to reach the battlefield and the guns were already blazing as five spotter balloons loomed into sight.

Callan's first image was the grey-brown scar that stretched endlessly to either side and forward for several miles. Every tree, bush, meadow, farmhouse, barn, church and home had been pulverised into a quagmire that had once been rich pasture and fertile agricultural fields. Thin black lines snaked over the shattered land, marking the trenches in irregular, jagged veins of abject human misery. The line of desolation stretched five hundred miles from the Belgian Coast to the Swiss Border.

Heavy guns roared from both sides and shells exploded, mushrooming into balls of smoke, shrapnel and ear-splitting blast-waves. As they crossed no-man's land, Callan saw black spots speckling the terrain. He knew they were infantrymen, but whether they were dead or alive was impossible to say. So far Mac Squadron flew above small arms fire, but once into German territory howitzers opened up. Shells exploded between the planes, although the squadron's luck held.

Only the flight leaders' planes had observer-operated two-way wirelesses installed. They were another recent innovation, still unreliable and limited by weight, short range, a long trailing aerial and the need for a Morse-key operator. So Callan just had to follow along, doing his best. As the Bristol Fighters reached machinegun range the German spotters leapt from their gondolas and parachuted to safety. All the planes were fitted with another mechanical inspiration, synchronised guns that fired through the propeller with far more accuracy than the wing-mounted Lewis guns.

While the Pups clawed the sky for altitude the Bristol Fighters remained at three thousand feet while their pilots selected a target, firing in short bursts. Immediately one hydrogen balloon exploded into a massive fireball. Callan missed on his first approach. Although he'd completed aerial gunnery with flying colours during training, the synchronised guns took some getting used to.

He banked the plane steeply as he flashed past, but his observer was an old hand and managed to get a burst off that struck home. Callan felt the heat of burning hydrogen as he turned the plane looking for a new target, but all the balloons had been reduced to flaming rags that drifted earthwards dragged by the weight of their tethering cables and copper communication wires.

The flight commander turned his Bristol Fighter for home and the others followed in tight formation just as a *Luftstreitkräfte jagdstaffel* of a dozen Albatros bi-planes pounced almost as if the observation balloons were a decoy. The rat-tat-tat of machinegun fire chattered above the roaring aero-engines. Callan's gunner blazed away, the spent shell-casings spraying into the front cockpit. Luckily Callan's thick leather flying kit protected him although the red-hot cartridges singed black marks into the sleeves.

Then the Pups dived into the fray. In the ensuing aerial melee, the Bristol Fighter flight leader took the opportunity to lead his planes out of harm's way — well, not entirely. He couldn't resist the temptation to harass the enemy once more.

As they approached the forward German positions he banked his plane south, running along the trench-line. Callan saw infantrymen spread all over no-man's-land, but so far none appeared to have made it to the German trenches. There was no doubting the flight-commander's intention. His plane descended to only feet above the enemy before raking the trenches with his forward guns while the observers picked off any targets that presented themselves.

The remaining Bristol Fighters flew in line-astern formation, spraying the Germans with a continual lethal stream of red-hot lead. Tracer and Buckingham incendiary bullets were other innovations, making machinegun fire far more accurate although it appeared the Germans were yet to adopt the technology. The planes also carried two twenty pound bombs each which the observers armed and dropped from the rear cockpit. As Callan's plane was last in line, he saw the bombs erupting, adding to the gouts of mud, equipment and human body-parts churned up and sprayed above the trenches.

And then it was all over. With engines roaring at full throttle the Bristol Fighters peeled away to the right and home base. Callan had been airborne less than an hour when he landed with his grinning observer patting him on the shoulder.

'Good show, old boy,' the observer yelled giving an enthusiastic 'thumbs-up' as the prop clattered to a stop. 'First flight is the hardest. It's all downhill from here.'

That might have been an unfortunate choice of words for an aviator to use, but Callan appreciated the support anyway. Afterwards both airmen and ground mechanics inspected the aircraft. Callan was surprised to discover a number of bullet-holes in the canvas fuselage and flying surfaces.

'I had no idea we'd been hit,' Callan said.

'Best that way,' the observer replied cheerfully. 'Things like that can make a bloke jumpy.'

The Pups landed shortly afterwards. Most bore battle-scars while one of the engines belched smoked and spewed oil all over the cockpit wind-screen, so the pilot made his approach by crabbing the plane sideward before kicking it straight with the rudder pedals at the last minute. The landing was hard and bouncy. The main undercarriage ripped away with the impact and the fuselage scraped along the ground, gouging a path through the grass. Fire trucks raced to the rescue, but the pilot jumped from the cockpit unharmed. His goggles dripped with oil and how he found his way back at all was a commendable achievement.

That afternoon the remaining half of Mac Squadron flew across the lines to inspect the results of the morning's work and take photographs. They returned with several planes damaged after losing two kites over no-man's land. To illustrate the battlefield's fluidness and confusion, both crews survived and while one pilot and observer were rescued by Indian ground troops, the other crew was captured by a German infantry patrol.

*

Day Two

'How did the push go?' Callan asked during the pre-dawn briefing.

The previous day's reconnaissance had been inconclusive.

'Satisfactory by all accounts,' Gene beamed. 'Our guys took the forward trenches and are holding on to those positions so far.'

'Yeah, but we've seen this all before,' one of the Yanks protested. 'The Boche will just bring up artillery and blast 'em out of there.'

'That's what we've been ordered to prevent. We'll get all the kites airborne at sun-up. Pups: escort — Bristol Fighter: bombs and cameras — one-and-a-halfers payload six twenty-pounders each — High command wants as many machines as possible in the air all along the front line from Verdun to the Somme.'

The task was two-fold: bomb the enemy artillery emplacements and photograph troop movements that might herald a counter attack. The 3-D cameras had been around since the American Civil War, taking two shots almost instantaneously to give a 3-D effect.

The planes were up as the sun cracked the horizon, revealing a cloud base of less than a thousand feet which meant the squadron would cross enemy lines within small-arms range. Added to that, visibility was reduced in passing rain showers.

The aircraft instrumentation was by no means standard as the aircraft had been procured from various sources. Whereas Gene had been cunning enough to enlist premier pilots, he had to take whatever planes he was given. Callan's Bristol Fighter was equipped with an airspeed indicator, magnetic compass, slip indicator and an engine RPM gauge. Probably the most useful of these was the slip-indicator which was just a dampened plumb-bob. Callan used his rudder pedals to keep the bob central on the gauge and achieve the best aircraft performance.

Bad weather might have hidden the squadron from prying German eyes, but Callan was now faced with a phenomenon that killed more aircrew than enemy action. Low visibility brought ice which formed on the wing struts and wire bracing, quickly building up and weighing the aircraft down. Subsequently the formation broke up and many planes returned to base — those flown by the most experienced pilots who knew a busted flush when they saw one.

Callan pressed on...

Chapter 29 — First Blood

The observer shook Callan's shoulder indicating it was time to turn around, but the rain front had blown through and the skies cleared. Only scattered showers persisted which were easy enough to navigate around. Callan pointed to the camera making it clear he wanted the observer ready to take photographs.

Callan saw trees and grass fields so he estimated he was at least five miles behind the German forward trenches which were surrounded by a stark muddy landscape. Next he spotted a railway terminal just under a mile ahead. Not only that, but several locomotives were lined up in sidings and troops could be plainly seen disembarking and forming into their respective units. At first the Germans took little interest in the Bristol Fighter — one plane looked much like another to them and they may not have seen the markings in the gloomy morning light.

'Right!' Callan yelled to his observer. 'One pass is all we'll get. Toss the bombs overboard as quickly as you can.'

His words were whisked away by the slipstream, but he observer nodded.

Callan banked the plane sharply and lined up on the central track. Steam engines and rolling stock lay ahead in orderly Teutonic rows. Callan dived as low as he dared which alerted the soldiers. Some — the smart ones — dived for cover, but others unshouldered their rifles and began loading the magazines. A few shots came Callan's way, but most were too late.

'Now!'

The bombs were secured in racks inside the rear cockpit, but the observer heaved them overboard with remarkable speed, so all six landed within two hundred yards of one another. Callan turned the plane once more.

'Get as many photos as you can,' he bellowed.

One pass was all they could hope for. As the smoke and dust cleared, Callan saw they caused commendable havoc. Bodies lay sprawled on the ground. A great deal of equipment had been damaged and some was ablaze. This time the troops were better prepared and a hail of bullets zinged towards the Bristol Fighter.

Callan lowered the nose and fired a short burst into the main troop concentration, but was forced to level off for his crewman to take his photos. Even Callan knew it was time to make himself scarce before the Germans called up their fighter *jagdstaffel*. The observer gave an enthusiastic thumbs-up, although Callan wasn't sure whether he was happy to be leaving, acknowledging the carnage below or he'd taken some good pictures.

Callan simply turned west and hoped he'd pick up some landmarks once they'd crossed the front. Whether other Mac Squadron planes had continued into enemy territory was unclear. Callan certainly saw no other aircraft for a few minutes, but a form gradually appeared just below the cloud base. Even at a distance Callan identified the aircraft as a German *Eindecker* monoplane.

The other machine was cruising at a slower speed than the Bristol Fighter. Callan set full power and gradually overtook the *Eindecker*. The plane was armed with a forward facing synchronised machinegun and had been devastatingly successful in shooting down allied aircraft during 1914-1915. It was now outclassed by newer machines and usually played a reconnaissance role.

As Callan closed in, the German pilot sensed his presence. Callan saw him turn and stare in disbelief before diving his plane to the ground. Callan followed and easily caught up. He was only twenty yards behind the *Eindecker* when he pressed the trigger. The first burst sailed ahead of the target — the second ripped the tail to shreds. Callan gave one further blast that hit mid fuselage.

Yet the German pilot still hung on. Struggling desperately at the controls, he managed to control the plane into a lazy left-hand, descending turn. The flight controls were badly damaged and it was all the pilot could do to prevent his machine spiralling in to ground.

The *Eindecker* hit the ground heavily, ripping one wing backwards as it dug into the quagmire. But the plane was not entirely destroyed and the pilot struggled with his seat belt to escape the wreck. Callan swept past and was amazed to see the German pilot raise a salute. More astonishingly Callan's observer saluted back.

Ruddy hell, do these blokes think they're playing sport — well, we'll see about that.

Callan gunned the engine with full-throttle, pulled up then let the wing drop just below the cloud base. He levelled the wings then dived towards the stricken *Eindecker* and, dammit the pilot was sitting on the undamaged wing — still waving.

Callan lined the plane and pressed the trigger.

The Bristol Fighter's machineguns blazed into the downed plane. Bullets tore the pilot to shreds and ignited the fuel tank. If the bullets hadn't killed him, the explosion surely incinerated him. Callan didn't wait to see the *Eindecker* reduce to ashes. He was pretty sure he'd done enough for one day and turned the Bristol Fighter west once more. As Callan turned for home, German infantrymen swarmed towards the wreck. They fired a few parting shots, but quickly saw they were simply wasting ammunition. As they converged on the smouldering plane it was obvious there was nothing to be done for the pilot.

Callan turned to the observer and gave a grin, but the crewman simple glared back with a look of black disgust.

What..?

Callan shrugged and concentrated on navigation. He crossed the front without incident, but had no idea where he might be. His observer, who was also the map-reader, was singularly unhelpful. Callan was seriously thinking of finding a field, landing and asking directions, when he spotted a church spire, which Bruce had explained was a useful orientation marker.

Gene McAlister watched the last Bristol Fighter touch-down and taxi to the marshalling area. He was interested to know precisely where young Callan had disappeared to before giving him a bollocking about staying with the flight. Playing lone wolf was just about the quickest way Gene knew to die on the front. It appeared Callan's observer felt the same, because they were in a heated discussion as they walked to the de-briefing tent.

'All I'm saying is that was damned unsporting. The fellow didn't have a chance and he wasn't armed.'

'He was a German. I'd have taken him prisoner if I could, but how the hell was I going to do that — lower a tow-rope?'

'What will the Boche think of us..?'

'I don't give a damn what they think. They're the enemy, man. If I can't capture them, then I'll ruddy well kill them. You did a grand job with the bombs and how many Huns do you reckon we killed then?'

'They were armed and firing at us.'

'I daresay, but the Boche is now one plane and one pilot less — one less resource to throw at us tomorrow.'

'Okay, you guys,' Gene said, 'what the hell's this all about?'

'Just a difference of opinion on tactics, sir,' Callan said with rather too much of a sneer in Gene's opinion.

The major turned to Callan's observer, who started to protest, but changed his mind.

'Right make your reports and I'll look 'em over.'

'We need to develop our photographs, sir,' Callan said. 'There's a build up about ten miles behind the German line. We dropped our ordnance on 'em, but there are still plenty left.'

'Battalion...Brigade..?'

'Division I fear, sir.'

'Do you have a complaint, Eric?' Gene asked the observer.

'No sir, like Mr McAlister says it's just a discussion about tactics.'

'Right then, I don't want to hear any more about this — whatever it is. If you have a problem, you come and see me, understand?'

'Yessir.'

'Good man, now get those shots developed and straight to the intel-o for analysis. Callan, you come with me.'

Once inside Gene's office, the CO didn't waste time.

'Take a seat and tell me what happened.'

Callan told him.

'You do see that if we start killing downed Germans they might be tempted to do the same to us,' Gene observed.

'Look, if he'd been on our side of the line, I'd have left him to be captured by our ground forces. Our job is to kill as many Germans as we can so they get jacked off enough to surrender.'

'Do you like killing, Callan?'

'Funny, you're the second person to ask me that. My old platoon sergeant Archie Blake wondered the same thing. The answer is, I don't particularly like killing people, but I seem to be good at it.'

'Many of the fellas here won't like your methods. They still have a sense of honour.'

'Honour — have any of 'em ever been in the trenches?'

'I doubt it.'

'You ever heard of a place called Lone Pine, Gene?'

'Can't say as I have.'

'It started off as just another Gallipoli ridge with a pine tree sticking out on top. When I got there Johnny Turk was entrenched all along the ridge-line. I was a signals courier for Colonel Monash when Billy Birdwood decided to attack the place. I was right where they planned the attack at the time — nowhere near my own brigade. Some smart-arsed subaltern ordered me to join his platoon for the attack.'

'You could have refused if he wasn't authorised.'

Callan shrugged.

'I was a corporal and it was just as risky there as on the left flank with Colonel Monash's brigade. The subbie got shot straight away, so I led his men by default. When we got to the trenches, Johnny Turk was still reeling from the artillery bombardment, but it didn't take long for him to recover. We had to bash in beams and fortifications covering the trenches while the Turks fired up at us. We held the place all right, but it took four days before the Turks stopped counter-attacking. Four days of close-up fighting with bayonets and hand-made bombs because we'd run out of grenades. Do you know what the best weapon was?'

Gene shook his head.

'A flamin' trench club. I found one on a dead Turk. It was like those maces knights in storybooks used — a spiked metal ball on a stick. I lost count of how many skulls I caved in. Bodies filled the trenches to the top.'

'So what you're saying is there are no rules in war.'

'I'm saying there's no honour. You do what you have to do to win. If that's not pretty enough for your private-school boys or offends their delicate sensibilities — well tough luck to them.'

'Is that what the MC's for?'

'No. I was awarded the DSM for killing Turks I had no particular argument with. The MC's for killing Irish nationalists I had no nothing against either.'

'The observers may not feel comfortable flying with you,' Gene suggested.

'I would have thought they'll do what they're ruddy well told.'

'You've only been here a couple of days, but shaping up to be too good a pilot for me to ground you, so maybe I'll think of something else...'

Dear Ma and Pa

I'm sorry it's been a time since I wrote, but this war continues to keep me fully occupied and therefore out of mischief. The winter weather is a shocker. The locals are calling it the worst and coldest winter anyone can remember, but we pilots or 'fly-boys' as our CO calls us have more time on our hands. The mechanics have to start the engines every day to keep oil running through the systems and stop them seizing up.

Our main task is scouring the area for firewood which is becoming a never-ending arduous task. Thank heaven for our flying kit. It's especially designed for insulation at high altitudes. Now we have to wear coats and fur-lines boots in the mess tent which is often as cold as an open cockpit at ten thousand feet!

Gene McAlister is our squadron commander who thinks we're distantly related. His dad was an Indian scout back in the Wild West days. He's a nice bloke and his men all like and respect him. He has a way of getting things done without being a pain about it.

I am now flying single-seat Sopwith Pup Scout planes, which are brilliant machines and quite the match for anything the Germans have although there are rumours of new planes being developed all the time. Some of our kites are due for replacement soon. Each new design flies higher and faster than its predecessor. (I don't know whether the censors will take that bit out).

My wounds have healed completely and I am now fighting fit, which is probably a good choice of words considering where I am. Try not to worry about me, I'm looking after myself and the food here is fine.

Give my love to Henrietta and baby George, who's probably toddling by now. I received a brief letter from Robert and he's doing well although he hates the cold weather.

Love from

Callan

Callan hadn't wanted to concern his parents about his wounds, but the Army had sent them a telegram, so he made light of it as best he could to put their minds at ease. He didn't bother telling them about the reconnaissance flight and the arrival of German troop-trains, but he wrote a detailed account to Archie Blake with whom he corresponded regularly. And the allied generals were pleased. Three French divisions were rushed to reinforce the front-line, which held against a number of German counter-attacks with the usual mass-carnage.

In his letters home, Callan also neglected to mention his first dog-fight...

*

It'd been a week after Gene had transferred Callan to the single-seat fighters to avoid any conflict with observers. In fact the opinion on Callan's battle attitude was mixed. By then many aircrew were so disenchanted, they also considered the only good German was a dead one.

The morning was clear and crisp with frost coating the landscape. Take-off was slippery, but soon the Pups were airborne and climbing to ten thousand feet. It was Callan's fourth outing in the beautifully responsive fast machine. On those past occasions cumulous clouds had billowed up forcing the pilots to pick their way between the storm cells to gain altitude. Impressive as this was to be above the cloud layer, the Pups saw no action and had to carefully descend through small breaks to return to the aerodrome.

Today the Bristol Fighters and one-and-a-halfers flew below in tight formation ready to shoot down artillery-spotter balloons, bomb the enemy's heavy guns and take reconnaissance photographs and generally make life unpleasant for the Germans.

This time the Albatros scouts were waiting.

A *Luftstreitkräfte jagdstaffel* loitered high over no-man's land, ready to swoop down on the approaching aircraft formation. A flight of German fighters dived towards the lower planes while the other half turned to tackle the Pup scouts. Some Pups chased the Albatros machines to guard the Bristol Fighters and one-and-a-halfers, while the remainder, including Callan, stayed at altitude to face the Germans.

Once the first bullets sprayed through the air, the dog-fight became an individual struggle between single planes taking any opportunity to surprise the enemy. Machines flashed past Callan from front and rear as friend and foe joined the fray.

An Albatros dived past with machineguns blazing. Callan thought he felt the bullets zing through his wing-struts only inches from the cockpit. He rammed the throttle fully forward. The engine roared and as the aircraft staggered for further altitude he continued to hold back pressure on the control-stick until he was inverted. He righted his plane, pushed forward on the stick until he was weightless. He'd gained precious altitude over his opponent who was now five hundred feet below him.

Using the altitude to gain speed, Callan aimed his plane towards the enemy. He was unaware of the melee around him where aircraft swarmed like enraged hornets in deadly combat. The enemy Albatros loomed ever-larger in Callan's gun-sight. The Pups were armed with a single Vickers prop-synchronised machine-gun — a reliable and accurate weapon.

Callan sprayed the Albatros with lead. The plane immediately erupted into flame and spiralled almost lazily earthwards. Callan saw a tiny dot drop from the doomed plane's cockpit. Only balloon observers were issued with parachutes in those days, so the German chose a quick death rather than being burnt alive in his machine.

But there was no time to reflect. An Albatros had latched onto Callan's tail and was closing fast. Callan didn't hear the guns, but several bullets ripped through his wing fabric. Luckily the damage was not enough to greatly affect the Pup's handling characteristics or performance.

Callan's plane was at maximum speed which he used once more to pull upwards, roll and turn to face the enemy. The manoeuvre was developed by German ace, Max Immelmann and was a great way of getting out of trouble, although not all pilots found it easy to execute and often stalled their planes into a spin which needed serious altitude for recovery.

Callan then found himself flying head on towards his adversary. In an aerial game of chicken the planes converged at two-hundred miles an hour. Callan held it as a matter of personal pride not to flinch — maybe he was just bloody-minded. At the last moment the German plane peeled away and pulled up, using his airspeed to gain altitude. Callan lost sight of that particular aircraft and cast around for others.

He dived back into the fray and chased an Albatros away from one of the Pups which was in deep trouble. As Callan flashed past, the pilot acknowledged with a thumbs-up.

Amid the whirling confusion, several planes spiralled to earth, smashing into the mud of no-man's land. Callan was unable to see whether they were German or British machines. With no immediate targets at hand, Callan flew towards the lower formation and damaged an Albatros which harried the Bristol

Fighters. But the Germans didn't have it all their own way. The observers blazed away with the swivel mounted Lewis guns, which often drove the Albatroses off.

The Pup flight had lost all cohesion and Callan found himself seeking a fight wherever he found it. The Pup had an airborne endurance of around three hours, but with the max-revs engine-straining flying of a dog-fight, it lasted barely an hour. Fortunately the Bristol Fighters and one-and-a-halfers' work was done and they were returning to base.

Mac Squadron lost two planes that day. One of the Bristol Fighter crews was presumed killed although a Pup pilot turned up in the afternoon having raced from one artillery shell crater to another, through barb-wire and back to the allied trenches under constant enemy fire.

Callan's plane was indeed damaged, but the ground crew, including Patterson and Simpson, agreed they'd patch it up in no time. The squadron flew a dozen other sorties before inclement weather grounded the planes. Callan shot down two more enemy aircraft — an Albatros and a Fokker scout.

'Looks like you're on your way to becoming an ace,' Bruce Adamson remarked when Callan returned from his mission.

'Yeah mate, it must be all that aerody you taught me.'

Chapter 30 — Ivy Goes to War

D'vere-Brown Country Residence, Shropshire — Late Winter 1917

'I do not know what to do with that girl, Dottie,' Meredith D'vere-Brown declared as she took morning tea with her good friend Lady Dorothie Fielding. 'She mopes around all day and barely utters a civil word to anyone and ignores me altogether.'

'Ah, but you have committed the unforgivable, have you not, Meredith dear?'

'If you mean forbidding her to communicate with that Anzac boy, then yes.'

Lady Fielding merely nodded and helped herself to another scotch finger biscuit which was very much her favourite. She spied Ivy through the French windows, strolling on the front lawn with a distant expression.

'Do you know even after I expressly forbade her, the little minx actually tried to write letters to Callan McAlister in secret? Luckily I instructed the servants to be vigilant for such mischief and I intercepted the missives.'

'And what did this correspondence contain?'

'Oh, just schoolgirl nonsense. The point is her intended beau never received those letters and has not written in return. Now she feels she has been spurned by her one true love.'

'Oh, haven't we all from time to time?' Lady Fielding observed urbanely.

'She needs some purpose in life instead of mooning around here dreaming about some Australian boy who is probably dead by now. I wish there was something I could do to buck Ivy up, but that young New South Welshman just won't do.'

'That is rather harsh, Meredith dear. Although perhaps I can offer an idea that may be constructive. I know I do not normally take gels under twenty-three, but Ivy does have her first-aid certificate and I understand she can drive an automobile.'

'Yes, she learnt in Ireland and has subsequently obtained her driving licence. I thought it would be a good diversion, but the elation was short lived.'

'Excellent! I would like her to join FANY.'

'Goodness me, Dottie — an ambulance driver! Wouldn't that be awfully dangerous?'

'Not at all, she'll probably never leave England, but we're always short of suitable gels. They have a habit of falling in love and getting married.'

'That is precisely what Humphrey and I are trying to avoid.'

'Not to worry, Ivy has yet to reach her majority and so must obtain your permission. I will keep a close eye on her in the meantime.'

Meredith still looked unconvinced.

'Look at her,' Lady Fielding said, pointing through the French-window. 'She's pining away here when she could be doing her bit to beat the Hun. I promise I'll see Ivy comes to no harm and

I'm not unconnected in London. I should be able to introduce her to some suitable prospects.'

The fact that most of the suitable prospects were being slaughtered in droves at the front appeared to be lost on Lady Fielding for the moment. Meredith D'vere-Brown obviously thought the same. But Lady Fielding wasn't really interested in match-making on Ivy's behalf. When she heard how her old chum, Meredith and her daughter had made their perilous way from Australia, Lady Fielding decided to actively head-hunt Ivy as an ideal candidate for her team.

Young, intelligent and cool in the face of danger were all qualities required for the First Aid Nursing Yeomanry. The British High Command in its usual infuriatingly pig-headed, closed-minded way had rejected FANY's services, declaring women had no place in war. The French and Belgians had no such out-dated prejudices however and accepted help wherever they found it.

FANY's main hospital was in Calais where wounded soldiers were delivered from clearing stations at the northern end of the front. There was no shortage of casualties to fill the hospital beds and many British and imperial troops were taken to Calais along with the French and Belgians.

Whereas Ivy didn't exactly embrace the notion, she didn't refuse either. Colonel D'vere-Brown raised no objections, but he too thought Ivy would serve with one of the UK based units, which would occupy her admirably.

'You speak French do you not, my dear?' Lady Fielding asked on the train-ride to London.

'Yes, Lady Fielding, but I fear I am rusty.'

'No matter, you will have time to brush up. I have text books and my other gels will get you chatting like a native in no time.'

'Very well, Lady Fielding, but I wish to be known simply as Ivy Brown, otherwise it's such a mouthful.'

'Of course — what a sensible young woman you are.'

Ivy didn't give Lady Fielding's comments much thought at the time, thinking wounded French soldiers would be evacuated to England along with British and imperial men. But after only a few weeks training, Ivy realised that if she pushed hard enough, she could well be posted to France. So she baled Lady Fielding up at the first opportunity.

'But I assured your mother, you would remain in England, dear. Do you not think my gels are not just as important here as on the Continent.'

'Absolutely, Lady Fielding, but I feel I can be of so much use to those poor boys at the front. Please, I absolutely have to go and do my bit.'

'What will I tell your mother?'

'Why nothing, Lady Fielding,' Ivy said artfully.

'Would that not be dishonest?'

'Absolutely not. It's only dishonest if you tell a lie. Saying nothing isn't lying and who knows when you'll see Mama again.'

'I will give the matter some thought.'

After a week's badgering from Ivy, Lady Fielding relented and assigned Ivy to France. Ivy packed a grip with two starched uniforms, underclothes, toiletries, nightgown, a spare pair of boots and very little else except her satchel of art and writing materials. Leaving Lady Fielding to wrestle with her moral dilemma, Ivy arrived in France just as the Allied April offensive began. The advance started around an ancient city called Arras, which had already been all but demolished by the ravages of war.

*

Flanders, April 1917

Sleet splattered the ambulance as Ivy peered forward through an inadequately small windscreen with ineffective wipers. The truck swerved in mud and only stayed on the track because of tyre ruts gouged by other vehicles making the road more like a railway. As she approached Arras ruined silhouettes of once proud structures loomed into grey grotesque images of three years devastation. Few buildings still stood and most were roofless ruined shells.

Soldiers, trucks, mule supply trains, artillery pieces all cluttered the approach to the city. Tanks lined the way in places, their crews brewing tea and smoking using the massive steel juggernauts as wind breaks. The tanks weren't particularly new, but the army was only now working out how best to use them. Right then the mud lay so thick even tank-tracks failed to gain traction.

Redcaps manned every intersection directing traffic — efficiently in some cases while others only created further congestion. French, British, Canadian and Anzac battalions were all involved in the allied advance. On seeing a battalion of Australians, Ivy thought of Callan — perhaps he would be among them — before dismissing the idea as nonsense.

There must be millions of soldiers in France. He could be anywhere — why hasn't he answered my letters. I explained why I was so cool when he left Ireland, surely he will forgive me. It's been a full year.

Ivy's thoughts returned to the job at hand when she reached the clearing station. It was her first assignment alone after being shown the ropes by experienced FANY veterans.

The Allied advance had started well although losses were horrendous. Now parallel wooden planks lay along the road to stop the trucks becoming bogged. Ivy smelt the trench stench before she saw the aid station. Mercifully the cold snap had refrozen the countless decaying corpses half buried in no-man's land, but hundreds of thousands of reeking, unwashed bodies, foul latrines and rotting garbage still lingered with an intensity that was almost visible.

How can there be so many sandbags in the whole world? There can't be a beach left anywhere...Dear God, Callan must endure this every day...if he is still alive...

Ivy closed her mind to that terrible realisation. To date she'd been so utterly occupied with her duties, thoughts of Callan were kept mercifully in abeyance.

She stopped the ambulance in a parking bay next to the clearing post marquee. There was insufficient room inside to accommodate all the wounded, so men lay in stretcher lines outside, tended by others with lesser wounds. Heartbreakingly many men sat in glum silence with their eyes bandaged, blinded by mustard gas. Others suffered from gangrene, missing limbs, burns and terrible disfigurement. Those most badly burnt were aircrews from downed planes although they were rare as most pilots and gunners died when they crashed.

Oh what have these poor boys done to suffer so? I don't know where you are, Lord, but you certainly aren't in Flanders, whatever the padres say.

As orderlies loaded those scheduled for evacuation into the ambulance, Ivy helped two gas-victims into the front cabin. She lit a cigarette for each man, who bore their torment stoically, remaining inconceivably cheerful. They started when German artillery shells exploded so close by, the shock-wave shook the truck and tugged at everyone's clothing. Seconds later Allied batteries opened up, trading salvo for salvo.

There were no orderlies to spare, so the men aboard would have to endure the bone-rattling ride back to Calais via St Omer unattended other than their walking wounded comrades who squashed into the truck between stretchers. The weather had cleared when she arrived at St Omer. Ivy knew the town was the RCF HQ where planes roared overhead in their hundreds whenever the weather permitted.

While Ivy arranged for her truck to be refuelled and procured food and water for her charges, a Sopwith Pup flight touched down in formation, bouncing across the grass which had only recently thawed enough to making landings possible. The pilots did not leave their machines.

A petrol truck rolled out to the planes which were immediately refuelled while armourers reloaded the planes' single-mounted machineguns. Mess orderlies brought the pilots tea and sandwiches and then a few aviators jumped from their cockpits to relieve themselves before clambering back aboard.

In less than half-an-hour the planes were airborne once more and heading for Arras. At the same time Ivy started the ambulance and drove north to Calais. She'd been too preoccupied to take any notice of the planes or the men who flew them.

St Omer was a mad-house of planes and support equipment. Twenty five squadrons were deployed there and at surrounding satellite strips to assist the ground forces at Arras. Most of the planes and pilots were new and they were being shot out of the sky within weeks or even days by the more experienced and better trained German pilots, although they only mustered five *Jastas*.

Ivy wasn't interested in the RFC, but kept an eye out for Australian units. She knew Callan had been associated with General Monash's 3rd Infantry Division, which could be anywhere. But as the battle around Arras raged Lieutenant General Sir Alexander Godley's II Anzac Corps arrived, including Major General John Monash's 3rd Infantry Division.

Yet Ivy's duties still remained with the French and Belgian wounded, while regular army medical units handled Imperial casualties. That didn't mean there weren't thousands of Australian troops in the area and whenever Ivy had a chance, she'd ask diggers if they'd heard of Callan McAlister. The answer was always an apologetic, 'Sorry miss, but I'll keep an eye for him.'

It's like looking for a needle in a haystack.

As the weather improved, engineers began tunnelling towards the German lines. Signal Corps technicians laid communication cables as they went. It was terrifying and desperate work. The signallers were in constant danger of cave-ins and attacks from German engineers, whose own tunnels often broke into Allied ones, resulting in hand-to-hand fighting in pitch blackness. One of those listed as missing, presumed dead, was Captain Bainbridge-Smyth.

But Ivy was once again diverted. In mid April General Robert Nivelle launched the French 3rd Army at the Germans holding a ridgeline along the Aisne River.

Against a continual background rumble of artillery, Ivy worked for ten days without rest as the butcher's bill soared and the French were beaten to a standstill. Aid stations were so overwhelmed, wounded men died before they could be treated. Surgeons, orderlies and nurses worked until they collapsed, but still the wounded kept coming. FANY ambulances were lined up at clearing stations twenty-four hours a day as men were squashed in so tightly some succumbed before reaching hospitals at the rear.

Ivy arrived at yet another clearing station while shells exploded only half-a-mile away. The blasts flapped the marquee canvas and the tent posts quivered uncertainly. Along with the stretcher cases a lone French infantryman stood silently staring blankly ahead. Ivy approached the fellow who had no outward signs of injury.

'Monsieur, are you hurt?' Ivy asked in French which she now spoke and understood fluently.

The soldier did not respond other than to twitch slightly. Whether it was because Ivy had addressed him or because of another shell blast was unclear.

'You must take cover, monsieur. It is not safe here.'

The soldier turned slowly towards her, but said nothing. Ivy looked around to see if there was anyone to help. The only person was a surgeon who dragged on a cigarette, his hands, apron and boots stained scarlet with blood. He was exhausted and Ivy wondered how many mistakes he'd made due to fatigue.

'He will not answer, mademoiselle. He is a malingerer,' the doctor sighed. 'We get them here every day. He has lost his grip, some call it shell-shock, but I do not know. It is happening all the time. Someone will come and return him to his unit shortly. They always do.'

'Is that any surprise with the conditions they endure out there? This man is on the point of collapse. He is in no condition to fight.'

'I do not make the rules, mademoiselle. I can do nothing for him. Now if you will excuse me I have *sick* men to attend to.'

He stubbed his cigarette out and returned to work leaving Ivy with the silent soldier.

'You had better come with me and we'll get someone to look at you in the hospital,' Ivy said, guiding the man to her ambulance which had finished being loaded.

Ivy helped the man into the passenger seat beside a soldier blinded by gas and she was uncertain which man was in worst shape. But as she cranked the motor, two men Ivy identified as military policemen dragged the silent soldier from the cab.

'What are you doing?' Ivy cried. 'That man is sick.'

'He is a deserter, mademoiselle,' the leading MP said. 'We will take him back where he belongs.'

'As I told the doctor, this man is unfit to fight.'

'No he is just unfit,' the MP said, grinning as if he'd made quite a joke.

The silent soldier was having none of it either, he shook off the MP holding him and dashed along the mud track towards the rear, slipping and stumbling as he went. The leading MP merely sighed, eyed the fleeing man with a bored expression. He drew his service revolver and before Ivy could react, he fired. The shot hit the silent man squarely in the centre of his back.

'You murderer!' Ivy screamed, racing to the fallen man.

She placed her fingers to his jugular, but there was no pulse. The silent soldier was dead. She turned to see the MPs were already striding back towards the front line. Two medical orderlies approached and loaded the dead man onto a stretcher. They took him to the long line of other corpses and laid him beside them. The MPs had gone, the orderlies returned to duty and the dead man joined a hundred more of the country's fallen.

On the 3rd of May the 2nd French Division was on the point of collapse. They'd had enough of General Nivelle sending them endlessly to futile slaughter just to massage his own ego. They were prepared to fight, but not simply to charge headlong into Boche machineguns and artillery and be mown down within a few yards. Soldiers refused to obey their officer, but offered no violence as in the Singapore mutiny Ivy had witnessed. The 2nd Division downed tools and in a few days more than half the French army joined them and went on strike!

Chapter 31 – Day of Reckoning

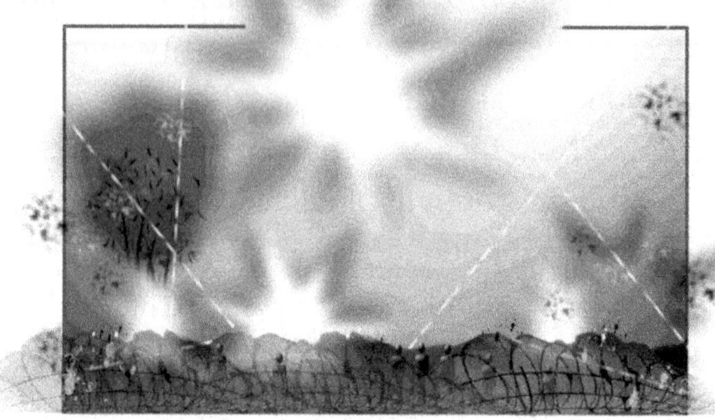

By May the Arras advance had stalled, and although some miles had been gained — remarkable enough by WWI standards — the mutiny crisis halted any chance of further French gains. Meanwhile the British and Anzac build-up north of Arras continued. But that did not mean the French were immune from casualties. German heavy artillery bombardments continued. Direct hits on concealed bunkers were not uncommon leaving dozens dead and wounded.

The only recent good news came the previous month when America finally decided to jump off the fence and declared war on Germany. They planned to send two million troops to smash the Hindenburg Line once and for all, but those men were as yet untrained and still many months away.

It was business as usual for Ivy. The FANY base at Calais was a casino where the girls ate, slept and worked on their ambulances. They were expected to perform all routine maintenance and change tyres. Some girls even learnt to conduct engine and gearbox overhauls and repair other systems.

A few days later Ivy returned to her regular clearing station only to find it had vanished leaving only a huge shell crater where the marquee once stood. With no other guidance, she drove towards the front. French infantrymen stood around idly smoking and looking decidedly sullen and defiant. About two hundred yards from where she believed the forward dressing station to be, she could go no further.

Ahead lay the massed barbwire bramble, interlaced with sandbags and a labyrinth of reinforced trenches. Just prior to the nearest trench opening another shell crater gaped hideously. It was filled with human and animal remains as well as the wreckage of a horse-drawn field ambulance. At that moment a machinegun opened up, peppering the crater rim and forcing Ivy to jump into the massive hole.

Seconds later two French privates leapt in after her. They took Ivy's arms and raced to the trench as bullets spat up mud and debris in their wake.

'*Mademoiselle*, you are crazy, *non*?' one of the solders said. 'The Boche gunners are just a hundred metres beyond our trench.'

'Is this the firing line?'

'*Oui*, you should not be here.'

'The clearing station has been wiped out.'

'So we understand.'

'Do you still have wounded men?'

The soldiers smiled.

'*Mademoiselle* we *always* have wounded men.'

'I have my ambulance close by. It will carry twenty stretchers. We'll take the worst cases first.'

'Come, *mademoiselle*. You must decide.'

Ivy followed the soldiers through the narrow trench, nearly knee-deep with mud. Troops were wedged into minute alcoves they'd cut into the trench wall and tried to cover with any materials available. As she passed she saw only abject despair in the men's eyes.

They're all like that poor fellow the MPs shot. These men are at the end of their tether. How can they possibly be expected to continue fighting?

They reached the wounded lined along the trench floor almost completely covered in water. In some cases men had drowned because their comrades were too exhausted to keep an eye on them. A careworn officer approached, sloshing his way through the mud.

'It is hopeless, *mademoiselle*,' he said. 'The men no longer obey. I cannot get these men to the rear. Our ambulance was blown sky-high last night. The Boche shoot anyone who lifts their head above the rim.'

'*Oui, monsieur*, they had a go at me, but these two brave fellows helped me to safety.'

'If we try to move the men to your ambulance, the Boche will kill everyone. We will not be quick enough carrying wounded. These men have seen so much death they don't want to be next. We must wait for nightfall. Even then the enemy fire flares.'

'An admirable sentiment, I don't doubt, but these men will be dead by nightfall.'

'Do you not have artillery for cover?'

'We have nothing.'

As if to emphasise the officer's point a barrage of German mortars exploded in quick succession. Everyone dived for cover, but still two shells landed directly in the trench, blasting half-a-dozen men to crimson pulp.

'Get on the field telephone. Demand help.'

'They do not care since the mutiny.'

But just then fate took a hand as a squadron of RCF Sopwith Camels hurtled along the German line at what would have been tree-top height if there had been any trees left standing. Taking the opportunity to cause mischief, they'd spotted the Germans and raked the trenches with machinegun fire. Bombs tumbled from brackets which held them to the underside of the wings.

The German trenches erupted in flames as the planes roared past. The Camels were the latest British scout planes equipped with the most modern technology for delivering ordnance.

'Quickly, before they recover!' Ivy yelled.

Her insistence galvanised the shell-shocked soldiers into action. They stacked as many injured as possible and loaded them into Ivy's ambulance.

'I shall come back tonight,' she promised. 'Bring another twenty stretcher-cases here under cover of darkness.'

She sped away just as the Germans recovered and started shooting again.

It was midnight when she returned to find the French had indeed brought their casualties to the rendezvous point. Unfortunately the Germans spotted the ambulance headlights and lethal red bullets streaked towards her. Ivy killed the lights, but was still some distance from the wounded men.

The Germans continued firing randomly and sporadically — perhaps their ammunition was precious, who could tell? The night was pitch-black, so Ivy crept along the wooden walk-way until she reached the stretchers. By this time her uniform was completely drenched with mud.

'Is anyone there?' she called, but only received a few moans from the casualties in reply.

'*Mon Dieu*, I cannot lift you all by myself.'

'We are here,' a voice called from the darkness.

Ivy barely saw them even when they were a yard away. Four walking wounded had volunteered to stay with the serious and critical cases until Ivy showed up. If she failed to appear they'd be caught in the open at daybreak. If the Germans fired a parachute flare overhead, they were also vulnerable.

One of the wounded had his arm bound and immobile, but he'd manufactured a sling he placed over his shoulder enabling him to hold the stretcher handles. It took three hours to move all the men, during which time the Germans did illuminate the sky with flares, but they were distant enough for the evacuation to go unnoticed. If fact, the flares proved a back-handed blessing, giving the stretcher-bearers a glimmer of light to work by.

As the ambulance lumbered away the Germans fired a few shots at its tail-lights, but Ivy soon drove out of range. When she reached Calais by mid morning, her head was spinning with fatigue. Two of her colleagues helped her to her Spartan room, ran a bath and took her clothes to the laundry.

'Go to bed, Ivy,' they admonished. 'We'll take care of your uniform. You're no use to anyone until you've had a proper sleep.'

They were right, Ivy's head hit the pillow and she slept for eighteen hours. She awoke famished, dressed in a fresh uniform and ate a hearty breakfast. She was enjoying her second cup of tea when two red-caps approached.

'Are you Miss Ivy D'vere-Brown?' the corporal in charge demanded bluntly.

'Just Ivy Brown will do nicely, thank you, corporal,' Ivy replied coolly.

'You are to come with us, miss.'

Ivy stared at the red-caps, noticing the Shropshire Regiment insignia on their collars and shoulder patches.

'Straight away, miss — them's our orders.'

'I have no say in the matter..?'

'Not when it comes to orders, miss.'

'May I ask where you're taking me?'

'Certainly, miss. Eleventh Battalion Shropshire Regiment headquarters. The CO wants to talk to you.'

*

How long Ivy figured she was going to get away with defying her mother was anyone's guess. It's unlikely she'd thought it through herself. Shropshire was not an insurmountable distance from London and FANY headquarters. When Meredith hadn't heard from her daughter for a couple of months, she took the train to Liverpool Street Station to pay a visit and perhaps patch up the coolness between Ivy and herself.

She wasn't particularly surprised to find Lady Fielding had ignored her request. Dottie had a habit of doing whatever she damned well pleased anyway. But Meredith was furious with Ivy and wrote to her husband explaining the situation leaving nothing out, although in fairness she did explain Callan wasn't the predator in the bedroom escapade.

The eleventh battalion headquarters was a couple of miles behind the forward trenches. The battalion sappers had constructed a canvas shelter over a roofless cottage where Lieutenant Colonel D'vere-Brown commanded his unit. Rows of tents stood neatly close by with the mess-tents, laundry, ablution blocks all sited in an orderly fashion. Colonel D'vere-Brown knew the value of hygiene and endeavoured to provide the best conditions for his men. Healthy, well-fed and rested men fought better and harder than exhausted, half-starved troops.

Ivy was appalled at how thin and drawn her father was. The eleventh had been in the front line for over six months and were only now being rested before they joined the Anzac left flank for the next assault.

The colonel dismissed the red-caps, rose and kissed his daughter lightly on the brow before asking her to sit in one of the chairs in front of his desk. He ordered his admin staff not to disturb him for half an hour.

So that is the time he has allocated me, Ivy thought. Her father stared at Ivy for a moment as if he was unsure how to deal with the problem.

'Are you not delighted to see me, Papa?'

'I don't think you understand the severity of the situation here.'

'It doesn't look as perilous as the French line I evacuated casualties from the night before last.'

'Don't be clever with me, Ivy. By "here", I mean the western front.'

'I have been doing important work. I hoped you'd be proud of me.'

'Yes, I am proud of what you are doing, but I'm not proud of the way you went about it. You deliberately disobeyed your mother and put Lady Fielding in an awkward position when she gave in to your wishes.'

'I think Lady Fielding is more than a match for Mama,' Ivy observed.

'You have become wilful, Ivy. It is not a characteristic I admire in my daughter. Do you think I have nothing to do with my time than deal with a wayward girl? I also know of your unseemly conduct with young McAlister...'

'That wasn't Callan's fault — I went to his room.'

'So I believe from what your mother has told me. Apparently Irish rebels saved the day. I do not blame Callan, but your behaviour was deplorable. I've a good mind to take you across my knee and paddle your behind.'

That's probably not the best idea here on the front line, Papa.

Colonel D'vere-Brown obviously thought so too.

'Think yourself lucky you're getting off lightly. I have made arrangements for you to be returned to England on the first available ferry across the Channel. I know you are on some hare-brained quest to try and find Callan McAlister, but that stops right here. I am sure he is unaware you're in France, I intend to see he remains ignorant of the fact.'

'You might be right. I wrote to him, but he hasn't returned my letters.'

'He never got your correspondence. Your mother intercepted them.'

Ivy stared blankly at her father then burst into tears.

'How could she?' Ivy wailed. 'Now he thinks I have cut him off. Oh, it has been more than a year. What will he think of me? He'll hate me forever. Oh Papa, how could you and Mama have been so cruel?'

The Colonel's attitude softened a little — sobbing women had that effect.

'Your mother and I only have your best interest at heart, Ivy...'

'I should be the judge of my best interest,' Ivy cried.

'Please lower your voice, Ivy. This is a military establishment.'

As if to emphasise the point, the battalion sergeant-major knocked and entered, snapping to attention and saluting with parade-ground precision.

'Beggin' your pardon sir, but a Major Blake from General Monash's HQ is here to see you. Says it's urgent, sir.'

'Very well,' the colonel said. 'Show the major in. Ivy wait in the orderly room please, we'll finish this discussion directly.'

As Ivy left her father's office she found herself staring at a familiar face.

'Archie Blake!' she exclaimed, flinging her arms around his neck and kissing his cheek.

'Why, Miss Ivy, what a pleasant surprise,' Blake replied nervously.

'You know one another..?' Colonel D'vere-Brown commented from his desk.

'Yes, sir. We met when young McAlister was recovering in hospital,' Blake explained.

'Is he still with General Monash?' Ivy squealed with delight.

'Why no, Ivy. He was so glum when he failed to hear from you, the General and I decided to transfer him to the RFC.'

'How is he?'

'Fine last time I heard, but the RCF copped a right bashing all through April...'

'Major, I understand you have information for me from General Monash, or did you just pop over for a chat and catch up on old times.'

'I'm sorry, sir. The general wishes you to attend a briefing at sixteen-hundred. I have the notes and maps here for you. The general wanted me to bring them personally rather than courier, in case you had any questions. We've had a few security breaches in the field telephone lines. I understand your Shropshires are to support our left flank when we next engage the enemy. General Monash would appreciate your input, sir.'

Blake handed Ivy's father a leather briefcase with the salient paperwork.

'Very well. Take Ivy to the mess tent while I look over these documents. Ivy, have some lunch before you return to Calais — and England. Report to me afterwards, Major.'

Ivy was agog with excitement as she tucked into bully beef and over-cooked canned vegetables. But she didn't care, Callan was alive and an aviator and now she knew why he hadn't returned her letters. How was she ever going to forgive her mother for that one? After telling her story, Ivy bombarded Blake with endless questions.

'Hold on, Ivy. One at a time. Firstly Callan's now a flight commander and has been promoted to captain. He's been stationed all along the front from time to time. Last I heard he was at St Omer...'

'St Omer — I go right through there almost every time I drive to the clearing stations. I always see planes flying in and out. Why he is only a few miles from Calais.'

'Yes, but the situation is fluid, Ivy. The planes can move at a moment's notice to where they're needed. We're getting much better at using the RFC these days.'

Maybe so, but allied aircraft losses had been horrendous during what was referred to as *Bloody April*. Bold offensive tactics deep into German territory caused huge losses. The *Luftstreitkräfte* knocked out allied planes at a rate of four-to-one with only about a quarter of the aircraft at their disposal. However according to Archie Blake, Callan was becoming an ace and his chances of survival grew better each day. The worst victims were young pilots on their first few missions. If they survived those, there was hope they might last the distance.

'How can I find him?' Ivy asked.

'I'll track him down for you,' Blake said.

'But Papa is shipping me back to England post-haste.'

'Look I'll tell him what happened and you can write to him care of Number 1A Auxiliary Squadron, RFC. Technically Callan's squadron is still part of the GSC, but I think they're due to be handed to the RFC at any time. It might take a week or two, but the mail does get through.'

It certainly will, Archie. Now that Mama isn't involved.

Archie Blake returned to the Anzac Division followed by Colonel D'vere-Brown in his staff car. Meanwhile Ivy was escorted by the two courteous, but resolute red-caps to Calais. She packed her grip and art satchel and found herself on a night ferry to Dover, vowing never to speak to her mother again.

Chapter 32 — Aces and Parachutes

The battle for Messines, despite heavy Anzac and British losses, was the Allies' most successful operation of the war. General Sir Herbert Plumber oversaw the action, which he planned with meticulous detail, greatly pleasing General Monash, who was a stickler for thorough preparation. Over two thousand artillery pieces and multiple RFC planes were involved in the week-long softening up barrage. The most spectacular event occurred when nineteen underground mines detonated, heralding the attack. The explosions were heard right across the Channel at Dover.

Allied engineers spent months tunnelling under the German front line to lay the charges. No one knows how many Germans were blown to smithereens during the blasts, but they were knocked off balance, allowing the Allies attacked and captured Ypres. Tragically gas caused heavy casualties among the Allies before the battle began just after 3 a.m.

The Auxiliary Squadron was involved, mostly in a photographic reconnaissance role, but Callan and Bruce Adamson both reached eight kills confirming them as the latest RCF aces. New Sopwith Camel scouts arrived to boost and modernise the squadron equipment. Their superior performance and superb manoeuvrability allowed RFC pilots to take on the German planes and gain control of the skies.

The French still reeled from the mutiny and were marking time. A few ring-leaders were executed, but the Army remained static under its new commander, General Petain, who wanted to wait for the Americans to give him a hand before committing his troops again.

Meanwhile the battle growled on from late summer through the autumn. German and Allied forces hammered away at each other around Ypres and Passchendaele, killing one another by the thousands, but by year's end the struggle had ground to a halt and the western front fell mercifully quiet for a time. Both sides suffered over a quarter of a million casualties each during the protracted fight.

For Callan there was new game in town. *Rittmeister* Manfred von Richthofen was a young man making a name for himself commanding *Jagdgeschwader 1*, which quickly became known as Von Richthofen's *Flying Circus*. His bright red Albatros D II fighters were becoming the scourge of the sky. Mac Squadron came up against them from time to time, usually losing one or two planes in the process, but Callan gave as good as he got with three scarlet planes to his kill-tally by year's end.

'I hear the Flying Circus is re-equipping,' Bruce Adams observed, perusing a week-old Parisian paper at breakfast.

'Says so in the morning news does it?' Callan replied.

'No, I can hardly read any of this *frog* anyway.'

'Probably better than practising on French whores — you don't know where they've been.'

'Yes, very droll, Callan, but the intel-o has reports they're getting Fokker tri-planes.'

Callan had heard of the development, but wasn't over-impressed.

'What're the specs?'

'Rumour has it they'll do one-fifteen mph and reach twenty thousand feet.'

'We can do that in our Camels, what's all the fuss about. It's not that much better than the D IIs.'

'The tri-planes are tough and manoeuvrable.'

'I understand the stall-speed is twenty miles an hour higher than ours. That's going to cause them grief in a dog-fight. We'll be able to pull tighter turns and fly rings around 'em. See, I've done my homework too, Bruce even while I'm sitting here quietly enjoying these boiled eggs.'

The squadron was taking a break in reserve at the rear at the time, but Callan knew the rest was only to be short-lived. The air war would once again rage as soon as the winter storms abated in the spring of 1918.

'Well good for you,' Bruce replied. 'Hey it looks like the mail has arrived. I'll see if there's anything from that girl-friend of yours.'

Callan always looked forward to Ivy's newsy letters. When the first one arrived explaining the whole sorry situation, Callan had already heard as much from Archie Blake. Ivy's correspondence was profusely apologetic, full of heartfelt anguish and begging Callan for forgiveness. Callan's reply saying it was fine — just a little misunderstanding that could happen to anyone — might have been a tad off-hand considering Ivy was an emotional girl.

Since then their letters were friendly and full of as much information as the censors would allow, although Ivy always used the greeting *Darling Callan* where as Callan settled for *my dear Ivy*. Callan tried to persuade Ivy to forgive her mother and resume their once close relationship. To date he didn't know if he'd had any success at all.

31ˢᵗ January 1918

Darling Callan,

I have just returned from Shropshire where I spent Christmas and New Year's Festival with Mama and Papa. The landscape was divinely peaceful with six inches of snow covering the entire countryside.

We exchanged gifts in front of a roaring fire. But how I wish you had been there to celebrate with me. I miss you so, dear Callan. I pray every night that you will return unharmed from this beastly war that just goes on and on.

Papa has finally recovered from being gassed at Ypres when his Eleventh Shropshires advanced with the Anzacs and Canadians. What a frightful weapon to use, which shows the Hague Convention is not worth the paper it's printed on. As you know he was blind for three weeks, but his other wounds have taken far longer to heal.

I doubt if he'll be fit to return to active duty. In any event the Eleventh was so decimated at Ypres that, it has been disbanded and its surviving troops incorporated into other Shropshire Regiment battalions.

Please tell me when you next have leave, Dearest Callan. Come to London and I will meet you there. I don't give a fig what Mama and Papa say, I ache to see you again. I still work for Lady Fielding at FANY HQ in

London. I often take patients to Harefield
Manor Hospital where you recuperated. The
nursing staff remember you fondly — they say
you were by far the most handsome officer they'd
ever seen. My you have turned some heads
indeed!

Most wounded now come from Dover by
railway, but we must then transfer them to
whichever hospital can accommodate them. There
are still so many young men arriving every day
with terrible injuries....

Callan read on as the letter moved from general news to endearments as well as alluding to the fact she would turn twenty-one later in the year and be free to do as she pleased. Well, they might just be in luck. Callan had not been on leave since his promotion, so he applied for a fortnight off before the weather improved. Gene approved the application, so what could go wrong..?

'Howdy, Callan.'

Gene had entered the mess-tent unnoticed. He bent over Callan and eyed him over Ivy's letter. Gene smiled, which wasn't always a good thing.

'Howdy yourself, Gene,' Callan replied suspiciously.

'Got a letter from your gal, I see.'

'Yessir.'

Gene was behaving a little creepily.

'Can I help you, Major, or do you just want to join me for a cuppa and a chat?'

'Coffee'd be swell,' Gene replied, hailing the duty steward.

'You look pleased with yourself,' Callan observed.

'Sure am. You wanna hear the good news or the bad news first?'

'Okay, I'll go with the good.'

'You've been promoted.'

Gene handed Callan two shoulder epaulettes with major's crowns embroidered in the material.

'What's the catch?'

'You're taking over the outfit, so it'll still be Mac's Squadron. Not bad for a kid who ain't even twenty-one yet. I've been seconded back to our boys. Apparently General Pershing wants me to help head up his Yankee aero squadrons. He's seen how the Brits got shot to shit because of inexperience. He doesn't want to make the same mistake, so he'll see his boys are properly trained and ready for a scrap when they get here. It's early days yet, but he's roping in guys from the *Lafayette Escadrille*. They need fellas with combat experience to show the new fly-boys the ropes. So Mac Squadron is all yours, pal.'

Gene beamed and spread his arms effusively.

'What about my leave?'

'That's kinda the bad news.'

'No offence, Gene, but I don't want the squadron.'

'You don't get a choice.'

'Jeez, it's mostly paperwork. Why not promote Bruce. He's much better at that stuff than me.'

'Not my call. They've thrown a DFC as a bonus. It's a brand new award for brave fly-boys — just out this year. There's one for Bruce too. You're growing quite an impressive row of gongs there on your chest.'

Gene and his pet cougar left a few days later. He wrote his contact details down for Callan, urging him to get over to New Mexico after the war. He planned to start a flying business and wanted Callan to join him. Callan promised he would — and he meant it. Flying was now in his blood. He knew the war must end eventually and he'd have to think to the future if he survived that long.

He rather hoped Ivy would share that future, but he still had an unsettling feeling that the English class system might get the better of them.

Over the next weeks, Callan did lead the squadron as often as possible, but he found administration tasks took up a frustrating amount of time. Then he hit on a brilliant solution. Instead of delegating the flying tasks to Bruce, he delegated the paperwork. The New Zealander didn't complain. He'd had a premonition that his luck would run out shortly, so he was happy to take a break from the front.

But on returning from a particularly spiteful tussle with the Flying Circus, Callan once more saw one of his men leap to his death from a blazing plane rather than be burnt alive.

'We've gotta get parachutes,' he declared as he entered his office where Bruce was holding the fort.

'Blimey, Gene tried for years and I've appealed to St Omer, but they reject the idea outright. The generals reckon it encourages pilots to abandon their machines needlessly.'

'I am sick to death of these bloody generals sitting up in their leather armchairs, throwing our lives away. It's almost as if they're competing for the highest body-count. They're not the ones trapped in a blazing wreck. Ruddy hell, Bruce, balloon spotters have been issued with parachutes since this show began.'

Bruce shrugged dismally.

'How many balloon units do you reckon there are around here, mate?' Callan asked.

'A couple close by, 'but there are dozens all along the front.''

'Right. Get hold of Patterson and Simpson. They're our two cagiest rogues...'

Equipment officers were a peculiar breed, who believed that stores in their care became their private property. As a result getting them to part with any of their precious hoard was a bit like shucking oysters. Full warehouses made equip-os happy without giving too much thought about those who might need the supplies. Nothing pleased an equip-o more than walking around a store house, packed to the brim with a clip-board in hand, ticking off his inventory.

But Callan had taken a leaf from Gene's book and decided every man had his price. He soon realised the top echelon in the equipment chain was incorruptible, so he despatched Patterson and Simpson to white-ant lower ranks, and there was nowhere better to go than a store's NCO.

It took a week touring every British, French and Belgian balloon unit for a hundred miles along the front. The two airmen carried a truckload of wine cases (any vintage), boxes of French cheese (especially Camembert) and numerous cash donations to any whorehouses within range. They returned with a truckload of parachutes.

Callan estimated it would cost him six month's pay, but Bruce held a whip-around among the aircrew who were only too keen to contribute. The ground-crew pitched in as well so no one felt excess financial pain and the squadron was now equipped with parachutes for all its aviators.

And contrary to the high-commands fear, over the next months Mac Squadron pilots didn't needlessly abandon their planes, preferring to make emergency landings or struggle to bring their embattled machines back to base even when riddled with bullet-holes. Only one S.E.5. crew bailed out of their burning plane, landing safely in the allied sector.

The rescuing American doughboys were puzzled when the pilot and observer insisted on bringing their parachutes with them. It cost Callan two more bottles of champagne to poach a fellow from the nearest balloon company to show the squadron ground crews how to repack the chutes.

Americans had been trickling into the front over the past nine months and had fought in some engagements, but the flood was still to be unleashed. However German General Ludendorff had other ideas. In October 1917 the Russians conveniently decided to have a revolution, arrested their royal family and replaced one repressive regime with an even more draconian one. In doing so they withdrew from the war, signed a peace treaty with Germany before Christmas and started butchering one another with the same gusto they'd shown against the Boche.

Alas for the Allies, that released eighty German divisions with supporting artillery and air power to the western front. Ludendorff planned one last go at the allied lines before the Americans could establish themselves in great numbers. In 1917 the allies attempted a spring offensive — now Germany planned to do the same in 1918.

Fortunately the French had pulled themselves together and reorganised into a fighting force once more. Just in the nick of time too. On 21 March Ludendorff unleashed sixty-five divisions supported by tanks, heavy artillery, mortars, machineguns and — hundreds of aircraft. And those Germans weren't rubbish reservists, but battle-hardened storm-troopers trained to fearlessly batter the enemy into submission, which is precisely what they did.

The first attack, called the Michael offensive, pushed the allied centre back for miles. French divisions and Monash's diggers were sent to staunch the leak as the British forces crumbled, while Callan's squadron soared eastwards to meet the Flying Circus.

On 9 April Ludendorff launched his second attack — Operation Georgette — to consolidate the advances so far. Callan's squadron scrambled into action. Every serviceable machine was airborne. As squadron commander, Callan wasn't expected to fly, but he was not a man to let others perform any task he was unprepared to do himself.

Both sides now used bombers and scouts in carefully planned raids, but once they clashed the battle became an aerial free-for-all. It was not unusual for fifty machines to swarm across the sky, tussling for the advantage and to get off a shot.

Planes came from everywhere in the melee, friendly or otherwise. Callan's head spun in the cockpit alert for constant split-second danger. Once he latched onto an enemy plane, he focused totally until the scarlet foe either escaped or spiralled to earth in a ball of fire. No sooner was a duel over when he looked for other German machines.

In battle all humanity was gone and he turned into a machine — to kill or be killed. So Callan endured one dog-fight after another and miraculously, or due to the fact he was now so experienced he'd had acquired sufficient rat-cunning, survived.

In late May the Germans struck again in the Blücher-Yorck Offensive which pushed the bulging front line just thirty miles from Paris. But in mid April an event occurred that changed Callan's life remarkably.

Chapter 33 — The Red Baron

'So, it looks like the rumours are true,' Bruce declared as he shuffled through a mountain of paperwork.

'What rumours would they be?' Callan asked.

'It's been a long time coming, but we're not in the army any more. General Trenchard has got his way. The RFC and the RNAS have been merged into the Royal Air Force! Maybe that's why they introduced the DFC so the RAF can have its own awards.'

'That's all we need is an administrative reshuffle with the Boche hammering at our gates. How exactly does that help us win the war?'

'Well...I dunno...but it actually won't make any difference to us, Callan.'

Bruce looked smugly from the desk he'd pretty well usurped from his CO.

'I take it that means we all stay here and slug it out with the Boche as usual.'

'Not us, sport.'

Bruce handed Callan a plump file which held his military record.

'The squadron is finally going to be absorbed into one of the RAF wings,' Bruce said. 'But *we* have been transferred back to the AFC. General Monash asked for you personally, it seems. You're been given a unit directly under his command and I'm to tag along as your 2IC.'

'At least we'll be working for a general who knows what he's about,' Callan said.

Callan left with mixed feelings. In truth he'd always felt like a stranger away from the Anzacs. Bruce Adamson was the only pilot he'd allowed to become a friend. The others were merely a sea of faces, some of whom returned from their missions while others did not. Although he cared for his men and did all in his power to see they were properly trained, resources were stretched to a limit where pilots and planes proved callously expendable.

Callan personally bade farewell to every squadron member, which took some time, but it was the way he liked to behave. He was especially sorry to part with Patterson and Simpson, who'd been his regular and reliable mechanics throughout, but it was time to return to the Diggers.

Knowing the RAF would probably confiscate the parachutes to ensure no 'lack-of-moral-fibre' infected their men, Callan and Bruce loaded them into a truck and took them to their new station.

*

'Welcome back, Major,' Lieutenant General Monash greeted as Callan stomped to a halt and saluted. 'At ease — take a seat.'

Monash had read the detailed reports Callan had provided. Archie Blake stood beside the general and was unashamedly pleased to see Callan back safe and more-or-less intact.

Monash had lost considerable weight since Callan had last seen him. But the general thrived on the challenges high command demanded. During the Gallipoli campaign, Monash had looked stressed and continually frustrated by the inadequacies of those generals running the show. Now he commanded an independent army corps and he was determined to see the job done properly. His Anzacs were not going to be used as cannon-fodder in a Boche shooting gallery if he had anything to do with it.

'I have a light reconnaissance squadron for you, McAlister,' Monash declared. 'Perhaps a major is high-priced help to lead what is essentially a blown-out flight, but I want someone I can trust. You'll have a mixed bag of equipment — Sopwith Pups and some French Nieuport 12s have fallen our way with a few brand-new Fairy IIIs thrown in. You'll report directly to Major Blake at this HQ. I understand you commanded a multi-functional squadron with the RFC.'

'We only did what other squadrons specialised in, sir, but I have no objection to commanding a flight,' Callan said sincerely. 'Captain Adamson's not only an ace pilot, but he's a first class administrator. I intend to go to the airfield immediately and check out my team.'

'Excellent, I want a unit who can think on its feet and take on innovative tasks without being bogged down with stick-in-the-mud senior officers. Archie tells me you're getting a good bunch, so I'm sure you'll lick 'em into shape in no time. I will need detailed intelligence on German positions in our area of operations.

We've slowed their advance, but who knows what else the Boche have up their sleeve.'

It was no secret the German spring offensive was planned to force the allies to the negotiating table before the threat of General Pershing's doughboys surging towards the front dashed any hope of a deal. Germany's finest storm-troopers still hammered away, but their assault showed signs of stalling. But casualties still mounted daily.

'We have to push the buggers back to the Hindenburg Line,' Blake sighed dismally.

'We have to push 'em back a damn-site further than that, Archie,' Monash said. 'We now have all the men and matériel we need for the job. I intend to get this right. I'm sick of those pompous leeches Bean and Murdoch white-anting my command.'

Monash had every right to be bitter towards Keith Murdoch and Charles Bean who were Australia's most influential war correspondents. They were also rampant chauvinists who opposed Monash's appointment as C-in-C of the Australian Corps simply because the general was of Jewish-German descent and didn't fit their notion of an Aussie stereotype. Unbelievably Murdoch and Bean influenced politicians and senior military staff when it came to army appointments.

'Flaming galahs think I'm un-Australian,' Monash complained. 'Did you know I met Ned Kelly in Jerilderie back in '74 when I was a youngster? You can't get much more Australian than that, can you?'

'What was he like, sir?" Callan asked because he wasn't sure how else to respond.

'He was a bit of a rebel like you, McAlister, but without any good qualities.'

Callan was surprised at Monash's candidness until Archie later explained the general's two favourite conversation topics were Ned Kelly and his hatred of journalists and the power they wielded. Mind you, Monash openly courted pomp and ceremony and had no objections when it came to mixing with the titled, rich and famous.

When the general dismissed them, Archie and Callan spent some time studying the maps of the front, which was fluid because of the German push which was sometimes successfully repelled, but more often than not gained precious territory, forcing the allies to retreat and reorganise.

'He wants guinea pigs, doesn't he, Archie,' Callan said as they studied the charts.

'It's a contradiction, I must admit,' Blake replied, 'but the general knows how damned unpredictable war can be and, yes he needs someone to test the waters. We've been keeping a close eye on your progress and reckon you're handy when the going gets tough.'

'Sacrifice a few forlorn hopes for the general good..?'

'Something like that, although we have every confidence in you.'

'Does General Monash think I'm so keen to look for glory?'

'He thinks you'll get the job done.'

'Why?'

'Because I told him you could.'

Callan took command of his flight on 20 April 1918, only two days after the RAF was formally established. He and Bruce spent the afternoon inspecting the flight and meeting the ground and aircrews, who turned out to be a cheerful and efficient bunch. The men were only too happy to have Anzacs in command, especially when they were issued with parachutes and shown how to use them.

Callan was pleased to see the squadron was in good shape and run by industrious conscientious NCOs. The accommodation, catering, engineering, supply and administration tents and marquees were all in order while the maintenance engineers appeared competent and keen. The pilots were mostly new-comers, but there were a handful of experienced survivors.

The following morning at dawn Callan led three Pup scouts to see what was stirring along the front. There was nothing much to report. The Germans occupied much of what had been allied territory forcing the Allies to hastily dig more trenches ahead of them. A few shots came from enemy machineguns, but there was nothing new in that.

On returning to base Callan filed a report for Bruce to forward to Monash's HQ. He then climbed aboard one of the Nieuport 20s to see how it handled. It was older and less powerful than the Pups with a Lewis machinegun mounted on the upper wing rather than synchronised through the prop. This made aiming more difficult, but was compensated with a swivel-mounted gun manned by an observer in the rear cockpit. On that occasion, Callan's observer was a teenage subaltern who didn't look old enough to be away from his mother.

The observer also handled a camera, so Callan decided to take another look at the front line in his sector. Callan pushed into an easterly headwind until he flew over the trenches. By this time things had heated up with Anzacs and Canadians engaged in probing skirmishes with a company of storm-troopers.

At that moment an RAF Sopwith Camel flashed just ahead of Callan's plane. It was in a steep dive. Several machinegun bullets ripped into the Nieuport's fabric while Callan's observer waved frantically and fired off a quick burst. Callan scanned all around as a lone scarlet Fokker tri-plane plunged after the RAF Camel, closely followed by another RAF machine.

Blimey! I'm in the middle of someone else's dog-fight and it looks like I'm the only one hit.

The damage to Callan's plane appeared minor. He couldn't see any other German planes so Callan remained at altitude and banked his aircraft to see the battle's outcome. All three machines were now so close to the ground they were the targets for small arms and artillery fire.

The RAF machines peeled away and headed west, taking advantage of a rare easterly breeze, but the Fokker looked in trouble. It flew haphazardly towards a small town in an area held by the Australians. By then it was too far away for Callan to make out details, but it looked as if the Fokker pilot had made a successful forced landing on a hillside paddock.

If you survived that lot, chum, looks like the war's over for you.

But now Callan had trouble of his own. Initially he thought he just sustained a few bullet holes in his wing fabric, but when he tried to change altitude he found the plane did not respond. His observer pointed to the tail where the elevators were badly shot up. They trailed in a neutral position, but failed to respond to the control column.

The Nieuport had lost some altitude in the turn and only stopped descending when Callan levelled the wings.

'Altitude control has gone!' Callan yelled over the slipstream and engine's roar. 'Looks like the bullets hit the tail section and shrapnel has jammed the cables.'

'I don't think I can climb back there and free 'em, sir,' the observer called doggedly.

Damn right there, mate. I sure as hell wouldn't.

'We still have enough height to jump,' Callan said. 'Make sure your parachute is strapped tightly.'

The observer stared back sheepishly.

'Sorry, sir. I forgot to bring mine — not used to having a 'chute, sir.'

Oh great! I should damn well jump out and leave him.

'OK, let's see what I can do to fly this crate.'

'You jump, sir.'

Yeah right — I'm going to do that, aren't I? Thank heavens for Bruce's aerody lessons.

Callan gingerly pushed the throttle forward and the Nieuport's nose rose slightly. He retarded the throttle and the nose dropped.

'Righto, I've got lateral control with ailerons,' Callan shouted. 'I'll try and use the engine torque for altitude. Keep an eye out for Huns and shoot at anything suspicious. It'll take all my concentration to fly this crate.'

Luckily friendly territory was close by and, aided by the tailwind, they crossed no-man's land heading for the airfield. At first Callan over-controlled the throttle, pitching the nose up and down in wild oscillations. In time he realised minute throttle movements were the answer — a skill he must master while there was still enough flying altitude.

Callan judged he was at about one thousand feet when he approached the aerodrome perimeter.

Okay, a rate one turn takes a minute to turn one-eighty degrees. Two minutes all the way round. Right...turn west...steady...fifteen degree left bank...easy...easy...throttle back a touch...

The Nieuport banked gently and began a slight descent. Callan adjusted the power as he judged his glide path. He was pleasantly surprised when he turned to line up into wind. The plane was in a good position — not too high or low. He'd clear the boundary fence easily and touch-down with plenty of room to pull up. The only problem was the Nieuport's airspeed. With no flight controls to compensate the machine flew at a constant speed, the only variable was its rate of climb and descent.

With the grass rushing up to meet him, Callan knew he only had one shot at the approach. He would be lucky to control a full-power go-around. Normally just prior to landing, he'd cut the throttle and raise the noise for a smooth touch-down. There was only one thing for it...

Callan cut the fuel-cock. The engine spluttered and died just as the main-wheels hit the paddock. The nose dropped instantly, driving the prop into the soft grassy surface. Fortunately it had stopped spinning and simply acted as a mighty brake. One of the blades snapped permitting the nose to smash into the ground forcing the fuselage to cartwheel and finally crash inverted.

Callan was dazed, but alive. He hung upside-down held into his seat by his tightly drawn safety-belt. He checked his body and discovered he'd sustained a few bruises, but was otherwise unhurt. His observer hung limply almost dangling from the rear cockpit. Callan flayed his arms and nudged the observer, but he didn't respond.

Callan was vaguely aware of the emergency siren's distant wailing. He shook his head to clear his mind. As his senses kicked back in, the first thing Callan recognised the stench of high-octane aviation petrol.

Bloody hell!

It was time to abandon ship — pronto as Gene would say! He unclipped his belt-release, tumbling onto the inverted upper wing. His mind flashed in horror as his next sense was the engine heat — still hot enough to ignite petrol fumes.

Scrambling to his feet, Callan grabbed the observer's shoulders and shook him. The man groaned, but appeared immobile or unconscious. Callan released the observer's restraining harness. The dead-weight flopped on top of Callan. It took all his strength to push the man over and roll free. Dragging an inert human was not easy, but Callan hauled the observer away inch by inch.

Just then petrol fumes wafted onto the engine cylinders and ignited. With a whoosh a trail of flames erupted, knifing towards the plane's petrol tank. The machine was engulfed in flame as two ambulance men grabbed the observer and yanked him clear. Other rescuers pulled up short and retreated when the Lewis gun magazines ignited. Bullets spluttered and sprayed randomly like Chinese fireworks. Callan staggered away vaguely aware of the racket behind him until Bruce took his arm and hurried him away from the burning wreck.

'Are you okay, Callan?' Bruce asked urgently.

'Yep, fine. What's the observer look like?'

'Bloody great bump on the head and singed eyebrows, but he's coming round. What happened?'

'I got between the RAF and the Flying Circus. Dunno who shot up my machine — knocked the elevators for six.'

'You did damned well to get back at all.'

'Yeah, we were going fine until the last bit. I only had engine revs to control my height.'

'Come on, you need a drink.'

Bruce drew up Callan's official report over a pint in the O's. Meanwhile the medics reported the observer had suffered concussion, but was expected to make a full recovery. Callan made a mental note to give him a right old dressing down about parachute discipline and impress upon his other aircrews they'd better remember their safety equipment or else.

Two other sorties took off during the afternoon. Bruce insisted Callan remain in the office and for once didn't get an argument. The flights returned unscathed by dusk, just as a motor-cycle despatch rider rattled towards the squadron HQ tent. A leather-clad corporal saluted and handed Bruce a buff-coloured envelope.

'Blimey, this is interesting,' Bruce declared.

Callan merely raised his eyebrows. Little about the war interested him anymore.

'According to this report, you got mixed up with Baron Manfred von Richthofen himself this morning. A couple of Canadian new-chums jumped him. He got the plane down in reasonable shape, but he was dead when our blokes reached him.'

'A pair of novices shot him down..?'

'Well, that's where it gets complicated. The Baron died of a single bullet-wound in his chest, yet everyone wants to claim the credit.'

'Well it wasn't me for a kick-off.'

'Some Diggers from the trenches around Vaux-sur-Somme claim one of them bagged him, so does a Yankee machinegun unit and a couple of artillery batteries as well as the Canadian flyers.'

'It was probably those damned Canucks who hit me and not von Richthofen at all.'

'Yeah, but you'd better keep quiet about that. You now have the honour of being the Red Baron's last victim.'

Chapter 33 — The Last Battle

General Monash's Anzac Corp HQ, Somme Valley — 30 June 1918

'It took four bloody months, but we've beaten the Boche to a standstill,' General Monash announced. 'And now it's time to give 'em a sound thrashing and maybe end this thing.'

All the unit commanders were gathered in a marquee surrounded by armed sentries. Monash had ordered the tent to be erected specially for the purpose of preparing for his next attack in total secret. All the infantry brigade and battalion commanders were also present along with tank, mortar and artillery battery COs, Signal, Supply and Medical Corps representatives and of course, the aviation squadron leaders. Officers from ten American infantry companies were present. The doughboys swelled the Australian ranks by two and half thousand men. Monash was thorough as ever, covering all the angles — or so he thought.

'You have your orders, gentlemen,' Monash concluded. 'We shall capture Le Hamel itself and the high salient points surrounding the village which command the entire area. Our infantry brigades will be supported by Mark V and Whippet tanks both for heavy gunfire and resupplying the front line. Artillery and night aerial bombing raids will soften up the Boche with a creeping barrage.'

Callan listened intently as the general went through his plan in precise detail, co-ordinating his forces in what promised to be the most synchronised attack he'd yet witnessed in the war. Mind you, so far the bar hadn't been set particularly high in that regard.

When he returned to squadron HQ, Callan briefed his men with equal care. His team was assigned reconnaissance and logistic support tasks. Resupplying ground troops from the air was something that had hardly been countenanced before, but General Monash thought the idea bore merit. Callan's Fairy IIIs and Nieuprot 12s were to carry ammunition and medical equipment in brackets under the aircraft wings and fuselage, while the Pups flew as escorts.

Since the idea was raised, Callan's pilots had trained hard and could now drop loads up to five-hundred pounds attached to static-line parachutes with commendable accuracy.

'We don't want to end up resupplying the Boche,' Bruce Adamson commented dryly. 'You know if we could get a strip close to the front we could evacuate casualties in quick time.'

'I can't see injured men clambering into the cockpit,' Callan observed.

'They wouldn't have to if we secured stretchers to the fuselage and strapped the wounded to them.'

'We have enough to deal with right now, but General Monash thinks the Mark V tanks may be able to do some evacuations as well as bringing supplies to the battle-field.'

'Are you going to listen to Billy Hughes' address?' Bruce changed the subject. 'He's touring the front the day after tomorrow.'

'No, I think I'll pass.'

'But he's come all the way from Australia...and....he *is* your PM.'

'Yeah, and he's going to tell us what flaming bonzer blokes we are and what a good job we're doing getting ourselves killed every day. If the Good Lord Himself came down and told me what a grand job I was doing, I can't say I'd be excited about it. You go and tell me all about it.'

Lately Bruce had noted Callan's indifference to everything other than fighting and correspondence from Ivy. The CO's changing attitude developed insidiously and probably went unnoticed to anyone other than Bruce. It was a distressing and alarming transition, which Bruce had no idea how to deal with. Could the war have dulled Callan's senses to a point where he simply didn't care enough to survive? Bruce wondered if Callan was losing his edge.

So Callan allowed the prime minister's whirlwind tour to come and go without him. And when Bruce returned, he reported the PM's speech was pretty much as Callan had predicted.

The following day was taken up with last minute preparations and reconnaissance patrols. Monash's information was also supplied by small ground patrols sneaking into German trenches and bringing back POWs for interrogation by specialist intelligence teams. That evening Bruce returned from Corps HQ in case there were any last-minute changes to plan...and there were.

'The damned Yanks have pulled out of the attack...'

'What? How can they do that? It's all arranged.'

'Archie Blake told me General Pershing has withdrawn his troops because he wants them to only fight with other Americans and not spread through allied units. Monash is spitting chips, he has to reorganise the entire attack plan, but it's still going ahead on schedule even if the Yanks can't be withdrawn in time.'

'Shit, another high-command cock-up. Is Monash the only general with an ounce of common sense?'

As it turned out two of the doughboy companies disobeyed Pershing's instructions and stayed with a Queensland battalion. It was significant because American companies were twice the size of Imperial units, so Monash still had five hundred Americans ready to fight for him.

Le Hamel Village district — 3 am 4th July 1918

Allied aircraft had harassed German positions throughout the night, strafing and bombing the enemy line. Then in the pre-dawn a massive artillery barrage opened up, pounding the German defences with high explosive shells, shrapnel and smoke bombs. The ordnance initially fell to the rear of the enemy line, slowly shortening range until it exploded only yards in front of Australian infantry and tanks then increased range as the Monash's corps attacked. Exploding artillery and tank shells dropped just ahead of the advance, splattering all resistance and gouging a path for the Anzacs and Americans.

The fight was on. General Monash estimated all objectives should be achieved in an hour-and-a-half. It took the Diggers and Americans ninety-three minutes to conquer Le Hamel and the surrounding high ground. General Pershing was left red-faced having withdrawn the majority of his doughboys from the most successful allied operation of the war.

All day RAF and AFC aircraft harassed the Germans, parachuted ammunition to the allies and helped navigate the troops through the trenches and barb-wire with marker flares and dropping maps with revised enemy positions as troop movements grew fluid throughout the day.

The Jagdgeschwader sent what they could to challenge the allied planes, but the German machines and crews were seriously depleted to only a shadow of their 1917 glory days. But they did shoot down several RAF aircraft and one AFC machine.

Major Callan McAlister flew five Pup sorties over the battlefield during the day and into the long summer twilight. He was last seen by a Fairy III observer strafing enemy troops to relieve a hard-pressed Aussie platoon, but he failed to return from that mission.

*

Harefield Manor Hospital, Middlesex — July 1918

Ivy had been busy all year. The German spring offensive had produced a flood of wounded soldiers who required moving to wherever they could be accommodated throughout the country. Imperial, French and Belgian casualties were now supplemented by a smattering of doughboys although they were quicky repatriated to America.

She fretted over Callan's lack of correspondence, but she'd heard about the battle at Le Hamel and knew he was involved. He was probably working day and night, but she yearned to hear from him again.

Earlier that year, Ivy was assigned to Harefield Manor where Callan had convalesced after the Gallipoli evacuation. Much of her work was transferring patients from London Hospitals to Harefield, but more rewarding was driving fully recovered soldiers to be reunited with their families. Of course many of the Harefield patients never fully recovered. Indeed their psychotic inner demons were often more complex and profound than their physical injuries.

Ivy visited her parents from time to time although she was still barely civil to her mother. Colonel D'vere-Brown was recovering steadily, but his mental scars were unlikely to ever heal.

During her first week at Harefield a staff car pulled up in the drive. A French captain got out and strode smartly up the manor steps.

'Pardon, mademoiselle,' he asked as reception assistant. 'Eet ees Mademoiselle Ivy Brown I seek. She is here stationed, *oui?*'

Ivy was surprised to see the young officer who snapped to attention, embraced her and kissed her on both cheeks. Ivy blushed slightly, but recovered quickly — that was just the French being French. The captain presented her with a small velvet-covered box and an envelope which contained a single sheet bearing a prestigious letterhead with ornate handwritten text in French.

Ivy's French was a little rusty, but when she opened the box she was in no doubt about the message. Lying on a velvet pillow was a green and red striped medal ribbon attached to a bronze cross and two crossed swords. A bronze star was sewn to ribbon.

'A *Croix de Guerre*,' Ivy whispered. 'Who's it for?'

The officer smiled.

'*Pour vous*, mademoiselle. For service most outstanding in aiding our wounded soldiers, a grateful nation thanks you most sincerely.'

'But I was only in France for a few months.'

'*Mais oui*, mademoiselle, but you performed a duty superlative. To the front line you came every day, risking yourself to save others. Mademoiselle, *vous êtes magnifique!*'

He embraced her once more, kissed her cheeks, returned jauntily to his car and drove away, leaving Ivy shaking her head. She studied the award for a few moments...

Well, why not?

She pinned the medal to her pinafore and proudly returned to duty.

The following day she delivered a group of wounded officers to Harefield and returned to her room for a well-earned bath and change of clothing. Two envelopes lay on her bed counterpane. She was disappointed to see neither was written by Callan and both were in an unfamiliar hand.

She opened the first envelope...

15th July 1918

Dear Miss D'vere-Brown

I must first introduce myself. My name is Captain Bruce Adamson, Callan's 2IC. He has often talked of you and how fond he was of you...

Was..?

I cannot say how much it grieves me to inform you that Callan's plane disappeared in action during the attack on Le

Hamel earlier this month. An extensive search has failed to reveal any trace of Callan or his machine and we have heard nothing to indicate he is a POW. We must therefore sadly reach the tragic conclusion that he was lost in battle and his machine completely destroyed.

Callan proved to be a magnificent squadron commander. He was also a true and wonderful comrade and friend. His courage and leadership are legendry among aviators. He was greatly admired and will be sadly missed by all the men under his command.

I know he held a special place in your heart, so please accept my sincere condolences and indeed those of the entire squadron.

If there is anything I can do to help further please do not hesitate to contact me through AFC HQ.

Yours sincerely

Bruce Adamson

Ivy felt an agonising stab through her heart. At first she was too dumb-struck to take in the horrendous information. She opened the second letter from Archie Blake which only confirmed what Bruce Adamson had written.

It was then the awful truth registered and grief overcame her. She threw herself face down on the bed and wept uncontrollably.

*

Ivy was a great favourite with the recovering officers at Harefield Manor. Her genuine concern, gentle manner, nursing and driving skills won everyone's hearts. Whenever she had time, she shared a cuppa or a meal with the patients, so it wasn't long before they were all aware she'd lost her sweetheart.

Whereas she still tended the men and performed her duties as before, an overwhelming melancholia shrouded her, giving an aura of distance and preoccupation. Yet she continued working diligently, hoping that by focusing on her job, she could somehow dull the pain.

As October drew to a close, the war finally looked like ending. One of the last patients Ivy drove to Harefield was Sultan Aashif Jalil who ruled his own principality known as Dera Jalil Khan in Northern India along the Indus River Valley.

Now that's someone you don't meet every day, Ivy mused vaguely.

Jalil had raised his own battalion which fought with distinction on the western front. The sultan, who was also the battalion colonel, was no slouch, leading his men in the true sense of the word. The battalion was particularly successful at reconnaissance raids in small sections. They captured hundreds of German prisoners, but also left hundreds more corpses in their wake. Jalil's troops were predominantly Muslim, but additionally he commanded a company of Hindus and Sikhs.

Jalil's men were fearsome, bearded warriors who liked nothing better than bayoneting their enemy at close quarters. Wisely Jalil kept his religious factions segregated to avoid sectarian violence, which was common enough back in the Himalayan foothills. For that reason Field Marshal Sir Douglas Haig and his chiefs-of-staff made one of their few sound decisions by keeping

Jalil's battalion in Flanders after other Indian regiments had been transferred to the Middle East.

The sultan had been seriously wounded during the Allies' assault on the Hindenburg Line. Military surgeons extracted five bullets from his body and were amazed he survived at all. Ivy had to admit that Jalil's chiselled features, piercing eyes, jet-black hair and clipped beard made him breathtakingly handsome and intoxicatingly alluring.

She shook such thoughts out of her head as she helped Jalil from the ambulance into a wheelchair. The sultan wasn't happy about being chair-bound — even temporarily — but Ivy wasn't putting up with his pride-driven nonsense.

'Colonel, you will not recover if you carry on as if you have not been shot,' she admonished, 'now please do co-operate.'

Jalil grinned, revealing his perfectly shaped, snow-white teeth.

'Then I obey my angel of mercy and may Allah smile upon you.'

'Well, he hasn't so far,' she said as she wheeled Jalil to his room.

Being a sultan had a lot of advantages. Jalil's household, including his wives, children and servants had all come to England for the duration while he served on the front. He'd leased a manor-house in Dorset where he spent what leave he'd been able to scrounge throughout the war. He intended to buy the property and make it his summer residence when the Indus Valley temperatures soared above a century Fahrenheit.

He also had a private suite at Harefield Manor, especially as he'd befriended Harefield's owner, Australian expatriate Charley Billyard-Leake. Rank had its privileges indeed.

'It seems to me Allah has blessed you with the fairest countenance of any young woman,' Jalil said with an unashamed candour, which Ivy found completely disarming.

She stared at him.

'Forgive me,' he said. 'I'm used to speaking my mind...'

'I suppose no one dares to contradict you in your palace or castle or wherever you live.'

'That is true, but I offer the compliment sincerely, for I only speak the truth.'

'Then thank you,' Ivy said, 'but comeliness doesn't necessarily mean your life is blessed...and...I am not in the mood for flirtation.'

'I see profound sadness in your eyes. This war has taken a loved one, has it not?'

'Which only makes me the same as everyone else in the empire.'

'Sadly true indeed, but if you wish to talk, I am a good listener and, as you see, I have time on my hands.'

Ivy smiled — for the first time since she'd heard the news of Callan's death.

'You're not what I expected a sultan to be like, Colonel,' she said.

'Four years in the trenches is a great human leveller.'

And that was how Ivy found a new job.

By war's end, Jalil had recovered sufficiently to return to Dorset. He and Ivy had talked often, and she found herself genuinely liking him. He appeared to be a devoted family man, talking about his wives and children with complete honest affection. Mind you, Jalil also allowing himself the pleasure of concubines, but that was the way sultans did things.

With the influx of wounded dwindling, Ivy felt no reservations when she accepted the sultan's offer to become his children's governess and tutor. The remuneration package was beyond her wildest dreams, but that was sultans for you. Ivy knew she would never forget Callan, but a sea-change could be a chance to try to rebuild her shattered life.

Part Five — Blood Stones of Jalil Khan

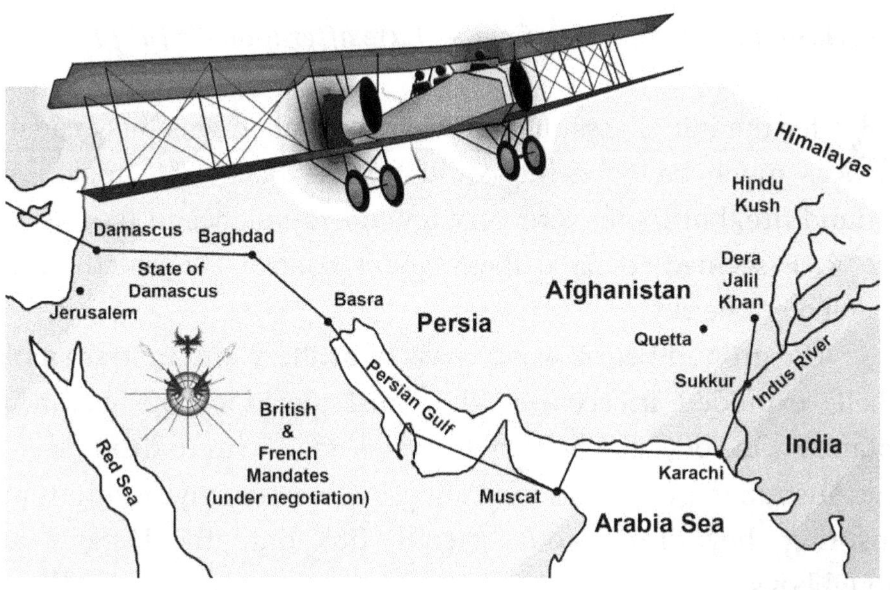

Chapter 35 — MIA

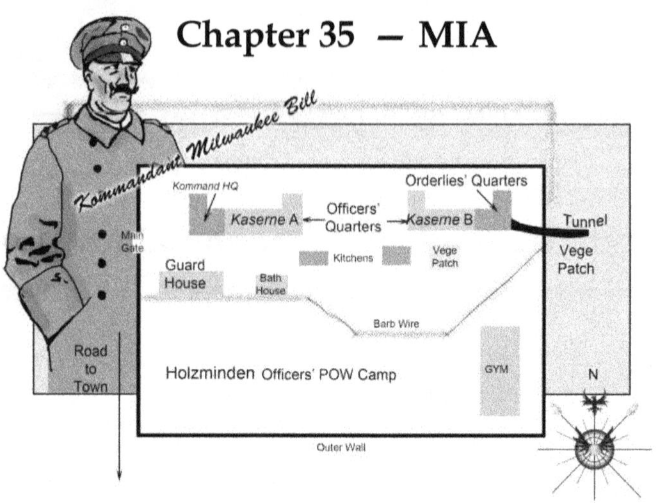

Overhead Le Hamel Battlefield — Late afternoon 4ᵗʰ July 1918

After the initial assault on Le Hamel, Callan was busy causing as much havoc as he could for the Boche. He took some ground fire, but there were very few enemy planes in the sky and the RAF seemed to have them under control. At last the allies dominated the sky.

The ground below was a mass of artillery and mortar smoke. Shells exploded in accurate lines just ahead of the advancing infantry. One of Callan's Fairy III crews' tasks was to drop maps to the Australian gun crews indicating the new enemy positions and ensuring they didn't pour 'friendly-fire' onto the Diggers and doughboys.

Amid the palls of smoke Callan spotted a column of German storm troopers advancing along one of the support trenches to reinforce their beleaguered front-line comrades. He marked their position on his chart, but before he returned to the artillery sites he couldn't resist one quick pass. He banked his plane sharply and lined up along the trench which ran at ninety degrees to the main defence line.

The Pup's wheels were barely above the barb-wire when Callan headed for the approaching Germans. His machinegun rattled and a trail of deadly lead scythed into the men in the trench. The Germans had nowhere to go. Soldiers fell into the muddy trench bottom — some ripped apart by bullets and some diving for cover.

Callan banked again and pulled the Pup skywards when he reached the point where the trench turned at right-angles again. But, if he thought the Boche storm troopers were going to take a pasting lying down, he was sadly mistaken. The survivors quickly clambered to the trench rim and a hail of rifle fire zinged after Callan's plane.

Slugs ripped through the canvas covered wings and fuselage, but the Pup was tough and still airworthy. As Callan registered the hits, he felt searing pain knife from his right ear across his temple. The pain was so sharp Callan immediately felt a peculiar vagueness, almost as if he wanted to go to sleep.

He'd received a head wound from a stray slug and momentarily passed out. The lurching aircraft jogged Callan back to consciousness as the nose dipped alarmingly earthwards. Instinctively Callan drew back on the control stick and the Pup reared skywards. Normally this would have been a simple manoeuvre, but in Callan's semi-aware state he grossly over-controlled, causing the plane to porpoise through the sky.

He was unable to recall if he came to his senses or drifted into oblivion and relaxed, but the plane stabilised and returned to level flight. The searing pain returned to his forehead, becoming so unbearable he lost all rational concentration.

From then on he flew by instinctively trimming the flying controls for level flight. Callan's vision was so blurred he could not make out his compass. He carried on for over an hour until his petrol ran out.

What he didn't realise was he'd been flying the wrong way — deeper into Germany all the time.

The wound may have been just a graze and Callan finally came to his senses when the motor quit. Maybe it was jolt that brought him round just in time to pick a field and land the machine.

Callan remembered clambering from the cockpit. There was no danger of the plane exploding as the petrol tank was empty. The next thing he was aware of was a crowd of bellicose locals rushing towards him. They were armed with farm implements including axes, scythes and pitch-forks along with a few shotguns and fowling pieces. There were a few militia and policemen with the crowd and they were armed with Mauser rifles. The males were either senior citizens or boys.

He may have been groggy, but Callan was smart enough to know it wasn't a welcoming committee. All pilots were issued with a Very-pistol as well as their service revolvers. Callan drew his Very- pistol and fired a flare into his plane.

Although there was no fuel to ignite, the fabric caught fire under the flare's intense sulphuric heat. As the oncoming crowd had no fire-fighting equipment, the plane was destroyed in moments. That enraged the locals and a couple of shots came his way, until the militia ordered a cease-fire. Callan raised his hands and walked towards the oncoming mob.

Callan expected a beating, but was treated well enough. It seemed the Germans had a benevolent attitude towards aviators, who they perceived as gentlemen of noble birth. Callan had no intention of letting them know he was a lowly farm-boy and played along.

He was escorted to the local *polizeistaion* and treated to a stein of beer, bratwurst with lashings of mustard and sauerkraut and pretzel-shaped bread. His captors were puzzled because he was over a hundred miles from the front. Callan merely shrugged and pointed to his wound, indicating it was just as big a mystery to him.

The following day an intelligence officer turned up and tried to pry any useful information from Callan. He asked how Callan was feeling and checked that his wounded was correctly dressed.

Aircrew were considered much more interesting than ground troops because they usually controlled cutting edge equipment, which the Germans wanted to know all about. They knew pretty much everything about the Sopwith Pup as they'd captured a few that had crash-landed. The German was far more interested in what might be in the pipeline, but Callan was able to claim with all honesty that he had no idea.

After that the Mister-Nice-Guy routine stopped abruptly. Callan was knocked around by the guard before being loaded into the back of a truck and transferred to Holzminden, ten miles south of the legendry 'pied-piper' town of Hamelin. The POW camp consisted of two four-storey mansions at the northern end of an estate known as '*Kaserne* A' and '*Kaserne* B', surrounded by a high wall and barbwire. As accommodation went, Callan had seen worse.

He was hustled out of the truck and marched into an interrogation room where he met the portly magnificently-moustached camp *Kommandant, Hauptman* Karl Niemeyer. He was dressed resplendently in a cavalry officer's uniform, a fur-collared trench coat, riding boots and spurs. Callan was surprised when Niemeyer addressed him curtly in a peculiar semi-German accent imbued with American slang.

'Howdy there, buddy,' Niemeyer greeted with a leering grin. 'Y'all gonna feel right at home here so long as you obey the rules.'

'What rules would they be?' Callan asked blandly.

'*Mine* rules!' Niemeyer snapped. 'You think you are a slippery customer, but I know how to deal with slippery customers. Damn right I do. I know about you Diggers. I know about Tommies, Canucks and doughboys too. You think I know damn nothing, but let me tell you I know damn all!'

'Handy to know, thanks,' Callan said barely able to contain a grin.

'You will not be laughing after a week here.'

'I can well understand that,' Callan replied truthfully enough.

Callan was dismissed after Niemeyer had established his alpha-male status, although Callan wasn't impressed. He joined the other POWs and was assigned quarters before meeting the senior POW officer, Colonel Charles Rathbone.

'I suppose welcome is an inappropriate greeting under the circumstances, Major McAlister,' Rathbone said urbanely.

'Whenever I think about my current living conditions, I compare then to the Gallipoli trenches and then I don't feel so bad, sir.'

'Well said,' the colonel nodded sagely.

'What about that crazy joker running the show, sir?'

'Oh yes, Milwaukee Bill,' Rathbone grinned. He and his brother lived in Wisconsin until America entered the war in 1917.

They felt obliged to return to Germany and were appointed POW *Kommandants* because they spoke English.'

'Some might dispute the speaking English bit.'

'Bill tries to make life unpleasant for the POWs, and he can be vicious occasionally. He's as bad with the guards and German support staff, which we use to our advantage as often as not. It's best to keep out of his way and he won't feel the need to make an example of you. Boredom will be your biggest worry though.'

'I was planning to spend my time working out ways to escape, if that's okay with you sir?'

'Yes indeed...and we may be able to help you there,' the colonel added enigmatically, but didn't elaborate right away.

Callan met other pilots who were able to exchange experiences, especially as several had been shot down by the Red Baron. Paradoxically they all seemed genuinely sorry von Richthofen was dead.

In time Colonel Rathbone's allusion to escape became clear. Being an officer had its privileges, among which was being assigned non-commissioned prisoners from other camps. These servicemen performed the menial tasks, prepared and served meals and generally looked after the officers' needs. That might have sounded tedious, but conditions at Holzminden were better than many other camps. So with reasonable meals and living conditions along with work to keep them occupied, the orderlies' lot was as good as any enlisted man's confinement.

With the orderlies' aid, the officers had been digging a tunnel for nine months from the *Kaserne* B to freedom and it was nearing completion. The orderlies' quarters in *Kaserne* B were off-limits to the officers, but it was closest to the perimeter fence. The would-be escapees built a hidden trapdoor from their end of *Kaserne* B to the orderlies' quarters where they'd dug the tunnel.

Just after midnight on 24 July Callan broke out of Holzminden through that tunnel. Callan was the thirtieth officer in line as the men squeezed into the tunnel with agonising slowness. A few torches dimly lit the tunnel as Callan crawled behind the heels of the man in front with major Jack Shaw impatiently right behind him.

Callan had never felt such a feeling of panic with barely inches to spare on every side, often brushing the tunnel walls causing dirt to pour from the pitifully inadequately shored roof.

Callan was about half way through when disaster struck. Twenty-nine men ahead had scraped and dislodged so much rock strata that the tunnel could no longer bear the stress. The tunnel caved in right above Callan, burying him completely. Grit and soil filled his eyes, ears and nose, although he heard Major Shaw groan with disappointment, as he was dragged backwards by his ankles by following POWs.

So that's it then, is it, Callan lad – buried alive in a flaming tunnel? – Not flaming likely!

Callan gouged his fingernails into the tunnel floor and heaved. To his terror he didn't move and he could barely breathe and would soon suffocate. He clamped his fingers even deeper and pulled again.

He moved an inch. He felt a wooden stanchion, grabbing it with one hand, he dragged himself forward a foot. Soil and rock spilled off his back and legs and filled the hole behind him. The stanchion came away in his hand and more of the ceiling collapsed. Callan was half buried again. He dug his fingers into the ground until they bled. So, inch by agonising inch, Callan found purchase and slithered forward until his entire body cleared the collapsed area.

Nothing was going to stop him then. He scrambled after his fellow escapees and emerged from the tunnel at the edge of a rye-field. Callan gingerly raised his head above the sea of cereal ears.

He saw no one in the moonlight. It had taken him so long to clamber out of the tunnel everyone else had cleared the field and gone. He shrugged and trudged forward, reaching the edge of the field as sirens began wailing from the POW compound. It was time to hot-foot it out of there.

As a late-comer to the escape plan, Callan was clothed in a civilian overcoat, with hastily prepared papers, which would pass a cursory inspection, but not close scrutiny. There were three avenues of escape:

- Catch a west-bound goods-train which was the fastest option provided the train kept moving.
- Cycle overland, but probably had the highest risk of detection.
- Steal a small boat and travel by waterways. The Weser River flowed through Holzminden town and joined an arterial canal system to the north. Hopefully all rivers would then flow to the North Sea.

Callan stumbled upon the river first so the choice was made for him. Finding a rowing boat was no problem at all. The riverbank was lined with small craft moored to pontoons and jetties. Callan didn't know much about boats, but found one that looked sound enough with a pair of oars and rowlocks.

He knew from the escape-committee's maps that he needed to clear Hamelin by daybreak or lay up somewhere until nightfall. Two black rye-bread loaves were stuffed in his coat pocket which would last a day or so and he'd have to drink river water whatever the risks might be.

And he didn't do too badly. The July weather remained mild and his coat was protection enough while the bread filled his belly. After the first night he pulled the boat into a huge patch of tall reeds, making him invisible from the main river and meadows along the bank. The wetland abounded with small fish and frogs stalked by wading birds.

I'm not ready to eat a frog yet.

But he was ready for sleep and hunkered down as comfortably as he could. He heard voices and distant traffic, but no one bothered him throughout the day. Callan drifted with the current all the following night, but was unable to estimate how far he'd travelled.

Without knowing, he passed Minden as the river flowed on towards Bremen which was a big town to be avoided. By dawn he rowed ashore in what looked like a rural area. Rye, barley fields, orchards, market gardens and cow paddocks stretched from the river on either side.

Callan realised he needed more food to sustain him, so he'd have to raid a farmer's garden and possibly a hen-house. He found another spot where willow trees dropped so thickly at the water's edge, Callan could hide the boat. From cover he spied a farmhouse with surrounding barns close by. Two teenage girls herded cattle for milking while a woman, who looked to be in her late thirties, chopped wood and took it inside.

Callan needed food before he continued that evening and had all day to wait for an opportunity. He was a farm boy after all, so how hard could it be? He found some raspberries close to the river bank, which tasted fine, but weren't particularly sustaining. Also

July can be a surprisingly sparse time in orchards. All the spring stone fruit was finished while the pears and apples were yet to ripen. Maybe he'd find a plum tree.

He waited all morning until everyone went inside the main house for a mid-day meal. Callan thought this was his best chance especially as he hadn't heard any dogs barking. Using bushes, tree trunks, fence-posts and anything else that served as cover, Callan edged stealthily towards the farm buildings. At least his Gallipoli experience was turning out to be useful for something.

He reached the farmyard without alarming anyone. His first stop was the hen-house where hens ranged freely during the day. A rooster strutted around like a German infantryman on parade. Keeping a weather-eye on the rooster, which could be aggressive, Callan purloined several eggs, placing them carefully in his pockets. Removing eggs from broody hens without upsetting them was something he'd done all his life.

He'd spied a fenced vegetable garden close to one of the barns where he might find some carrots and spuds. As he turned from the henhouse he stared straight into the eyes of an Alsatian dog.

The Alsatian eyed Callan with some hostility, snarling menacingly. The dog didn't bark, but then neither did it have to. As Callan raised his eyes he saw the woman approaching with a pitch-fork raise chest high. He was about to make a bolt for it when the teenage girls appeared on either side one was armed with an axe while the other levelled a single-barrelled shot-gun at his chest.

They'd approached so stealthily and with such speed, Callan was taken completely by surprise and now they were only feet away. Wedged up to the hen-house behind him, Callan had no escape route. He had no way of knowing how good a shot the girl was and he'd never outrun the Alsatian anyway.

Blimey, I'm losing my touch. I'd have heard Johnny Turk a mile off. Flaming aero-engines have made me deaf.

The woman said something to the dog and it calmed down. She also said something to Callan which he didn't understand, but allowed himself to be escorted to the farmhouse kitchen especially after a couple of prods from the pitch-fork tines. Strangely Callan didn't sense any deep-rooted hostility from the three Germans, but more nervous curiosity. Even if he did make a dash for it, they'd raise the alarm in no time.

Once inside, the woman urged Callan to sit at a table spread with bread, milk, cheese, tomatoes and pickled gherkins.

'Ich bin Frau Wolff. Sitz — essen — gut, ja?'

Callan realised she was inviting him to be seated for a meal. He didn't need to be asked twice.

Chapter 36 — A Warrior Returns

D'vere-Brown Country House, Shropshire — New Year 1919

'Madam, there is a person at the door who wishes to speak with you and the colonel,' Beatrice, the new parlour maid announced.

How quickly the other household staff had either become betrothed or married, hoping to snap up what few eligible young men were left. Beatrice was barely sixteen — the only girl left on the agency books. She was sweet, well-meaning, eager, but inexperienced and bobbed a lot.

'A person..?' Meredith D'vere-Brown ventured.

'Yes, madam. He is bearded and dressed in a faded uniform. He is powerfully thin and pale, but looks tough and mean.'

Oh my goodness, not another tramp posing as a war veteran or indeed a genuine ex-soldier looking for a handout.

'Is he just looking for a hot meal, Beatrice?'

'He didn't say, madam, but insisted on speaking to you and the colonel. I told him to use the tradesman's entrance, but he said he only used the front door.'

'I'll come.'

Meredith followed Beatrice through the hall. The caller stood silhouetted against the door frame. The morning sunlight was behind him so at first Meredith was unable to recognise him.

Oh, dear God...it can't be...

'Good morning, Meredith,' the visitor drawled. 'I hope you don't mind familiarity, but I'm all out of protocol right now.'

'Callan...Callan McAlister...We thought you were...'

'Dead?'

'Yes.'

'A little premature, I'd say, but not from want of trying by every damned Hun on the Western Front.'

'Mind your language with madam present,' Beatrice admonished with commendable pluck.

'I'm sorry, but like I said, I'm out of practice with social airs and graces.'

Callan was still dressed in a faded, but clean AFC uniform, but his wings insignia, medal-ribbons and major's crowns were still easily identifiable. His peaked cap was battered although the kitbag he carried over his shoulder looked brand new.

'Sorry about my appearance. The repatriation desk-jockeys wanted me to get a new dress uniform tailored in London, but I told them it'd wait. I had things to do.'

'You'd better come in before you catch your death.'

'If four months in Southern Saxony didn't kill me, a little west country chill won't bother me much. Blimey, Germany can be flaming cold.'

'Yes, but we don't want you catching Spanish flu,' Meredith insisted.

A particularly virulent flu first noticed in Spain was sweeping Europe, and as if the war hadn't claimed enough lives, hundreds died of the disease daily. Meredith hustled Callan inside, asking Beatrice to prepare tea and anything nourishing she could rustle up. Callan entered the parlour to be greeted by Colonel D'vere-Brown. Ivy's father walked with the aid of a cane nowadays and had lost much of his past vigour.

'Congratulations on your promotion. I believe you have had quite a distinguished wartime career.'

'Yes sir, I can remember many of the highlights, especially killing Turks, Germans and Irishmen I had no argument with, shooting other young men out of the sky and spending my twenty-first birthday on the run.'

'On the run? I don't understand. Everyone thought you'd been killed in action. Ivy was devastated of course.'

'I'm not surprised. Germany was a mess in 18. The paperwork must have gone astray — simple as that, or the fact I wasn't in the POW camp for more than a couple of weeks before I escaped.'

'Escaped — what happened to you?' Meredith asked, almost spilling the tea as she poured.

'A bunch of us broke out in July. Later I found out over half were re-captured, but I was caught by a farmwife and her daughters. They'd lost all their men folk at the front and needed someone to help work the farm. I'd had enough fighting to last a lifetime and everyone knew the war was finally coming to an end. I was happy to see out the war helping out. I am a farm boy remember.'

'You can't just opt out of the army whenever you feel like it,' Colonel D'vere-Brown observed. 'There will be people who might say something about dereliction of duty, cowardice, aiding and abetting the enemy or even desertion.'

'I don't consider innocent women and teenage girls my enemy,' Callan countered. 'The German military came and confiscated most of their produce anyway. I knew the family needed my help or they'd starve through winter.'

'I do not think anyone can accuse Callan of cowardice, dear,' Meredith said, eyeing the row of medals on Callan's chest, which now included a DSO.

'What did General Monash make of it all?' the colonel asked.

'Frankly sir, I left out most of the details. As far as the general is concerned I was a POW. Right now he's far too busy demobilising his army to be bothered with niceties. I'm telling you on trust.'

'We will not break your confidence,' Meredith stated resolutely in case her husband had other ideas.

'I guess I was out of the system when the Red Cross inspectors called at Holzminder, so I was sort of overlooked or that bastard *Kommandant* Niemeyer couldn't be bothered telling anyone,' Callan said. 'No one knew I'd been captured and oh boy, were they surprised when I turned up after the armistice. General Monash had recommended me for this gong posthumously, so he insisted his staff telegraph my Mum and Dad immediately.'

'Thank heavens they've been notified,' Meredith remarked.

'My brother Robert is still at sea on his way home,' Callan said. 'He may not hear the news until he gets there. *Frau* Wolff and her girls were keen for me to stay at the farm to help out, so I did until after Christmas then made my way back to Blighty. The army wanted to send me back to Australia straight away, but I said I had to make a call first. Good old Archie Blake pulled some strings for me. He got me fresh kit. It's a bit threadbare, but he's booked me up for a posh tailor next week.'

Blimey, I've blabbed on long enough.

'Where's Ivy?' Callan asked — demanded actually.

The colonel gave him a pained look and Meredith burst into tears, which wasn't what Callan expected.

'She's not here,' Colonel D'vere-Brown said flatly, while Meredith sobbed into a lace-edged handkerchief.

'Not here..?'

'That's what I said. She has barely spoken a word to her mother for over a year and is only civil to me because of my ill-health.'

'I'm sorry, but...'

'It was my fault,' Meredith wailed. 'I intercepted her letters. It was wrong I know.'

'She did mention that,' Callan replied dryly, 'but I rather hoped she'd cooled down a bit.'

'Will you forgive me, Callan?'

'How about we do a deal? You tell me where Ivy is and we'll forget all about any past differences.'

'She's in Dorset,' Meredith said flatly.

'That's not too bad then. I'm sure there's a line through Swindon. Someone told me every train in England goes through Swindon.'

'She has taken a position as governess to an Indian sultan's family. Apparently he is paying her a small fortune.'

'That's sultans for you — loads of dosh to chuck around.'

'What are your plans?' the colonel asked.

'Do you mean, are my intentions honourable?'

'Our daughter is very precious to us,' Meredith said.

Precious enough for you to stop her mail, Callan thought, but didn't say anything.

'I'm going to ask her to marry me,' Callan beamed. 'I assume a decorated AFC major is more acceptable than an Anzac private farm-lad?'

The colonel and his wife looked sheepishly at Callan. The war had changed much and cutting off their daughter's inheritance because of her romantic choices was no longer on the agenda.

'Tell you what — if she says 'yes', I'll tell her she'll have to forgive and forget.'

'Let me see if we can find that railway timetable and I have the full title and sultan's address around here somewhere,' Colonel D'vere-Brown said, extending his hand as Meredith kissed Callan gently on the cheek, which he took as a positive sign.

*

Much as he wanted to go straight to Ivy, Callan returned to London and took up Archie Blake's offer of a new uniform. Even a NSW bumpkin knew you fronted royalty in your best clobber, even if that royalty was a tin-pot ruler of some end-of-the-world principality. Also if you want to go courting, you should at least dress up for the occasion.

Callan wasted no time heading to Savile Row as General Monash was footing the bill. His first call was Dege & Skinner at No 10. William Skinner had only joined the firm two years earlier when the firm specialised in military uniforms. A bevy of assistants looked on uncertainly when Callan entered the premises.

Snobbishness and elitism were rampant on Savile Row, but major's pips and a chest-full of awards went a long way to breaking down barriers.

'May I be of assistance?' one of the counter-men offered uncertainly before adding, 'sir.'

'How long will it take to make me a new uniform?'

'Sir...we...er...are an establishment...er...with royal patronage...'

'That's not what I asked,' Callan replied with a smile.

'What I mean, sir is we have a certain expectation of our clientele.'

'I'm sure you do, but I understand their lordships are famous for not paying their bills on time. I, on the other hand, am underwritten by General Sir John Monash, Commander-in-Chief of the Australian Army Corps and he pays up promptly. So — how long does it take to make a uniform?'

'Normally for bespoke gentlemen's attire, if we make an appointment for an initial fitting later in the week, we expect the final fitting in six weeks.'

'Six flaming weeks — do you shear the sheep yourself?'

The assistant shrugged.

'You know I've heard they can knock up a suit over-night in Hong Kong and Singapore,' Callan said.

The assistant looked appalled.

'In that case I suggest you visit Chinatown, sir. Dege and Skinner do not...knock up garments.'

'Four flaming years fighting the Boche with guns, bombs and bayonets and I'm beaten by a bloke with a needle-and thread,' Callan declared, throwing up his hands in exasperation.

But the assistant's advice proved faultless. By lunch-time the following day, dressed in an immaculately fitting uniform, Callan boarded a steam locomotive express at newly renovated Waterloo Station bound for Weymouth.

Best fiver's worth ever, he beamed. *The general will be pleased.*

As the steam locomotive chugged through the bleak winter countryside that looked so verdant in summer, Callan's thoughts were not only of Ivy. In the last four months of 1918 he'd rediscovered contentment in productive hard work. Frau Wolff and her daughters, Kikka and Magnilde were typically attractive no-nonsense blonde-plaited fair-skinned Saxons. It was quickly established that if Callan earned his keep, they wouldn't turn him in. The choice was a no-brainer. If Callan was to be a captive, he knew where he rather be imprisoned. Over time Callan picked up enough rudimentary German to discover Frau Wolff's husband had been killed somewhere along the Somme in the war's early weeks. Her sons, Gustav and Oswald were buried under a million tons of mud after the first mega-mines exploded to herald the Messines Ridge assault.

There was a time when Callan would have simply thought, *well you shouldn't have started the flaming war in the first place*, but he was over that now. Like the Wolff family it was unlikely one German in a thousand wanted to march off and conquer the world. Wasn't he just like Gustav and Oswald, only luckier?

German military commissariat teams roamed the country side, foraging for anything they could. There was always ample warning before they arrived, giving Callan time to hide. Once the harvest was baled the soldiers' sweeps became less and finally stopped altogether and the Wolff family had squirreled enough away to last through winter.

There was no task Callan couldn't perform. He'd been born to farm life after all and being a crack-shot, he bagged numerous rabbits to supplement their diet. Yet as September rolled into October and the days shortened an event occurred that still left

Callan with mixed feelings. While Frau Wolff and her daughters occupied the two upstairs bedrooms, Callan slept in the loft where warm air from the hearth wafted upwards keeping him snug.

They were a naturally cheerful family despite the horrors and their losses during the war. They loved to sing traditional oompah-pah folk songs accompanied by a button-accordion and cow-bells. Despite everything, Callan still possessed his Hohner harmonica and enjoyed nothing better than playing along.

One night when he was about to turn in Frau Wolff climbed the ladder to Callan's loft. Nothing was said as she slid beneath the blankets beside him. It turned out she was a passionate woman and four years had passed since Herr Wolff proudly marched away to war.

After that night, she visited Callan regularly, although he never presumed to go to her bedroom. In a way he was glad the good Frau introduced him to experiences which would be handy to know when the time came for his own marriage bed. But also a lingering guilt that he'd done the 'wrong thing' hung over him. He smiled as he peered through the carriage window.

Yep, it was fun though and there was little enough of that during the flaming war.

When he left there was a flood or tears, but Callan knew he must go. Frau Wolff even hinted she'd throw in her daughters to sweeten the deal if he stayed. She was a pragmatic woman who thought Germany needed a new generation of young men just as quickly as possible. So after many hugs he bade the Wolff ladies farewell, knowing he'd left them in good shape for the coming year.

Callan caught a train heading west for the Dutch border. At every station thousands of hope-sapped sunken-eyed German veterans crowded the platforms waiting for eastbound trains to carry them home. After four years carnage there were still some young men left who might accommodate Frau Wolff and her daughters.

He reported to the first Allied unit he came across, which was a company of Canadian sappers who were repairing a bridge. They were surprised to see an Anzac marching out of Germany, but gave him a lift to divisional headquarters and back to England.

*

Callan caught a bus at Weymouth Station. It was only a short trip to Dorchester where the sultan's house stood at the outskirts of town, bordering the countryside. The 'house' was more of a mansion in the centre of a ten acre estate surrounded by a stone wall.

Callan eased the wrought iron gates open. Nobody attended the coach-house so he crunched along the frost-encrusted gravel driveway. No cars were parked by the front steps, but then if you're stinking rich with a fancy Roller or Bentley, you'll put it in the garage out back, won't you?

He hammered on an ornate gargoyle door-knocker.

And if just one toffee-nosed servant tells me to use the tradesman's entrance, I'll thump 'em in the jaw!

Callan was surprised when a rather normal looking fellow dressed in a standard suit answered the door.

'Good afternoon to you sir,' he greeted civilly enough — no hint of the back door. 'How may I be of assistance?'

'I've come to see Miss Ivy D'vere-Brown. Is she home?'

'I am afraid I am not acquainted with that lady, sir.'

'I understand she is governess to the Sultan Aashif Jalil's family.'

'Oh, yes indeed, but there is no one here at present.'

'When will she be back?'

'I am sorry, but that I cannot say, sir.'

Callan stared at him blankly.

'You see sir, his highness felt sufficiently recovered from his war injuries to make the journey back to India. He has duties there I believe — repatriating his battalion and so on. They left early yesterday morning. I have been commissioned to prepare this property for lease for at least twelve months.'

'And everyone went with him?'

'Indeed, sir. The entire household. Only a caretaker remains. We have hired a cleaning service to visit monthly and keep everything shipshape.'

It appeared the factor was conscientious in his duties.

'And the governess, Miss D'vere-Brown has gone with them.'

'I have heard nothing to the contrary, so I would understand that to be correct, sir.'

'Then I must hurry. At which port do they intend to board the ship? I must catch up.'

'Goodness me, sir I fear you are too late already. As I said they left yesterday for embarkation at Southampton. Their steamer sailed with the morning tide and I estimate she will be in mid-Channel as we speak.'

Of all the flaming sour luck! I could have been here yesterday when I was poncing around with fancy uniforms..!

Chapter 37 — Air Race

***Director-General of Repatriation and Demobilisation HQ, London
— January 1919***

'I have to get to India, Archie,' Callan pleaded with newly promoted Lieutenant-Colonel Blake, who was now a permanent fixture on General Monash's staff. 'I mean like right now.'

'Look Callan, don't be in such a rush and do anything foolish,' Blake advised. 'You could be looking at a successful career in the AFC. I mean you're a twenty-one year old major. Dammit, I'm twice your age.'

'But how can I get to India if I'm still in the AFC unless they post me there and the only postings right now are to Russia to fight the flaming Bolsheviks. I don't even know which part of the sub-continent this Sultan Aashif Jalil lives in.'

'I can help you there,' Archie said, spreading a map over his desk. Our Intel boffins have investigated. It wasn't hard. Apparently his battalion were right larrikins and have more gongs between them than practically any other unit. He runs a sultanate called Dera Jalil Khan. Here it is — along the Indus River north of Karachi.'

Callan studied the map.

'It shouldn't be too hard to reach if I can get to Karachi,' Callan said.

'Tell you what. I can organise six months leave without pay and let's see how you feel then. How you get to India is your business, but you have a hefty back-pay nest-egg.'

'Can I access the money?'

'No worries, we can get the paymaster to open an account with Lloyds Bank. They have worldwide branches, which might be handy from what you say.'

Blake handed Callan a mountain of paperwork to sign before the men shook hands and said farewell.

'I knew you were a goodun, back in Lismore,' Blake smiled.

'When was that, Archie, maybe a thousand years ago?'

'Feels like it, doesn't it. Good luck, mate. I hope you find your girl. She's a little corker if you don't mind me saying.'

'Not at all. Thanks for everything, Archie and thank the general too.'

'I will.'

As Callan left Blake's office he passed an RAF captain about his age in the hallway. The officer walked with a marked limp.

'Excuse me, Major,' the captain said. 'You're Callan McAlister, aren't you?'

Callan stopped and faced the young stranger, trying to recall the face. His accent marked him as Australian but other than that he was in no way familiar.

'I'm sorry...have we met?'

'Just once in passing, but you won't remember. I'm Charles Kingsford-Smith and if it's not impertinent, I'd be honoured to shake the hand of a true Australian hero.'

'Thanks, but you're no slouch either, judging by that MC ribbon on your chest.'

Callan extended his hand.

'It seems aviators either get decorated or die over the Western Front,' Kingsford-Smith observed. 'Got shot down myself in seventeen and lost a chunk of my foot. Bally thing gives me hell in damp weather.'

'What are you doing now the show is over?'

'I've just been demobbed. Cyril Maddocks, a Tassie mate of mine has started a joy-flight business up north with war-surplus crates. They're going dirt cheap right now.'

And that gave Callan an idea — a pretty ambitious one with a lot of details that needed to be ironed out, but an idea nevertheless...

*

Callan joined Kingsford-Smith, who was a fellow Gallipoli veteran, at Maddocks Aeros Ltd in Northern England.

Primarily because Callan couldn't think of anywhere else to stay for the time being, but he also needed Cyril Maddocks' help and advice. So he signed up as a casual pilot with Maddocks, spending some time taking thrill-seekers for joy-rides, while he hunted around for a suitable plane of his own.

'Buying a kite is child's play,' Maddocks said. 'Keeping the wretched thing licensed and air worthy are the killers. You need a mechanic and support.'

And then one morning a possible opportunity presented itself.

'Ten thousand quid reward for the first plane to fly from Hounslow Heath to Australia within a month. Billy Hughes has just authorised the Australian Treasury to put up the dough,' Kingsford Smith declared, perusing the *Daily Mail* while dunking toast soldiers into his boiled eggs.

'That's just the ticket,' Maddocks declared.

Callan stared at him.

'Come on Callan, don't you see?'

'I don't see what it has to do with me buying a plane and flying to India.'

'We'll enter the competition. It's only a hundred quid entry fee and we'll get government help for refuelling, maintenance and accommodation along the way. I'll hunt around and I'm sure I can dig up sponsors, especially from the *Daily Mail*. Lord Northcliffe will be up for it. He was as keen as mustard about air races before the war.'

Maddocks' enthusiasm was infectious and he arranged not only financial backing, but procured a *Luftstreitkräfte* Gotha G.V. twin-engine, pusher-prop bomber and arranged for it to be ferried to Hounslow Heath.

'Bought it for a song, but I had to get in quickly,' Maddocks said. 'It looks like our blokes are hell-bent on destroying all the German military hardware they find. What a damned waste. I've got a few deals for Fokkers as well. It looks like there is money to be made from the second-hand aircraft market.'

At first Callan thought Kingsford-Smith and Maddocks would join him aboard the three-crew plane, but they pulled out after pressure from the Royal Aero Club and Australian

Government who thought they were too inexperienced for the enterprise.

'Anyway, you don't want more pilots, you need maintenance men,' Maddocks said. 'We've had some press coverage from the *Mail* and local press. I'll put out an ad for a crew.'

Callan was delighted when he discovered who answered the advertisement and turned up a few days later.

'Charlie Patterson and Bill Simpson, as I live and breathe!' Callan declared shaking both men's hands warmly.

'Yessir,' Simpson replied. 'We saw your name in the paper and thought you'd not get ten miles without us.'

'You're hired. Now we use first names? I'm Callan from here on.'

Bill Simpson and Charlie Patterson were of the old school where a man knew his place and didn't try to get above it. While they only winced slightly when Callan addressed them with such familiarity, it would be some time before they'd bring themselves to abandon his 'sir' title.

'I'm just a New South Wales farm kid after all,' Callan insisted.

'Yes, sir,' both men replied in unison.

The Gotha wasn't the fastest plane around, but it was reliable and had over a five-hundred-mile range which was the minimum needed for any hope of making the flight. Callan told Patterson and Simpson they'd share the £10,000 prize if they made it.

'So as I understand the plan, sir,' Simpson surmised. 'We take part in the air race, pick up your lady along the way and wind up in Australia.'

'That's about the size of it, Bill.'

'India's a bleedin' big place,' Patterson observed.

'Take a look here,' Callan said as he unfolded one of the many charts he had prepared for navigating to Australia. 'This is our route: Paris-Rome-Athens-Cyprus-Damascus-Baghdad-Basra-Muscat-Karachi-a quick detour up the Indus River to Dera Jalil Khan then on through Delhi-Calcutta-Rangoon-Bangkok-Penang Island-Singapore-Jakarta-Denpasar-Kupang-Darwin, how hard can it be?'

About then they hit their first snag — well their first three snags really.

In his enthusiasm to make history Maddocks failed to read the small print in the competition rules. But the Royal Aero Club officials who oversaw the race from the British end were sticklers for details and instantly disqualified Callan. Actually they didn't disqualify Callan, but Patterson and Simpson weren't Australian nationals and the Gotha G.V. had not been built within the British Empire. Those were two essential requirements to enter the race. National pride rated highly in Prime Minister Billy Hughes' priorities.

Maddocks claimed as Patterson and Simpson were British subjects, which automatically made them Imperial citizens, they were therefore Australians. It was a stretch, and might have been arguable. The Gotha, on the other hand, was not only made beyond Imperial boundaries, but also by the Empire's mortal enemy.

'We'll have to change the plane and crew,' Maddocks declared undismayed.

'No, there's no time to get a new machine. I'll go alone,' Callan said.

Everyone in the hangar stared at him.

'You can't go by yourself,' Kingsford-Smith protested. 'No one can.'

'You ain't goin' nowhere without us,' Patterson said as Simpson nodded with determination.

'There won't be any prize money,' Callan explained. 'We'll lose our sponsorship. It'll take all my cash just for fuel.'

'Maybe not,' Maddocks said with his usual *glass-half-full* attitude. 'Look even if you're not part of the race, mate, you'll still be a sensation when you get to Darwin. I reckon I can persuade most of our backers to stay with the project. And I'll make ruddy sure we get our hundred quid back.'

'What's in it for them now, Cyril?' Callan asked.

'Never under-estimate the value of prestige, Callan. It looks like you'll be first away and the *Mail* is itching for the scoop. So Lord Northcliffe will be happy — he likes scoops. We also have men of vision who've put up varying sums. All you have to do is get to Darwin. The prize-money will be small-change by comparison.'

On 31 March 1919 the Gotha G.V. with three crew, rations, maintenance kit (including parachutes) and extra fuel tanks carried in the bomb compartment, lifted off from Hounslow Heath. Quite a crowd, including most of Maddocks Areo Ltd staff, turned out to see the adventurers depart. Standing beside a staff car, General Sir John Monash and Colonel Archie Blake watched the plane lift through a thin cloud layer and disappear southwards.

'I hope that's not the last we'll see of young Callan,' Archie said under his breath.

'I wouldn't count on it,' the general smiled. 'He does have a habit of popping back up, doesn't he?'

*

Sultan's Palace, Dera Jalil Khan Province, Indus Valley foothills — Late March 1919

Ivy was just finishing a sketch of the panorama towards the mountains. The sultan's children always marvelled at her talent. She spent hours teaching them the basic techniques, but as yet none of the youngsters showed any particular artistic talent.

At first glance Jalil's home did indeed appear palatial, but on close inspection — like what little else of India Ivy had seen, the building was rather down at the heel and in need of a coat of paint. This seemed to be a result of the harsh climate rather than lack of attention. Jalil certainly had funds enough for lush carpets, expensive drapes and quality furnishings, not to mention numerous household servants.

So far Ivy had been spared much of the squalor that was rife in India although she often gazed from one of the many palace balconies towards the hovels that made up the shanty-town outside the gates. Begging seemed to be the population's chief industry.

Ivy had settled in well and enjoyed tutoring the royal children in English, maths, basic science (which was all she knew), history and geography (which she knew a great deal about). She still carried her satchel even though the sultan spared no expense in supplying whatever equipment she wanted.

The women of the house consisted of Jalil's three wives who were all in varying stages of pregnancy and half a dozen concubines who were not. Jalil had been busy during his leave breaks from the western front. His wives had dutifully produced seven heirs so far. There were four rather charming girls and three rather tiresome boys who were altogether too full of their own self-importance.

The eldest son ibn-Jalil was by far the worst. Although he was just thirteen, he knew he was destined to rule the Sultanate in due course. He neglected his lessons and was only interested in horse racing, hunting, cricket, hockey and falconry. Ivy also noticed he took an unsavoury interest in the teenage servant girls, but who was to gainsay him?

One irritating aspect of Islamic regal life was that Ivy was expected to wear a hijab. Jalil's wives had approached Ivy, saying it was the Sultan's wish, although face veils were not required inside the palace walls. Actually she got used to the head scarf and found it far more comfortable than a heavy bonnet. She had a large selection of colourful silks to choose from and wore a different one every day.

The women were all quartered in the palace harem, which was a spacious multi-roomed area consisting of bedrooms, common rooms, kitchen, female servants' quarters, lavatories and a communal bathing area. Initially Ivy was tentative, but the harem women were quite at ease bathing naked together. But dammit Mohamed — *may Allah smile perpetually upon the great prophet —* had made a rule for everything.

You washed your private parts with your left hand, you prayed countless times a day whatever you were doing, you had to wear different clothing at different times depending where you were. Most dogmatic of all was you were required to shave (or pluck — ooh) your under-arm and pubic hair at least every forty days.

Forty days! Who made that one up?

Whereas Ivy liked to keep her under-arms neat, it wasn't something that concerned many English women. Ivy hadn't thought too much about 'down there' as the whole subject was still taboo in polite society. However she found the idea appealing — why should she not pay as much attention to all her body hair as she did to her head. She especially liked the smoothness of her freshly shaved legs which was an emerging fashion in Europe as Paris haute couture decreed rising hem-lines and sheer silk stockings.

At first she saw little of Jalil, but after a couple of weeks his work-load slackened off and he spent more time with his womenfolk although he never ventured into the harem. All contact with his family was done strictly by appointment.

He was interested in his children's education, knowing they'd need to reach a high standard if they were to compete in India or the world beyond. Ibn-Jalil was ear-marked for a prestigious British boarding school in Simla at the Himalayan foothills.

And that will do him no harm at all!

Then another insidious and more disturbing development occurred. At first Jalil left Ivy to her duties and barely spoke to her other than a passing greeting. But soon he began to seek her out, asking her opinion about general topics and updates on the children's health and schooling. It was not like the sultan to engage in small-talk.

'You must remember, your highness,' Ivy reminded him, 'I am not a trained educator, I can only try to teach what I know.'

'Come now, Ivy ibnatu Humphrey D'vere-Brown, your experience is vast and eminently interesting.'

'Oh the children don't mind hearing my war experiences, although they are time-consuming, but they are less receptive to algebra and conjugated verbs.'

Jalil laughed.

'I'm sure you enchant them continually. You have bewitched the entire palace with your charm and beauty.'

Is he flirting with me..?

'I try to be friendly with everyone.'

'Including me..?'

'I'm sure that goes without saying, your highness.'

Over the following days Jalil would often take Ivy's arm or place his arm around her waist when they walked together. Whereas the experience wasn't necessarily unpleasant, it still made Ivy feel uncomfortable. She tackled Raym ibnatu Mumbais, Jalil's *panguian* or chief wife when safely back in the harem.

'His highness is becoming very familiar,' Ivy suggested, wondering what the court protocol might be.

'It is as my lord — *may Allah smile upon his revered form —* wishes,' Raym replied with a look of disbelief that someone would question anything the sultan did or said.

'I am getting the feeling he is courting me.'

'Goodness me, of course he is.'

'You know? Don't you mind?'

'It is not my place to mind, but my lord — *may the grace of Allah shine upon his face daily* — has discussed the matter with me and his other wives.'

'Discussed what..?'

'The matter of your betrothal. Safwha ibnatu Abdul Ahal and Maryah ibnatu Abdus Samad and I have no objection.'

'Okay, this is spooky. Jalil's three wives have no objection to..?'

'You becoming his fourth wife, in fact we'd be delighted for you to join the family.'

'May I ask why he has discussed the matter with you and not me?'

'It is a matter of harmony within the seraglio. You have noticed that we all get along together, have you not?'

'I'm sorry to disappoint you, but I have no intention of marrying Sultan Jalil.'

'I doubt if you will have a choice. He — *blessed by Allah on high* — already had three advantageous unions with the daughters of three powerful caliphs — *may Allah smile upon them* — and now desires a union with the British Raj.'

'Not this part of the British Raj, he won't.'

'The nuptials are already being planned.'

'I don't believe it. He hasn't even asked me!'

'The sultan — *praised in the eyes of Allah* — does not feel obliged to ask for what he desires.'

'What if I refuse — which I will — is he going to take me to his bed by force.'

'That is unlikely. No woman would be foolish enough to refuse the Sultan — *may he be favoured in Allah's sight*. However, to take you by force would be a great loss of face, so he will be patient — but only to a point.'

'I've got news for him. This woman will refuse.'

Ivy stormed from the harem and broke about every protocol when she barged into Jalil's work chamber. Ivy was so mad she failed to notice the looks of absolute horror on the faces of Jalil's advisors, military officers and courtiers.

'How dare this woman..?' one of the chief ministers blustered.

'I beg your pardon, your highness,' Ivy said as calmly as she could, 'but there is a matter of utmost personal importance that cannot wait.'

Jalil waved his men away. He stared at Ivy with eyes as black as coal.

Chapter 38 — The Great Indus Valley Rubies

Damascus — April 1919

Callan discovered having a mega-national daily newspaper backing him had enormous advantages. True to Cyril Maddocks' prediction, Lord Northcliffe, the *Daily Mail's* eccentric and aging owner gave Callan's project his full support. *Mail* agents and correspondents met the Gotha wherever it landed and eagerly interviewed the crew members.

Company factors arranged fuel, food and accommodation for Callan, Bill Simpson and Charlie Patterson. True, the sleeping quarters were sometimes under the plane's wing and the food exotically spicy, but there was always a bathing tent with a portable shower with ablution facilities. Callan had no complaints as each mile drew him closer to Ivy.

The *Daily Mail* reporters used a sophisticated communications network, allowing Callan to wire ahead and order fuel, oil and rations. Spare parts were always problematic, but so far Bill and Charlie had kept the engines running smoothly although they used oil copiously.

The Gotha attracted some interest from local Arabs who often turned up in camel-trains, eyeing the plane with a mixture of curiosity and suspicion. Callan received support from British and French units still stationed throughout Mesopotamia.

Bill and Charlie had grounded the Gotha for a few days, while they worked on the plane. It was frustrating for Callan, who thought the machine ran perfectly.

'That's the whole point ain't it, Guv?' Charlie said.

He and Bill had dropped the 'sir' title, but were not yet ready for 'Callan'.

'What point?'

'The plane goes perfectly Guv, because we keeps it in tip-top condition, don't we?'

'Yes...I know that.'

'We don't wait for summut to go wrong, Guv 'nor,' Bill explained. 'It's called preventative maintenance. We change the oil and air filters before they get clogged. We change the oil before it gets gritty. We drain the water from the fuel tank before it can build up. We...'

'Yes chaps, I get the message. You blokes are little mechanical angels.'

'We are that, Guv,' Charlie beamed. 'Also it gives you more time to study them maps proper and make sure we get where we're going.'

Callan couldn't argue with that logic. Much of the navigation was via coastlines or using unique geographic features. So Callan studied his charts, drinking tea and munching a bully-beef sandwich supplied by a British catering unit billeted in tents a few miles from Damascus. Callan had landed at an air-strip often used by transiting RAF squadrons patrolling the Levant.

Callan was so engrossed in his study he failed to notice an approaching figure until a shadow fell over the map. At first Callan couldn't make out the silhouette against the sunlight.

'Greeting, Callan my old friend,' the stranger greeted, dressed in traditional Arab thobe and ghutra.

'Blow me down, Hassan al-Wazir!' Callan cried, jumping to his feet and embracing his old comrade. 'How did you know where I was? How did you get here?'

'Well met, Callan. It pleases me Allah — *may his name be praised* — has spared you through the war.'

Callan was about to say something about doubting whether Allah had anything to do with it, but remembered how touchy Hassan was about his relationship with God.

'Your name and picture are in all the papers,' Hassan explained. 'I knew at once it was my old friend and comrade-in-arms. I have followed your progress from London. You have made good time by all accounts. My home is Jerusalem, only a hundred and thirty miles away. The train service is still unreliable so I had a stout mount to bear me here. Come see.'

Hassan usually rode a camel, but this time he was on horseback. Once again Callan was gob-smacked. Hitched to a handy rail stood Flash-Jack.

'Flash-Jack saw his young rider safely through the war,' Hassan explained. 'It broke the lad's heart when he was sent home and had to leave his horse.'

Callan threw his arm around Flash-Jack's neck and stroked his mane. Even after four years, the waler seemed equally pleased to see his old rider. He snorted a little while nuzzling into Callan. Hassan explained Flash-Jack was to be sold to the Indian Army or destroyed. Fortunately Hassan had ridden with the Light

Horsemen as they advanced through the Sinai, Gaza and joined them on their historic charge at Beersheba. So he'd been at hand at war's end to pick up some equine bargains, Flash-Jack among them.

Bill and Charlie had built a fire and were brewing tea when Callan introduced them. They shared a meal and a brew while Hassan filled them in on the situation in Asia Minor and he was an unhappy man.

'We tribesmen fought the Ottomans beside Lawrence when we could have simply stood aside. Now France and Britain have carved Arabia into their mandates. There is even talk of a Zionist state in Palestine to accommodate Jewish refugees fleeing the Russian pogroms. If that occurs there will be civil war and trust me, the Palestinians will never surrender their homeland.'

Callan sympathised. He had firsthand experience of Hassan's contribution to the war effort. Maybe the tribesmen only sided with the allies to get rid of Turkish oppression, but they were still being ignored in the name of global politics called the Sykes-Picot Agreement, thought up by a pair of hitherto unknown English and French diplomats. Although the document had not been officially adopted, it was the basis for post-war mega-power negotiations and the locals were nervous about the outcome.

Once Hassan had aired his grievances, Callan told him about his quest for Ivy.

'So how do you plan to retrieve your lady?' Hassan asked.

'I don't think that's a problem,' Callan replied. 'I am going to ask her to marry me and take her to Australia.'

'What if she is no longer in a position to do so?'

'What do you mean?

'She thinks you're dead...'

'...and she's made other plans?'

'Possibly, or Sultan Aashif Jalil has made other plans for her.'

'You mean...kidnapped her..?

Hassan shrugged.

'Do you have room for another man in your plane?' The Arab asked.

Charlie and Bill exchanged glances.

'We can fix a temporary seat in the rear-cockpit, Guv. It'll take a day or so, but shouldn't be a problem.'

'You'd drop everything and help?' Callan said.

'I remember I owe you my life, Callan,' Hassan recalled the incident at An-Nekhel in the Sinai so long ago.

'There are no debts between friends,' Callan reminded him.

'You might need someone who thinks like a Muslim.'

'We won't be coming back this way.'

'Making my way back here is no problem. I have travelled the spice roads many times before. I shall leave Flash-Jack with a friend who will care for him until my return. I will see you tomorrow. You could have sent the girl a letter or a telegram, you know.'

'Cyril Maddocks thought a plane would be faster than a steam-ship. The railways are still a mess from the war and Army intelligence reported bandits have cut the telegraph lines down between Karachi and Quetta. We reckoned this was the best way and Cyril was all fired up to get the publicity.'

'He sounds quite the entrepreneur,' Hassan observed, mounting Flash-Jack.

Callan said what he knew was a final goodbye to his trusty steed before returning to the Gotha to help Bill and Charlie with the alterations. The Gotha rear crewman's station had an opening in the lower fuselage enabling the gunner to bring his Lewis gun to bear on enemy planes attacking from below. The rear Lewis gun had been dismantled, but by boarding up the lower gun-port there was extra space for another crew seat.

Initially both guns had been removed from the Gotha, but Callan thought it wise to be armed going into possibly hostile territory. They'd acquired a surplus Lewis gun in Cyprus and mounted it on the forward gunner's platform. Charlie and Bill had also rigged restraining straps in the bomb compartment which now contained petrol cans, food, drinking water and the crew's kitbags. It was potentially an airborne fire-bomb, but that was the nature of aviation at the time.

The following morning the Gotha took off with a four-man crew on an easterly heading for Baghdad. Callan's flight plan was to hug the north shoreline of the Persian Gulf to Muscat and the Arabian Sea coast to Karachi with refuelling stops at military outposts en route. Fortunately spring weather was mild and, apart for isolated rain showers, visibility was unlimited.

*

Aashif Jalil's stateroom Sultan's Palace, Dera Jalil Khan Province — late April 1919

'I could have you stoned to death for your conduct,' Jalil said evenly.

'That would defeat the purpose of the fate-worse-than-death I understand you have in store for me.'

Ivy was so angry she didn't think to be afraid because she was in great peril indeed. If there was one thing she'd observed,

455

Muslim men were a volatile lot, prone to fits of rage over trivial matters. She deduced it was a result of always getting their own way so they acted like spoilt children.

Jalil smiled.

'So you consider a life of luxury in my palace a fate worse than death.'

'It would have been nice to hear the news firsthand.'

'Unfortunately your father is not here to negotiate a dowry, so I have waived the requirement.'

He'd probably have paid it too, Ivy thought bitterly.

'I will give you time to consider,' Jalil said as if he was being unusually considerate.

'Your highness, much as I am honoured by your offer, it is not my intention to be any man's fourth wife. If I choose to marry I will be my husband's first — and only — wife...and I shall marry because I love him.'

'Are not prestige, honour and position important to you?'

'Not without love,' Ivy declared.

'As I said I will be patient because our culture is as yet unfamiliar to you. But you will learn and embrace your conversion to Islam — *may Allah shine enlightenment upon you.*'

Conversion to Islam!

Ivy was speechless and that was a rare condition for her, but only for a moment.

'I am quite content to remain C-of-E, thank you your highness, where we feel it only necessary to bother God once a week for a short time only.'

'As I say, 'Jalil continued, 'I am patient, but not eternally so. You will become part of this household. A British wife will enhance my prestige in the Raj. Until such time you reconsider your position, you will be permitted free access to the women's areas of the palace, but you will be escorted at all times.'

'So I am a prisoner. You planned this all along, didn't you?'

Jalil shrugged and nodded.

'How do you think you'll get away with this? What happens when the British authorities discover I have been kidnapped?'

'It unlikely they will. As a sultan, no authorities dared interfere with my return to India. No one has checked our papers and no one but my household servants and advisors know you are here. They also know I will cut out their tongues if word goes beyond these walls. I am beyond the Raj within my province. British authorities will not seek to meddle in Dera Jalil Khan unless there is a threat of uprising and I can assure you I will not permit that.'

'This is unacceptable...'

'The reality is there is nothing you can do but accept. In the meantime I have two gifts I wish you to wear at all times.'

Jalil took an ornate jade box from the top drawer of one of several davenport desks around the stateroom.

The box contained two blood-red rubies. One was set in a golden pendant and chain and the other was the centre stone of a ring. Both pieces were encircled with diamonds. Ivy was no expert when it came to jewellery, but she knew these two pieces were priceless.

Jalil clipped the pendant chain around her neck and placed the ring on her left-hand ring-finger. She didn't resist — what was the point and she was momentarily overwhelmed by the sheer opulence of the rubies and their settings.

'These are the Blood Stones of Jalil Khan,' the Sultan whispered with just a hint of awe in his tone. 'They have been in my family for centuries and are said to have been given to my esteemed ancestor — *may Allah show him eternal peace* — by a Mongol chieftain as a tribute after being defeated in battle.'

'Wouldn't these treasures be more appropriate for your *panguian*, Raym ibnatu Mumbais?'

'I alone decide all matters within Dera Jalil Khan Province. I have bestowed a great honour upon you...'

'And you expect me to be awfully grateful? Are these to mark me as your newly acquired possession or to bribe me into submission?' Ivy said, suddenly regretting she may have pushed him too far.

'I do not need badges to display what is mine, but it pleases me to see you adorned by these treasures. However your beauty overshadows the stones to a point where they are mere trinkets.'

Oh, you're smooth with the compliments, Jalil, but sweet words won't win this gal over. But exactly what I can do about it is a complete fog to me right now — '...what is mine indeed...'

'They are my betrothal gift to you,' Jalil added urbanely as if selecting a woman was his God-given right and the nuptials a mere formality.

Ivy was met with a mixed reception when she returned to the seraglio. There was a marked change in Jalil's wives, who were both shocked and resentful. Ivy was just an infidel blow-in and now she wore the coveted Blood Stones. Each of Jalil's wives had been younger than her predecessor, which hadn't been a problem because Jalil didn't played favourites. The harem was content for Ivy to take on the subservient role of wife No 4, but now she posed a threat to the status-quo.

Admittedly Jalil had concubines for amusement while his wives' loyally incubated royal progeny, but now he was obviously smitten by the English rose, permitting her to behave outrageously. Obviously declaring their approval for the sultan's — *may Allah show him the error of his ways* — potential fourth wife had been ill-advised. Well, the harem had ways of putting upstarts in their place and the infidel bitch would be no exception.

And that afternoon a monumental event occurred which gave Jalil's wives just the opportunity they needed to get rid of Ivy D'vere-Brown.

The town surrounding the palace erupted in pandemonium. Men, women, children and livestock scattered hither and yon as a mighty roaring shadow flashed overhead, circling several times. The monster flew at head height clearing everyone from the fields before bumping to earth in a cleared paddock.

Three stubble-faced men climbed from the machine accompanied by a shivering man dressed in Arabian robes wrapped in a blanket. After the initial shock, curiosity overcame the townsfolk and they edged towards the four men. The strangers were armed with revolvers and rifles, but indicated they were friendly.

After a brief discussion accompanied by intense gesturing, the Arab determined they were at the right place.

'Okay, gents. Charlie, will you please guard the kite while we go and pay a visit on his highness the sultan,' Callan said, striding forward as the crowd parted.

Chapter 39 — The Heist

'Blimey, Guv, this place is straight out of a Douglas Fairbanks film,' Bill declared, eyeing the palace domes, minarets and mosaic facades. 'It looks like we're back in the flamin' Middle Ages.'

'You are, Bill,' Hassan remarked grimly. 'Even though the British have nominal control of India, the sultan has absolute power on his home turf — as you Tommies say. It is part of the deal. Aashif Jalil keeps the peace in exchange for territorial autonomy. Don't expect any help from Karachi or Quetta unless Jalil asks for it.'

The palace was at the centre of a partially walled town. The sultan's actual residence was surrounded by a rampart guarded by a pair of sentries. The main entrance consisted of two elegant wrought-iron gates within a stone portal framed by two 19th Century cannons. Jalil's troops were dressed in western khaki uniforms with ghutra headgear. It looked as if the British had reclaimed the modern weapons leaving Jalil's men armed with ancient jezails and curved janbiya and khanjar knives.

A row of prestigious automobiles stood in the courtyard. Callan recognised a Bentley, Mercedes and Rolls Royce among others. Each car sparkled in immaculate condition. A team of cleaners laboured endlessly ensuring not a speck of dust sullied the paintwork.

'Nice motors,' Bill observed.

The townsfolk didn't follow through the gates — they knew better. Callan and his companions didn't get much further either. A stern looking bearded officer dressed in a scarlet tunic stepped forward, raised his hand to bar any further progress. He wore three captain's pips on his epaulettes.

'Who dares enter the sultan's domain uninvited?' the officer demanded.

Callan recognised a veteran when he saw one and knew this fellow was no ornamental guardsman. It was time to flash a bit of brass. Callan casually opened his leather flying jacket revealing his major's uniform and medal ribbons. He knew military men set great store by fellow valiants.

'My name is Major Callan McAlister. My colleagues are Hassan al-Wazir and the honourable William Simpson.'

Callan wasn't averse to laying it on thick although Bill wasn't so sure about his elevated status. As far as he knew 'honourables' were all politicians and he didn't have a high opinion of them, but he let it slide.

'What is your business here?'

'Actually we have come to talk to a lady, Captain,' Callan replied glibly.

The captain frowned. This utterly stumped him. Why would anyone come untold miles to see a woman?

'You are English..?' the captain suggested as if that explained everything.

'Australian, but close enough.'

Now the captain was really confused. He was well aware of the sultan's decree regarding the English woman, but this foreign infidel already knew she was in the palace.

'That will do, *Risaldar*,' a voice commanded with absolute authority.

The captain heaved a sigh of relief, snapped to attention and saluted an approaching man dressed in pristine white robes. Callan offered a salute when he noticed the guards froze at attention. The bystanders who had business within the palace, bowed before edging away into oblivion. Callan was pretty sure this fellow was the sultan, so he remained silent. He'd heard somewhere you wait for royalty to speak first.

'Well, well, young man, you have made quite an entrance with your noisy flying machine which appears to have scared my subjects witless and scattered their livestock.'

'A thousand apologies, your highness. Finding a suitable landing strip is one of the major challenges for an aviator.'

'Indeed.'

Jalil didn't introduce himself, he naturally expected minions (which included everyone below the status of baron) to know precisely who he was and learn his correct form of address before bothering him. There was a slight pause until Callan realised the sultan had no intention of offering him his aristocratic hand.

'I do beg your forgiveness for this intrusion, your highness and I certainly won't inconvenience you any longer than necessary. I have come to see a young woman in your service.'

'Indeed?'

'Yes, Miss Ivy Brown. I understand she is working as a governess.'

Jalil frowned and looked as puzzled as his captain.

'No, there is no one of that name in my household that I know of.'

Technically that was true. Callan had dropped Ivy's D-vere prefix, so Jalil did have some justification for telling a whopper when Allah — *may his name be exalted on high* — challenged him at the gates of paradise.

'You have no governess?' Callan insisted.

'Not to my knowledge.'

Again Jalil could rationalise the lie because Ivy was no longer a mere governess, but his future consort.

'But her parents told me she'd taken the job before you sailed from Southampton.'

'Oh, yes indeed, but she is no longer in my employ. She must have changed her mind and left my service at some time.'

Now that was stretching it a bit thin. Allah in his goodness and purity might have a thing or two to say about that one.

'You don't know where or when she left?'

'It is not a sultan's business to follow the minute details of his servants. Now I tire of this interrogation. I have indulged you as one war veteran to another, but I have other business to address, as do you I am sure.'

Callan was about to say more, but Hassan pulled gently on his sleeve.

'Thank you, my lord,' Hassan salaamed with appropriate humility and obsequiousness. 'We beg forgiveness for taking up your most valuable time, effendi. May the Lord of All Light rain blessings upon you and your most worthy household.'

'He's lying,' Callan muttered as they were escorted past the gates.

'Through his teeth,' Hassan agreed.

'What now, Guv?' Bill asked.

'We need a plan, but I have no idea what it will be.'

They reached the Gotha and explained what had happened to Charlie.

'Pity we didn't bring any bombs with us,' Charlie lamented.

'I think I've killed enough people for a lifetime,' Callan reflected although Hassan had no such reservations.

'I think the only way is to fly to Quetta and get the army in on the act,' Callan said. 'That'll sort out the Sultan-flaming-ruddy-Jalil.'

'It shouldn't take long to reach Quetta. It's just on the Afghan border.'

But no one flew to the large British base at Quetta.

Right then a peasant girl approached the airmen. This was unusual because local women were usually shy, furtive and steered clear of strangers. She moved so quickly Callan barely noticed her as she slipped past, dropping a piece of paper at his feet before hastening away from the palace.

'Hey you dropped...'

Callan retrieved the paper and unfolded it. There was a single line to the note:

Midnight tonight under the wall right of the gate

Callan passed the note around.

'Does this mean what I think it does, Guv,' Charlie asked.

'There's only one way to find out, but I think we should take the kite a few miles away out of sight.'

'You mean make that sultan bloke think we've given up and buggered off.'

'Precisely.'

*

Raym ibnatu Mumbais, Jalil's first wife was not a vindictive woman. In fact she was a gentle and caring soul, who truly wished for a life of simplicity and harmony. The English woman's arrival threatened that tranquillity. Raym liked Ivy, but already saw the threat of cultural clashes, which could disrupt or even tear the family apart, not to mention her husband's unseemly infatuation. Was it just the fact that he was in the mood for another chaste maiden or had he truly been bewitched by the ivory-skinned infidel?

At first Raym thought she'd have to discipline Ivy, but she found beatings distasteful and unsettling. Now it looked as if there might be another way to resolve the dilemma. Obviously Ivy would be unhappy in the Jalil household anyway, so why not help her achieve a different path. It wouldn't be a case of disobeying her husband — *Allah forbid* — but simply doing something he was unaware of.

Raym quickly wrote a note in her neat hand-writing. She summoned one of her most faithful maids, instructing her to deliver the message and then continue to her family home close to the Indus Banks. She wanted the innocent girl out of the way for several weeks in case Raym's plan back-fired.

Raym told no one, thinking that if Jalil discovered what she was up to, no other members of the harem would be punished if they were ignorant of her plan. Not that Jalil would think mere women were capable of intrigue other than palace gossip.

Now for Ivy. Her accommodation was an annex to the harem, guarded by a sentry with orders to admit no one to the chamber once Ivy retired for the night. The sentry was a problem especially for Raym's identity to remain secret. Someone else was needed — hence the note.

Raym knew she couldn't simply guide Ivy to the gate and let her sneak away into the night, especially when she heard the Englishman's aircraft engines rev into life. She rushed to a balcony just in time to see the plane lift off and head back towards Karachi. She wondered if they'd lost heart and abandoned the quest, but when her servant did not return, Raym decided to go ahead with her plan anyway.

Before turning in, Raym took Ivy aside.

'Be ready tonight. Midnight — be ready!' she whispered.

'Be ready for what?'

'Your man will come for you. If I was him, I would.'

'Callan!'

'I believe that is the name he gave my lord sultan. Apparently he is not as dead as you thought.'

Callan.

Ivy wanted to ask Raym more, but the *panguian* urged to silence. The less said the better.

'Just act naturally and patient,' Raym admonished.

What with my heart beating so fast I can hardly breathe? Calm yourself, Ivy. Your love will take you away from this nightmare.

*

Callan found a suitable landing site among many in the fertile Indus Valley. The river was still low so much of the floodplain was dry. The Himalayan spring ice-melt was still in its early stages, while summer's flooding monsoonal rainfall was still three months away. He left Charlie and Bill with the Gotha and instructions to 'expect anything'.

'Put this on,' Hassan told Callan, tossing him his spare thobe and ghutra. 'That should do to stop you standing out like the Dandy you are.'

'Nothing wrong with keeping up appearances,' Callan retorted with a grin.

Hassan and Callan loaded their revolvers and checked their water canteens were full before hiking back to town. They arrived well into the night and headed straight for the palace wall. The main gates were already closed, but Callan had no idea if the sultan shut up shop at a regular time or ad hoc.

Two guards patrolled the inner courtyard, but there were no patrols beyond the palace wall. Some town stalls and streets hawkers still plied their trade, but it looked like the town had settled down for the night. No one took any notice of Callan and Hassan, who were just two robed figures walking the streets.

Callan owned a wrist watch which had become popular during the war. They replaced clumsy and fragile pocket-watches for convenience and their luminous dials.

'What is the hour?' Hassan asked.

'Just after ten,' Callan said. 'Two hours to go.'

'Stay here and do not talk to anyone. I am going to ask around.'

Callan became worried when Hassan hadn't returned after an hour, but just as he was seriously concerned, the Arab appeared beside him.

'You know this place isn't as strong as it looks,' Hassan said.

'Looks pretty strong to me.'

'Perhaps, but there are few guards. All Jalil's troops have returned to their farms and businesses. So many men have died, those remaining are sorely needed. Less than half of his elite palace guards survived the war and practically every home is in mourning. Word around town is Jalil has barely twenty men.'

'So we're not up against a horde of thousands? Those jokers in the courtyard are probably the only ones on duty.'

'It seems not.'

Callan's watch showed the time was approaching midnight. He was uncertain how accurate either his, or the palace clocks were, so all he could do was wait.

Yet within minutes of his watch hands coinciding at midnight, Callan and Hassan heard a thump some yards to their right. Edging along the wall, they felt a rope dangling from the ramparts. Callan tugged the rope which was secure and knotted at about three foot intervals.

'I guess they want us to climb up,' Callan whispered. 'Feeling fit?'

Hassan nodded.

'And we're not killing anyone unless it's absolutely unavoidable.'

Callan was already half way up the wall, so he was unaware of Hassan's response.

Both men were over the wall in moments. To their surprise they were met by a lone woman whose face was covered by a veil.

'No questions,' the woman hissed. 'I will show you where Ivy is. I can do no more. Follow me.'

With his heart beating at the thought of seeing Ivy again, Callan also wondered why this woman wanted to help. But time for that later. As they entered a side door to the Harem, the woman turned, placing her finger to the lips behind the veil.

'If the Sultan finds us in the women's quarters,' Hassan whispered, 'he will castrate us before tying us to those courtyard cannons and blowing us to smithereens.'

'Nice to know, thanks,' Callan replied grimly.

'There,' the woman pointed to the door to Ivy's bedroom, guarded by a single sentry. 'He took his station at midnight, and will be replaced in one hour.'

Hassan and Callan exchanged glances, when they turned to the woman, she was gone. There was no time to reflect how she'd vanished in a flash, but drapes on the wall beside them fluttered gently for a second.

Hassan pointed to his chest indicating he would deal with the guard. Callan didn't argue. He knew Hassan was the expert in this field. Callan's experience of hand-to-hand combat tended to be unsubtle and extremely noisy. Hassan was only feet away when the bored guard noticed him. By then it was too late.

Callan had no idea how Hassan dealt with the sentry. In a split second he was lying still on the marble floor. Hassan had overpowered and disarmed the man without a sound.

'He's not dead, is he?' Callan hissed.

Hassan shook his head and placed his finger to his lips.

The door had been locked from the outside, but the key was still in place. Hassan turned the key and gentle pushed the door ajar. The two men slipped inside. The room was spacious and luxurious.

Ivy stood in the centre dressed in a shirt, leather jacket, riding jodhpurs and hiking boots. She'd strapped her precious satchel to her back.

'I knew it was you,' she whispered and rushed into Callan's arms. 'I heard the plane and the harem girls said a man was looking for me and how dashing he was.'

'No time,' Hassan warned. 'You can get reacquainted later.'

Ivy stared quizzically at Hassan.

'Later!' the Arab insisted. 'Follow me.'

The plan was to follow the same way they'd come in. Callan was sure Ivy could clamber down the rope. They'd be back at the Gotha by dawn and on their way to Karachi before the palace even woke up.

And that would have worked just fine, except a vigilant sentry patrolling the rampart stumbled upon the rope coiled beside the wall. Callan, Ivy and Hassan crept along the rampart, arriving at their escape point as the guard picked up the rope and examined it suspiciously.

Chapter 40 — India by Night

The sentry peered over the rampart wall, shone his torch onto the street below, shrugged and re-examined the rope. The knots were a give-away. He flashed the torch around in time to illuminate Callan's face as he rushed in, dived and rugby tackled the guard.

The sentry slammed into wall, and was instantly winded. He released the rope which dropped over the wall to the ground. Hassan used his pistol butt to club the guard who was already only half-conscious. Hassan took the guard's jezail which had been converted to a single-shot breech-loader. He also found spare cartridges in the fellow's ammunition pouches.

'It's too far to jump,' Callan said. 'And we won't get half a mile before this bloke sounds the alarm.'

Hassan's eyes narrowed.

'No, we are not going to finish him off.'

'What then?' Hassan challenged.

'What about one of those getaway cars?' Ivy suggested.

'I can't drive a car,' Callan admitted.

'What — you fly aeroplanes?'

'That's different. I always had a driver to chauffeur me around.'

'Horses and camels for me, sorry,' Hassan shrugged.

'It's just as well someone can drive then. Come on we'll take that open-top Roller. I bet it has an electric self-starter. I can't see his highness using a crank handle.'

'That's what minions are for — let's get going.'

The three figures tried to keep to the shadows as they crouch-ran along the rampart to the closest steps. There was a sentry on duty beside each of the cannons in the entrance courtyard.

'We'll have to silence those blokes,' Callan whispered. 'Ivy, get the car going while we tackle the guards.'

Hassan and Callan were instantly in stealth mode. Memories of Lone Pine flooded through Callan's mind, although Hassan remained inscrutably calm. The sentries were facing the gate where of course they'd expect trouble to come from. Hassan took the furthest one, while Callan grabbed the closest and thwacked him across the skull with his pistol-butt. The guard groaned and slumped to the ground.

There was a sentry post at either side of the gate which was padlocked closed. Callan searched for a key on the unconscious guard, but came up empty.

'No keys on this one either,' Hassan whispered. 'I'll check the guard boxes.'

Callan dragged the guards against the rampart wall where they were less conspicuous. By the time he'd finished Hassan was inspecting a row of keys on a board inside the second guard post.

'Which one?' Callan asked.

'I don't know.'

'Why the devil not? Look the names are written above each key in Arabic.'

'It is not Arabic, it is Urdu.'

'What's the difference? It looks the same to me.'

'Different like German and English. Same script — different words.'

'We'll have to take 'em all then and try each one. Some will obviously be wrong.'

About then the point became academic.

To her dismay all the cars in Jalil's fleet were pre-war models without an electrical self-starter amongst them. She selected the Rolls anyway because she located the crank handle straight away. Ensuring the gears were in neutral and the hand brake engaged, she set the throttle and choke to what she judged would be their correct positions.

Cranking motors was nothing new for Ivy. None of the ambulances she'd driven had self-starters. After two attempts the engine rattled into life accompanied by several back-fires.

Cripes, the mixture's too lean!

The exhaust farts sounded like gunshots in the calm night air. At the same time the stunned guard on the rampart staggered to his feet and started yelling for help. Ivy jumped behind the wheel and crunched the gearbox into submission.

The motor roared as the Rolls lurched towards the gate. Callan turned in dismay to see the recovering guard raise his rifle and aim towards Ivy. Callan fired a pistol shot which blasted the masonry at the guard's feet. He flinched as he pulled the trigger forcing his shot wide.

Hassan fumbled with the padlock, but still had not located the correct key. He tossed the other keys aside, drew his revolver from his belt and fired into the padlock.

It fell apart on the third shot just as half a dozen guards raced from their quarters. Most were still in their underwear, but they all carried rifles with their ammunition bandoliers slung over their shoulders.

Callan and Hassan dragged the gates open allowing the Rolls to pass through.

'Get in!' Ivy yelled.

Hassan and Callan didn't need a second invitation. They stepped onto the running boards on either side and clung to the door-posts. Several bullets zinged past, so Callan fired the remaining three shots from his revolver while Hassan clambered into the back seat for a steadier aim. By then the Rolls was well clear and rumbling out of town.

Later, reports, town gossip and harem rumours indicated the palace was in confusion for at least half an hour while the guard captain tried to sort out the mess. It seems Sultan Jalil stormed onto the scene only moments after he heard the gunfire. By this stage the three guards were in various stages of recovery. The men at the gate had no idea what happened except they'd been ambushed from behind.

It took time, but the third guard finally remembered the knotted rope, which of course was no longer on the rampart. Jalil immediately sent men to inspect the outer wall. Once they returned with the evidence, its significance was still unclear.

'The flier!' Jalil was reported to have raged. 'He came for the English woman.'

They quickly found the fourth guard who still lay semi-comatose outside Ivy's empty chamber. At first Jalil wondered how the Englishman could have found the Harem annex, but although the area was forbidden, it wasn't a secret location. Anyone in the town could have told him. His Arab partner-in-crime probably had the skill with a rope to lasso a battlement and climb up. Apparently it never occurred to him that one of his wives would dare betray him. The thought was inconceivable, so simply beyond his consideration. And the idea they'd be able to tie a rope was even more ludicrous.

But it did occur to Jalil that if the Australian aviator had kidnapped his bride, then his flying machine must be close by...and...about then he remembered he'd given Ivy the Blood Stones of Jalil Khan!

When a search of Ivy's apartment failed to discover the gems, Jalil ordered his cavalry to mount up. He led the troop himself, baying for blood.

*

Ivy and Callan were feeling pretty smug about getting clean away. She chattered away to Callan, relating her adventures while Hassan remained silent in the back seat. He regularly cast his eyes behind the car, certain the sultan wasn't about to give up without a fight — Hassan knew he wouldn't.

Ivy drove slowly because the road was badly in need of grading and pot-holes threatened to puncture a tyre at best or break an axle at worst. But with headlights to guide her, she avoided any major obstacles.

'Ivy, this is Hassan al-Wazir,' Callan said. 'He is a true friend and a bloke you want on your side and not the other way round.'

'So I've seen,' Ivy said thrusting her right hand over her shoulder causing the car to swerve alarmingly.

'Salaam, Miss Ivy, I am delighted to finally meet you,' Hassan replied with commendable gallantry as he gently took Ivy's hand while she wrestled with the steering-wheel.

He breathed a sigh of relief when she released his hand and resumed control of the car.

Callan had to admit the plan hadn't been worked out with General Monash's precision. In fact it hinged on a vague assumption that someone inside the palace was prepared to help them and they'd improvise as they went along. And that was pretty much what happened, although a motor car wasn't part of the original concept. Callan had anticipated they'd escape over the wall undetected, and then walk back to the Gotha, arriving around first light.

Even though Ivy drove with extreme care they still reached the plane at least four hours before dawn and that posed an unexpected problem.

After introducing Bill and Charlie, it was time to consider their options.

'A night take-off is not a great problem,' Callan explained, 'but unless I have an aerodrome with some illumination to guide me down, a night landing is out of the question.'

'You have landed in cornfields, beaches, roads, goat-tracks, cow paddocks, race-tracks and cricket-pitches before,' Hassan said.

'True, but they were all in daylight. For a night landing I need a minimum of touchdown point lighting or flares. Strip lighting would be even better.'

'Which means..?' Ivy asked.

'Which means we have to arrive at our destination after first light. Quetta has an illuminated airfield, but they won't light the flares if they don't know we're coming.'

'Wouldn't they 'ear our engines over'ead, Guv?' Charlie suggested.

'Maybe, but I don't want to chance it and it'd still take time to get the flares set up and lit.'

Another problem was fuel. They had enough aviation petrol to last just over two hours, so simply flying to a landing site and circling overhead until it was light enough to land was not an option either.

'I don't want to risk Quetta at night anyway. The place is surrounded by hills and it would be a shame to bump into one after coming all this way.'

'It would be a shame to bump into a hill anytime,' Bill observed.

'We could always negotiate with the sultan,' Charlie suggested.

'I don't think Jalil will be in a mood for chit-chat,' Ivy said. 'I've sort of taken something he gave to me as a wedding gift.'

She opened her satchel and produced the rubies.

Callan let out a low whistle.

'He gave you those...blimey, that's generous.'

'Yes, but I think the condition was *he* would be the groom.'

'You could simply return them,' Hassan suggested.

'Not likely,' Ivy said. 'He was going to force me to marry him and make me his slave. If Jalil wants to treat me like a commodity, he can jolly well pay for the privilege.'

'Okay, it looks like there won't be any deals. Bill, stow Ivy's satchel safely in the plane, please. We don't have enough petrol to reach Karachi. I'd planned to stop at Sukkur which is about half way. So this is what we'll have to do...'

*

Ivy checked the petrol tank before cranking the Rolls engine into life. Hassan sat beside her with his rifle while Charlie took the back seat with the jezail Hassan had taken from the palace guard. They drove for about a mile before Ivy executed a three point turn and stopped in the centre of the dirt track. It was only wide enough for a single vehicle anyway.

The motor chugged at idle.

'We need silence,' Hassan whispered.

Ivy cut the motor. That was a bigger deal than it might have sounded in an era when motor cars — even a Rolls Royce — were far from reliable and prone to starter tantrums.

While Charlie peered into the darkness with the jezail level along the road, Hassan stepped from the running-board, and knelt down, placing his ear to the ground. Ivy wondered if he was about to recite the Fajr chant early in case he didn't get time later, but Hassan remained silent. After a few minutes he rose and stepped back into the car.

'They come,' he said.

*

Back at the Gotha, Callan and Bill checked the plane for take-off. They poked their torch beams inside the engine cowls, checked the oil sump levels and control cables were free and ran smoothly over their pulleys. The Gotha was parked on the road, which looked like the best take-off area. There was a sharp bend behind the plane, so the only take-off direction was straight ahead towards the palace.

'Guv, you know we're pointin' the wrong way, don't you? We could taxi a mile up the road and turn the kite around.'

Just then they heard the distant popping of rifle fire.

'I think it's a bit late for that, Bill. Stand by to spin the starboard prop.'

*

Jalil's cavalry advanced slowly. His fifteen horsemen rode carefully in the darkness. A horse could easily trip in a pothole and break a leg. It took two hours to close in on the Gotha.

A sound like a faint whistling sound whizzed past Jalil's ear followed by a thud. One of his men grunted and tumbled from the saddle when Jalil heard the gunshot. Another shot followed. One of the horses reared and snorted, throwing its rider. The animal wasn't badly hurt and cantered back along the palace road.

Jalil ordered a halt before sending two scouts ahead.

By now Hassan's night-vision was owl-like. He sensed the pair of approaching riders and fired twice while Charlie reloaded. He doubted if his shots had done much damage, but the riders turned their horses and retreated into the darkness.

'Time to get goin', Miss Ivy,' Charlie said, taking the crank handle.

The engine spluttered into life again. Charlie jumped onto the running-board as Ivy gunned the motor and the Rolls sped away. Hassan fired a steady dose of lead from the back seat. The Rolls flung up grit and a dust cloud in its wake which hung in the still pre-dawn air.

*

'Contact,' Callan yelled. Bill spun the prop and the starboard engine roared. He race behind the tail to the port prop.

'Contact!'

Both motors coughed and trembled at idle power. Callan advanced the throttles slightly until both engines ran smoothly just as the Rolls rumbled towards the Gotha. Bill scrambled into the rear cockpit and crawled along the access passage that led beside the pilot's station to the front gunner's position.

Ivy swerved the car off the road at the last second. Charlie, Hassan and Ivy leapt out.

'Watch the prop!' Charlie yelled to Hassan, who gave him thumbs-up. Using the main wheel as a step he climbed onto the front of the wing and into the rear gunner's station.

Being sliced to shreds by the prop in all the excitement was a common early aviation tragedy. Charlie took Ivy's hand and led her to the plane's nose. He grasped her waist and heaved her upwards. Bill grabbed her hands and hauled her into the gun-station beside him. It was a tight fit, but Ivy squeezed in.

'Sit down please, Miss,' Bill yelled above the growling engines. 'Stretch your legs down the gangway, so your 'ead don't get in the way when I swivel this gun.'

For once Ivy did as she was told. She looked up saw Callan's goggled face. He grinned and then mouthed, *I love you.* She reached up and touched his knee. As soon as Charlie was safely aboard, Callan moved the throttles to take-off power and the Gotha lumbered forward. As the plane picked up speed, Callan switched on the landing lights recessed into the front of the engine nacelles.

When the beams lit up, a line of horsemen flashed into view on the road too close for Callan to take off before the Gotha reached them — in a matter of seconds! Bill's Lewis gun blazed into action, slicing lead into the horsemen. Ivy yelped as red-hot spent cartridges sprinkled around her.

Jalil's cavalry milled in confusion. All they saw were the brilliant headlights which blinded the men and terrified their horses. Some riders fired their rifles, but who knew where the shots went?

And then the flying monster was upon them. The noise, vibration and wind blast confused Jalil and his men into panic. They scattered as the Gotha's wheels whooshed past at head height. It was all over in a flash as Callan accelerated the plane to climb speed, reduced the throttle setting and turned onto a southerly track.

Now Callan estimated he had just enough petrol to reach Sukkur and stay airborne until first light. He'd filled the petrol tanks at Sukkur en route to Dera Jalil Khan and the oil company factor was expecting him on the return trip.

Chapter 41 — The Finishing Line

Raffles Hotel, Singapore — A late evening in early May 1919

'You know I really enjoyed shopping this afternoon,' Ivy said. 'Singapore maybe hot and sticky, but I love the markets. Do you know it was four years ago when I was last here during the sepoy mutiny?'

Of course Callan knew the story, but Charlie and Bill were interested in Ivy's odyssey from Cocos to Ireland.

'I wonder if Hassan has made it home yet,' she changed the subject suddenly as she savoured the hotel specialty, a gin-sling, while Charlie, Bill and Callan enjoyed ice cold lagers.

'He said he'd hang around Karachi for a bit to see what news came out of Dera Jalil Khan,' Callan reminded her.

'He was nice bloke for an Arab,' Bill remarked.

'He was a nice bloke for an "anyone",' Callan grinned. 'I dunno if we'd have pulled it off without him.'

Once they returned to Karachi, Cyril Maddocks had wired funds for the remainder of their trip. He was thrilled by their progress although it looked as if they wouldn't make Darwin within the competition deadline, but then they weren't in the completion anyway, were they? They were met by reporters whenever they landed, whose interest intensified when they discovered Ivy had joined the team.

Bad weather had slowed them through Burma, Siam and Malaya, restricting them to fly only in the early morning. Monsoonal thunder-clouds built up every afternoon forcing Callan and his crew to find shelter for their plane. The inclement conditions were a phenomenon known as the Inter Tropical Convergence Zone. A line of thunderstorms encircled the globe, which moved north and south of the equator within the tropics depending on the season. From May to October the storm fronts lay north of the equator, so Callan expected flying conditions south of Singapore to improve significantly.

As Callan and his friends studied their proposed route to Darwin, a bell-boy approached carrying a telegram on a silver platter.

'Major McAlister,' the bell-boy announced, 'this just arrived.'

'Thank you.'

Callan opened the telegram:

```
Jalil sending agents after you stop
seeking help from Sultans of Borneo Brunei
Johor and Indonesian sultanates stop
beware believe he means to kill you stop
God be with you stop Hassan
```

'Looks like he's calling his Muslim buddies for help,' Bill said. 'He'll have cabled Batavia for sure.'

'Indonesia is a Dutch colony. The authorities won't allow anyone to interfere with us, will they?' Ivy said.

'You notice Jalil hasn't gone to the British, or we'd have been arrested by now. He's not interested in the due process of law,' Callan said. 'No, this is personal. I believe we're in danger of either being murdered in our beds, or kidnapped and spirited back to Dera Jalil Khan in the hold of a tramp-steamer.'

'Sounds like we need to get out of town and disappear,' Charlie suggested.

'I think you have a point, Charlie. These jokers will never give up.'

'What do you reckon?' Bill asked.

'Let's sleep on it and make a plan when we're fresh in the morning,' Callan said.

There was a very good reason Callan was keen to turn in, because that night was to be the first time he and Ivy shared a bed. Nothing had been said and until then, they'd slept separately, and to tell the truth they were so exhausted after many arduous days flying, sleep was all they desired. Ivy, like Callan, loved to be airborne and enjoyed nothing better than standing in the forward gunner's turret, with the cold wind in her face as they cruised at five thousand feet.

They'd booked a double room and an adjoining suite in one of the two-storey wings. The luxurious accommodation had an inter-connecting door for Bill and Charlie. Both rooms shared a balcony divided by a low ornately carved partition. It was a very convenient set up when it came to planning the next leg of their journey.

Ivy wasn't in the least coy about undressing in front of Callan, reminding him of the occasion in Dublin so long ago. He wasn't sorry either — she was exquisite!

'You asked me to marry you and I agreed,' she stated in her typical matter-of-fact way. 'I love you, so now I shall *make* love to you. As our lives seem to be in constant danger, I have no wish to die an old maid. We can sort out the formal details of becoming Mrs McAlister when we reach Australia.'

'What if you become pregnant?'

'I have no objection to bearing the children you father, my darling, but I have come prepared.'

She rummage in her satchel and produced a packet of condoms.

'Apparently "rubbers" are much favoured by the French,' she explained with disarming candour and a charming smile. 'I bought these from a Chinese medicine store when I was shopping in Bugis Street today.'

She smiled as she surveyed the naked man beside her.

'They wanted to sell me potions and powders to help everything along, my darling, but it seems to me you will manage perfectly well *au naturel.*

Callan turned out the electric light leaving only moonbeams to bathe the room through the open balcony window.

Callan couldn't have become distracted at a worse time, because the assassins came that night. Around midnight two men scaled the wall via drainpipes, creepers and balcony balustrades. They moved with the stealth and agility of cats with night vision to match. Both men were bearded, bare-footed, bare-chested and dressed only in loin-cloths, carrying their curved knives in their teeth. They'd abandoned any clothing that might hinder their progress and agility.

They slipped silently onto the balcony of Callan and Ivy's bedroom suite. The ceiling fan rotated languidly as the assassins crept towards the mosquito-net enshrouded bed.

The leading assassin slowly pulled back the net, raising his knife to strike. He froze then staggered away from the bed. A bayonet handle protruded from his rib-cage with the blade buried to the hilt. The second man turned and slammed into Bill who rammed his revolver barrel into the assassin's belly and pulled the trigger. Bill muffled the gun with a pillow so the discharge made a pop not much louder than a champagne cork.

Bill switched on the light. Both men lay dead with a good deal of blood staining the bed and carpet.

Ivy sat frozen on the bed. For a moment she was stunned by the sheer brutality and uncompromising ruthlessness of the fight. Callan had lost none of the edge which had kept him alive at Gallipoli. Charlie and Bill may have been mechanics, but they'd both endured trench combat back in '14 and '15 and knew how to handle themselves.

Ivy quickly wrapped herself in a bed-sheet before Callan gently placed his arm around her.

'I'm sorry,' he whispered. 'It's not how a girl should spend her wedding night.'

Bill winked and grinned.

'You keep a bayonet beside the bed?' Ivy stammered.

'Sorry, it's a hangover from Gallipoli. Something Archie Blake taught me in case Turks come sneaking down your trench at night.'

'What if I'd had to go to the ladies room? You might have stabbed *me*!'

'No chance, Ivy. Those blokes smelt bad. Believe me, you have a lovely smell.'

Indeed many women — and men — would have been reduced to hysterics by what they'd just seen, but Ivy wasn't just any woman. Certainly she was passionately romantic, possessed a sentimental heart and gentle nature, but she was tough. Soft-heartedness had its place, but she knew it was time for toughness.

'The maids won't be happy,' Bill observed, switching on the light and eyeing the blood-stained rug.'

'It could have been worse,' Ivy said. 'Both men died instantly and stopped pumping blood, but we will not be able to pass that off as a ruptured hymen, will we, darling?'

The two men stared at her.

'What..?' Ivy said. 'I do not know why you look so shocked, Callan. You are standing there stark naked. I think you should at least put your shorts on.'

Ivy gave them one of her sweetest smiles.

Charlie entered the room through the balcony door. He was also armed with a revolver.

'The coast is clear. There are no more of the buggers,' he reported.

'Just as well Charlie and I decided to take turns keeping watch,' Bill said.

'That settles it,' Callan said. 'We need to get out of here as soon as possible. Yesterday would have been good.'

'What about this mess, Guv?' Bill asked. 'What about the deaduns? The last thing we want are the rozzers involved.'

'And now we *really* need to disappear,' Ivy said. 'I mean vanish from the face of the earth.'

'I have been giving that some thought,' Callan said and told them what he had in mind.

'Blow me down, Guv,' Charlie said. 'We're gonna need a bunch of help. We're gonna need local knowledge.'

It was then Ivy remembered a promise made four years ago.

'Any time you're in Singapore, Missy Ivy. You visit Ze Yu.'

'I might know someone who is street wise, if I can find him,' Ivy said.

'Okay,' Callan said, 'there is no time to lose.'

*

Two days later the *Straits Times* as well as tabloids in Australia and Great Britain splashed the headlines across their front pages. Nowhere was the disappointment greater than in Darwin, where a grand celebration had been planned. The anticipated arrival of Major McAlister's plane drew dignitaries and curious spectators from all over the territory and southern states.

What a thrill to see the first aeroplane land in the Northern Territory all the way from England.

So when the bombshell hit, the reaction was disbelief, profound grief and loss.

How could such a disaster happen on what was considered the easiest section of the flight?

How indeed..?

*

THE NORTHERN TERRITORY DAILY STAR

(1d)

DARWIN'S INDEPENDENT BROAD-SHEET

ANZAC WAR HERO LOST IN JAVA SEA

Decorated Australian Flying Corps ace, Major Callan McAlister and his intrepid crew have disappeared somewhere in the Java Sea south of Singapore. After taking-off from Seletar field in the pre-dawn darkness. The plane and its crew were never seen again.

A thorough sea search will be conducted by the Royal Navy, but there is little hope is of finding any survivors.

Major McAlister and his crew were endeavouring to be the first to fly an aeroplane from England to Australia. They were on schedule to achieve this goal until the unfortunate tragedy two days ago.

Major McAlister's crew were Mr Charles Patterson and Mr Clive Simpson who were both Londoners. It is rumoured that a young woman was also thought to be accompanying the expedition, but as yet her identity remains a mystery.

Major McAlister was one of Australia's most decorated war heroes, having been awarded the DSO, MC, DFC and DSM. His distinguished service included the Sinai, Gallipoli, Ireland and the Western Front.

The Gotha GV Bomber

Reports of Major McAlister's plane flying overhead are sketchy, but several local fishermen believe they heard the engines passing above. Bad weather has been ruled out as a cause of the alleged crash. Forecast conditions were fair with only isolated showers in the area, which local aviators insist would have been easily avoided.

Major McAlister's parents who own a property in northern NSW are said to be devastated as is his brother, Robert McAlister, who also served with distinction throughout the war.

This paper wishes to pay tribute to a bold aviator and true blue Australian.

Having survived four years of the horrors of war, it is an even greater tragedy that Major McAlister should be lost after his great adventure when he was almost safely back on Australian soil.

Ze Yu would soon be seventeen and ran a gang of street kids whose activities ranged from legitimate small-time enterprises to some areas just scraping the cusp of legality. These days Ze Yu had distanced himself from the Triad Clans who'd moved in from Hong Kong and were at constant loggerheads with the police.

In Ze Yu's opinion crime might pay, but it was too risky and took up vast resources to stay one step ahead of the law. He even made a little extra on the side as a police informant, but that was something he did sparingly and in secret.

The eyes and ears of his agents were alert all over the island, so Ze Yu knew instantly that an English woman was asking for him at the quayside. He also knew exactly who she was by the description his lookouts gave.

Ivy and Callan had been looking for less than an hour when Ze Yu approached them along the wharf where his father's fishing boat was docked.

It was still dark and the docks were not brightly lit, but Ze Yu recognised Ivy immediately. Ivy embraced him — Ivy was a great hugger.

'Good gracious, Ze Yu, you've grown into such a handsome young man.'

'And you are just as lovely as I remember, Missy Ivy,' he replied, which was pretty suave for a sixteen-year-old.

'I'd like you meet my fiancé, Callan McAlister,' Ivy said.

'Shame on you, Missy Ivy,' Ze Yu said as he shook Callan's hand. 'I was rather hoping you had come back for me.'

'She's a handful,' Callan said. 'But right now we're in big trouble and Ivy says you're the chap who might help us out of this fix.'

Of course, Ivy remembered a twelve year old kid whose extended family might point them in the right direction for what they planned, but Ze Yu proved far more pro-active than that.

'Okay,' Ze Yu said when he heard the situation, and relishing the challenge. 'First we remove bodies and then replace rug.'

'How are you going to do that?' Ivy asked.

'Leave that to Ze Yu and chums. The Raffles front-of-house staff are big snobs. They don't know what goes on out back at the laundry, garbage-collection, maintenance and kitchens. Look the part and no one questions you.'

Before room service began, an eight-man gang entered the Raffles via a discrete tradesman's door. Four men carried two rolled carpets. The team left barely a quarter of an hour later, also carrying two rolled carpets, although this time it took all eight men to bear them away.

Shortly after breakfast Callan and his companions checked out of Raffles to be met by a fleet of trishaws which transported them and their luggage to the fishing marina. Next the trishaws pedalled across town to Seletar field on the north side of the island where Callan had parked the Gotha. The field was also a Royal Navy radio station, so the aircraft was well guarded by RN patrols.

Charlie and Bill oversaw the unloading of the plane including the Lewis gun and spare petrol cans. A RN sub-lieutenant watched the activity with interest, until Callan told him they were taking the equipment for last a minute inspection before departing for Australia. He also explained he would take the Gotha for a final test flight the following day before the long journey south.

Once the sub-lieutenant returned to his duties, Ze Yu's team manhandled the carpets into the bomb compartment.

'Those two men are assassins and not just burglars,' Ze Yu explained. 'They have cobra tattoos meaning they belonged to a killer brotherhood. Each clan has a predator symbol — snake, tiger, dragon and so on. No one will know about their disappearance, so there will be no reprisals.'

The next part of the plan was critical.

'You must be exactly in the right place,' Ze Yu said. 'My father will take his junk to this position here.'

He indicated an island fifty miles south of Singapore.

'It is uninhabited other than passing Malacca pirates maybe.'

'Comforting to know,' Charlie said.

'There shouldn't be a problem with that big gun of yours mounted on the junk. My father knows most of the pirate crews anyway. You have flares?'

'Yep, a whole box full.'

'Then we'd better set sail,' Ze Yu announced. 'We'll be waiting for you.'

'Right, you lot get back up to the harbour. I'll spend the night here. I'll take off at first light. Everyone else, enjoy your voyage.'

Ivy clung to Callan before she left.

'Can't I come with you?" she begged.

'No Ivy, we've talked about it. I don't want to put you in more danger.'

'What if something happens to you?'

He kissed her again.

'I'll be fine. Now get going with Charlie and Bill. I'll see you tomorrow.'

Ze Yu's father's junk was a three-master with an auxiliary motor which made five knots with ease, so they'd reach their destination in good time. It may not have been the most luxurious craft and smelt fishy, but it was reliable and well maintained.

Once his friends had left Seletar field, Callan felt unexpectedly lonely. He'd always had his crew with him when he flew the Gotha. He ate dinner with the RN sub-lieutenant in the radio station wardroom and slept through the night in the officers' quarters.

At first light he checked the fuel tanks and made a pre-flight inspection of the plane. The next part was tricky, because he'd have to spin the props himself before clambering into the cockpit. None of the RN sailors were trained as aircraft mechanics, so Callan didn't want to risk one of them slicing his head off. He didn't want anyone around anyway. As it turned out that wasn't necessary.

'I'll spin those props for you, skipper.'

Ivy's head popped up from the gunner's turret.

'What the blazes, Ivy? You should be on the boat with the others. How did you get here?'

'Trishaw of course, my darling. I wasn't going to let you do this alone. I slept in the plane's gangway, which was okay when I didn't think about those two dead chaps in the bomb bay.'

Callan was speechless.

'I brought a parachute,' Ivy said. 'It is too late to do anything about it now. The junk set sail yesterday, so I *am* coming with you.'

'It's too dangerous.'

'And staying here and waiting for Jalil's murderers is not?'

'The boat was safe.'

'Callan darling, I want to spend the rest of my life with you. I do not think I could bear to live without you. If we go, we go together.'

'Crikey Ivy, you're impossible.'

Callan jumped to the ground, kissed her and ensured her parachute was strapped on tightly.

'Okay, when I call "contact", swing the prop and don't chop your pretty head off.'

Shortly the Gotha lumbered into the morning sky and headed south. After forty-five minutes Callan identified his island destination. He descended to two thousand feet and circled the junk anchored below. A flare shot upwards and exploded before floating to earth, confirming the rendezvous.

'Right Ivy,' he yelled. 'Remember just like I showed you. Hold the rip-chord as you go out. Count to three and pull the flaming thing as far as you can.'

The Gotha wasn't designed for abandoning aircrew. Callan climbed to five thousand feet. He figured that should give him enough altitude. He undid his safety harness while Ivy stood in the forward gun turret.

'I'm going to roll the plane over, Ivy,' he yelled. 'Let the force push you out.'

She smiled and gave him a thumbs-up.

Callan heaved the control wheel into his belly and swung full deflection to the right. The Gotha had never been intended for aerobatics and every bracing-wire, strut and wing fabric groaned as they warped, stretched and buckled. As the plane became fully inverted he cut the fuel-cocks and the props shuddered and froze rigid.

At that second Ivy squealed involuntarily as she dropped from the gun-turret. Callan had no time to think, he let go of the control wheel as the Gotha's nose ducked almost vertical. He leapt from the cockpit, bounced against the upper wing then tumbled into mid-air.

One...two...three...

He pulled the rip-chord.

Whoosh! The parachute spewed from its case.

Plop! The canopy ballooned open, breathed once and settled, before gently drifting down. With a sigh of regret, Callan watched the Gotha spiral into the sea and disintegrate upon impact.

Where was Ivy? He cast his eyes all around, but all he saw were his feet and the sea below.

The junk manoeuvred under Callan as he descended. Ze Yu's dad did a pretty good job too and Callan plonked onto the deck. Charlie and Bill gathered the silk canopy which Ze Yu thought might make a decent sail.

'Where's Ivy?' Callan cried. 'I didn't see her 'chute.'

Charlie and Bill merely looked up and pointed. Ivy's parachute was passing about one thousand feet.

The junk steered towards the dropping 'chute. Ivy waved enthusiastically and appeared to have enjoyed the entire experience. Callan shook his head and glared accusingly at Ze Yu, Charlie and Bill who looked sheepish.

'You knew she wasn't aboard the junk, didn't you?'

The boys shrugged, but were admitting nothing.

'We might just reach her before she gets her feet wet,' Ze Yu grinned.

'Serves her right if she gets drenched,' Callan said.

Ivy dropped into the sea only yards from the junk. She unbuckled her parachute harness and trod water until Ze Yu and Charlie hauled her aboard. She hugged and kissed everyone including Ze Yu's dad.

'My, that was exhilarating,' she gushed. 'Next stop Australia!'

Epilogue — Merimbula NSW

Danny McAlister's property Southern NSW — present day

'Callan forgot to look up, didn't he?' Angela said, scanning Ivy's journal. 'She says here she pulled the rip-chord as the Gotha dived past her. Her parachute had already opened when Callan bailed out so she stayed above him.'

'I wonder why the RN blokes at Seletar weren't suspicious,' I said. 'Callan told them he was just taking the plane for a test flight.'

'According to the *Straits Times*, they assumed Callan had changed his mind as the plane was fully fuelled. When they couldn't find Charlie or Bill, they thought they'd returned to the plane and taken off together. Everyone was pretty miffed, because they wanted to see the plane depart for Australia, but weren't excited enough to get out of bed for a mere test flight.'

'Then Ivy and Callan dropped off the radar,' I said. 'If radar had been invented then, of course.'

'Yes, it looks like it. We have a tonne of material, but nothing between 1919 and 1921.'

'I wonder why.'

'Obviously they wanted to cover their tracks from Sultan Jalil, but you'd have thought they'd have been safe enough in Australia.'

'Did they reach Australia?'

'They must have,' Angela insisted. 'Otherwise where did all these documents come from? I mean we have diaries, Callan's log books, Ivy's artwork and news clippings.'

'Yep, my grandma Henrietta had all this stuff,' Grandpa Danny said when we asked him what he knew. 'Great Uncle Callan must have left it with Robert and his family while he and Ivy travelled around. I remember my grandma mentioning it, but it was long time ago and I didn't see much of her anyway. When Henrietta died my mother must have inherited the stuff because there was no one else to give it to. George, my dad, had already disappeared in New Guinea.'

I remembered Danny telling me that his grandfather, Robert, had tragically committed suicide shortly after the war. He was one of thousands who simply could not live with the horrors they'd endured.

We had explored most of Callan's and Ivy's stuff, and there were several interesting items. Here are a few:

Excerpt from a letter [certified copy] to Cyril Maddocks —
November 1919

> *Colson, Colson & Colson Ltd*
> *Lawyers, Factors, Estate Agents and Accountants*
> *Rooms 12a & 12b, 2nd Floor, 34 St George's Terrace,*
> *Perth, Western Australia*
> *My dear Mr Maddocks*
> *I have been instructed by our clients in the utmost confidence to forward this Lloyds Bank draft in your favour for the sum of £1500.*
> *Our clients, who wish to remain anonymous for matters of their own safety, hope this will in some way compensate you for the loss of your property earlier this year.*
> *Our clients have instructed us to divulge no further information.*
> *I remain, sir*
> *Your obedient servant*
> *Reginald Jenkins*
> *For Colson, Colson & Colson*

'Well, no prizes for guessing who "our clients" are,' I remarked. 'Surely Cyril Maddocks would have known that.'

'Maybe it was a less than gentle hint by Callan suggesting Cyril keep quiet about the payment,' Angela said. 'I guess it worked.'

'It looks like Callan and Ivy paid their debts, but where did they get the cash?' I wondered. 'I mean fifteen hundred quid would have been a fortune back then.'

'Perhaps they sold the rubies,' Angela suggested.

'They'd be hard to move, wouldn't they?'

'Maybe they just sold the diamonds. Who knows?' Danny said.

Cyril Maddocks would have been grateful too, because in November, pilots Keith and Ross Macpherson-Smith with crewmen James Bennett and Wally Shiers made the flight from Hounslow Heath to Darwin in a Vickers Vimy bomber and split the prize money four ways. Although the Gotha's disappearance made news for a while, it soon became fish 'n' chips wrapping. So any profit Cyril hoped to make from the air race was dead in the water — literally.

He and Charles Kingsford-Smith had moved on to barnstorming by then anyway.

There was another letter Callan wrote to his parents who must have kept it for sentimental reasons. He told them he was alive and had married a nice English girl, but swore them to secrecy other than letting Robert and Henrietta know.

'Callan and Ivy never came back to work the Lismore farm,' I observed.

'Not from the city records. Ma and Pa McAlister sold out just in time before the '29 crash and moved to town. They bought a suburban cottage and retired comfortably. We have no idea whether there was ever reconciliation between Ivy and her mother.'

'I'd like to think so,' I said. 'Ivy didn't seem like a vindictive person who'd hold a grudge.'

We found another poster amongst the memorabilia:

Major Gene McAlister

Presents

the 1921 Summer Spectacular of Aerial Thrills

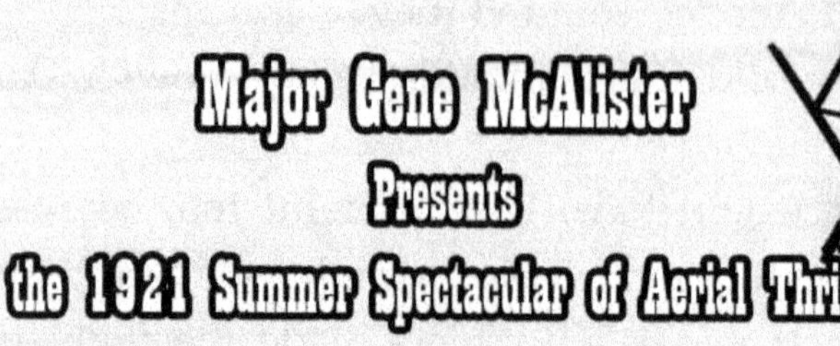

featuring Great War Air Aces
Callan McAlister & Charles Kingsford-Smith

Introducing
the World's most Glamorous & Daring Wing-Walker
Miss Ivy Brown

Marvel at the Aeronautical skill of
Dogfights – Aerobatics – Aerial Stunts
& Much, Much More

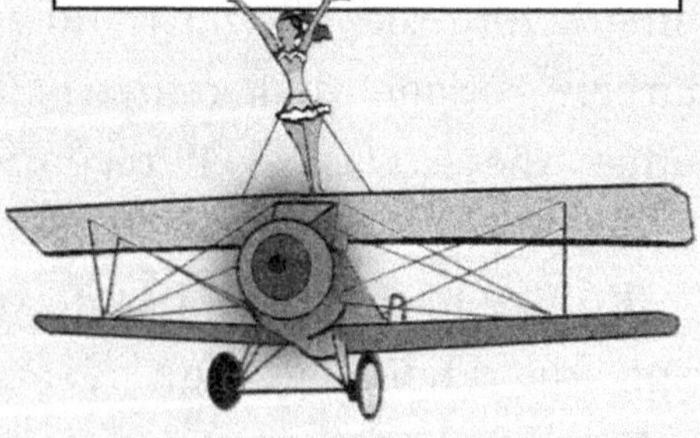

Tickets Just 50c

Memphis	28th May	Sacramento	16th July
Houston	1st June	Carson City	23rd July
Dallas	11th June	Salt Lake City	30th July
El Paso	18th June	Denver	6th August
Santa Fe	25th June	Kansas City	13th August
Phoenix	2nd July	Indianapolis	20th August
Las Angeles	9th July	Cleveland	27th August

'This is dated 1921,' I said. 'So Callan and Ivy had come out of hiding by then.'

'I think I know why,' Angela said, peering into her laptop. 'Look there was a huge earthquake in '21 — 7.5 on the Richter scale — there was massive devastation in the Western Indus hinterland.'

'*Dera Jalil Khan* must have been right at the epicentre.'

'Maybe that's what finished Jalil off. It certainly revved Callan and Ivy back into action.'

'I wonder if they had kids,' Danny said.

'We haven't turned up anything yet,' Angela replied, 'but they certainly had a rip-roaring good old time judging by this barnstorming poster.'

'You know, we still don't know what became of the Blood Stones of Jalil Khan. I mean they're priceless rubies, there must be a trail.'

'No, we don't,' Angela sighed, closing her laptop, 'but right now, my two darling boys, I think we've worked hard enough on this project. Now I deserve a glass of one of your splendid Aussie wines while we sit and watch the sunset.'

The End

The Author

Richard Marman was born in Swindon, UK. His father was a RAF pilot who had served with distinction during WWII. His family moved from base to base after the war, including four years in Germany. They immigrated to Fremantle in 1962. Richard attended six primary and three secondary schools, so he is familiar with the 'new kid on the block' status.

After school, Richard joined the Royal Australian Air Force and trained as a pilot. He served for nine years, including a tour in Vietnam and a significant time flying in New Guinea. In 1975 Richard left the RAAF to fly with Ansett Airlines until the company closed in 2001 at which time he was a Boeing 767 captain. Afterwards he trained Singapore Airlines cadets on Lear Jets until 2007.

Leaving aviation behind, Richard completed a Diploma of Visual Arts at Tewantin TAFE and a Bachelor of Arts at the University of the Sunshine Coast, majoring in creative writing and graphic design. Many of Richard's book ideas have stemmed from University projects.

Richard lives on Queensland's Sunshine Coast with his wife Judy. They have twin daughters living interstate.

For more information visit:

www.richardmarman.net and www.richardmarman.com

The McAlister Line Reader Reviews

'...Masterfully handled and quite eloquent...wonderful.'

'I like this book [McAlister's Way] it covers issues that need to be addressed.'

'Waiting for the sequel'

'*McAlister's Spark* is a fast-paced, action-riddled amazing read you will struggle to put down.'

'A great action read for teenagers and great graphics...a great literary effort.'

'...with pirates and secrets set amongst the northern tropics, you're in for a delightful read. With a good sense of place and the voice to the detail it's [*McAlister's Way*] a very fast-moving action story that will have you wanting more.'

'*McAlister's Way* is a fast-paced, page-turning read — the kind of read where you lose track of time. Absolutely enveloping! Highly recommended!!'

'Through the non-stop action and the integration of history, new cultures and wars the reader is kept engaged from beginning to end on a literary roller coaster ride they won't soon forget.'

Wave and Web Series

Illustrated for Rita Hayward　　　**Illustrated for Elle Burton**

The dreaded dragon, Brimstone is terrorising the sleepy village of Oak Tree, so it's up to Prince Roger and his sister Princess Crystal to hunt down the fiery beast.

They are aided and hindered — as the case may be — by an evil knight, a mysterious good-guy, the local sheriff, loyal men-at-arms, forest brigands, a pair of trusty — and not so trusty — chargers, ogres, trolls and Oak Tree's citizens with a bunch of attitude.

There are thrills, spills, romance and a heap of rollicking good fun to be had by all.